RUDOLPH DELSON

Maynard & Jennica

MARINER BOOKS
HOUGHTON MIFFLIN HARCOURT
BOSTON · NEW YORK

First Mariner Books edition 2009

www.hmhbooks.com

Library of Congress Cataloging-in-Publication Data
Delson, Rudolph.
Maynard and Jennica / Rudolph Delson.
p. cm.
ISBN 978-0-618-83448-8
1. New York (N.Y.)—Fiction. I. Title.
PS3604.E4475M39 2007
813'.6—dc22 2007008520

ISBN 978-0-547-08571-5 (pbk.)

Book design by Melissa Lotfy

PRINTED IN THE UNITED STATES OF AMERICA

DOC 10 9 8 7 6 5 4 3 2 1

This comedy has five unequal parts, and what follows is

THE FIRST PART.

It is quite brief, and purely introductory.

JOAN TATE, *tipsy after another revelatory lunch with her son, illustrates her point (early August 2000)*:

Here's a famous story. And remember that I am his *mother*, so the fact that I am the one telling you this—that tells you something. It's a famous story, and it shows you what kind of a person Manny is.

The year was—. Well, Scott and I had just sold the place on 72nd Street, so it was 1973, and Manny would have been nine years old. We were living in a three-bedroom on West 10th. It was rent-controlled and had twelve-foot ceilings, and you don't want to know what we paid. We paid one-fifteen a month.

And when we lived on West 10th, Manny would wait for the school bus on 6th Avenue, on the corner, in front of Balducci's. He went to school uptown, and the school had its own buses. So Manny and Dave Fowler and the other kids whose parents lived in the Village would all wait on that corner together, in front of Balducci's, for the little squat yellow school bus. There was an air vent that blew warm air onto the sidewalk, and on cold mornings in the winter the kids would all fight over who got to stand under that vent. Dave Fowler, with his little backpack, would time the other kids on his wristwatch so they would all get their turn.

Except for Manny, who didn't want to stand under the vent, and who never wore a hat, and who wanted to wait for the bus twenty feet away, in the ice and the snow, shivering.

Well, I asked him about it, and he said, "The air comes from Balducci's cheese counter. It smells like what Dad eats." Scott had this one unpasteurized Camembert he liked, which smelled like—which you just had to have smelled. Manny said, "Smells are the result of microscopic particles in the air, and I do not want microscopic particles of cheese hitting my head like meteors." I told him that if he would just wear his stocking cap, then the smell wouldn't get into his hair. And he said, "Stocking caps are undignified." Well, I was his mother, I knew better than to try to argue with him about that, but I did ask him whether there was any kind of hat that he would consider dignified. So that he might wear a hat in the cold. And he said, "A bowler." That was how we settled it. I made Scott take Manny uptown to find him a bowler.

It just goes to show you what kind of a nine-year-old Manny was. And it also goes to show you that he was the same then as he is now: fussy about the unlikeliest things, and picky, and obstinant—obstinate, and prepared to suffer for the strangest reasons. And so now, now when he tells me over lunch that he wants to change? Well, I am his mother—of course I am elated.

He says that the motes—the scales have fallen from his eyes. He says that he is tired of making things difficult for himself, that he's tired of being in debt. This is the first I have heard about him being in debt, but he's tired of it. He even told me he wants to take his romances more seriously. Might it be that now, now that Manny is thirty-six years old, I am finally going to get to meet one of his girlfriends? What kind of women is he even attracted to?

JENNICA GREEN, *who never has any luck on Valentine's Day, describes the evening of her boyfriend's arrest (mid-February 2001)*:

This is so going to make me sound like one of those women, and I so am not one of those women.

All afternoon it was as if the city was as oblivious as I was to what was happening. Right up until two minutes before Arnie called from the police station, the city was, like, intent on being gorgeous. With the snow, and the serenity, and my first afternoon off in months. Deceiving me, you know? All afternoon

I'd been communing peacefully with the awnings and the fire escapes and the lampposts. The elegant side of Soho. The wet black iron and the fresh white snow, in relief against each other. The sapphire light, the deep-sea light of a snowy day.

But sure enough, at five o'clock, just as I need to get a cab and get home and get packed, the snow . . . devolves into sleet.

The pretty drifts on the fire escapes and lampposts? Melting and drooling down, onto me. All the snowbanks on the sidewalk? Melting, simultaneously. The gutters are inundated. Frothing up this . . . filth. Ice, cigarettes, cellophane, flooding the street. The sewer grates are overcome. Spewing dirty water. Of course my umbrella is funneling the sleet straight into my shopping bags. And it's dark, and my cell phone starts ringing, but I can't get it.

Bear in mind, I'd been at work that morning. In my decent clothes. My black zipper boots? Sopping. My black coat? Sopping. The sleeve of my sweater? Like a wick, just sucking all this clammy, icy whatever straight from the stem of my umbrella up to my armpit. If you come from San Jose, California, it doesn't matter how long you've lived in New York, you feel so . . . vulnerable to shabbiness.

I get to 6th Avenue, looking for a cab. And of course on 6th Avenue the wind tries to mug me. It has its fists wheeling. Wham, across my face. Wham, my bags are flailing around everywhere. And I'm trying to fend it off with my umbrella, but my umbrella is doing that gagging thing. You know, that thing umbrellas do when the wind gets them? Where they look like a cat coughing up a hairball? The only way I can keep my umbrella alive is by pointing it directly into the wind, which blocks my view down 6th Avenue, practically. And my cell phone is still going off, but I suddenly see this cab.

I don't have a free hand, so I hail it with my umbrella. Getting myself even more drenched. But the cab starts flashing its turn signal. So it's my cab, right? I got soaked trying to hail it, so it's my cab. Right?

Which is when the crazy German woman materializes.

The cab had stopped . . . ten feet away from me? Fifteen? But from nowhere this crazy German woman has appeared and is opening the door to my cab.

She is dry. She has a cigarette in her hand, which she is putting out, and she has a muffin, which she is putting into her pocket. Getting in my cab. Huge, curly, wheat-blond hair with lots of ringlets, all pinned up like a diva's. Getting into my cab. And, let me describe this coat she is wearing. It's rubber, first of all, and white, and it goes down to her knees, with a belt and buttons but with a huge fur collar. Like, white rabbit fur. And she is wearing it with a mustard-yellow scarf and turquoise pants. Dry, and getting in my cab. It's as if she had been waiting in a doorway for me to hail a cab for her. So I lose it. I'm like:

"Hey! Hey! That's my cab!"

And she just gets in. Just opens the door, gets in, and reaches over to close the door. Ice is splashing me everywhere. My umbrella finally gags on its hairball and dies. My bags are beginning to tear. So I absolutely lose it. I scream, and I do mean scream:

"You fucking cunt . . . that's my cab!"

And, all right. I don't want this story to make me sound like one of those women, so let me tell you why I was in a hurry. Which only matters now to prove that I am not, whatever, a horrible person. So, my plan:

Step 1, at eight o'clock on Thursday night I would meet Arnie, with my bag packed.

Step 2, at eight-thirty we had reservations at Four Noodles, because we'd been warned to have one good meal before we left. Including by Rose, Arnie's globetrotting grandmother Rose, who told us: "The first thing you do when you get to the island is go to a grocery store. They have avocados the size of my handbag there. You can eat them for breakfast, or lunch with cottage cheese and paprika. Because let me tell you, there is not one restaurant on that island you are going to enjoy."

Step 3, by ten-thirty, get back from Four Noodles and go to bed at Arnie's.

Step 4, at seven o'clock Friday morning, the cab comes to take us to JFK.

Step 5, by Friday at noon we are with my parents in San Jose, so that they can meet the man who fathered my cat.

Step 6, early Saturday morning, we leave San Jose for Hawaii, where neither of us has ever been.

Step 7, by Saturday at two o'clock we are on the Big Island, for Valentine's week.

Notice that there is no step that involves me making bail for Arnie. But the point is, Step Negative One was to go to Soho to purchase a linen top and sunglasses and sandals. And nice soap, because who knows what will be in our condo on the island. And at five P.M., Step Zero was to get into a cab and get home and get packed. But instead this German woman is stealing my cab and closing the door on me, and so I'm screaming at her:

"You fucking cunt!"

Which is when I realize what the German woman is doing. She isn't closing the taxi's door on me, she's pulling it in so that I can squeeze past the puddles and climb into the cab too. And what she says to me, from in the cab, with her Marlene Dietrich accent, is:

"I thought that we share the taxi, if you go uptown."

Human kindness. She wants to split the cab. I am mortified, because I just called her a fucking cunt. But what am I going to do? I get in the cab.

It's an Israeli cabbie, or maybe he's Russian. He's sort of eyeing us, like, Who are these two nut cases? And, okay. Normally, when you sit down in a cab in winter and get out of the snow and into the heat, it's like . . . taking a trip to Hawaii. A hot, mobile island. But in this cab? You sit down, and what you experience, before you even feel the heat, is the driver's cologne. So heavy, you feel like it will give you a rash. Which is in addition to the rash I'm already getting just from the tension with the crazy German woman. Anyway, I tell the driver Lexington and 83rd. And the crazy German tells him she's going to 65th at 3rd Avenue. Like, directly on the way, if we go through the park. How convenient, right? What a coincidence, right? And the cabdriver says: "I take 8th Avenue, is faster on West Side."

So, 8th Avenue in a sleet storm. The cabbie is muttering to himself, but fine. The crazy German woman is eating her muffin and sitting there all prettily, like I didn't just call her a fucking cunt. And just as I am getting ready to apologize to her, my cell phone starts ringing again. The call is from some unknown number, but it's Arnie. So I'm like:

"Hey, baby! Where are you calling from?" And he says:

"Ah . . . a precinct house."

"Oh no! What happened? Did you get mugged?" He's offended:

"Me? Mugged? No, Jennica, listen, I've been arrefff."

Because 8th Avenue has the worst reception for my phone. So I tell him:

"What? I'm not getting reception."

The German woman? Cringing. The smelly cabbie? Cringing. Because of course I am being shrill. Of course they are thinking that I am one of those women. But Arnie is like:

"Fff arrested, and I need you to call David Fowler."

"Arrested? For what?"

"Fff!"

"What?"

"Mff!"

"Murder?"

And the smelly cabdriver and the crazy German woman both cringe, in a different way. Because now they aren't sure if I'm one of those women or if I'm a spoiled Mafia moll.

"But Arnie? Who are they saying you . . . ?" And he's like:

"Allegedly, Jennica, allegedly. Fff! Fff!"

"Arnie, I can't hear a word."

Which is awful. It's like, is he all right? Is he getting out? Am I supposed to call Gran Rose and make bail? Am I supposed to call the airline and cancel everything? A minute before I had been worrying about, like, How do I apologize to the crazy German woman? Should I really have spent seventy dollars on that white linen top? Did I remember to give Julie the key so that she could feed the cat? Some worries are a privilege. And all Arnie is saying is: "Call David Fowler! Call David Fowler!" And, David Fowler? He's a terrible lawyer. Look what happened the last time Arnie went to him. And that was only money, not, like, murder. I tell him:

"Arnie! I don't want to call David Fowler. Let me call Gran Rose. She probably knows somebody who can . . ." But he says, totally clear:

"Do not you dare call Gran Rose! Call David Fowler!"

And at this point the taxi's pretty much at Times Square. I realize I have to get out of the cab; I have to get to a ground line; I have to figure out David Fowler's number; but mostly, I have to get out of this cab. So I say:

"Driver, I need to get out here, there's been a change of plans. Arnie, if I'm going to deal, I have to get to a better phone. Tell me exactly where you are." And he says:

"They say they're taking me to . . . the tombs." Totally creepy.

While he's saying this, I'm splashing back out onto the sidewalk where the cab dropped me. Outside, everywhere, it's sleet, and, just, cataracts of ice. But already I've spotted the hotel I'm going to make a dash for, and I'm strategizing how to deal with the concierge, what to tell him so he'll let me use a ground line. And the cabbie is saying:

"Is okay, you two figure out money, is okay."

I've got bags everywhere. I'm dripping all over the seat. But the meter is at almost eight dollars, so I give the crazy German woman a five. Because it's either that or a twenty. And, totally blasé, she's like:

"*Ja*, fine."

Oh, and as I close the door, I tell her:

"I am . . . totally sorry that I called you a fucking cunt." I meant to apologize to her, and that's what came out. So embarrassing. And when I get my cell back out of my pocket, I realize that I managed to hang up on Arnie.

Right?

So I'm clopping across the sidewalk, sopping wet, sleet running down my neck, trying to make it into a hotel lobby where

I can borrow a ground line to call David Fowler, when I hear the cabbie, from up 8th Avenue:

"You are a fucking cunt!"

I turn around, and there's the crazy German woman, half a block up, on the sidewalk. Like, she decided to get out of the cab too, except she's making a dash for the subway station. And the cabbie is standing there in the sleet with his flashers on, watching her and calling her a cunt.

She jumped the fare. The crazy German woman jumped the fare.

So I run half a block up, through the sleet, to pay the driver, because, whatever, it's what you do. The crazy German woman hadn't even given him my five. And while he's making change for my twenty, he tells me:

"This is why she wanted to get out on 65th. She was going to let you pay for her. She is very smart. But you? Coming back and paying me when you were already out of the car? Not so very smart."

Like, thanks. Did I mention that you smell? But anyway, what I want to know is: Who was that woman?

ANA KAGANOVA, *safe in the Berkshires and inspired with a fraudulent scheme, decides how to conscript her husband into her plot (September 12, 2001)*:

Like every American, I sat yesterday on the sofa and watched CNN. Yeah, eventually people called my cell phone, but my instinct was not to answer. Perhaps I liked the idea that they did not know whether I was alive. I left Monday for the country without saying goodbye, which is what I do when I stay at my husband's grandmother's cabin.

All day yesterday I thought, Nobody knows that I was not on the ninety-first floor. But, *weiß' du*, at the same time I thought, Nobody knows that I had any reason to be on the ninety-first floor. This is the lay of the land.

In the end I turned off the television, because it is always the same thing that they are playing, and I turned on AM radio. The callers all wanted to know, "Where can I send money?" These rednecks in Massachusetts call AM radio to ask other people what to do with their money.

This is when I realized that these people who were in the towers would be rich. There will be millions of dollars of charity, and there will be millions of dollars of lawsuits, and there will be millions of dollars of reparations, and anyone who was in the towers when they fell will be now rich.

You see who I thought I should in such a circumstance perhaps contact? In order that someone should report me missing? After all, Gogi is my husband. He should report that I am missing, and this is all there is to it.

I went outside, and I had a cigarette, and I threw my cell phone into his grandmother's pond. Because if I was going to pretend that I was on the ninety-first floor, I would need to destroy my cell phone, without a clue. And yeah, have you ever thrown a cell phone into a pond? In September, the pond is nothing but lilies. The cell phone landed on a lily, and it floated. And I thought, This is my shit luck, the floating cell phone from Finland. Why are the Finns making cell phones that float? I thought, Perhaps there is a kayak? And I can drown this cell phone by hand? But then it sank finally into the pond.

And then I drove half an hour to a pay phone and bought one of these calling cards. I spoke with myself for a minute, in order to get the accent correct, and then I called my husband to tell him that his wife is dead.

And this is

THE SECOND PART.

It is longer, and consists nearly exclusively of statements made during the summer of 2000. However, the dead and the inanimate also have their say in this part, and there are press clippings. Please note that despite interruptions and digressions, eventually everybody comes to their point. A list of the speakers in this comedy, should you like one, appears at the back of the book, after the Fifth Part, on page 293.

MAYNARD GOGARTY *tells us what happened on the subway and dissects a dilemma (early August 2000)*:

There was a woman with beauty spots, and a misunderstanding with the authorities—all on a Lexington Avenue local, uptown. She was one of these women who strike your heart and leave it resounding, like a bell. It's a simple story. But may I give a preface, a brief preface, and then we can discuss what I did wrong?

A preface:

You step onto the subway, the subways constituting a borough unto themselves, with different hostilities and different hopes, a whole mobile county of curiosities, and—there she is! This creature with angelic blood, and a cup of iced coffee, and the scent of some recherché shampoo, and her smile just so. Her halo quivering every time the subway rattles. And you must decide what to do. Do you say something, or do you say nothing?

Dignity would seem—dilemmatically, to require both and yet to permit neither.

The subway is, after all, one of the most dignified places to open an affair. Love should contain a constituent element of irreducible destiny, and destiny is exactly what is lacking when—. When Battery Park businessmen ransom dates with chesty socialites from commercial matchmakers in midtown. Or, or when idle and gelatinous West Side freelancers, suctioned to coffee-shop tables like sea anemones, filter through the classifieds in the *Village Voice* for ads reading "Woman seeks Manly Polyp." And destiny is what is lacking when, after months of inhaling one another's dander, the mustard-breathed attorney commences his case, his lascivious case, against his homely, hot-doggy paralegal. Or, or when the bag boy at Gristedes propositions the Gristedes cashier. Love should not be the spoils of a deliberate campaign or the convenient alliance of a war of attrition. Love should be an instant and supernatural uproar in the soul. It should be the resounding of a bell.

So on the subway, with a beautiful girl, dignity demands action and condemns silence. Because—when the girl with the halo sits down across the aisle from you, it is your one chance for truest love!

However, and contrariwise, subways or no, dignity demands that we, as rational apes, reject delusions, including comforting delusions, in favor of the truth. And it is a comforting delusion to think that every time a beautiful woman sits down across from you on the subway, destiny is trying to bring you happiness. Destiny does not manifest itself in the form of chance encounters with beautiful women. Destiny manifests itself, always, in the form of hobbyhorses, pet phrases, pet cats, nosepicking, and credit card debt. And Sunday crosswords, and the pursuit of "fun." In other words, your destiny has been riding across from you on the subway for much, much longer than you can ever imagine. Beautiful strangers do not each represent a new form of happiness. Beautiful strangers are like everybody else—dull, demanding, violent, and malodorous.

So when a beautiful woman sits across the aisle, dignity condemns action and demands silence. Because—when you fail to say hello to a beautiful stranger on the subway, you have triumphantly avoided yet another form of—human misery.

To say something, or to say nothing? This is the anatomy of the dilemma presented by love and dignity on the subway, and this concludes the preface.

I was on an uptown local on the Lexington Avenue line, a subway that was doomed to stall at 33rd Street.

I had boarded at the City Hall stop, still woozy from a breakfast meeting with the woman who wants to buy the rights to my movie, and I was taking the contract uptown, to my attorney. It was my quadrennial half-pint of success. I was *in media res* in the worst way, running an errand for my meager movie on a wet furnace of a morning. My armpits were—have you ever used a droplet of water to test the heat of a wok? While I was waiting on the platform for the train at City Hall, my armpits were informing me that the wok was ready. The woman next to me on the platform at City Hall was wearing a yellow muumuu and carrying a Bible and a blue-ice freezer pack. Bible shut, freezer pack against her chest. Fundamentalist heat, this.

The subway was empty, naturally, when it finally rolled in, since City Hall is the first stop on the line. But I didn't take a seat. I took off my jacket, draped it over my—moist shirtsleeve, and stood like a jack under the air conditioner, to expose myself to as much as possible of that good dry air. Though I did leave my boater on my head, to protect my scalp.

So! The subway leaves City Hall. And as it makes each stop, the doors open, the beastly day seethes into the train, the doors close, and cool order returns. By Spring Street the woman in the muumuu has cooled off enough to start reading her Bible, and I extract my handkerchief and begin to mop myself up, when I notice—a crucial detail. At the far end of the subway car, the alarm for the emergency brake is sounding.

But I do nothing about it—yet.

Spring Street, Bleecker Street, Astor Place. Our train arrives at Union Square simultaneously with an express train. Fatefully, I decide against doing that bounce across the platform to catch the faster train. I am too hot, and am in no hurry. My lawyer can wait. The fundamentalist in the muumuu leaves, however, thumps away to catch the express, and into our car, from the express train, slips—the woman with the beauty spots. A shapely twist of a woman, dressed in black, with two beauty spots on her right cheek. The doors shut. She sits down at the other end of the car, directly underneath the colicky emergency brake.

Twenty-third Street. Twenty-eighth Street. Shadows and stiff air. The beautiful woman's halo is vibrating in time to the trill of the emergency brake siren. Thirty-third Street. And just note the pointlessness of the place and time. Thirty-third Street? Ten twenty-five A.M.? In the midst of a primordial heat wave? At 10:25 A.M., 33rd Street—is harrowingly bland. It is nowhere.

But—33rd Street. The train pulls up to the platform, but the doors don't open. And then, as was foreordained, the train stalls. The electricity weakens and dies, the lights dwindle and quit, the air conditioning expires. We, the passengers, are experiencing the subway as it was in the age of reptiles. The only things still functioning are the alarm on the emergency brake and the public address system, the latter of which the conductor is using to scold us. She is accusing someone of having pulled the emergency brake. "This *train* is going to be *held* in the *station*." Apparently she is planning to go car to car, looking for the culprit.

Now, you can tell a lot from this conductor's voice. She is black, young, and calm, but not necessarily always calm—you can hear the potential for impressive intemperance. "People, listen *up*. We have a *brake situation*, so you are going to have to be *patient*. Be *patient*, please."

So we sit there and, without the air conditioning, commence to sweat, and we listen, in the darkness, to the whine of the emergency brake. Outside, growing restless, are all the damned souls on the platform at 33rd Street, waiting to get into the train, waiting to be pardoned and released into the cool interior of the 6 train, or rather, the ever-less-cool interior of the 6 train.

The woman with the beauty spots is sipping an iced coffee, at peace in her seat. She is wearing leather sandals, but her feet are enchantedly clean for someone who has been walking about Manhattan in weather hot enough to sublimate the concrete. Her hair is thick and wavy and blackish, pulled back under a knotted white handkerchief, a pristine handkerchief. Eyes closed, soft features, and two beauty marks on her right cheek. Maybe she is Spanish, or maybe Jewish. A sleeveless black shirt made out of something elastic-y, stained in the faintest half-moons of perspiration, right along the bottom of the armholes, which is very sexy, and billowy black linen pants. Sipping her iced coffee through a straw. No milk; she's drinking it black. And the condensation is dripping onto her hands. She's got a napkin, a bundle of paper napkins, that she's using to mop the condensation from the side of her plastic iced-coffee cup and that she's then holding against her forehead, so she can feel the coolness. Freckles on her shoulders.

Her seat is at the other end of the car, directly under the noisy emergency brake. And I—I see my opportunity. All I need is one teaspoon of courage, in order to do her the dignified courtesy of shutting off that alarm.

JAMES CLEVELAND, *age twelve, describes what Maynard looked like under the air-conditioning vent on the uptown No. 6 train (early August 2000)*:

He was just some tall white guy dressed like an old man. Except he wasn't old, as in old-old. But he had on old-man clothes, like one of those brown checkered jackets that looks like a tablecloth, and a white straw hat with a brown stripe around it, and a red tie with one of those silver clips to hold it to the shirt. He looked like the geezer who sits all on his own at church and who thinks he behaves better than everyone else and who stares at you and your sister to let you know it. And that was the thing with this white guy—he had a face like he was surprised at something. And when he raised his eyebrows, he had about five hundred and fifty-five wrinkles on his forehead. You know how they add extra lines in music for the high notes? His forehead was like music that has all kinds of notes that are going way, way, way too high.

Chief was like, "Son, he look like he just step in something nasty, son."

And I said, "Son, you be saying *son* far too much, son."

And Chief said, "Your mother be saying it too much. He got a face like something cold just touch his balls."

But the point being is, ain't nobody going to pay attention to you unless you make a problem for them. And Brittany and

Juney and Shawna were trying to make a problem for the white guy, to see if Chief and me were scared enough to run away. So they got the guy's attention, and then they flipped him off. And I think the reason they picked him was because of his face.

MAYNARD GOGARTY *continues undeterred with the story of what happened on the uptown No. 6 train (early August 2000):*

So, now, out on the platform, waiting to get in, are five black kids, two boys and three girls, twelve or thirteen years old, and they are waving at me through the window. Or at least the girls are waving. Only twelve-year-olds could muster such brio in such heat. These three girls are absolutely—conjubilant. And bear in mind, these kids are perfectly the age to do something simultaneously adolescent and childish: go on a double date, yet wave at strangers on the other side of the glass. They have the look of cutting class—some infinitely tedious summer band camp, perhaps, since the boys have trumpet cases with them. They feel daring for skipping class, for being on a date, and so the girls are giving themselves courage and teasing their young escorts by waving at me. Well—! Naturally I wave back. Naturally I wipe my sweaty brow and wave back.

Which is when the girls show me—their ring fingers. If a twelve-year-old black girl shows you her middle finger, you know what it means; but what does it mean if she shows you—her ring finger? So, after a brief moment of racial disharmony in America, the three girls run away, up the platform, laughing. Their escorts watch them vacantly and then look at me vacantly. If you spend enough time as a teacher, especially if you are as subtle a disciplinarian as I am, then you develop a certain indifference to these things. I can see that the boys' opinion of the three girls isn't much higher than my own—and then I realize I have accumulated one teaspoon of romantic courage. So I put on my jacket, pick up my attaché, and stride down the subway car toward the woman with the beauty spots, determined to silence that jeering alarm.

Now. A digression on the nature and construction of the cars that run on the Lexington Avenue line. Redbirds, I think they may be called. Anyway, a digression:

At the front right and rear left of every redbird car are the emergency brakes, each of which consists of a little handle shaped like an upside-down letter *T*, dangling on a wire. The brakes aren't very sturdy, apparently, because to prevent anyone from yanking one down accidentally, they are protected by metal covers, hefty boxes with hinges at the top that have to be lifted before you can gain access to the brake. If you lift the metal cover, an alarm goes off—or not an alarm so much as a high-pitched electric buzzing, a crude, piercing whistle. *Nnneeennneee.* It's flat of A sharp. *Nnneeennneee.* The alarm doesn't mean that the brake has been pulled—it means the cover has been lifted. A sharp bump in the tracks will sometimes jolt one of the covers open, setting off the emergency siren until some gallant and savvy rider—*par exemple, moi!*—has the mind to slap the brake cover back into place. End of digression.

So! I stride down to the emergency brake, and I draw to a stop in front of the beautiful woman. Her eyes are closed, but they flutter open when she hears my footsteps coming. I draw to an emphatic stop—and administer a single, decisive whap.

The alarm falls silent. The woman looks up. For one twinkle, I enjoy her pretty eyes. She is about to say something, presumably thanks, when a drop of sweat from my wrist falls onto her pristine white handkerchief. We both watch it fall together.

"Pardon me—I just meant to—ah."

Because I am who I am, I had paused dramatically to demonstrate what I was doing. I had frozen in place with my arm next to the brake box, to show my gentlemanly intentions. So there is time, while I am stuttering my apology, for—a second drop of sweat to fall on her handkerchief. Gah! She gives me a crushing look—a look that means, in Manhattan, *Stay away, you crazy*—a dumbfounding look when delivered by a woman with two ideal beauty spots. It was as though I'd spat on her while asking her to spare me some change.

So I retreat. And I think to myself, as I retreat, What is this beautiful woman doing on an uptown No. 6 train at 33rd Street at 10:25 A.M.? But I retreat. I retreat, and I take a seat, and I sweat, and I straighten my hat, and I settle my defeated face into a frown. At which point, in a rage, looking for her culprit, enter the subway conductor.

JENNICA GREEN *fails to explain what she was doing on an uptown No. 6 train at 33rd Street at 10:25 A.M. (early August 2000)*:

I was going to buy a six-hundred-dollar cat. Which, I know. But hear me out.

I live on the third story of a red brick walkup on Cark Street, in the West Village. You've seen these sorts of buildings. The kind with tiny black-and-white tiles on the floor of the entryway and coppery mailboxes. Where the copper has this gummy feeling from the scraps of glue left behind where the previous tenants have taped up and then torn off their names over the decades. With a narrow cinder-block stairway painted chocolate brown ... like, Hershey-quality chocolate brown. I have a rear unit, with a view of the backs of some brownstones and their gardens and some ailanthus trees in the alleys, and with a fire escape leading down into the courtyard. Which supposedly makes my apartment ideal for burglary. I moved in, and my mother said ... like, forget that the apartment is spacious and bright, and has parquet floors except in the kitchen and bathroom, and has some redeeming features even if it is too expensive ... like, forget all that, what my mother said was:

"It sounds ideal for a burglar." I said:

"That's why I have renter's insurance, Mom." And my father was like:

"Those policies are a scam. And insurance can't protect you from a determined rapist." It's like, Thanks, Dad, for reminding me.

Anyway, the six-hundred-dollar cat.

On Monday I got home. It was seven-thirty, about. And it was one of those dusks in July and August where the sky is thick and white, the color of a poached egg. I had walked home from the subway slowly, so that I could look at everyone in their heat-wave clothes, and when I got home, there in my copper mailbox, I recognized her handwriting immediately, was a letter from Nadine Hanamoto.

Nadine Hanamoto, who was my best friend in San Jose, California, in 1989, and who was my first cosmopolitan friend. And, okay, cosmopolitan in San Jose, California, in 1989 . . . so, cosmopolitan with caveats. But Nadine Hanamoto, who I haven't heard from in I don't know how long, and whose feelings I think maybe I unintentionally hurt. So I start reading her letter before I am even up the stairway as far as the first landing.

> Dear Jenny,

She's the only one who ever called me Jenny, so already it's kind of poignant, right?

> I'm sorry to send you such a possibly weird letter.

She said she called my parents to ask for my address. She was so happy and impressed that I was still surviving in New York City. What was my neighborhood like? What was my apartment like? Was it "illustrious"? The letter was handwritten in green ink, six pages long, and so I flipped through it, just assessing the volume of it. And on the back Nadine had drawn two blue-ink boxes around one green-ink paragraph, to make sure that one paragraph would catch my eye, if nothing else did.

> George (<u>that</u> George) just bought an apartment in Manhattan, and he says he wants to meet you. He says he forgives you for standing him up in 1989. How hilarious if the two of you hit it off.

My parents apparently told Nadine I was single.

I'm reading this as I open my front door. And, I leave my air conditioner off while I'm at work, to conserve electricity, so when I walk in, my apartment feels like, whatever. Poached. But I put my bags down and sit on one of the barstools at my little rolling kitchen island, and I'm reading Nadine's letter in the heat. So it's absolutely silent in the apartment, no air conditioning, no television, no loom construction going on next door. Even my refrigerator, which is so huge and so poorly insulated that it spends twenty hours a day in the summer rattling its fan, just to keep my whatever, my mixed salad greens from wilting . . . even my refrigerator was quiet. So I'm reading in silence, and then there is this noise. Like, a burglar in my apartment.

MITCHELL *and* SUSAN GREEN *discuss their daughter's aspirations to illustriousness (early August 2000):*

M: She was reading those particular books that high schools still think teenagers need to read, *Wuthering Heights* and *Jane Eyre* and *Great Expectations.* And she came away with the lesson that we as a family had done something wrong that there wasn't more intrigue in our lives. She read *Madame Bovary,* and the lesson she came away with was that Emma Bovary was a perfectly reasonable woman.

S: What she really enjoyed were all of those books by J. D. Salinger.

M: "The Greens are not illustrious." There were about six months when that was her refrain, her constant refrain. She thought it would be romantic if there were invading armies we had to flee, or if we were . . .

S: She wanted to join the leisure class.

M: . . . or if we were winning a fortune shipping boatloads of spice on the high seas, or if the family was harboring an assassin, or if there was incest secretly afoot.

S: And there was incest afoot, on your side.

M: What, Simmy and Lala?

S: Well?

M: That was no secret. They bragged about it. My father's parents were first cousins.

S: Jennica thought we led boring lives. What do you tell a sixteen-year-old? "Be grateful you live in peace and comfort"? And expect that to be the end of it? "Nothing interesting ever happens to us. All you and Dad ever did was go to college and buy a house and have us." I told her she could say whatever she wanted to us, since we were her parents, but she shouldn't just go around telling other people that she thought they led boring lives, because she would hurt someone's feelings. She said, "At least hurting someone's feelings would be interesting." What do you say to that?

M: And it's not as if our family is notable for its ordinariness. I mean, the stories your family has about the war?

S: Or that cousin of yours.

M: Cousin of mine?

S: In Israel, with the skin disease and the spa.

M: Oh, he is a freak. Robby, with his friends from EST.

S: Robby. Oh, he was awful. Those showers we had to use.

M: Nineteen eighty-one. Susan and I went to Israel and left the kids with Susan's parents. We visited my cousin Robby at his spa, outside Haifa. These people, at the spa. They thought that magnetized mud would halt the spread of certain cancers. This kind of pathetic fantasy. People dying for their ignorance. Just losing weight and disassembling their minds out there in the desert. Talking in EST jargon about the chemotherapy conspiracy, over dinner in their communal cafeteria.

S: And what dinners. Quinoa with yeast sauce. Kelp salad.

M: Robby's spa was macrobiotic. He served seaweed grown at some awful kibbutz somewhere that he wanted to take us to visit. The only Jewish socialist solar-powered aquaculture tanks in the world. In his converted Toyota pickup, he wanted to drive us halfway across Israel with his Russian girlfriend. Who was the worst of them all. A wraith of a woman, talking about Talmud and rising signs versus moon signs and Kabbalistic poetry. As if she'd only learned English from Robby himself.

S: Oh, I am so glad we got that ticket to Rome instead.

M: What a tragedy we left Gabe and Jennica behind. That trip would have taught her something about illustriousness.

S: We told her, my mother and her parents escaped Hitler, your father's grandparents moved to the Bronx from Russia with nothing and worked in cigar factories and pencil factories, my father's family has that whole fascinating side in Venezuela, the ranchers, and the one cousin in New Zealand. And she says, "It's just you guys who are boring, it's just my parents. The whole Green family is interesting except my parents." What do you say to that? But you see what it is she likes about New York City.

M: And since when aren't we interesting?

NADINE HANAMOTO *weighs whether or not the Greens were illustrious (early August 2000)*:

I don't think Jenny ever appreciated that she lived in a house where no one was insane. I mean, you'd go over to the Greens', open their refrigerator . . .

My family's refrigerator was, like, some gross, burned fried rice that my mom made, my dad's beer, and some limp celery. You know ants-on-a-log? Where you fill a celery stalk with peanut butter and sprinkle it with raisins? If you made ants-on-a-log at my family's house, the celery would be the least crunchy part.

But you'd go over to the Greens', open their huge new refrigerator, and in the condiments compartment, like: pickled herring, pickled grape leaves, four kinds of mustard, *salsa de nopales*, anchovy paste, smoked Riga sprats, some jar filled with Susan Green's homemade mayonnaise, every single possible variety of salad dressing. Susan Green's homemade jams, with these labels that Gabe created with their dot-matrix printer. And that was just the condiments. In the meat drawer, all these white packages, deli wrapped: smoked salmon, Havarti, roast beef, head cheese, two different kinds of salami, a whole, real liverwurst, blood sausage, Gorgonzola, three kinds of Brie, deli pickles.

You open up their pantry doors: Nutella. Three kinds of rye bread, six different kinds of vinegar, and a complete Tupperware dream set filled with three kinds of rice and two kinds of sugar and four kinds of flour, and whole-wheat wagon-wheel pasta and tomato-infused fettuccine and spinach-infused spaghetti and a mountain of ramen. The Tupperware sales guy would open this pantry and stand tippy-toe with pride.

This is the Greens' kitchen.

I'd be over there, and I would be pleading with Jenny to let me eat, but there was always some reason why we had to wait. I'd be like, "Please, just let me put some blue cheese on these Wheat Thins." Jenny'd be like, "No, I think my mom is making *Schmüchlblärchl* tonight, so we should wait. You can have an olive maybe." So I'm devouring the Greens' olives, famished. Jenny's eating nothing.

Susan Green would come in with a paper sack full of groceries. I'd be like, Why? Why? Why is she buying more? When there is this whole gorgeous picnic in the fridge? And Susan Green would be like, "Well, Nadine, you can have those olives if you want, but tonight I'm making *Schmüchlblärchl.*"

It didn't matter what was for dinner, it was always worse than what was already in the fridge. Because Susan Green cooked some weird shit. Jenny and Gabe were totally brainwashed. Susan would be like, "You should stay for dinner, Nadine. Tonight we're having the Apricot Dish." And she'd be chopping apricots into a frying pan full of ground turkey sautéed in cumin. And Mitchell Green would come home from work and be like, "Smells like the Apricot Dish! Let's put on *La Traviata.*" Then they'd all start arguing about which opera to listen to while eating the Apricot Dish. Gabe would say, "So long as there are no arias in a minor key, because minor keys inhibit digestion." I'd be like, What are these people talking about? And Jenny would be saying, "The best thing with the Apricot Dish is the goat's-milk yogurt." And Mitchell would be like, "I agree," and start burrowing through their fridge for the goat's-milk yogurt.

Jenny and I would set the table. With napkins and napkin rings and wooden bowls for the salad. And then, at seven P.M. sharp, they'd all sit down together at this table for six. Susan, Mitchell, Jenny, Gabe, me, and one chair where they would balance all nineteen kinds of salad dressing they had brought out for Susan's shiitake mushroom and red bean salad. And out would come the *Schmüchlblärchl* and the Apricot Dish and some mashed potatoes. They'd all be like, "Yum! The Apricot Dish!" I'd be like, Why? Why are we eating fried apricots and turkey with goat's-milk yogurt? When there is deli meat right in the fridge? And rye bread in the breadbox? The Greens aren't insane, like my family, so why, why must we suffer? Meanwhile, Mitchell would be like, "Nadine, this is an important aria. This is where Violetta declares the folly of love," and he starts singing along. And I'd be making myself swallow the *Schmüchlblärchl* and thinking about the pastrami and the mustard.

At my house, dinner was at eleven P.M. My mom would burn some rice and eat it in front of the TV. Setting the table meant asking my sister to move over on the couch. My sister, who would be eating ants-on-a-log.

JENNICA GREEN *again fails to explain what she was doing on an uptown No. 6 train (early August 2000)*:

And here's why I can't explain it just like that: because I have to explain about California before I can explain about New York. Or, like, about San Jose before about Manhattan.

I mean, San Jose.

I am from San Jose, California. A city of never quite one million people. Well, city? Municipality. Sunny, and quiet, and always a little brisk at night, and the summers never humid. With lawns and lanes, all spread out sort of low, across the flats of this valley, the Santa Clara Valley. Where before I was born there were orchards.

And there was such a sense of shame about the orchards! The first mention by any of my teachers of, like, the deportation of San Jose's Japantown in World War II? Junior year of high school. But the first mention of the annihilation of Santa Clara Valley's orchards? Second grade, Ms. Rappe, Trace Elementary. We thought Ms. Rappe was mean, because she made us do multiplication a year early. And because she yelled at us sometimes. She had an allergy to chalk dust and so she used the dust-free kind, which was shinier and crumblier than regular chalk and which made that horrible noise on the chalkboard, but if we even peeped when her chalk inevitably scratched, she would yell at us. And she would yell at us if we called her Mrs. instead of Ms., like, "I learned your name, you should learn mine." But despite all that, she still maintained some popularity because of her two Great Danes, these mammoth Great Danes that she would bring to school a few times a year and let the smallest kindergarteners ride like ponies during recess. For example, Nadine Hanamoto was tiny enough to get to ride Ms. Rappe's Great Danes when we were in kindergarten, although she and I only became friends later, in the ninth grade, when we had English together. Anyway. Ms. Rappe was forever nostalgic about the orchards. Cherry and apricot and pear orchards. And, along the ridges of Santa Clara Valley, to the south and east, cattle ranches, on estates granted by the king of Spain. She was forever waxing sappy, and forever making us do coloring projects involving the Spanish missions and local fruits and fruit blossoms. She told us it was our civic duty to save the coastal redwoods because they were the last real trees left.

The history is, between the world wars, developers started cutting down the fruit trees in Santa Clara Valley and subdividing the orchards. So by the time I got to high school, in 1986, you could tell the age of the shade trees in San Jose by the age of the houses. Like, "That's an Eichler from the fifties, so that maple must be in its thirties." Eichler was this notorious developer, to be mentioned only with distaste. It was a point of ridiculous pride in my family that our house was built in 1924 and was in the Rose Garden District, which Eichler hardly touched. And that our house had wood-frame windows, not aluminum. And that instead of having a swimming pool in our backyard, we had cherry trees, and a cement fountain of a shepherd pulling a thorn from his foot that came from a 1920s Sears, Roebuck catalogue. I knew about all of this before I knew how to multiply, about Eichlers and wood-frame windows and fruit trees versus shade trees.

And if there was a big earthquake, I knew how to turn off the gas.

I mean, just, this atmosphere of desolation, in San Jose, as a teenager. In 1985, when I was thirteen, the City of San Jose started a redevelopment campaign, "San Jose Is Growing Up." With a purple-and-pink logo that was the exact color combination I would have picked for my bat mitzvah if I'd had a bat mitzvah. The city planted these sycamores, these gangling sycamores, along 1st Street and San Carlos Avenue. And they proposed a new downtown convention center and a new downtown shopping concourse and a new downtown light-rail corridor. And the Fairmont built a twenty-story hotel on Market Street. It was San Jose's tallest building. Twenty stories, salmon pink, with an open-air swimming pool on its fourth-floor patio. After the graduation ceremony from middle school, Herbert Hoover Middle School, the dare was to sneak into the Fairmont Hotel and go for a swim. Except no one would admit to knowing what county bus line would get us from our graduation ceremony at the Rose Garden over to Market Street, because familiarity with the county bus lines was shameful. So instead we all walked over to the Rosicrucian Museum, twenty or thirty of us, in our navy blue vinyl graduation gowns. And we kicked each other with the chlorinated water from the fountain surrounding the Rosicrucian statue of the hippopotamus god. And then we went home and felt exquisitely desolate and waited for high school to start.

This is San Jose. This is where I am from.

MITCHELL *and* SUSAN GREEN *explain about the bat mitzvah (early August 2000)*:

M: She complained and complained, and we relented.

S: You relented. I never needed any convincing. She said, "I don't believe in Torah, you don't believe in Torah, what's the point?" And I said, "Look, you're missing the chance to have a big party and make some money." She said, "I'll get a job if I need money." And I thought, What more can you ask from an eleven-year-old? Jennica is very sensible when she needs to be.

M: But can we say we would have let Gabe quit? Would we have let him, as a boy, at age eleven, drop out of his Hebrew classes? We tried very hard to be evenhanded, but would we have let Gabe quit?

S: Well, Gabe never complained, so it was never an issue. But Jennica hated those classes. And I can't say I blame her. She never became friends with a single one of the girls at that synagogue. Nor did Gabe, I might add, with the boys. And, the mothers. These women were just so . . . Asking me wasn't I anxious about keeping the kids in public school. Good riddance. I told Jennica, You may not marry any right-wing evangelicals; otherwise, as far as religion, do what you want to do.

M: It's more than that. She should marry a Jew.

S: Mitchell has some opinions about this.

M: I don't have some opinions, I have one opinion. Jennica should marry a Jew. I had the same opinion about Gabe, and his wife is Jewish. And it's just my opinion. I'll let the fiancé know my opinion, and then I'll keep my mouth shut.

S: And Jennica did get a job, when she finally did need money. Not just in college, but very early on in high school. She wanted to join the Los Gatos Rowing Club, but Mitchell put his foot down about the fees, which were very high. Hundreds and hundreds of dollars, to join a rowing club. So Jennica got a job at Yogurt U.S.A. and paid her own way for three years. Because she wanted to be on a rowing team.

M: She said that there was no point in being Jewish in California. Remember this? "Why won't the Green family admit that there is no point in being Jewish in California? We aren't wandering in the desert." And then she joins a rowing club.

JENNICA GREEN *succumbs to nostalgia; the uptown No. 6 train, forget it (early August 2000)*:

All of which is background for why it was so . . . poignant to get a letter from Nadine about her brother.

I said Nadine was cosmopolitan. Which . . . fine, caveats . . . but sophistication is always relative. What I mean is, by the time Nadine and I became close, in high school, she had tastes and some opinions. She was nearly through with her parents and was buying herself a used car, with her own savings, she said. And she was making her own arrangements with a city, on terms she seemed to be negotiating for herself. Which was impressive to me. It was like she was the sole proprietor of her own flea market. All these curiosities, these five-and-dime thrills. She would always be chewing on hard candies with indecipherable Asian wrappers. Licorice? Sesame? Taffy from, like, Korea? Or Thailand? She wouldn't tell me unless I put one in my mouth. She bought them at Vietnamese and Salvadoran groceries, and she wore such a straight face as she defied me to eat them that I would laugh until I choked, practically, out of anxiety about how rancid they would taste. Her car radio was incessantly tuned to this one schizophrenic station, KFJC, that never played any song you knew, so riding in her car there was always some unrecognizable noise happening in the background. I would be like:

"Who listens to this?" And Nadine would be indignant:

"Who cares who listens to it? The point of music isn't to be able to tell other people that you listen to the same things they do."

"The point of music also isn't to be able to tell other people that you *don't* listen to what they do."

"How about the point of music is enjoying yourself?"

"How about I only enjoy myself if I actually recognize what's playing once in a while?"

"So listen to KFJC more often."

When she was fourteen, Nadine had lied about her age and gotten a job at a Subway Sandwich, so that by the time we were sixteen, when I was earning $4.25 at the yogurt place, Nadine was already working at the artsy movie house in Los Gatos for, like, $6.85 an hour, which seemed like a fortune in 1988. But which in retrospect . . . it should have been obvious that Nadine's finances didn't really make sense.

She shopped secondhand, of course, which was a revelation to me. I mean, how did she know about the Salvation Army in Redwood City? I guess it was a revelation to me in general, how much one could know about a city. Every Goodwill or Savers in Santa Clara Valley, Nadine had been there and knew what they had. Nadine was the first one to start wearing vintage T-shirts. Like, faded blue, child-sized Garfield T-shirts. She squeezed into them by cutting off the collars. This one Garfield shirt that she wore, when my brother saw it, he was like:

"Garfield?" And Nadine said:

"Garfield's cool." And my brother was bewildered. He couldn't tell if she was kidding. And then there was Nadine's Peugeot.

GABRIEL GREEN *tells us about Nadine's Peugeot (early August 2000)*:

I have these conversations with my sister that I don't have with anyone else. And one theory is that it's because she's my sister, but another theory is that it's because in Santa Cruz I don't meet a lot of people who lead the kind of life Jennica leads in New York City.

Take how Jennica eats.

Rachel and I have visited Jennica in Greenwich Village a couple times, and there are definitely some pretty good grocery stores near her, but the food is *so* expensive. *Five dollars* for a pint of supposedly organic strawberries. *Two-fifty* for one bunch of kale, and they don't even have lacinato kale out there, or purple kale, or rainbow chard, or even red Swiss chard, so Jennica's basically eating monoculture greens. She buys "mixed salad greens" for *seven dollars* a bag, triple-washed with who knows what. And to get this stuff home, which is only two blocks away from the grocery store, Jennica throws all of it into plastic bags. There is a *husk* on her corn, corn that Jennica's store sells in *April* . . . there is a *rind* on her grapefruit, grapefruit that gets flown in from *Florida* . . . but still, Jennica puts the corn and the citrus into plastic bags. Her supposedly organic red peppers, which cost *six dollars a pound*, come in a foam tray under shrinkwrap, but she puts them in a plastic bag. And then the checkout girl puts all of Jennica's little plastic parcels into two or three *more* big white plastic bags, and then Jennica walks the two blocks home, where she unpacks all the bags and then throws them in the same trash bin where her cornhusks and citrus rinds go, because they don't do compost in New York City.

The last time we were out there, Rachel and I gave Jennica a whole set of hemp shopping nets as a present, to use instead of plastic bags. Jennica was like, "They won't let me use these! Not in New York!" Instead she hung the nets up on her bedroom doorknob, and now she uses them to dry out her dirty gym clothes.

I mean, Jennica drinks her water from a so-called water purifier. Which means that she only drinks water that has been sitting for hours on end in a plastic Brita jug. I told her that New York City has the best drinking water in the country, except maybe for water from rain-catchment devices, and what she said was, "Obviously I know that, Gabe. But you can't trust the pipes in old buildings." What she really meant was, "Everyone I know drinks their water from a Brita water purifier." So yes, Jennica buys her organic fair-trade coffee, but when she makes it, she makes it in a drip machine, with Brita water, with a plastic cone, and with a reusable nylon filter, so she's basically pouring boiling hot plastic water through a membrane of plastic and then ingesting it straight.

Not that the consumption of plastic polymers that mimic human hormones *necessarily* will play the same role in modern America that lead poisoning played in ancient Rome, or *necessarily* contributes to infertility or dementia. But it's possible. I'm only saying it's *possible.* So that is another theory about Jennica's phone calls: dementia.

Anyway. Jennica will call me up. It will be four-fifteen in the afternoon for me, but in New York City it's seven-fifteen, so Jennica will be walking home, and she'll be all perky and needy. But in California, I'm still at work, and in my IT Department, four-fifteen is the catatonic hour. I'll be like:

"Beh." And perky Jennica will be all:

"Gabe, I need you to tell me everything you can remember about George Hanamoto."

And then it's my job to tell her everything I can remember about George Hanamoto. We don't talk about Rachel, or the baby, or the latest ridiculous thing that Mom and Dad said about the fact that Rachel and I are having a baby, or anything else; we have to talk about George Hanamoto. What I remember about George Hanamoto is pretty much nothing, except the fistfight with Old Man Bersen on the day of the Loma Prieta earthquake. Jennica's on her cell phone, walking through New York City. In the background, what I'm hearing is sirens and screaming people and drivers leaning on their horns and trucks with no suspension hitting potholes and motorcycles without mufflers. It sounds basically like Jennica is walking through rush hour in the apocalypse, but what she wants to talk about is George Hanamoto. Or, like, my phone will ring:

"Beh."

"Gabe, I need you to do that voice that Nadine Hanamoto used to do with her Peugeot."

When we were in high school, Nadine had this Peugeot, some mid-seventies model. It was a loud car, and when Nadine drove it, she would always be coaxing it along, like, "Oh, you want to be in third gear, don't you? You want to know why I won't take you out of second, don't you? Oh, poor baby. You wish Mommy would give you the unleaded gasoline, but Mommy can only afford the regular. Let Mommy put you into third. Yes, yes."

Jennica hated the voice, because she couldn't do it right, which became a joke in itself. But now, ten years later, Jennica suddenly wants to hear me do the voice. It's as if she can't cross the street in New York without thinking about California. Where is all this nostalgia coming from? And yes, *one* theory is that all siblings have these conversations with each other, but *another* theory is that Jennica just isn't happy in New York City.

JENNICA GREEN *continues to fail to explain what she was doing on an uptown No. 6 train (early August 2000)*:

About the letter from Nadine.

Nadine's father was Japanese and her mother was Mexican. Which is fascinating, come to think of it, but which I hardly thought about at the time; at most, I envied how exotic Nadine looked. Her father was hardly around, but Nadine's mother, Perla Hanamoto, was always there, and always formidable, with huge reserves of energy to direct against Nadine. Unless she was making the effort to smile, Perla had these deep lines from her nose down to the corners of her lips, the lines of discontent. Whenever I went over to their house . . . this ranch-style house with aluminum windows, at the border of Willow Glen . . . she always interrogated me about my academic plans, as a way to needle Nadine. Was I planning on graduating with my class or taking the equivalency exams to graduate early, like Nadine? Was I going to a university or to a community college, like Nadine? Was I going to Junior Prom or was I skipping, like Nadine? She would open the door to Nadine's bedroom, her boxy, eastern bazaar of a bedroom, to nag Nadine about something, and Nadine would just say:

"Later, Mom, okay? Bye."

That was alien to me, that refusal to engage your parents. But Perla Hanamoto certainly loomed judgmentally enough around that house, and Nadine's older sister, Theresa, was their mother's, like, deputy.

And, Theresa and Nadine. Really, they were the funniest people I had ever met. It's hard to explain, but when they got going with each other? Like, Theresa would come into Nadine's bedroom because, whatever, their mother was angry with them about the refrigerator. And Theresa would have a plastic takeout box with her, holding it like clinical evidence. She'd kick herself a path through the Salvation Army sheets that Nadine had hung from her ceiling and whatever random mannequin parts Nadine had lying around her floor, in order to get to Nadine's bed to confront Nadine with the takeout box.

"Nadi, regarding this specimen from the fridge." And Nadine would be like:

"I said I'm going to eat it."

"Right. You said that . . . last week."

And I would recognize the box. It would be from a month before . . . some enchilada from El Cacique, which was Nadine's favorite taqueria. Theresa would be like:

"Nadi, when I asked you about this specimen of enchilada last week, I figured you knew about . . . the mold. I told myself, Nadi's not squeamish, she'll scrape the mold away. I figured, Nadi is tough enough." And Nadine would say:

"Would you just shut up and put it back in the fridge? Because the longer it stays out, the faster it will go bad." And Theresa, like, pressing ahead:

"So, Nadi. Last week the mold was only on the left, on top of the rice. Now I observe three kinds of mold, all of which have spread from the moist lower regions where the rice was to this large lump in the middle, which I believe to have once been an enchilada. I am going to attempt to lift the lump." She'd be, like, prodding the enchilada with the handle of a fork and making a face. "I have successfully lifted the lump. And my question is, Nadi, have you smelled this? Are you . . . tough enough?" Like, pressing the tray in Nadine's face. And, Nadine would fix her face against the odor and say:

"I'm totally going to eat that."

Which, maybe you had to be there.

And then there was their brother, George. The oldest sibling. Who had been gone for ten years. He had run away to San Francisco when he was fifteen or sixteen, and he was never mentioned. And the day his name finally came up was the day of the Loma Prieta earthquake.

MAYNARD GOGARTY *tells the story of what happened on the uptown No. 6 train (early August 2000)*:

Enter the subway conductor.

She is young, black, with one of those tight, heavy MTA uniforms on. She is a buxom conductor, but her uniform has compressed her chest into a flat breastwork of civic authority. And—the redbird trains are designed such that the conductor has to hustle back and forth from one car to another, depending on whether the train has pulled up to an express platform or a local platform. I mention this because apparently we were in the car that the conductor used as her headquarters at express stops, so the fact that the conductor was investigating our car implied that she had already searched one entire half of the train looking for her culprit, the entire down-track half of the train, and had found nothing.

So! Enter the subway conductor. Those doors between subway cars are always hard to get apart, but she just thrusts them wide with one wrist and shouts at the whole carload of us, "Anyone here touch the brake?"

The woman with the beauty spots—looks at me. She wants

to verify that I will confess that I did in fact close the cover of the emergency brake. I realize that either I turn myself in or I will be denounced. So as the conductor is hurrying past, I say, "Madam? The cover on that brake there? It was open, and so I shut it."

The conductor looks at me with—wrath!

"You touched the brake."

"No. The cover was open. The little metal box, the cover. I shut that."

"You touched the brake."

"No. This was after the train had stalled. I shut the cover. Because the alarm was sounding."

"The alarm was going off," she said with disgust, "so you decided to touch the brake."

So then—then! She turns away from me and reopens the box over the brake.

What the EMERGENCY BRAKE *has to say for itself (early August 2000):*

Meee!

MAYNARD GOGARTY *tells the story of what happened on the uptown No. 6 train (early August 2000):*

The conductor pretends to inspect the brake, but—what is there to inspect? The woman with the beauty spots just sits there, underneath the conductor, eyes shut, wishing for her privacy back, until finally the conductor gives up, turns to me, and asks, "You think maybe the alarm was going off for a reason? Like something is wrong and you shouldn't be touching the brake?"

She hasn't properly shut the cover, so the alarm is still bleating at us. But she leaves it bleating and unlocks the closet in our subway car, her little closet for the express stops, and she goes inside, saying, "I am *not* done with you."

"But I did nothing wrong."

"I'm telling you, I am *not* done with you."

At first she is tinkering with some of the controls, shouting with the motorman over a telephone. But then—the lights and air conditioning come back to life. She leaves the closet, leaves our car, and then the side doors spring apart and 33rd Street heaves its flames into the subway car.

Over the hoarse public address system comes her voice: "Thirty-third Street. Grand Central next. Stand clear the doors."

In her voice I can hear, she is not done with me. But as I am awaiting my trial, the two black boys—who knows where the three girls were hiding themselves—the two black boys with the trumpet cases board the subway car. One of them is chubby, the other one is skinny. They sit down not far from me, open up their trumpet cases, and begin admiring each other's graffiti pens. That is what they were toting in their trumpet cases—vandal-sized permanent markers.

JAMES CLEVELAND *talks television (early August 2000)*:

Brittany and Juney and Shawna flipped off the white guy. I said, "Why you all trying to get us in trouble?"

And Chief said, "You a coward, son?"

I hated that, because it was like he was trying to prove something that didn't need to be proved. But when the subway doors finally opened, Brittany and Juney and Shawna ran to get on a different car, and so it was only me and Chief that got on board the same car with the white guy. And Chief was talking all loud, like, "I'a fucking show you, son, I'a fucking show you." He was talking loud, and I couldn't tell whether Chief was scared or not, which I also hated. He was saying, "Son, it is fucking hot in here."

And yeah, it was hot on the subway. My jeans were like they just came out of the drier. And the white guy, when we got on, he was right there, like he was on safari, in his mad layers of clothes. I saw this show on thirteen about the Sahara. "Funding was provided by the Corporation for Public Broadcasting." It was about slaves in the salt mines and Timbuktu and camel caravans and all that. The nomads keep cool by wearing lots and lots of layers of clothes. And that was what it looked like the white guy was trying to do with his mad layers. But it is bullshit about layers being cool, because the white guy had a whole Congo River of sweat coming down his face. That was probably what the cold thing was that touched his balls—it was probably sweat.

The only seats were right next to the white guy. So that was where me and Chief sat, right next to the white guy. And Chief, he was trying to show off he wasn't scared, so he opened his case and took out the pens. And he whispered, "Who the coward, son?"

Everybody was looking at us, so I tried to look normal, like, "Ain't nothing to see here, folks." Pretending the pens weren't nothing special at all. But I was holding the pen in my hand, and the train conductor walked right in.

MAYNARD GOGARTY *tells the story of what happened on the uptown No. 6 train (early August 2000):*

The doors close on 33rd. The train leaves the station like a dog on a leash—lingering behind to sniff the stains on the platform, then jolting ahead, down the tunnel, already smelling the urine of Grand Central. And I, like the rest of the train car, am gawking at these boys and their pens, and their—bravado in displaying them. They are, I believe, quite illegal under Mayor Giuliani.

Reenter the conductor, to execute me right there on the linoleum floor of the uptown No. 6 train with her MTA-issue revolver. She is sturdy-footed, quite obviously used to riding in trains without holding on. She straightens her uniform with a tug at the belt—as if anything that tight could really become displaced—and seeing her, the chubby boy claps his trumpet case shut and the skinny kid shoves the pen he's holding between his legs.

YVETTE BENITEZ-BIRCH, *the conductor, quotes her brief lecture (early August 2000)*:

Jonas was the motorman, and he found the problem up front. It was just a brake in the third car, and so once Jonas found it, we were back up and running. Whatever that gentleman had done, that condescending gentleman in the white straw hat, it wasn't responsible for stopping the train. But there was something about him that made me think he needed a talking-to.

I told him, "Mister, I don't know where you're from. Maybe where you're from they let you touch the emergency brake. But here in New York City, we ask our customers not to touch the emergency brake. Understand?"

He said, "But madam! I am from New York City."

I told him, "If you are from New York City, then you should know not to touch the brake."

He said, "But touching the brake is exactly what I didn't do."

I was thinking, I do not have time for this—I do not have time to be called "madam." But there were two little boys sitting there, and one of them said, "Hey lady, he lying."

I thought, Now why would this skinny little boy call the man in the white straw hat a liar? I knew the man in the hat hadn't pulled the brake, but like I said, there was something about him that I did not like. I thought, Let's see what the boy has to say.

MAYNARD GOGARTY *presses ahead with the story of what happened on the uptown No. 6 train (early August 2000)*:

The skinny kid says, "Hey lady, he lying." This is a tone of voice I recognize from my students—the sanctimony of a child who is trying to cover up his own misbehavior.

His chubbier friend says, "Shut up, son."

But the skinny kid insists, "No. This is what happen." And then he tells a tale to be reckoned with: he tells the conductor that he and his friends were outside the train, that the girls were teasing me, and that I got mad and pulled the brake so that I could make a citizen's arrest. A citizen's arrest—such is the fancy of youth. But in the midst of this tale, and timed perfectly to corroborate, the door between our car and the next car up lurches open and the three black girls appear—looking for their lost escorts, no doubt. The instant they see the conductor, all three girls squeal "Oh shit!" and scurry back the way they came—letting the heavy door lurch shut behind them. But they had served destiny's purpose: they had corroborated the boy's story.

The conductor may be masterful at being bossy, but—she's gotten in over her head here. She grabs the overhead bars, blocking up the entire aisle with her skepticism and her grimace. The train is slowing down, as the trains always do in that last stretch before Grand Central. The two black kids clearly think they've told the truth, but they do not know what the adults are going to do.

I say, "Madam, I have no idea what these children saw."

The skinny boy says again, "He lying—he the one that pull the brake."

And this is when the woman with the beauty spots speaks.

She says, "Excuse me? I saw it from right here. All this man did was close the box. Those boys are the real, like, troublemakers."

That *like*—very sexy. Sexier than the sweat rings in her shirt. *Like*, the watchword of eternal youth. But—what a gorgeous and irrepressible snitch! Cooperating with the authorities! To save my sweaty and luckless hide! Again I ask you: What *was* she doing there?

JENNICA GREEN *still fails to explain what she was doing on an uptown No. 6 train (early August 2000)*:

All right, so, the letter.

> Dear Jenny,
>
> I'm sorry to send you such a possibly weird letter.

And then Nadine tells me everything that's happened to her in the last ten years. She got a divorce four years ago from the guy she married when we were twenty, so maybe it's for the best that I didn't go to that wedding after all, she says. She doesn't know if I ever realized how upset she was at the time, that I didn't come. She apologizes, anyway, for having been angry with me; she knows I was at Princeton and it was hard for me to find the money to fly home on short notice. Anyway, she promises to forgive me if I come to her next wedding.

> His name is Oscar Seventeen-Other-Last-Names Dicochea.

She says he works as a counselor in the prisons and he is devoted to fixing up Mustangs, which is how they met, and he is an avid birdwatcher. Also he has two kids from his first marriage, who stay with them weekends. She adores the kids, who are super-smart firecrackers, but it's hard, she says, because by the time the kids get used to living by Nadine and Oscar's rules, the weekend is over and they have to go back to their mother. Also Nadine is pregnant, due in late December. Oscar's kids are convinced that they get to name the baby, and they want to call it Dick O. Dicochea. Also Nadine and Oscar bought a house in Fresno, which needs a lot of work.

This kind of a letter. Your best friend's life story.

The whole thing just gives me this feeling that I am . . . unreachably far away from the place where real life is carried on. And that I have nothing to report. Like, what have I been doing here in New York? Playing with water? While everyone was back in California, working with . . . redwood? There are as many kinds of homesickness as there are kinds of common cold, and that's one of them: the sudden feeling that you could have been so much happier if only ten years ago you had stayed put.

> I almost forgot the best thing!
>
> George (that George) just bought an apartment in Manhattan, and he says he wants to meet you. He says he

forgives you for standing him up in 1989. How hilarious if the two of you hit it off.

And it was like, am I finally going to meet George Hanamoto? And will he be as funny as Nadine, and as exotic and good-looking? So I am thinking this . . . in my perfectly silent apartment, my broiling hot but perfectly silent apartment . . . there is this noise. Like, someone is in my apartment. A burglar is in my apartment.

And, from my kitchen and bedroom, you can hear everything that happens in my neighbor's kitchen and bedroom. I tell people that I can hear what happens in my neighbor's bedroom, and they immediately think, *Ooo!* As if what you hear from your neighbor's bedroom is always *Ooo!* It's more like, if your neighbor has a dog, you can tell when the dog needs its nails clipped. Or, in my case, you can hear your neighbor building his loom, or whatever. But all the noises that come from my neighbor's apartment are muffled in this particular way, and this sound, the burglar sound, as I'm sitting at the kitchen island with Nadine's letter, is not muffled at all. It's crisp, it's in-the-room-with-me crisp. Someone is standing in the alcove behind my refrigerator, where the recycling is, which is the one part of the kitchen I can't see, and is taking a knife out of a crinkling plastic bag.

And my reaction? My brilliant reaction? I freeze. Not, like, I grab my cell phone and run out the front door. No, I freeze. I sit there and wait to get hit over the head by the intruder. And then there it is again, the noise. The burglar is definitely in the alcove, and he definitely has a knife in a plastic bag. And apparently he's having serious problems getting the knife out of the plastic bag . . .

So anyway, it's a mouse. In my recycling.

I don't even try to actually spot the mouse. I just leave Nadine's letter on the kitchen island and run to the pet store on 6th Avenue. And I do mean run, because it was almost eight o'clock, and I didn't want to wait another day for my cat. Because I've always wanted a cat, and I'm tired of never doing the things I most want.

GABRIEL GREEN *discusses whether or not his sister does the things she most wants (early August 2000)*:

After college, she didn't take any time off; she didn't go to Thailand or Peru or anywhere. Three weeks after graduating, she started her first job, as an analyst for Hoffman Ballin. And the result was, for three years she never left America, never had a real vacation.

I would tell her, "Jennica. Take a leave of absence. Go to Thailand for a month. You can have massages every day, you can do an intestinal cleanse, you can take cooking classes, you can go to a yoga retreat on the beach." She said she couldn't take off that much time until she quit, and she didn't want to quit until she found a new job in the arts, because the arts were her passion. I would tell her, "So start applying! You need a vacation." But she didn't want to start applying until she had paid off her student loans and saved up an emergency fund. I told her, "You don't need an emergency fund. In an emergency, you can move to Vietnam. You can live the life of Riley there on *nothing*, on, like, *three thousand dollars* for six months."

But no. Instead she had an apartment in Greenwich Village without any roommates, and she bought herself clothes, and every month she put the maximum amount into her 401(k). And so it took her three years to finally pay off her student loans and quit her job at Hoffman Ballin.

And yes, then she got herself a job in the arts, doing "development" at the New York Public Library. Meaning she was organizing parties for the library's rich donors. But between when her job at Hoffman Ballin ended and when her job at the library began, she only gave herself ten days of vacation, which she used to go to Paris. And because of how little the library paid, she converted her emergency fund into an emergency clothes-and-restaurants fund.

And after barely two years at the library, she decided to quit. She said, "The library has some serious staffing problems." What she meant was, "I am the best employee the New York Public Library has ever had; I'm the last one to leave every day; I do my own work and everyone else's work too; I'm working harder at the library than I did at Hoffman Ballin." She said, "If I'm living this sort of life, I might as well be making enough money not to have to deplete my emergency clothes-and-restaurants fund." It's like Jennica is so concerned with living sustainably in some financial-slash-prestige sense, but she doesn't even think about whether she is living sustainably in an emotional sense.

See? She makes interesting decisions. She always wants to dress and eat and live so that everyone will think, "Oh, she's friends with successful people." But at the same time she wants to pay her own way. Rachel says, "A lot of women feel like that; money is different for women than it is for men. Women aren't raised on the assumption that they will always be able to just *make* as much money as they want." That's one *theory*, but another theory is that Jennica is a Green and that we Greens all have money issues. If you put a Green in New York City and tell her to pay her own way and keep up appearances, of course she is going to work all the time.

For years, whenever Jennica came out to San Jose, which were the only vacations she would take, Rachel and I would beseech her to move to Santa Cruz. Last year, when everyone in America was moving to the Bay Area, we told her that if she moved to Santa Cruz, I would teach her Web design and Rachel would teach her to surf, and Jennica and I could go into business together doing Web stuff and Rachel and Jennica could go to the beach together every morning for exercise, and we could all buy a bungalow together somewhere, and all go shopping at the Staff of Life together and restock our communal dry goods . . . But Jennica wanted to stay in New York. "I feel like I haven't done everything I want to do there yet," she said.

When she finally quit the job at the library, she went back to

Hoffman Ballin, this time to run their personnel department. She said, "Gabe, I promise I'll quit Hoffman again as soon as I have a down payment saved." Fine, a down payment . . . *in Manhattan.* You want your older sister to be happy, but you also know that there are certain things your older sister is never going to be able to do. She lives out this self-fulfilling prophecy of anxiety. She's successful because she works hard, but she only works hard because she is stressed out about being successful. She's only happy *because* she's unhappy. Right? I mean, I don't mean to be harsh. But what could ever happen that would let her *prove* her success? And Jennica can't live in California, because she thinks that successful people only live in New York.

JENNICA GREEN *nearly explains what she was doing on an uptown No. 6 train (early August 2000):*

You may know this pet store. It's on 6th Avenue and it displays Jack Russell terrier puppies in the window, or whatever's in style. And it has this gigantic, bitchy, hoary macaw at the front of the store that sits dead still until you are right next to it and then screams its name in your ear.

I got to the pet store just before eight P.M., but it turned out that it was open until nine, so I sort of . . . perused. The aquarium section was very dreamy: like, dark, except for the purple lights in the tanks, and with that bubbling sound from the fish toys and with that weirdly good, silty smell? So I was dipping my finger into the water to pet the aquatic plants . . . Touching the turtle's feet. Crinkling my nose at the mice. They had this whole pen of mice just beside the aquarium aisle, living in an inch of sawdust and tunneling into a stale loaf of oat bread. You feel bad for pet-store mice, since they obviously are sold as food for snakes, but I guess not bad enough that you aren't going to buy a kitten to kill the house mouse that's in your kitchen. Because, if it wanted to, my house mouse could go live in the loom next door, or whatever it is that guy is building, but pet-store mice have no escape.

I was working my way toward the kittens when the owner lady finally came over. She was like:

"The last time you were here, you were expressing some reluctance. You said you had issues with spontaneity and indulgence, and that you were concerned with how cat ownership by single women was perceived by single men in New York. We were discussing whether or not you should premise your day-to-day decisions on the likes and dislikes of the hypothetical male love interest."

I like this owner. Very student-radical-feminist-turned-small-businesswoman-divorcée. Mid-fifties, obviously hanging around the Village since college for who knows what reason. You know, still smokes two cigarettes a day, wears these earthy clothes she bought in the early eighties. So I said:

"Well, he's not hypothetical. His name is George and we're being set up on a date by his sister." I mean, I didn't want the owner to think I was utterly hopeless. "Plus, I heard a mouse." And she said:

"Okay, so you've reached a stage where delay is no longer emotionally viable. That's healthy. Is there one of these kitties you have your eye on?"

And there wasn't, really, which was one reason I kept going back. Because, I don't want just some random cat. I want a hulking cat. One that will kind of spill over the edge of whatever he sits on. And a very intelligent cat. Because some people have these airhead cats, who obviously are unsettled by everything that is happening around them, and antsy. I don't want one of those. I don't want a cutesy cat, or a spastic cat. I want a cat that's jaded. Affectionate, but coy. And I want a cat that is world-weary and a little wry. I want a well-read cat, a fat and autodidactic cat. I was trying to explain this to the lady, who . . . I like her, but she was giving me this look, like, Am I going to make a sale? Finally she asks me:

"Have you been to Practical Cats?" Which is their sister store, on Lex and 78th, and which only sells cats. A kitten from Practical Cats can cost from five to eight hundred dollars, but, for example, they have cats where they guarantee the cat will learn its own name. They've bred them for that. So she gives me their card and sells me a litter box and a bag of litter and one of those catches-the-mouse-alive traps that don't work. And as I am going, the macaw, like, hollers in my ear.

What THE MACAW *hollered (Summer 2000)*:

Ho, Ho, Ho Chi Minh!

JENNICA GREEN *finally explains what she was doing on an uptown No. 6 train (early August 2000)*:

Anyway, that was Monday night. When I got home from the pet store, I set up the mousetrap, turned my air conditioner on low, and ate my leftover falafel salad out on my fire escape. Where there are no parquet floors radiating heat, and where there is a breeze to keep me cool while my air conditioner gets started, and where the only wild rodents are pigeons. And squirrels. I decided that I liked the idea of going on a date with George Hanamoto. We could get white wine at a rooftop bar somewhere; I'd been fantasizing about rooftop bars since the start of the heat wave. Maybe there was one with a pool, like on the fourth floor of the Fairmont. Anyway.

And I decided that I liked the idea of a store called Practical Cats. I could take a few hundred dollars out of my money market account, which supposedly is the account I use to save up for my down payment, but whatever. And I work in midtown, where Hoffman's administrative offices are, but Tuesday morning I had a meeting at the downtown office, where our traders work, so after that meeting I could take an early lunch and go shopping for my five-to-eight-hundred-dollar cat. Which is why I was on an uptown 6 train at 10:25 A.M. on a Tuesday.

MAYNARD GOGARTY *comes within a whit of finishing the story of what happened on the uptown No. 6 train (early August 2000):*

So! Half a minute south of Grand Central on an uptown No. 6 train. The skinny black kid has denounced me to the authorities, and the woman with the beauty spots has in turn denounced the skinny black kid to the authorities, saying, "Those kids are lying, and their cases are full of graffiti pens."

The conductor decides to take charge. She says, "Miss, I know that Mr. Peanut here"—meaning, alas, me—"didn't pull the brake. It was someone at the front of the train." Apparently she heard this from the motorman when she was in her booth. "I am just telling Mr. Peanut to keep his hands to himself with the brake box." Meanwhile she is considering the boys' trumpet cases, and so now she says, "Show me what you've got."

Well—then I have my brainstorm. Oh, it cut right through the old hot and humid brain haze, this brainstorm of mine did. Follow me: if I could confuse the situation for just a moment, the conductor would have to go back into her closet to announce the next stop. Then the boys could escape when the train doors opened at Grand Central, and then I would have a lovely segue into conversation with the beauty-spotted woman on the way to 51st Street. And I knew that the woman with the beauty spots would stay on the train at least as far as 51st Street, because if she were getting off at Grand Central, why would she not have stayed on the express train back at Union Square? Ah-ha! Is my brain not infallible?

I say to the conductor—audaciously, "You are not going to search the boys' trumpets."

The conductor says, "Mister, I have had enough from you, and I have heard enough of your so-called opinions. Either everyone wants me to call the police in here or these two boys will show me what they've got."

So! Pointing my attaché at the woman with the beauty spots, I say to the conductor, "Madam. The lady here misinterpreted what she saw. There were no graffiti pens. Very likely she saw two rambunctious black kids—."

And just as I'd predicted, the conductor goes back into her booth to announce Grand Central. All right—*mea culpa! Mea* own regrettable *culpa.* I shouldn't have implied that bigotry was at work in what the beautiful woman said. I shouldn't have implied that she was only denouncing the black kids because they were—black. But I meant only to diffuse the situation. I would apologize to her on the way to 51st Street.

What I'd forgotten was that the black boys had dates in the next car up, so naturally they weren't going to get off the train, not without their girlfriends. And I also didn't account for another possibility.

YVETTE BENITEZ-BIRCH *announces that the train is going express (early August 2000):*

You cannot make it too clear for these people. I said, "Forty-second Street, Grand Central Station. Transfer to the 4, 5, and 7 trains and the shuttle to Times Square. *Ladies* and *gentlemen,* listen up. Listen *up,* people. This train is making express stops only to 125th Street. *Express* stops *only.* This train will *not be stopping* at 51st Street, 68th Street, 77th Street, 96th Street, 103rd Street, 110th Street, or 116th Street. If you *want* to *stop* at 51st Street, 68th Street, 77th Street, 96th Street, 103rd Street, 110th Street, or 116th Street, *get off this train and get on the local immediately behind.*"

You cannot make it too clear for these people.

When we had left 42nd, I went back into the car to straighten things out. The condescending gentleman in the hat was still there, and the two little boys who had called him a liar were still there, but the woman in black was gone. She'd exited the train at 42nd to catch the local. God's truth be told, I was relieved that the woman was gone. I do not need all this insanity. I got enough grief.

I said, "I am only surprised that you *all* didn't get off the train." I told the boys to leave the TA's property alone, and I gave the condescending man in the hat a look to say, Mister, you are not forgiven, but you are dismissed. And then I went back in to announce 59th.

JAMES CLEVELAND *tells the stupid ending to the story (early August 2000)*:

It's a stupid ending to the story, I'm warning you.

For example, if you make a show about camel caravans in the Sahara for thirteen, you better show me two caravans crashing into each other in the desert and fighting. If they don't want to fight, it's your job to make them fight. The point being is, don't tell stories if they only have a stupid ending, and I'm warning you that this story has a stupid ending.

Everyone left the car but me and Chief and the white guy. And the white guy had a look on his face like this all was just about what he had been expecting.

So I said, "Hey, mister."

And Chief said, "Son, shut up!"

But if the guy in the tie wanted to get us in trouble, he would have done it already. I said, "Hey, mister, they not trumpets."

And the guy said, "I know."

So I said, "Then why you said they was?"

And he said, "I was trying to be nice. Stay out of trouble with those pens." And he wanted to know where we got the cases from and if we did play the trumpet.

So I said, "We in band camp."

And he said, "I thought maybe so." And then he said, "I'm a musician too, and we musicians need to stand up for each other. But the trumpet is a noble instrument that deserves your respect. Don't you neglect it."

Making me feel guilty, like I was supposed to be practicing trumpet all day. I told you it was a stupid ending. The interesting part was later, after me and Chief ditched Brittany and Juney and Shawna.

MAYNARD GOGARTY *provides an epilogue to the story of what happened on the uptown No. 6 train (early August 2000):*

I have no epilogue to the story of what happened on the uptown No. 6 train. So may I untangle myself from the *res* that I am *in media* of here and tell you about how I sold the rights to my film, or do you demand an epilogue?

Fine, then—an epilogue:

Prevailing wisdom—that oxymoron—prevailing wisdom has it that there is something exceptional about New York, some ineffable spirit to Manhattan Island, an *esprit de pays* above and beyond that *esprit de corps* that supposedly typifies New Yorkers. The *esprit de pays* is the notion that Manhattan cannot be improved upon. It has something to do with how the city manifested itself in 1948 or 1957 or 1994. When, six weeks after moving into student housing at NYU, some aspiring bachelor of arts condemns as "gentrification" a proposal that a reviled East Village pervert parlor that sold only beers and massages be replaced with a bright Duane Reade that sells floss and floor polish and flowers? That's the *esprit de pays.* When salaried Democrats braggadociously complain about the twenty-six thousand dollars they spend so that their child will not have to participate in the public schools? That's the *esprit de pays.* When levelheaded retirees send lachrymose letters to the *Times* bewailing the fact that the MTA is retiring the horror-show redbird subway cars in favor of sleek, airy trains designed in Osaka? That's the *esprit de pays.* I reject this lunacy. Because if you subscribe to the *esprit de pays,* then of necessity you also subscribe to the belief that the only way to be happy is to leave New York.

One form that the *esprit de pays* takes is the insistence—by the young and the lusty—that missed opportunities are romantic, that it is romantic that in New York no one meets anyone twice.

Bosh! *Esprit de pays!* It is not romantic that no one meets anyone twice in New York—it is appalling! Because it means that if you believe in being reserved, you must always be alone.

So there is your epilogue, you—optimists. There is the epilogue to the story of the woman with the beauty spots whom I met—once—on a No. 6 train, uptown. Where was I?

I believe I was about to tell you about my visit with David Fowler, my lawyer, my pro bono lawyer, who will be advising me on the contract to sell the rights to my movie.

There has always been an air of default about my friendship with David. We are friends because—after knowing each other for three decades, what else can we be? Our fathers collaborated on this and that, and our mothers were always of a mind, when we were children, as to the merits of a particular teacher or the imbecility of a certain principal. In other words, I was always sent to the Fowlers' to play—board games.

It was revolting and infuriating. David and his younger sister chewed on all the game pieces. We would play Monopoly, and when I finally controlled an entire run of properties and could begin the development of Pacific Avenue with those little green Monopoly houses that represent the first wave of urban renewal, the eaves of my newly erected units would not be properly aligned because David's sister had gnawed on the roof lines. We would play Risk, and when David amassed an army of little plastic cubes to pour across the Bering Strait from his stronghold in Alaska, it was an army riddled with teething marks. The things children are expected to endure! Obviously, David always won. He knew all the rules to every game—he loved the rules—and if you ever threatened his victory, he would surprise you with some new rule that prevented you from doing what you wanted to do.

By a certain age—eleven, twelve—I anyway preferred my own company, and the piano, to anything else.

And in high school David became an enthusiast of role-playing games—of games that required you to fill out paperwork.

The purpose of the paperwork was that, once complete, you were permitted to pretend that you were an elf in an iron bikini or a dwarf with a "plus-two ax." David immersed himself in this, and when we were fifteen and going to Chatham, he tried to recruit me into his—coven, a coven which, it seemed, consisted of just him. He would sit in his room alone all summer, memorizing the rules but never actually playing the game. He even would draft his own proposed rules—how to battle ghosts, how to build a golem—and he would submit them to the publishers of these rulebooks, hoping that his bill would become a law and soon every elf in America would have to follow the Fowler Amendment when calculating the rate at which rust accumulated on her iron bikini. This—is my lawyer.

DAVID FOWLER *does not tell a sockdolager about Gogarty (early August 2000)*:

Fellow I know from the City Bar works in entertainment law. Smart guy, doing very well for himself. Says, "It's not entertainment *law* that's interesting, it's entertainment *clients.*" All right, Gogarty isn't a client exactly, he's a friend, but wait until you hear this sockdolager about him.

Manny Gogarty calls on Monday. And you know, if I have free time, which thankfully isn't always the case, I lend him a hand, pro bono. I tell him to come by, and Tuesday morning he shows up in my reception. Comes in, covered in sweat from the subway but still looking dapper, as always, with his briefcase and his hat. And I guess he hadn't seen my new office, which I share with a few other attorneys, other solo practitioners, because the first thing he says is, "I like this space, it suits your utilitarianism."

I say, "It's respectable."

"Absolutely! Artificial ferns. Wall-to-wall carpeting, no doubt very easy to vacuum. Eight-foot ceilings with the asbestos tiles, very easy to rewire."

I tell him, "Look, don't scare me, those tiles aren't asbestos. I don't want a place that makes the clients think I'm wasting their money."

"David," he says, "I have never felt that you're wasting my money."

There is no talking to Gogarty except you feel like he's passing judgment on you. Him telling me "I have never felt you're wasting my money"? When he's never even gotten me a thank-you gift? Yes, Gogarty, in fact, I do run a business, and I do have paying clients.

He says, "I think you've found your niche here, David. This office really goes with your look."

"My look? What look?"

"Your shoes."

"My shoes."

"Black 'leather' tennis shoes with black stitching, black nylon laces, and thick black rubber soles."

"What, Gogarty, you've got a problem with my shoes? I can wear them for anything. I can wear them running, I can wear them to court with a suit. I own one pair of shoes, they cost me forty dollars."

"And this office space meets the same criteria. That's what I'm saying. You are an indefatigable ascetic."

"How's your mother, Gogarty?"

"I am her only disappointment."

"Your grandmother?"

"The same. Strong as a tortoise."

Never does he ask me about my kids or my wife. You know, he's good at heart, but he's got such a stiff manner. Is it that he's morbidly shy? Is it that he doesn't want to intrude? Is it all part of his endless philosophy of dignity? Anyway, he gives me the contract. I tell him, Look, I can tell you what this says as a legal matter, but I can't tell you whether it's a good deal as a business matter—I know nothing about this industry. He says he just wants to understand what he's signing away and how much money to expect. I tell him I'll take a look. But I ask him, out of curiosity, Who's the attorney who wrote this?

FRANNY CLEMENT, *the attorney who wrote it, gives us a tour of the reception area of Herman Nathaniel LLP and tells us about her meeting with Maynard Gogarty (early August 2000)*:

In our reception area, along with the white leather chairs and the white marble coffee tables and the white, muggy view of Jersey City, New Jersey, is an enlarged replica of a famous Japanese bonsai. Now most bonsai are planted in earthenware trays that are as shallow as wasabi dishes, but the trough holding *our* bonsai is made from marble and is over two feet deep. And instead of being only a few inches high, *our* bonsai trees are over twelve feet high. And instead of dwarf pines, the trees in *our* bonsai are fully mature junipers. But otherwise our bonsai is a to-scale replica of a planting of seven trees that was given as part of a famous dowry in seventeenth-century Japan. Welcome to Herman Nathaniel LLP; our receptionists are allegedly happy to bring you a beverage while you wait.

Now, Mr. Gogarty did not exactly look at home in our lobby. He was standing on an open patch of white marble tile, as far as he could be from our bonsai and our chairs and our receptionists, with his old brown briefcase leaning against his calf as if he were afraid to set it down on any of our four white marble coffee tables. And he was ventilating himself, one hand pumping the breast of his jacket in and out to get air to his chest, the other one beating his hat up and down beside his cheek to get air down his collar. He was dressed for summer, but so was Gene Kelly in *Inherit the Wind*.

But let me come to the point. The reason I had invited Mr. Gogarty down to our offices was that one of my clients is ITD Records, of Long Island City, New York. ITD stands for "intent to distribute." As in "possession of a controlled narcotic with." Obviously, ITD is a pro bono client. And they had just signed a new performer who was so very, *very* prolific, but so very, *very* unconcerned with copyright difficulties. Puppy Jones! Now, for the most part I had been able to track down permissions for Mr. Jones, but Mr. Gogarty seemed to hold the exclusive rights to his own music, and seems to have sold Mr. Jones a CD at Sundance for five dollars, with no contact information.

Isn't that quaint? And isn't that the sort of thing I want to spend my time on, at one in the morning, after I am done with the work for our paying clients? And isn't it generous of the partners in the Intellectual Property Department at Herman Nathaniel LLP to allow their sixth-year associates to take on as much pro bono work as they like, but only as long as it "does not interfere with other assignments"?

MAYNARD GOGARTY *moves right along (early August 2000)*:

I knew from her voice on the phone that Franny would be black, but I wasn't expecting her to be so—short. An air of seriousness about her, which I always trust and admire, but it was beaten in with sarcasm, which I sometimes distrust. She had extravagant artificial braids affixed to her scalp by one of those mysterious methods hairstylists have, involving seared knots. But her skirt was a conformist gray, and her blouse was that ditto-ink purple that people are wearing this season, and wrinkled at the elbows. So—a short, sarcastic woman carrying an accordion folder.

She took one look at me and my boater and decided to hustle me out of her office. She insisted that we—talk—over breakfast, and she led me to a deli a block and a half away, just far enough to vanquish any reservoirs of cool I had gathered in my shirt while in her lobby. May I tell you what she ate for breakfast, this woman who wants to buy the rights to my movie?

Bivouacked in the middle of the deli to which she led me was—a breakfast buffet. Many different dishes, each one isolated, like radium, in a deep aluminum pan and suspended above a steaming bath of water. One hundred dishes, one single uncanny smell. Uncanny because it is the same smell that is in every deli in Manhattan now, a mixture of dishwater and barbecue sauce. Some dishes had their own aluminum spoons or tongs; other dishes did not. So, for example, if a man wanted a late breakfast of waffles and bananas, he would have to use the tongs from the sausage links to pinch up each—sodden waffle, and would have to use the spoon from the ranchero-style scrambled eggs to fish bananas out of the fruit cocktail. Did I mention, too, that there were chicken wings? Not a popular breakfast item, chicken wings, but, aswim in their sauce, in their oily red and fatty brown sauce, very psychedelic.

For breakfast Franny had stewed strawberries over Belgian waffles, with ketchup-coated hash browns on the side—except the hash browns were more like hash pales. When she attempted to stab one of her stewed strawberries with her plastic fork, the strawberry would slip away from her and bolt for safety toward the hash browns. But Franny would not give up. She would pursue the strawberry, with her fork, into the mire of the ketchup, where she would be able to spear it at last, and then—she would eat the ketchup-covered strawberry. This is how breakfast is taken by the woman who wants to buy the rights to my movie. Me, I drank coffee.

While Franny ate, she felt she could be casual with me. She said, "Now, shame on you, Franny, shame on you, but—I have not seen the movie."

I told her, "It's not too late. It's playing on Saturday at the Pioneer Theater, the one behind that—pizzeria. You should come. It seems there is a problem with the pizzeria's piano; otherwise I would accompany the film live."

"Like a silent movie!"

"Or, well, when I think of a silent movie, I always think that something is missing. A silent movie is a movie that is missing sound. I prefer to think of *Unseemly* as missing nothing. *Unseemly* is not so much a movie minus sound as a piano recital plus miraculous light show."

"The proud father! But tell me what it's about."

That question, always that question, that question of what something is—about. So I told her what my movie is about, and I gave her the long version, including how I built the hidden camera and how I set my ambushes. Then came the awkward moment. It always comes.

She said, "It sounds like the kind of thing I'd never see on HBO."

And I said, "Yes, well, a dignified life does, after all, involve very little television."

And she said, "We all have our weaknesses."

And I said, "I suppose so."

There we were, she looking at me as though I had insulted her, and I baffled as to what I had said wrong. Something in my expression makes people believe that I am not—nice. Something in how I look at the remains of their buffet breakfasts.

Franny finishes her ketchupy strawberries, and out comes her accordion folder, and out comes her contract, and out comes the truth. Her client is not interested in buying all the rights to the movie, only the rights to the music. He is not even interested in buying all the rights to the music, only the right to use certain samples—in hip-hop. In other words, she wants me to sell *Unseemly* for scrap. She explains the terms to me, and I—.

Hope is the most private emotion. I won't bore you or embarrass myself by relaying all that I had hoped. But I had hoped, without telling anyone, for so much. Despite all the backwater film festivals and despite all the debt—I had hoped for so much. And now *Unseemly*'s run was nearly through, and—there it was: Franny Clement represented a record label that represented a singer who wanted to sample my music. That was what my hopes had been reduced to. I told her I would look the contract over, but—I knew I was in no position to refuse. How could I refuse? My personal credit card debt from the movie being another *res* that I am *in media* of.

We said goodbye, and I slogged over to the No. 6 train with the contract in my attaché case, in order to go uptown, where David Fowler could help me assess my quadrennial half-pint of success.

PUPPY JONES *recounts his trip to the Sundance Film Festival (early August 2000)*:

Mr. Maynard Gogarty! The man changed my philosophy.

I was living in Venice at the time, Venice Beach, California, and I had my little thing going on as Deejay Peejay. At the time. And some friends had some friends who had a condominium in Park City, Utah, and they told me they would give me five hundred dollars, plus tip, plus drinks, plus a bed, if I would spin at their Sundance party. Five hundred dollars was equal to my rent in Venice. At the time. They told me, "You can get a ride to Park City with Bez, the half-Asian bisexual." You see what I'm saying.

I'm saying fourteen hours in a Mercedes from Venice Beach, California, to Park City, Utah, with a half-Asian bisexual actress named Bez Bekamilui. Dreadlocks, industry talk, daddy is in real estate, boyfriend is in Sydney, Australia. Complaining about being celibate because her boyfriend is in Sydney, Australia. You see what I'm saying. We left at seven in the morning. She did her yoga, she didn't shower, she got in her car, she picked me up in Venice with the equipment I rented, and we drove to Utah. Fourteen hours, smelling her unshowered bisexual hooch-naynay yoga sweat. My feet up on the equipment I rented because there's not enough room in her trunk. Bez talking about pornography, eating her McDonald's french fries. Dipping the McDonald's french fries in the Thousand Island dressing, telling me it reminds her of come. You see what I'm saying. I'm saying Jones is still smelling her hooch-naynay over the smell of the french fries.

We get to the condo in Park City, Utah, which turns out to be nowhere near Park City, Utah. It's late at night, and they assign me to a loft bed. A loft bed in the living room. This is the bed that the families put the eight-year-old in when they rent the condo for skiing. Puppy Jones in the baby bed, Bez Bekamilui in a bedroom all by herself. No respect for the deejay. You see what I'm saying.

The next morning at nine A.M., Bez comes into the living room to do her yoga and her chanting, and she wakes Jones up. Rest of the condo sleeps through it, but Jones wakes up. Half-Asian bisexual yoga going on six feet underneath Jones? Half-Asian bisexual ass in the air, with the incense burning? Who's Jones making coffee for? But Bez sez: "I don't drink coffee, I brought my own yerba maté. I'm into the maté latte."

Bez sez she's going to see all the short films that morning after her mate latte. Who's following behind her? Who's following behind her like a good little puppy dog? That's all I'm saying. All I'm saying is at twelve noon, Jones and Bez go sit in the dark together. Where they see a short film by a Mr. Maynard Gogarty.

Mr. Maynard Gogarty: director, cinematographer, pianist, destroyer of worlds. Here is a man who is doing the work! In the theater, in the dark, Bez expropriates Jones's box of jujubes, puts it between her legs. A jumbo box of jujubes is right up in there next to the hooch-naynay, and Jones doesn't even notice. I don't even notice, because I am being shown *Unseemly*, by Mr. Maynard Gogarty. And when the movie is over, there is some Q and there is some A.

Bez wants to leave, but I tell her, "No, I want to hear the man." So we hear some Q, we hear some A, and I sez to Bez, "The man is a genius."

And Bez sez, "He's just full of himself. He was insulting the other directors, and they knew it. It was rude."

Bez did not want to hear the message. Mr. Maynard Gogarty's movie was addressed to her soul, but her soul was not ready for the work! But Jones's soul? Ready for the work! I'll finish off the story for you about Sundance. I do my Deejay Peejay thing at the party. A little of this, little of that, home at four A.M., five hundred dollars in my pocket. Plus drinks. Plus tip. Minus the cost of the cab to take me and the equipment back to the condo, because Bez never came to the party to get me.

But next morning, nine A.M., there she is with her yoga and her chanting, burning the incense and waking me up. Who's out of his cradle in the treetops, making coffee and maté latte?

"Sorry I didn't see you last night, Bez. Want some maté latte?"

And she tells me, "Yeah, sorry. I wanted to come to your party, but I was tired. Also, I met this guy last night? Who needs a ride back to L.A. today? So do you think you could find another way back to Venice?"

On a normal morning, what would Jones have said? Because Jones is such a puppy dog? "Okay, Bez. I'll find another way back to Venice. Just like I found another way back to the condo last night. I'll just ignore that you've been swinging your hooch-naynay in my face for three days and that you promised to take me back to California."

But this is not a normal morning. This is New Year's Day. Year One, Post-Gogarty. Seeing the man's film and listening to the man's A when the man got a Q, it changed my philosophy. So when Bez sez, "Do you think you could find another way back to Venice," I say, "No, Bez, no, I do not. You were supposed to take me back, you shall take me back. You shall inform the other dude of your mistake, and you shall take me back."

Do I even need to tell you that she took me back? Do I even need to tell you that she is not being faithful to the boyfriend in Sydney, Australia?

DAVID FOWLER *delivers his sockdolager (early August 2000)*:

The sockdolager. On his way out, after he's given me the contract, I ask Gogarty if he's seeing anyone these days. He draws to a halt, theatrically. Takes off his hat, which he had just put on.

"Is what I'm telling you confidential?"

"Gogarty. It goes without saying."

"I'll be needing your help with a divorce in a few months' time, David."

"Who's getting divorced?"

"I am."

"You are. From who?"

"My wife."

"Your wife. This is some sort of metaphor, Gogarty, or did I miss something? For example, the wedding? Your wedding ring is what, invisible?"

"That's why this is confidential."

"Okay. I apologize. Start from the beginning."

"Remember Ana, the German girl, the photographer, the maniac?"

"Very vaguely. She was in your life, when, mid-nineties?"

And I did remember her. She lived with him at the place in Gramercy. She was a gorgeous girl, but a bit terrifying. When she learned I was a lawyer, she said, "How can you stand all these typical days you must have?" A real charmer. But then again, maybe the bad attitude is what she and Gogarty liked about each other. Gogarty starts to tell me about this divorce he needs, and within two sentences I cut him off, because I don't want to be disbarred. Not for some INS bullshit!

ANA KAGANOVA *defies a polite question about what her typical day is like (early August 2000)*:

Typical days are for other people, *weiß' du?* You want to see my typical day? Here, here is my typical day:

STEFAN MAYR *reports on the front page of* Berlin Blick *(June 27, 1979, translated from the original German)*:

EXCLUSIVE! ONLY IN B. BLICK!

"I Came from an Ape"

EAST GERMAN BEAUTY ESCAPES COMMIES
INSIDE WORLD-FAMOUS GORILLA

BERLIN, 27.6: When the 1.8-meter-tall, eighteen-year-old Venus from Karl Marx Allee walked into the police station in Wedding last Tuesday, the officers on duty could not believe their eyes. But when she told them how she escaped from the

East, it was their ears they could not believe! In an exclusive interview with **B. BLICK**, Ana Kaganova told of her flight to freedom—inside a gorilla!

"I always dreamed of life in the West," said Ana, who sat with a **B. BLICK** reporter this weekend and unfolded a harrowing tale of intrigue, romance, and courage! "I only needed an opportunity."

Love gave her the opportunity in May, when her West German boyfriend, a student whom she met at a youth conference in Danzig last winter, made contact with a smuggler named Wolfi.

"Wolfi wanted six thousand marks to bring me west, which my boyfriend was able to borrow from his parents and his friends," Ana said, enjoying an American cigarette and a French café au lait at a bar off the Ku'damm. "The next step was for Wolfi to meet me in the East. For several weekends we met for beer in Marzahn, where he traveled on a fake day pass as an Austrian diplomat. He wanted to establish a pattern, so that we would not raise suspicions on the day of the escape.

"On the fourth visit, he told me he had a plan. I was to meet him the next Saturday morning at ten o'clock, but he would tell me nothing more!

"I couldn't tell anyone what I was doing, or thinking, and yet I had so many people to say goodbye to! How could I tell them that I might never see them again? And yet I was in love, and I had so many hopes for my new life of freedom!"

When the appointed day came at last, Wolfi arrived in a truck, accompanied by a stranger named Klaus. All three climbed into the truck's rear cabin, and they closed the door behind them.

"At first I didn't know what to expect. Wolfi still had not told me the plan. I thought that maybe he was going to hide me inside the wheel panels; I had heard of such escapes before. But I never could have expected what was waiting for me instead!

"Inside the truck was a stuffed gorilla!"

It was Bobby, the prize possession of the Commie Museum of Natural History. Bobby the Gorilla was born in French Africa in 1924, but in 1928 he was purchased by the Weimar authorities at the Berlin Zoo. Bobby was among the first great apes to arrive in Europe, and his gentleness and size made him the zoo's favorite attraction and Berlin's leading citizen. Even as the dark hour of Nazism descended on Germany, Bobby provided hope to decent Berliners, an ambassador of peace in troubled times.

When Bobby died in 1934, at the young age of ten, all the newspapers in Berlin ran obituaries commemorating his heroic life. And so, in a bald play for public sympathy, the Nazi authorities had Bobby taxidermied and put on display in the Berlin Museum of Natural History.

Ana picks up the story from there: "Wolfi had impersonated a museum curator from the West and had convinced the head of the Museum of Natural History to lend him Bobby for one week, as part of an international exhibition on the history of taxidermy in Germany. And the museum believed him!

"Wolfi had faked many documents, including the necessary insurance bonds from the West. And he had all the necessary paperwork from the East to bring Bobby through the checkpoint. All we needed to do was get me inside Bobby!

"Klaus was an expert taxidermist brought in especially for the operation. It took Klaus four hours to open Bobby up, carve out a place for me to curl into, and then sew Bobby shut again. But this is exactly what he did!

"It was very uncomfortable inside the ape. Bobby smelled like chemicals, and it was hard to breathe. I had to sit with my head between my knees, because that was the only way for me to fit inside Bobby's belly." The Amazonian Ana demonstrated this feat for **B. BLICK**'s photographers, in the full-color recreation attached.

"At the border, I was very nervous! I heard the border guards questioning Wolfi, but all the paperwork checked out, and so they let us through! Then it was just a matter of letting me out and sewing Bobby back up.

"For the next week I hid in a hotel room in Wedding with my boyfriend, until we heard from Wolfi that Bobby had been safely returned to the East. And then I went straight to the police to tell my story! I was so happy to be free at last!"

Both "Wolfi" and Ana's boyfriend declined to be interviewed by **B. BLICK** for fear of prosecution by the West German authorities for their roles in faking the necessary paperwork. The Museum of Natural History could not be reached for comment.

ANA KAGANOVA *addresses, sort of, a polite question about what her typical day is like (early August 2000):*

This is the sort of typical day that I had in 1979. Now my typical day, I have to get from Hano a donkey head.

I do have in actuality the one typical thing, which is to go to the bodega and buy coffee in a paper cup. This is the true symbol of America, the paper cup for coffee, with the plastic lid so that the coffee is not spilling. In America you can hurry while you drink a cup of coffee. So there for you is my one typical thing.

But today my goal was that I needed to charm Hano so that he would give me the donkey head. He already promised that he would give it to me, but when he made this promise, he sounded reluctant. I think perhaps he does not trust me with it, because I have told him too many stories and he thinks I am a criminal. I told him for example what I do when I must style a shoot that has no budget and we need for example an anonymous black sweater: I buy it from the Gap, and I use it in the shoot, and I make sure that the model is not stinking it up with her armpits when we are in the sun all day on the beach at the Howard Johnson's at Asbury Park in New Jersey, and then I return the sweater to the Gap for the full refund. Hano said, when I explained this to him, that one day I would be arrested. He is never alarmed, but this story about the Gap alarmed him. And I think when I asked him would he give me the donkey head, he thought, Oh no, Ana will lose it to the police.

My idea was to bring therefore breakfast to Hano, as a charm, because he goes always early in the morning to his studio without eating. So I stopped at a Chinese bakery and spent ten dollars on rolls. Ten dollars buys a gargantuan bag of Chinese rolls, but even after I bought the rolls, I felt that I needed more of a charm. So I bought also crabs at the Chinese fish market. The blue crabs, that are alive. They were very hale, and did not have even bubbles at their mouths, even though they were in a tub without water and it is August.

With the crabs and the rolls I arrived finally at Hano's lobby, and got the visitor pass, and took the elevator up. He has a studio on the ninety-first floor of Tower One at the World Trade Center. It is so tall, this Tower One, that you must change elevators at a sky lobby on the seventy-eighth floor. And you meet always the ugliest people there. But this is where Hano has his studio, down the hall from the boys who did the balcony thing. I came to his door, and he was at work on something that was built from glass.

"Hi, Hano! I have brought you breakfast."

"Hi, Ana."

"What do you mean, 'Hi, Ana,' as if every day I am coming and it is not a surprise to see me. You! How are you?"

"You called ahead and I am getting you past security, so it cannot be a surprise."

"You can try despite this to be happy."

This is how he is, always not impressed. To make his point he scrubbed his glass sculpture for a while still before he got up to kiss me. Hano has all of his hair shaven off, and he has the eyes that often gay men have. *Weiß' du,* the deep eyes, with dark eyelids and very feminine eyelashes. With these eyes and his hair shaven off, Hano looks like a man from the future. He said "Hi" while he kissed my cheeks.

"Hi."

"Hi."

"Yes, Hano. Look what I have along for breakfast! Delicious."

"God in heaven! They live. They are a wonderful blue. We perhaps can boil them alive in my coffeepot?"

"Do not be this way. Act surprised at my crabs. What sort of demon are you that you every day eat blue crabs for breakfast and are not surprised when I bring you beautiful crabs as blue as the sky?"

"Look, Ana, it is August and the sky is gray. I am surprised. Do you have butter for these crabs?"

"Do not be this way. I have also along twelve kilos of Chinese pastry."

"God in heaven, breakfast!"

"Now you act surprised."

We sat on the floor and ate the Chinese pastries. Hano makes recreations. He sewed a recreation of the golden dresses from this painting by Klimt with the many girls and then hung them on a rack under the plastic dry-cleaning bags. This sold for many thousands of dollars. He did the same for this Raphael with all the philosophers. But now he is tired of clothes and dry-cleaning bags, and he wants to build a glass freezer. What he imagines is to recreate the menu of a Dutch still life, with pheasant and fruits and bread. And then he wants to put all of it in Ziploc bags and freeze it in a glass case, like leftovers. But this was very difficult. Because his freezers have mist and icicles. So while we ate, we put the blue crabs into one of his failed glass freezers.

HANO MOLTKE *explains the pantomime eyes (early August 2000):*

Ana had seen the donkey head at one of my parties in Red Hook. When she asked if she could borrow it for a shoot, I said by all means. I only wish that she had not made this gesture with the blue crabs. What does she want me to think? "Oh, Ana, you are so surreal, because you brought me live blue crabs." I already knew that she was a little bit of a fiend, without the crabs. She is proud that she is a fiend. In the morning, if she needs to go downtown, she waits for a businessman to hail a cab on 2nd Avenue, she asks him if she may share the cab, and when they have gone almost all the way downtown and have stopped in traffic, she gets out and walks away. She does not say anything or pay anything, she only walks away. She thinks that businessmen will not chase her, because they are too rich and too busy. I told her that someday she would be arrested, and she laughed at me. So she is a little bit evil, I think.

But the donkey is a little bit evil too. Michael and I bought it in Honduras, and I paid too much. But one feels silly in these villages trying for a bargain, and how could I resist a stuffed donkey's head? Originally it had glass eyes, with corneas that were orange, but those I took immediately out, because they made the whole donkey look haunted by regret. When we were back in Red Hook, Michael and I had it over our dishes, with no eyes. It was very spooky. But then the cord that held it up over the dishes snapped, and the donkey head in the middle of the night fell down and broke Michael's porcelain. Also the hide got wet and started to smell funny. Michael said that the donkey was therefore a thing of evil and must go to my studio.

But it was Michael who found for me at a yard sale the plastic eyes from a pantomime horse, which I sewed over the original eye sockets. And now the pantomime eyes give the whole donkey head a comic appearance.

I asked Ana, while we ate the Chinese breads, for what did she need to borrow the donkey head, and she said, "It is for the *New York Times Magazine.*" This is standard for her, to hide at first her true motive, until you have agreed to her plan. Ana asked me to do her a favor and lend her the donkey head, but in fact the favor is not for Ana, it is for the *New York Times Magazine.* Someone has a new line of denims for winter, and Ana wants to do a shoot inspired from *A Midsummer Night's Dream.* So she needs my donkey head, because of this donkey man who is in *A Midsummer Night's Dream.* She wants to have a model in her shoot who will be naked, except that he will wear the jeans, naturally, and the donkey head. And he will float in the middle of a flock of fairies, who will be nude except for their wings. It all seems very crass to me, but Ana must have quite a budget, and so for her it must be a triumph. Every photographer whom I know is obsessed with this *New York Times Magazine.*

ANA KAGANOVA *explains her obsession (early August 2000):*

Tja, I have to make money somehow.

NADINE HANAMOTO *explains Jennica's obsession (early August 2000):*

Jenny hasn't told you how obsessed she was about George when we were in high school, and it's because she's embarrassed. It didn't start on the day of Loma Prieta, either. Loma Prieta was just what brought it to the surface. We were sitting in my car a few minutes after the earthquake, listening to KGO. And the callers and the reporters were like, the earthquake was magnitude 8.0; the Bay Bridge has had an epileptic seizure and has fallen over into the bay; there has been an avalanche in Santa Cruz and the redwood grove at Elfland is now on top of the roller coaster at the boardwalk; the seventeen ounces of plutonium that they store at U.C. Berkeley have melted down and now Telegraph Avenue has become the new Chernobyl; this was the big one. And we believed it, because it was on KGO. And so I said, "I wonder if my brother is okay." And because Jenny was obsessed, it became her mission to find my brother.

The thing was, in Jenny's insane world, no brother could vanish without a sinister subplot. In Jenny's world, every family except her own was constantly having climactic fights out of *Death of a Salesman* or *A Long Day's Journey into Night.* Like, Jenny thought that the night George left, my mom was screaming, "Spite, spite, is the word of your undoing," and my dad was in the background, all strung out on morphine. I would tell Jenny, "George was just an asshole. He moved out when I was seven, and he told us he didn't want to have anything to do with us, and that's it." But in Jenny's mind, it was impossible for my brother to be just sitting around S.F. State and smoking weed. She was convinced he must be illustrious. That was San Jose, a town so quiet that even the idea of moving to San Francisco seemed illustrious. Loma Prieta just became Jenny's excuse.

Anyhoo. The week after the earthquake, when they had all the photos in the *San Jose Mercury News* of the damage, Jenny kept asking me, "Do you even know where exactly George lives in San Francisco?" I told her, "We really don't hear from him, Jenny. You don't have a single asshole in your family, so you don't know. The only time anyone gets in fights in your family is when Gabe gets beat up by Old Man Bersen."

But she was obsessed. And so a few weeks later, Jenny called information in 415 and got George's address and telephone number. He was listed. So she gave me George's number, and she made me call him on the phone in her bedroom. She was like, "He's your brother, it is your duty to be in his life."

The thing with the phone in Jenny's room, though, was that the buttons were on the handset. You could hang up without anyone seeing that you had hung up. So I dialed George's number while Jenny sat across the room, and I got George's answering machine, and I secretly hung up, but I pretended that I was leaving him a message. Like, "Hey, it's your little sister calling, I want to come up and see you, call me at work, here's the number, let's make arrangements!" And then, because Jenny kept obsessively asking about it, a couple of weeks later I told her that George had called me at work but that he could only meet up on a Tuesday or Wednesday morning. I figured that would be the end of it. But Jenny said, "Let's cut class." Unfathomable, right? Jenny Green suggesting cutting class? Jennica "I shall not smoke weed, I am going to Princeton, I have to be home for my mom's crazy dinner at seven" Green? How could I not say yes?

MITCHELL *and* SUSAN GREEN *describe the limits of their liberality (early August 2000)*:

M: They played hooky and drove to San Francisco.

S: At maybe three-thirty in the afternoon, I get a collect call, at my office, from Jennica. Yes, I'll accept the charges. "Mom, Nadine's car broke down and we're stranded in this ghetto." I thought, It's Jennica being dramatic. What ghetto is there in San Jose? But she wants to know, "Can I put a tow truck and a taxi on the credit card, and Nadine will pay us back?"

M: We'd given Jennica a credit card, on our account but under her own name.

S: I ask her, Have you called Nadine's insurance company? "Nadine doesn't have insurance." I say, If Nadine's car is registered, she better have insurance. Jennica says, "Nadine let the registration expire on her car, because she couldn't afford the insurance." Oh really? Jennica says, "I just found this out myself, Mom. Nadine is having a panic attack." Well, have you called Nadine's parents? "We can't reach them." Why don't you just lock the car and take a bus home? "We can't really leave the car here." And where exactly are you that you can't leave the car there? "San Francisco." And what are you doing in San Francisco? "We decided not to go to school today."

M: Which does and does not answer the question.

S: "We decided not to go to school today." And out it comes that Nadine is going to get in trouble with her parents if they find out that she's in San Francisco. I tell Jennica, Young lady, I am not willing to lie to Nadine's parents on your behalf. You tell Nadine she should call her parents herself and deal with the consequences before she starts asking me to lie for her and pay her bills. Was I ever mad.

But you have to admire Jennica's tenacity. She can be tenacious when she's in a corner. She says, "Mom, do you want to lecture me, or do you want to lecture Nadine? If calling Nadine's parents were an option, we would have done it. Her credit cards are all maxed out. If she loses this car, she doesn't have a way to get to school or to work. So how about you agree to let me put the taxi and the tow truck on your credit card, and we'll work out the money later? It's creepy here, and we want to go." So now I'm beginning to wonder if maybe they aren't in a slum somewhere. So I ask her, Where exactly are you? "Hunter's Point." So I tell her to put it on the credit card.

M: And then you called me and told me that Jennica was stranded in the ghetto. This is the same week that Jennica had sent her application to Princeton. Every other day I am proofreading her essays for Yale, Swarthmore, Columbia. She refused to apply to Berkeley. It wasn't illustrious enough.

S: Ten minutes later, Jennica calls back. Again collect. A taxi to San Jose will be some exorbitant sum. Hundreds of dollars. "Can you come and pick us up? We're right off the freeway." I tell her, You can ride in the tow truck. She tells me that they already tried that and the tow truck company won't let them. I say, If you want me to come get you, you can wait until I get off work. Go sit in a McDonald's until seven-thirty. "But if we do that, Nadine's parents will find out she was in San Francisco." I say, I am through with you, young lady. Take the train home if you don't want to pay for a taxi, or call your father and harass him, because I've had enough. Was I ever mad.

M: So Jennica calls me and harasses me, just like her mother told her. And I leave work to pick them up. Some ghetto. They were three blocks off of Highway 280. I told Jennica, "Look, as long as your grades are good, your mother and I don't care if you cut class, we only wish you would tell us, so we know where you are if something happens." She said, "Well, something did happen, and I did call you, and now you and Mom are freaking out about the cost of a tow truck."

S: Which was true.

M: And Nadine chimed in to say she could pay us back in six weeks. I told Nadine that I wasn't taking her money, I was taking Jennica's money. They were both furious. We should ask Jennica if Nadine ever paid her back.

S: Nadine's parents. The father we didn't know, but the

mother. Ever since she and I were in PTA together at Trace Elementary, she had no interest in being friends with me. She was never rude to me, but she had absolutely no interest in making conversation with me, or with any of the mothers. Always this very sour set to her face. And when she came for Nadine that night . . .

M: Flames licking her nostrils.

S: We did not see much of Nadine after that.

M: You forget how some people are with their kids. Even I felt bad for Nadine. I told Susan, "That girl just met perdition." And not a word from the mother about money, either. It was okay with her if we paid for the tow truck.

S: It probably never occurred to her. She had more important things to worry about. She probably thought that we were in cahoots with the girls.

M: And we were liberal, but not that liberal. On the way back down to San Jose, to lighten the mood in the car, I asked them, "Good day in San Francisco at least?" They weren't accepting any peace pipe from me. Nadine said, "We went shopping." I asked, "Oh? And what'd you buy?" She said, "Nothing worthwhile." And you could hear in her voice the sound of a door closing. Oh, Nadine knew what she was in for.

NADINE HANAMOTO *describes what was not her finest hour (early August 2000)*:

The morning we go, the Peugeot is smoking a little, but, hey, I'm cutting class with Jenny Green, a little smoke is not going to stop me. So Jenny and I drive to George's address, which turns out to be this apartment in Daly City, one of those duplexes with a bad paint job and bad parking. But George's name was on the bell, so it was the right address. And of course George wasn't there when we rang his bell at nine in the morning on some random Tuesday, because of course he had no idea we were coming, because of course I had never actually called him, because unlike Jenny,

I was not obsessed. But Jenny couldn't believe he wasn't there. She said, "We have to wait. Ring again. Maybe he works the night shift and is just getting back."

It was like, Do I tell her he's not going to show up? That he has no idea that we're coming? That I never left a message for him? So that at least we can go drive into the Haight and see some record stores before we have to get back down to San Jose and establish our alibi? But Jenny was all patience. The idea of family is Jenny's own private god. So we sit there for an hour, just wasting our day. Jenny only agrees to leave after I tape a completely nonsensical note on George's door, saying we'll try calling him around two.

Anyhoo, we go into the city. The Peugeot is still smoking.

And at two in the afternoon Jenny makes me call George from a pay phone in the Haight. And he's there, George is there. He and I have this lunatic conversation. He was like, "Nadi! You can drive! You have to come by right now! It's crazy, you sound exactly like you did as a kid, except an adult! Where are you? Haight Street? Do you smoke green bud? You have to come by!" I was like, "We're coming!"

I tell Jenny it's a misunderstanding, George is home now. And so Jenny and I spend half an hour trying to get on a freeway, since they were all closed from the earthquake. Up and down every hill in the Haight and Potrero Hill six times, trying to figure out what to do, and then we missed the turnoff from 101 to 280, and then there was no denying it anymore, the Peugeot was on fire.

So we have a fight about whether to pull off the road, because we're in Hunter's Point. But Jenny starts to scream that the car is going to explode, so we pull off. And then we have a fight about what to do, and I have to tell Jenny I have no money, that I can't afford a tow truck. So we call Jenny's parents, and Jenny's parents tell Jenny that if we get a tow truck, Jenny has to pay for it. So then Jenny and I have another fight, about money. Because Jenny thinks she needs her money to pay for her rowing club, which she thinks she needs to be in if she is going to get into

Princeton, and I need my money to pay off my credit card and move out of my parents' place.

We completely blew off George, completely forgot to call him and say we had an accident. It was so bad. I didn't even call him to apologize until, like, six months later. It would have been so great. It would have been so great to see Jenny's face when she realized that what the Hanamoto siblings wanted to do at their reunion, after not seeing each other for years, was smoke the green bud. Which is what George and I did at my wedding reception, three years later. But Jenny didn't come to that.

It wasn't . . . the end of our friendship. But obviously the trip to San Francisco was not my finest hour. My parents had no idea how broke I was, because I wanted them to think I could manage my money so they would let me move out of the house. The point is, it took me a year, but I did pay Jenny back. I sent a check to her at Princeton. I called her parents to get her address, and they were like, "Oh, Nadine, she'll be so happy to hear from you!" And I was like, You Greens have no idea what it's like, do you? Because when Jennica left to go to Princeton, she left. Left, off to her dreamland, where she can meet all her illustrious people, and work every summer to pay for school, and never have any time to meet up with anyone on her trips back to California. And the next thing I know, it's ten years since I've seen her.

JENNICA GREEN *presents the facts and the figures (early August 2000)*:

So I didn't get a cat.

I took the No. 6 train to Practical Cats that morning, and once I had seen the Maine coon kittens they had there, I wasn't going to be able to settle on some cheap tabby from the place on 6th Avenue. There was this one, for six hundred dollars, with such huge teeth and such an adorable little face . . . But I just can't bring myself to take six hundred dollars out of my down-payment fund to buy . . . a cat. And once I realized I wasn't going to buy a cat, it became that much harder to call Nadine up and thank her for her letter, because, like, what news did I have, at all? So her letter just sat on my kitchen island, making me feel guilty. And I didn't e-mail George, because it felt too unfair to e-mail him before I called Nadine, even if I was sort of excited to have a white wine date.

But then, a few nights after I got Nadine's letter, the noise from the loom was out of control. At three in the morning I am rudely awakened, or, like, lividly awakened, because once I hear the hammer knock on the loom for the first time, there is nothing to do but fume and listen alertly for it to happen again. It's three in the morning, I am lucid with anger, and also . . . sort of terrified. Because, what if there's something dangerous going on behind the wall? Violent men at work, like, clandestinely? Like, constructing an occult machine for use in dark rituals? I'm pretty pragmatic during the day, but night is full of scenarios, for me. Which, if I had a boyfriend, we'd wake up, and I'd make him go deal with it. A boyfriend could go into the hall and knock on Mr. Loom's door and make Mr. Loom shut up. Or a boyfriend could pound on the wall for me and shout obscenities at Mr. Loom.

And a boyfriend could go in with me on the down payment to buy an apartment. An apartment with, like, impregnable walls. And impregnable floors. Hardwood floors, finished a little darker and more orangey than is in style these days. And impregnable ceilings, ten feet high at least, painted milk white, so that when it's afternoon and the sun is coming in the window, you can look at the ceiling and find faces in the shadows of the uneven plaster. And a bathroom where you could install your own doorknobs instead of the ugly ones that come with the apartment, and a kitchen where you didn't have to accept the landlord's uncleanable linoleum and eternally broken refrigerator.

But there's no way for me to do it alone, buy a place. And I have always lived alone. Because, I haven't exactly been lucky in love. Which is not a segue for me to, like, list the names of all my boyfriends, along with why we broke up, and along with, like, yes or no, was he Jewish, and yes or no, could he have prequalified for his half of the mortgage? But which is also not to say I don't have similar lists. I'm into lists.

Okay, so maybe this all was a segue:

ESTIMATED RELATIONSHIP LENGTHS (1990s)

	Dates (EST.)	Possible Additional Dates	Length (EST. DAYS)	Possible Additional Length
Christian Harris	9/1/90–10/1/90	*misc.*	30	10
Ethan Broom	4/15/91–8/1/91		107	
Amar Jai Kak	5/1/93–7/1/93		61	
Hunter Edam	7/1/93–10/1/93	4/1/94–6/1/94	92	61
Joshua Dauer	5/1/95–12/1/95, 3/1/96–5/1/96	12/1/95–3/1/96	275	91
Amadeo Rosmarin-Sanchez	6/15/96–7/1/96, 9/1/96–9/15/96, 2/15/97–3/1/97	7/1/96–9/1/96, *misc.*	43	75
Ethan Drangle	1/15/97–2/13/97		29	
Jonathan Sunshine	3/15/97–5/1/97		46	
Vitaly Luskin	3/1/98–8/15/98		168	
Felix Von Ulm	7/4/99–9/3/99		61	
TOTAL			912	237

To summarize: During the 1990s, which were 3,652 days long, I was definitively in a relationship 24.92 percent of the time, definitively out of a relationship 68.53 percent of the time, with the remainder being technicalities. For example Amadeo, who that whole rest of the year I kept seeing, but only when he was stopping over between L.A. and Madrid, and who I never called in between at all. The longest relationship was with Joshua, of course. So then I worked out the median and the mean and mode relationship length:

Mean = 91.2 days
Median = 61 days
Mode = 61 days

Since the median is lower than the mean, we know that a couple of long relationships are skewing my numbers upward. I realize it is pathetic to make these kinds of calculations, but once you get some figures, it's compulsive to play with them. The same way it's compulsive to work on your finances. Except with your money you can make assumptions about the market and see where you'll be in five years. With love, there is no way to tell. And really, I don't believe that I deserve anyone's sympathy. I indulge myself with these tables of data, but I don't think my life is as sad as, like, *Wuthering Heights*, or *Love in the Time of Cholera*, or Dave Eggers, or whatever. But I am the only person I know who is practically thirty years old but who has never had a relationship last more than a year. Obviously I am doing something wrong. That, or I am unlovable.

I mean, I can look back on each of my ten relationships, and I can say why each of those ten had to end. But that doesn't tell me why there wasn't an eleventh relationship that wouldn't have had to end. And I can say that I felt happy, mostly, being single and going to work and going on walks and going shopping for cats and whatever, but it doesn't mean that if you had told me on December 31, 1989, that I would be lonesome for 68.53 percent of the 1990s, I would have thought that it would be . . . a good way to spend that decade. What *am* I doing wrong? I didn't *want* to be just playing with water in New York. I don't *want* to be the friend who calls Nadine and has nothing to report. Does every Mr. Eleven see something bad in me that I don't see in myself?

Anyway, I don't mean to . . .

At least I have data, I guess.

Anyway, last night, it was five in the morning and I was awake, so I decided to go into work and go on the Internet and at least see what kind of an apartment I could buy if I used all my savings as a down payment. Which is why I came into work at six this morning. And of course all I was finding were these lame studios on the Upper East Side. And so of course I went back to the mortgage calculator home page. How much would my parents loan me for a down payment? Ten? Twenty? And so of course, by about seven-thirty, I was realizing yet again that I cannot afford to buy an apartment on my own. And I was like, I really need to relax and be a happy person. I need to spend some money on myself, immediately. I'll save that much less this month, and I will actually buy myself exactly the cat I want.

Furthermore, what I want to do this weekend is see a sad movie. About New York. In black-and-white. Something sad and romantic and arty. So I looked around on the Internet until I found something. And furthermore, I am going to write George Hanamoto an e-mail. Maybe he'll go to the movie with me.

GEORGE HANAMOTO *talks shop (early August 2000)*:

Jim, my boss: brilliant banker, rock-solid guy, totally loyal to the group. But Jim runs a high-wire act, as in big top, no nets, three rings. The way Jim got to be where he is is that he took care of his favorite clients. He took care of his babies. If it happens that all of Jim's babies want to do a deal the same week, which is what happened that week Jennica e-mailed, then me and all the rest of the clowns have to be out there on our unicycles, pedaling around the high wires and swinging from the trapeze, 24/7.

The first week of August was madness. Some analyst is e-mailing me to ask if he can order deal toys in the shape of toilet paper rolls for the FlushPro deal. Which was one of Jim's babies. My guys in Syndicate are fighting with the client over the allocation for the AllMaxia block. Which is one of Jim's babies. And my guys in Credit are telling me that I have to be on some call with S&P because they got it in their head to downgrade TDX. Which is another one of Jim's babies. Middle of all this, boom, an e-mail from Somebody Green at Hoffman Ballin.

And I'm thinking, Fuck! Hoffman Ballin? Hoffman Ballin? What deal do I have with Somebody Green at Hoffman Ballin?

And then I remember: it's the girl Nadi was telling me about, Jennica Green. An old friend from San Jose who is now a beautiful, single, Ivy League superstar in search of a Prince Charming, and who works at Hoffman Ballin. The kind of girl who actually might understand what it is I do and why it's fun being in this traveling circus.

Her e-mail says we should get a drink. It's sort of a cute e-mail, and it's one of these things where if I don't call her right away, I'm never going to call, so I call her right away.

"Jennica Green."

"I can't believe my little sister's best friend runs Personnel at Hoffman."

"George Hanamoto!"

So we talk, and she sounds great.

I tell her, "Here is an institutional challenge that you and I both have to address: finding dates for Nadi's wedding next summer."

"It is a challenge!"

"Because otherwise, when you get the invitation and it says 'George Hanamoto and Guest,' you feel as though you've failed."

"My RSVP will be like, 'Jennica Green plus whoever she can scrape off the sidewalk [x] will attend. [1] salmon plate(s), [1] chicken plate(s), [0] vegetarian plate(s).'" And she says it so that you can hear where all the check boxes and parentheses are on the RSVP card. Which is funny. And how often do you really meet a funny girl?

I tell her, "Well, we'll address our institutional challenges, right?"

"We'll get a drink!"

And I apologize that my August is crazy, but let's calendar something for September. So we both sit there at our desks and type it into Outlook to e-mail each other after Labor Day. Two banking geeks, right? But we've got a date in September.

JOAN TATE, *waiting for her son, beats the ornamental celery stalk dry on the rim of her first bloody mary and tries to lower expectations (early August 2000)*:

He asked me to meet him for lunch to hear his resolutions, but I am not exactly holding my breath, and so you shouldn't be either. Manny has new resolutions at least biennially—twice a year. And of course because I am his adoring mother, I am always happy to listen, but this time I said, "Let's do it on a Saturday. Let me take the car in from Montclair, let me do some errands in the morning, we'll have lunch at Phoebe's, they have good air conditioning in this heat, and I won't have to worry about hurrying back to the Foundation after forty minutes." And I also won't have to worry about having a drink—ha-*ha!*

Oh, I shouldn't joke. But let me tell you about his resolutions.

The first time he came to me with one of his ideas was when he had been back from college two or three years. This was the era when a cup of coffee in New York cost only fifty cents but was always so bad that you had to take it with milk and sugar. Manny loved that. He was just enamored of the fact that in order to get your coffee with milk and sugar, you ordered it "regular." He would sit around practicing his New York accent, just like Scott used to do: "Regula'. Regula'." Well, Manny does it better.

If Manny's idea had been to sell everyone better coffee, then he might have made a millionaire of himself, and the rest would have been history. But the rest is not history, because his idea was not to sell better coffee but to sell worse muffins. "Mother, everyone has learned to accept such spartan coffee. They can learn to accept the Spartan Muffin." He wanted everyone to forget that they had ever tasted a bagel, or a doughnut, or a croissant, or a Danish, and he wanted them to eat, every morning, a bran muffin. And Manny was resolved to be the baker who baked that bran muffin. You can't fault him for ambition—or for lack of ambition. Manny may not have inherited the famous Gogarty sense for business, but he certainly did inherit the Gogarty pence for—propensity for—schemes. Manny dreamed that Spartan Muffins would become a New York institution, with a factory in Queens and a secret recipe and his own fleet of little delivery vans. And he wanted to sell his awful muffins for fifty cents apiece, just like the awful coffee. So he lost a few thousand dollars on that.

Well, at least he followed through! Last year his inspiration was "e-Shrines," an idea that came and vanished. The whole thing may have been some sort of a joke about the Internet; sometimes I don't understand Manny's sense of humor. He wanted to make money by building makeshift shrines. He had a portfolio of clippings from the *New York Times* that he showed me, comprising—comprised of—stories about murders and hit-and-runs, all of them mentioning makeshift shrines. What fascinated Manny was that whenever there was one of these sudden deaths, the poor family of the victim would build a makeshift shrine, with balloons and teddy bears and poems and photos and candles and flowers. I told him, "Please tell me you aren't sharing these stories with your girlfriend, if you have a girlfriend," which offended him, though I was only trying to help, because having that portfolio of clippings made him seem morbid. And he isn't morbid, at least by disposition! Manny wanted to open a Web site called e-Shrines. The families of victims would pay a flat fee and give him the location and victim's name and the cause of death, and Manny's company would go and tape up the poems and light the incense. Maybe I should be grateful that idea went nowhere.

One year he resolved to become a rehearsal pianist, but after one season Manny quit, because he said he hated all the musicians and "their Inwood lives," whatever that was supposed to mean. One month he resolved to become a subway motorman with the MTA. I thought that was a joke, but he was convinced it was his calling. "Forty stress-free hours, Mother, then I can go home and do as I please." Stress-free! They used to call the 4 train "the Muggers' Express." I just told him not to tell Gran Rose.

His job at Chatham was the only job he ever held on to for more than a couple of years. He taught music at the Chatham Academy, and everybody there loved him: the administrators, the parents, the kids. They wanted to promote him to music director, but Manny quit before they could. He said it would have been too much stress. Instead he had resolved to make a movie. And that was his first movie, the one about dog shit.

His movie about dog shit is another example of his sense of humor that I do not understand. I suppose a mother shouldn't second guess an artist's temperament. But after that movie was done, Manny wouldn't go back to teaching at Chatham, because he was already filming his second movie, which is the one that went to Sundance.

What has paid his keep, year in, year out, is piano lessons. Every autumn another dozen women on the Upper East Side decide that their child is a piano prodigy, and they are the women who pay Manny's rent. But does he ever complain about them! "The mothers only want their kids to play piano well enough to be accepted into the right day school. The kids only want to play piano well enough so their mothers will let them stop practicing and play video games. So the mothers brag to me about what school their kid is going to get into, and the kids brag to me about what video game level they are going to get up to. Whole dynasties based on bragging."

Well, it is always funny to hear Manny complain—I only wish he felt satisfied with himself. And it seems to me that he doesn't. But that's the sort of thing he doesn't like to hear.

And then there were all of his decisions to relocate. There was Mexico and India and Brazil and Portugal and Italy. I didn't mind so much when he moved to Italy, because I could visit him there. But when he moved to Guanajuato, outside Mexico City, he didn't stay long enough to invite me to visit. He sent me postcards of the Virgin Mary once a week, saying, "All is well in Mexico, Mother! More soon!" And then, after three months, he left. He called me up from his apartment in New York to tell me that he was home again, because he couldn't get into a good routine in Mexico, and because there was nowhere to buy coffee, and because the Spanish newspaper didn't have a local section to compare to what was in the *Times*. I didn't even know he read Spanish for pleasure, much less Italian or Portuguese or Hindi—Hindu?—Hindi?—you know what I mean. He borrows language tapes from the public library and teaches himself new languages in the evening so that he can fulfill his resolution to move away from America. But he only survived in Bombay for two months, because he couldn't find anyone to teach piano to. He couldn't get a work permit in Lisbon. I forget what the problem was in Rio de Janeiro. He did enjoy Genoa and Rome, but he had visa problems there as well, eventually. Also, I think he got lonely, away from New York, with no one to talk to. And what is he running away from, after all? I told him I would be happy to pay for him to see an analyst, if money was the issue, but he said, "Mother, I assure you, my objections to psychoanalysis are not based on price."

Those are his resolutions. Can you blame him for thinking about his Grandmother Rose and all of that Gogarty wealth she is just sitting on? If I were in his position, I would think about it too.

ROSE GOGARTY *shares the secret to prosperity (early August 2000)*:

It's no secret—vigor!

Don't you tell me there is a generation gap. Don't you tell me that Manny's generation is different from my own. Because I have heard about these generation gaps for three generations now, and I don't see the first evidence for them, not the first evidence. Just you look at the newspaper, the *New York Times.* You read about the same kind of businessmen as you did fifty years ago, when Manny's grandfather Jack was making a living. Where is the generation gap in the business section? Or in the wedding section? In the Sunday paper there are wedding photographs. They used only to photograph the bride, and now the grooms are shown with their brides, but where is the generation gap in the wedding section? The world does not change where prosperity is concerned.

A successful man in his thirties has always been out of bed five days a week, in a shirt and jacket, commuting downtown. I don't care how he cuts his hair or whether he wears a tie. But not indolent, not thinking of himself as an exception to any rule. He is hardnosed, finding opportunities. Don't tell me these men do not exist anymore, because I see them in the paper, and I see them hailing cabs in the morning, and I see their wives at Saks, and I see the nannies with the babies in the strollers, just like always. Money is made today the same way money was always made: by showing up every day, with zest. And vigor is what Manny lacks. In 1930 he would have been in the breadline. He already owns the right clothes for it.

JOHN GOGARTY (*1792–1893*), *great-great-great-great-great-uncle of Maynard Gogarty, who made his small millions in tontines and industrial trusts, explains the secret to prosperity (spring 1892)*:

Prosperity is born of Longevity, and the parents of Longevity number three,—a Lust for Hygiene,—a Love for Beauty,—and a Luck in the Eradication of your enemies.

MILTON GOGARTY (*1872–1959*), *great-grandnephew of John Gogarty and great-great-uncle of Maynard Gogarty, a railroad and real estate millionaire, explains the secret of prosperity (summer 1956)*:

Prosperity? You must learn to charm—charming people! And I have met charming people in the most curious of circumstances.

I once met a wonderfully beautiful woman during a revolution.

I said, "Was that gunfire? And if so, why aren't you, ah, running away from it?"

She said, "It was gunfire, and I am a librarian. I have to get to the palace to save the president's library from the mob."

I said, "Don't be silly. You are beautiful, but not beautiful enough to stop a mob. Have a glass of wine with me instead. It will be your first glass of wine as a, ah, liberated librarian."

We found a bottle of wine, and by the time we were through, the police had put down the revolution. Charming.

JOHN MAYNARD GOGARTY (*1909–1991*), *nephew of Milton Gogarty, grandfather of Maynard Gogarty, and banker to the insurance industry, explains the secret to prosperity* (*autumn 1978*):

Let me tell you about Sam Standish.

In 1960, Sam Standish and I lost some money in railroad bonds. And Sam was having a rough time of it. More than anything, he was upset about his divorce, but he had filed for bankruptcy and was at his wits' end. He tried to burn his own house down to collect the insurance. But the house wouldn't catch, and the police arrested him for attempted arson and insurance fraud.

I told him, "Standish, you're a damned fool. We've been losing money in rail bonds for twenty years. You can't let it bother you now." I told him, "Clear your debts—your name is always good with me. I'll give you money even if you are a bankrupt bachelor at the age of sixty." We were downtown, getting lunch. He was eating turkey pie and a Coke, and pouring his own rum into the Coke. He said, "Jack, losing my money is bad. But losing my wife is worse." I said, "I offered you money, Standish, now you want me to offer you Rose?" And he said, "Say that in front of her, and next time the fire will be at your house."

That was Sam. He passed away last year. But he did fine for himself in the end, and he got remarried too. So that's the secret—never panic.

JOHN SCOTT GOGARTY (*1936–1974*), *son of John Maynard Gogarty and father of Maynard Gogarty, flips through the scrapbook his mother kept of his years as a child pianist and explains the secret to prosperity* (*winter 1972*):

Here's a clipping from when I was seven, from the society pages. It's about Mrs. Flemm, my piano teacher, who maybe was a charlatan, or who maybe was just some dowager from somewhere who knew how to play piano. We should ask Mother where she found her. "Mrs. Flemm reports that young Scott can sight-read Liszt's *Transcendental Etudes.*" That is a bold lie; I managed to memorize a few of them.

Here's something from the *Times.* Nineteen forty-four, so I was eight. As soon as the war was over, no one was fooled by my mother anymore, but here they're quoting me. "I vow to your readers that I shall memorize all of Beethoven's piano sonatas within the year." Mother must have put that in my mouth. I mean, she must have. It is an impossible thing for me to have said. I was never that good, and anyway I always hated Beethoven.

Here's the photo of me and Rubinstein. Mother knew someone who knew Arthur Rubinstein, and he came to one of the recitals at 69th Street. The only thing I remember about that night is Mother being high-strung. She made me wear rouge and lipstick, because she thought I looked pale, which is why I look so strange in the photo. Rubinstein was Mother's biggest coup. Mother is convinced that she and I are going to be featured prominently in the autobiography that Rubinstein is supposedly working on.

Here's the album cover to my one recording, two waltzes by Chopin. We had them made for Christmas in 1947, a run of two hundred. So—Scott Gogarty, boy prodigy. The secret to prosperity apparently involving, for the most part, good PR.

ROSE GOGARTY *discloses another secret (early August 2000):*

We own that apartment that Manny thinks he is renting. Oh, don't you go thinking I'm not sly. Fifteen years I've outsmarted him.

When Manny came back from college, he was doing just what his father did thirty years earlier. Scotty was an incontestable prodigy; whether Manny has any musical talent to justify himself with, I leave that for the world to judge. But both of them did the same thing after college, scrambling around the city like cats in a carwash, no jobs, no prospects, renting apartments and tossing out money each month like garbage onto the curb. Thousands of dollars a year in rent, for nothing. You hate to see it.

Jack and I bought the place on 72nd Street for Scotty, and did we ever learn our lesson. Because the instant Scotty had no rent to pay, there went any incentive for him to make anything of himself. Suddenly he was writing operas, light operas, about cripples! That was one mistake there was no need for Jack and me to repeat, letting a twenty-four-year-old musician live rent-free.

I will tell you what I did for Manny instead. Oh, I bought him an apartment, just like I did for his cousins. I even bought it big enough that he could marry and put a couple of children in the spare bedroom. But I didn't tell Manny what I'd done. And he still doesn't know what's what, any better than a fly in a bottle. I paid two hundred eighty thousand and transferred title to a joint trust. Two hundred eighty thousand, in 1986. A steal! Fourth floor, three bedrooms, on Little Cooper Alley, off of 19th, with a view of the German Lutheran Cemetery, which is a city park and which, I will have you know, is consistently rated among the best-kept secrets in New York. Fourth floor, pre-war, view across a park, two eighty, 1986. Don't you let them tell you that I am not shrewd.

Manny has no idea that this apartment is anything other than a rental. Mr. Ruggeri and I have made certain of that, and I give Mr. Ruggeri a nice present every year to keep it that way. You tell me how smart a man is, in his late thirties, and outsmarted half his life by his own grandmother. I've given Manny a reason to earn his way, and his money isn't just flushed into the harbor like spit. Fifteen years, he has never asked how it is he's living in a rent-controlled apartment in a building full of condominiums. So much for the famous Gogarty real estate instinct.

SAL RUGGERI, JR., *explains about the eradication of your enemies (early August 2000):*

The truth is, I'll explain it. Mr. and Mrs. Gogarty, the grandparents, God bless her and God rest his soul, they own a number of properties. And when they bought that unit up on four, that unit Manny's in now, they took me aside, and they told me, Sal, here's the deal, can you help us out? Sure, I can help them out. Hey, how they work out their money as a family, that's their business.

He's a good guy, Manny. He had that girlfriend up there for a while, paying the rent with him, the foreign lady. I liked her. And I've seen Manny's movies. The guy is funny as hell! Fucked up, but funny as hell! He thinks he owes me, for keeping his rent down, is the funny thing. So he helps me out sometimes, fixing the heater, painting the hallways.

Or, give you the best example. Mrs. Wong on two. She tells me how much she hates the mulberry trees in the cemetery. The mulberries are falling all over her windows, she gets no light, the mulberries bring the birds and the squirrels, the squirrels are eating her flowers, there are ants, she hates these trees. I told her, What's it worth to you? A tree is a tree, and two trees are two trees. I won't tell you what she said, in terms of dollars. She talked to some of the owners on two and three and four—you get the idea. In the end, they all chipped in some money except for crazy-face Mrs. Gladys on three. So I told Manny, We got to eradicate those mulberry trees. We do one a year, one this year, one next year. We poison them in the winter, they die in the spring, the city comes in the summer and saws them down. We drill a few holes into the trunks, pour in the herbicide, it's over. We do it at night, in the middle of January, February, nobody knows.

Mrs. Gogarty doesn't care if her grandson has to work a bit, I figure.

Here's the story we've been telling him. He was twenty-two, twenty-three years old at the time, just back in the city after college. Mrs. Gogarty tells him she's heard about an apartment, that a friend of hers got sick and had to move in with family in Florida and has an apartment to sublet. Mrs. Uphampton is what we called this lady. We told Manny that the Uphampton family wanted to hold on to the apartment, it's a rent-controlled apartment, and wanted a subletter until Mrs. Uphampton was able to move back to the city. So Manny comes by to look at it. I'm telling you, tall, skinny kid, just back from college. I tell him, as though I am letting him in on a secret, I hate to break it to anyone, but Mrs. Uphampton is not coming back to this apartment, not at her age, not in her condition. I tell Manny he can have the place, but the whole deal has to be kept quiet. I tell him the rent is three hundred a month. Three hundred, for that place, the kid's going to take it. Three hundred barely covered maintenance, but the kid wasn't asking any questions. Twenty-two years old, someone gives you a place that big for three hundred dollars, even in 1986, you don't ask any questions.

The one question he asks, Where is her furniture? I tell him, Oh, her kids came and took it. That satisfied him. I'm telling you, he wasn't asking any questions.

He moves in, and every month I deposit his check for three hundred dollars in the account Mr. and Mrs. Gogarty set up, and every month their maintenance bill gets paid out of that same account, automatically. They had some good lawyers, those two, no doubt about it. They were getting some sort of tax break, definitely. A couple of years go by, Manny has a piano put in there, he starts buying furniture, starts giving lessons.

A couple more years go by, and I decide enough is enough. I get Mrs. Gogarty's okay, and then I tell Manny, Mrs. Uphampton passed on, but her kids still want to hold on to the place, in case any of the grandkids ever want to move to the city. I told him, Between you and me, Manny, it's never going to happen—this place is yours as long as you want it. And between you and me, the owner doesn't ever need to know that Mrs. Uphampton isn't still in this apartment. I left it a big mystery who the owner was. I told Manny, Thing is, a place like this, on the open market Mrs. Uphampton's kids could be getting a couple thousand a month for it, and so they feel like maybe three hundred just isn't reasonable anymore.

That's how I've been raising Manny's rent over the years. And he thinks he owes me a favor, for keeping his rent down. It's funny, when you think about it.

MAYNARD GOGARTY *describes lunch with his mother (early August 2000)*:

So—Phoebe's! A restaurant where the only natural light is what sneaks past the coat check. On a Saturday afternoon, when you walk into Phoebe's to meet your mother for lunch—and the reason you are meeting her for lunch there is because she still cannot forget a particularly scrumptious salad that they served her once thirty-five years ago—you see the shadows of the waiters tumbling under one another to hide in the kitchen. The carpeting is royal blue and gasps like a dry sponge under your shoes. The ceilings are low, as is the mood: when you see your own deathly reflection in the gilt mirrors at Phoebe's, you find yourself singing the "Edward" Ballade, by Brahms.

I arrived, heavy with orange-colored perspiration. I always try to impress my mother by dressing nicely when we meet for lunch—in peppy cottons, et cetera—simply to give her something to be hopeful about, to give her hope that her son is not as lonely as he seems, and instead I always arrive looking malarial.

My mother was sitting at the bar, barefoot, drinking liquefied steak tartare and smoking. If she had been at the bar for long, then I wouldn't be able to afford to pick up the tab, so we were off to a bad start. And when my mother stood up from her stool and squatted down to slap her sandals out from under the bar, she had to steady herself by clinging to one of my pant legs. She was—tipsy, let's say.

So. We move to a table, and one of the spidery waiters, in his black vest and decommissioned black bowtie, brings us the menus. My mother already knows that she wants the chicken

Caesar salad, and I order a tonic water and the gazpacho, *muy auténtico*, with Worcestershire sauce. When the bread comes, my mother starts gobbling it down with seagull swallows, not even pausing to chew.

"Mother," I say.

And how to continue? Normally there are two forces—two predominant yet opposed forces—at work when I speak with my mother: her greed, her insatiable greed to hear everything about me, no matter how tedious and discouraging, and my hope, which never diminishes, to preserve my privacy and my dignity by only telling my mother things about me that are—objectively newsworthy. But at Phoebe's, I am feeling resolved. Even if my mother is tipsy, I want to try to make her happy, I want to try to tell all. But still, how to continue?

"Mother," I say.

Mother, what if your son isn't—nice? All these mistakes over the years, the jobs that didn't last, the girls that didn't last either, the times that I probably wasn't easy to get along with—. I always justified it by saying that I was doing what I was doing because of my music. The justification for all that debt, all that credit card debt I have from my movies, was the hope that it would serve—my music. But what if rather than occasionally doing things that weren't nice for the sake of my music, I actually only pursued music because being nice was so trying, for me? For reasons I cannot explain?

Mother, if I give up music now, how do I apologize for thirty-six years of subjecting everyone to my—vanity, my perverse vanity?

Mother, have I disgraced myself?

Mother, I think that—I think that I regret that you and Dad taught me to play the piano. How else am I to feel except sad that the one pursuit I admire unreservedly is a pursuit for which I have no real talent? I was never a concert pianist, we all knew that. But I have also never been much of a composer. What if I had discovered Schubert's lieder and Debussy and Brahms at age thirty-five? Then I would have been old enough to admire them and love them without feeling like I needed to imitate them. Except the happiest moments of my life *have* come from the piano. They have. And—. Mother, I've been sad. And I feel like with or without the piano, I would have been sad. And I want to stop feeling like—there is no way for me to be happy. I want to apologize to you, for not having been happy.

For half an hour I try to make myself clear, and finally all I can say is, "Mother, I want to start being nice to people! Today!"

"I don't know what you're apologizing for, Manny. You've always been one of the politest, best-mannered—."

"No, Mother, I haven't. Listen to me. I want to stop feeling that I have to protect you from what I am really like. Namely, pretentious, monastic, and nasty. I've been unhappy, Mother, and I've wanted to preserve you from that. But I don't want to anymore. And not because I want you to accept what's unacceptable about who your son is, but because I want, as your son, to simply—be good, do well, cast off delusion, live without affectation, make money, pay taxes, have friends, contribute charitably, mail Christmas cards, subscribe to the Met, and be loved and spread joy! I want never again to have to protect you from who I am, because I want to become the son you want me to be! And I want you to smile and say you're glad!"

I tell this to her, in those precise words, and what is her reaction? She is—miserable. Miserably putting chicken Caesar salad into her mouth, miserably eating bread. I am telling her that I am about to become the son she has always wanted, and she isn't just impassive, she's—deject.

JOAN TATE, *asked at the end of lunch whether she was miserable, denies it (early August 2000)*:

Miserable? No, no, I thought he was going to ask me for money. Where else was I supposed to think it was going, when he was telling me about his credit card debt and how unhappy he is? Or I thought he was going to ask me to ask Rose for money on his behalf, which is one thing I would never do. Rose has never been anything but extremely generous to Manny and me, but to her—I'm still just the coed from Barnard, Scott's ingenue from Newton, New Jersey. Manny clearly had something he wanted to tell me, but I'll tell you the truth, by the time he was done talking, I wasn't exactly following all the ins and outs of his inner pain anymore. I am an adoring mother, but after two bloody marys, in the middle of a heat wave, what do you expect? Here, come, step over to the bar with me so I can have a cigarette, and I'll tell you a famous story.

MAYNARD GOGARTY *describes lunch with his mother (early August 2000)*:

"This is why you thought we should have lunch? To tell me you're unhappy with your life?"

"Mother, no, not unhappy, resolved." And why exactly is it that I am—never understood? "I want regularity, Mother. I want stability. I want to stop worrying. Did I tell you that someone wants to buy the rights to the music in my movie? I'm going to sell it to them, I don't care who they are or what they want to do with it. I'm through with forever worrying about—gah!—art." None of this seemed to be what she wanted to hear. "I think maybe I would like to get married, Mother."

"Well." She sighed, and this was a sigh with a difference. "You need to find a girl first."

"I can't argue with that."

"Are you seeing someone? Is this what you're telling me?"

After all the honesty, I couldn't do it. I couldn't tell my mother the truth about how single her son has been.

"I am seeing someone." It was a lie, but I could not stop myself. Oh, the indignity of lying, and being lied to. "And I think you'll like her, Mother. It is very recent, so you will have to be patient, but I do think you will like her."

So. What exactly am I to do now? Call up Ana?

ANA KAGANOVA *reminisces (early August 2000)*:

There is a good word for Gogi in German: *konsequent.* Which means consistent, but also grave and stubborn. It is hard to give examples, because no celebrity is *konsequent* today anymore. Israeli prime ministers almost always are *konsequent.* Ernest Hemingway. Käthe Kollwitz. Diane Arbus. But not for example William Wegman, and not Annie Leibovitz, and not Cindy Sherman. It is very hard for Americans to be *konsequent* about anything except money. But Gogi was very *konsequent.*

This movie about dog shit, for example, that he made while we were together, with his hidden camera. The movie was how we met, in actuality, because I heard the camera clicking inside his suitcase when he sat next to me on a bench, waiting for dogs to come and shit. A movie about dog shit is the movie of a man who is *konsequent.* This movie had four parts. First part: footage of men and women who pick up their dog's shit with plastic bags and put the plastic bags into trash cans. Second part: footage on a windy day, of plastic bags that are blown out of trash cans and into the air. Third part: footage on a windy day, of plastic bags that float down the street, in the air, and become caught in the trees. Fourth part: footage on a rainy day, of men and women who walk under a tree that has plastic bags in the branches. The lesson was that we walk always through a rain of dog shit. The movie was silent, with, as a soundtrack, Gogi's piano music.

Americans think that the Germans have no sense of humor. But to make a movie about dog shit is very much in the German sense of humor. It is the joy of when you show other people their illusions.

Gogi has lived his entire life in this city, but despite this he is not patient with how other people live. I feel often this same way. How can you live in New York and not think, Hey, all of you are good for nothing! For a couple of years, then, it was fun to live with Gogi and to keep each other company. At the same time, it was always peculiar to live with him in the apartment in Gramercy. He was too polite with me, even when I am living there two years. I wished he would argue with me more often, and say what he thought. But he liked instead to sulk. He liked his own company. Even when we lived together two years, he said always that he felt lonely. Perhaps he is more easily lonely than I am, but this is not a good indication, to hear that the man with whom you live is lonely. And so when one day he tells me I must move out, there was no warning, but I did not feel such a tremendous surprise. I simply moved out.

JULIE LASALLE, *a doctoral candidate in comparative literature at Columbia University, having just seen Maynard's movie with her friend Jennica, hits the nail on the head (early August 2000)*:

One of Jennica Green's most often remarked-upon characteristics (and I think I speak with some expertise, having known her since freshman year of college) is that all, or nearly all, of the enjoyment she takes from an experience comes not from the experience itself, but rather from the anticipation of how enjoyable the experience is going to be. She is quite cerebral in that way, and it is endearing once you get used to it (though when we were all in college together, it drove us to distraction how evasive Jennica could be, in terms of actually doing things with us, spontaneously or not).

The canonical anecdote concerning this feature of Jennica's character being the nude beach story. "Which" (as Jennica would say), to make a long story short: Five of us, including Jennica, drove to Maine together during the summer before our junior year of college and spent a week at a country house that one girl's family owned. Jennica anointed herself as our Maine recreation specialist and managed to exert, if not programmatic, then systematic control over our itinerary in Maine simply through her superior command of Maine's recreational options. She wasn't necessarily pushy, but she was excessively well informed about things to do and not to do, in Maine, recreationally. And among the things she recommended that we, five single undergraduate women from New Jersey, do was drive to one particular nude beach that she had found. Which, to make a long story short, we did. However, as soon as we had disembarked upon this recommended nude beach, Jennica informed us that she would not be taking her clothes off. It seemed that Jennica was chicken. We weren't upset; we thought it was hilarious.

We told her, "Jennica, you do what you want to do, but we are taking our clothes off."

Jennica replied, canonically, "I was only recommending that we come to this nude beach. I was not proposing that we participate in the nudity."

And, living in New York, I continually witness Jennica Green's inability to enjoy the very things she imagined she would enjoy. Six weeks will elapse, during which Jennica won't call or send me any e-mails, and then in the course of one afternoon she will leave me three messages telling me that she has learned of, let's say, a Greek Orthodox church in Jersey City that is having a festival and pageant. She will insist that I go there with her. She will be emphatic about the attractions: fried fish, baklava, ouzo, folk-dancing lessons, a petting zoo. I will call Jennica, and I will pledge to go, and I will cordon off an afternoon, and I will ride the PATH train to Jersey City with her. And so I will find myself with Jennica Green in a churchyard, in the company of all of Greek New Jersey. Grandmothers in huge T-shirts, babies in huge strollers, teenagers with voices the explosive force of which you would have to measure in megatons, young men with their shirts off. Ouzo, music, goats in pens.

But no sooner does the folk dancing start than Jennica will say, "Let's go."

"What? We have to drink and dance with these people."

"Let's go."

"But Jennica, this is fun."

"This isn't how I thought it would be. Let's go."

Coming, then, to last night. Jennica had discovered a short film festival in the East Village. There would be three movies and a Q & A with the directors afterwards, and a virgin caiphirinia bar, BYO Pitú (Pitú being, as Jennica informed me, the brand name of a Brazilian sugarcane liquor, akin to but not identical with rum, which I would have to pick up in Little Brazil on my way downtown). Jennica advertised all this in a series of e-mails to me, and because I was free that night, I told her I would go. And so she and I met for dinner (which, since I am so poor and she is so frugal, meant spaghetti with meatballs at Two Boots) and then went to watch the films.

And, if I may hit the nail on the head, metaphorically, over dinner at Two Boots, Jennica was telling me about some guy she is being set up with, an investment banker who is the brother of a friend from high school, a fellow named George Hanamoto. Jennica, based on one phone call, had an assessment, to wit: "He seems funny, and wouldn't it be magical to actually fall in love with this person I've known about for years? But am I really interested in an i-banker? What if he's boring? What if he's totally conventional? What if he isn't cute?"

I had to tell her, "Jennica, you're agreeing to a first date, not to marriage."

But, and this is the nail the head of which I have just metaphorically hit, Jennica takes the same approach to men that she does to everything else in her life. It's all cerebral for her; within a minute of meeting a guy, she is imagining how it would be to marry him. But once she actually finds herself involved with him, her instinct, sooner or later, is to run away, because the reality is different from what she had imagined. Which brings us to the three films we saw.

MAYNARD GOGARTY *describes his film* (*early August 2000*):

So, the movie! My second movie. *Unseemly.*

I shot it surreptitiously, in New York City, over the course of three years. This necessitated a soundproofed briefcase with a mount for the camera. The soundproofing was necessary because it became clear when I made my first film that people could hear the camera operating. It was sixteen-millimeter film, an expensive decision. I jury-rigged two knobs near the handle, to start and stop the camera and adjust the focal length, but the exposure had to be calculated in advance, before the briefcase was shut. That was also an expensive decision. But with the addition of the soundproofing, it was the same briefcase I used for my first movie, *Pet Peeve.* Or, as my mother called it, *Manny's Movie about Dog Shit.*

The lens of the camera rested in a circular aperture cut into the top of the briefcase, and the aperture was camouflaged so that it looked like the cover for a lock. A fancy lock. In fact it was a one-way mirror. The exposure of the film had to be calibrated to compensate for the—reflectivity, is it?—of this mirror, to make sure there was enough light. When the camera worked, I could film people with the briefcase on my knees. But even with two years of practice, I got clear footage only about two thirds of the time. Another—spectacularly expensive aspect of the film.

These were good constraints, and necessary; I accept that the expenses were of my own making. There is no one for me to resent but myself that the interest rates on my credit cards are so punitive.

So, the movie has four acts, or four—movements.

First movement:

Shot on a downtown No. 6 train in June of 1998 at about eight-thirty in the evening. I filmed, for nine consecutive minutes, three women sitting side by side underneath—an advertisement for Banana Republic. White women, late twenties, boisterous, squeezed onto a single bench. None were wearing engagement rings, but all three wore black heels. Two had on indigo pants—jeans, dark jeans—and the third, the one on the right, had on black trousers. And they were talking with tipsy animation. They crossed and uncrossed their legs, they tapped each other's knees, they leaned forward and backward to look at each other when they talked. At every stop they craned around each other to see where they were. A suspicious man walked past, and they all gave him the same suspicious look.

Their pants were all cut so that the cuffs fell in a mantle over their high heels. Do you know this look? It is still prevalent, the cuffs of the pants that hide the crotch, the intimate crotch, of the high heels. All three women had their pants cut the same! All three pairs of pants were tailored to hide that nameless, secret groin where the sole of the shoe vaults up from the toe to meet the slender heel, that innermost thigh of a shoe. They chatted for nine minutes, and then they left the train.

This footage, naturally, was silent. The sound, my invention, was dubbed later.

Second movement:

Shot in the spring of 1997 from the benches around Astor Place and Sara D. Roosevelt Park, the long park along Chrystie Street. I accumulated an hour and a half of footage of women who wore—pants underneath skirts. Do you remember this look? For a while the majority of such pants were dungarees. But then, over the course of June and July, while seated at the café across from Cooper Union, I shot forty minutes—forty minutes!—of women specifically wearing black silk slips, specifically over blue jeans, specifically with flip-flops for shoes. And ten minutes of that—ten!—was of women specifically in the act of waiting to cross 3rd Avenue. Almost all of them, by the way, while waiting to cross, adjusted their skirts. Ten minutes, in a single summer, of dozens of different women waiting to cross the same street, in the same outfit, all filmed from the same table in front of the same café, making, for the most part, the same gesture.

Third movement:

In October, November, and December of 1998 I documented two hundred—two hundred!—two hundred!—heterosexual couples on the No. 1 and No. 9 trains between Columbus Circle and Columbia University. Each couple—each couple!—was identically dressed, the man and the woman both wearing shiny black shoes, black leather jackets, and blue jeans that were powder blue or lighter. And I filmed each couple doing exactly the same thing: occupying the seats next to the door, underneath the MTA map. Some of them squished together; some of them had to duck when someone came to look at the map. Some of them looked at the other passengers. One couple gave each other ear kisses. It was madness. I was forced to give up only owing to expense. There were hundreds of them. Hundreds!

And then the fourth movement:

April of 1999, during a heat wave that brought June in eight weeks early. I filmed a young woman through the crowd on a D train. Oh—this girl. She was beautiful, with long, thick, curly hair. Her face was like the face of Joan of Arc in that painting by Bastien-Lepage at the Met. Potent is what this footage was.

She was crying. And she kept swallowing her woe, and wiping her nose on her finger and then wiping her finger on her purse. Someone had just broken her heart. Across the Manhattan Bridge and all the way to the Houston Street stop she sat, with her knees exposed between her boots and her skirt. And then! Then she stood to let an elderly woman sit. She—a girl—stood up! Never, never before seen! And when she stood, her clothes adjusted. Her skirt then hid her knees, but because she held the overhead bar, her shirt then lifted to expose a crescent of naked hip.

Other passengers kept moving past her, jostling her out of frame, and she smiled pathetically at everyone who bumped her. I nearly wept. She was—so, so sad. Someone had broken her heart minutes earlier, and now she just wanted to get home and cry in private, but still, in the way of the heartbroken everywhere, she was trying to be kind to strangers. She got off at 14th Street, and—who knows what became of her. Joan of Arc, heartbroken.

I edited all of this footage into four silent seven-minute-long sequences. Excerpts of the three women with their heels, a montage of women crossing 3rd, a montage of straight couples sitting on the Broadway local, and the heartbroken woman on the train from Coney Island. And only then did I compose the accompaniment. I composed it and arranged it over the course of two months: a long piano sonata, with four movements. A scherzo, *allegro molto,* full of gaiety. That was for the three women on the downtown 6, under the Banana Republic ad. An andante, *ma non troppo*, sort of gray and impatient. That was for the women with skirts over jeans, crossing 3rd Avenue. Then a prestissimo, gleaming and joking, for the couples wearing the uniform of the Upper West Side, the black jackets and black shoes and jeans. And then—dazed and, and heartbreaking!—an adagio sostenuto, for Joan of Arc.

I recorded the entire piece in a studio that was specially furnished with a projector and screen so that I might watch the film while I played. I knew the twitches of this film sinew by sinew. I knew the moments when the three women in heels all leaned to see which station they were at. I knew the moments when certain couples would finally stop wiggling into their seats on the downtown Broadway line. The music was all impromptu—the delays and the flourishes, the fermatas, the tremolos. The bursts and the sobs of each movement coincided with the jump cuts in the footage, and with the rattlings of the subway, and with the expressions and gesticulations of my subjects, their shudders and their laughs.

And that's *Unseemly*.

PUPPY JONES *paraphrases what Maynard Gogarty said when asked at Sundance about immortality (early August 2000)*:

My jujubes were getting warm between the thighs of Bez Bekamilui, but I was paying attention only to the Q and the A. I was ready to receive a change of philosophy, is what I'm saying, and I was ready to receive it from Mr. Maynard Gogarty. Because when you are a musician such as a Deejay Peejay and when you hear a musician such as a Maynard Gogarty, it makes you a little nervous. It makes you a little jealous. It makes you regret how you have been using your time. When a Maynard Gogarty is asked a Q that you, a Deejay Peejay, could not yourself answer, you listen up, is what I'm saying. Here is a man who has done the work, and it was the work that I myself wanted to do.

The moderator asked Mr. Gogarty, "Are you worried that your movie might quickly be dated, because it is so topical, because it has so much to do with fashion? Are you worried that no one who sees it next year will get it? Do you want to achieve immortality through your art?"

Mr. Gogarty says, "Do I hope to achieve immortality through art?"

And he clears his throat.

He says that fashion happens because people want to define themselves. He says that the desire to define oneself will last forever, not just one year. He says that the easiest way to give a definition to oneself will always be to play a role.

He says, "People stop asking themselves whether they are *enjoying* what they are doing or wearing, and instead ask themselves whether they are *supposed to be enjoying* what they are doing or wearing. They ask whether they are in role."

And I say to myself, That's right! Speak it!

He says, "It's as if these people have gone into a grocery store with a list of things to buy, and it doesn't matter if it's their list or someone else's list, because what is giving them pleasure is not eventually eating the food that they are buying but the fact that they are checking off every item on the list."

He says, "Think of all the human types. We all play a few dozen types at any time, giving the illusion of originality, but most of us are no more unique than a spread of tarot cards is unique. Most of us are nothing more than a recombination of the same old cards."

He says, "For example. The working girl who wants a rich boyfriend to pick her up in a Mercedes and drive her off to an expensive dinner. The regular guy who wants to drink a beer in a lawn chair on the beach. The married couple who want once each season to go hear an opera at the Met. Does that girl enjoy that meal? More than she would enjoy one cooked at home? Does the guy enjoy the beer in the chair? More than he would sobriety on a towel? Does the married couple enjoy what they hear at the Met? More than they would oldies?"

No sir!

He says, "But people do enjoy the sense that they are playing a role. 'Oh my god, he took me on such an *amazing* date!' '*Dude*—a beer in a chair on the beach.' 'Oh, we just *love* going to the Met.'"

He says, "And that's how you achieve immortality. You achieve immortality by being a cliché. Because if you are a cliché, then even though you may die, you have lived on."

Hallelujah!

He says, "If I wanted to achieve immortality through my art, I would have made a genre piece. The directors who make horror films or high school comedies or action thrillers, and the screenwriters who write them and the musicians who do the scores—they are immortal. Because when they die, there are already dozens of other directors or writers or musicians who are doing exactly the same work. They cannot die, for they constantly have risen."

He says, "And these people in my film, they cannot die. The Upper East Side princess, the Upper West Side liberal, the East Village hipster—they cannot die. The doting mother, the pedagogical father, the fashion victim, the happy couple, the rebellious youth, the Hollywood director—they cannot die. Pick your cliché, they will live forever, because whenever one generation of them dies, another generation of them has already risen to take their places."

Hallelujah!

He says, "So no, I do not want to achieve immortality through art. Art is what I hope will let me rest in peace."

Yes! Yes! This is a man who is doing the work! This is a musician who has stopped playing along! The time has come for Puppy to stop playing along! The time has come for Puppy to do the work! Yes, yes, yes!

And I sez to Bez, "The man is a genius."

And Bez sez to me, "He's just full of himself."

JENNICA GREEN *describes a fraught moment at the movies (early August 2000)*:

I recognized one of the directors, the one who made the movie with the piano music. His was so the best movie they showed that night. The scene at the end? With the lonely girl on the D train who was so devastated? Did she have to leave New York, and her boyfriend wouldn't leave with her? Did someone she know just die? I mean, there was no way to listen to the music and to watch her crying and trying to smile and not to . . .

But then there were other parts of his film that were just so . . . funny. Like, there was this one phrase of music that kept returning over and over. The director had arranged everything so that every time that phrase returned, it was as if the people on camera heard it and asked themselves, "Did I miss my stop?" The phrase would return, and instantly, whoever was being filmed would make the same frightened face. "Did I miss my stop?" The whole theater was laughing. It was really one of the simplest and purest films I can remember seeing. And it didn't have a single line of dialogue.

When the movies ended, they turned on the lights, and the programming woman for the movie theater invited the directors up to the front to answer questions from the audience. And I recognized the director who made the movie with the piano music, but I didn't remember from where. And normally, when you recognize someone, it's at some event or some function, and so you have to immediately, like, conjure up their name and what they do for a living and the fact that at some previous function six months ago you talked with them about their seventeen-year-old dog. And if you can't remember what their name is, it means you're self-involved and antisocial and unethical. They'll be like, "I can't believe you forgot me! I remembered you! And now my dog is dead." As if it's your fault. But in this case, the director who I recognized was standing at the front of the whole movie theater, and me and Julie LaSalle were just sitting there anonymously, sunk down in our seats, sipping on our individual-sized bottles of Pitú, so it felt like I could safely gaze at him until I had him placed.

Except that he caught me staring at him, twice.

He was one of these people who . . . you see his face and you sort of instantly and secretly like him, because it's obvious that he has all sorts of unspoken and subversive opinions. Meaning, an expressive face. With these very interesting wrinkles along his forehead. When the programming woman was introducing the other two directors, reading their biographies and filmographies, he frowned, and cocked his head to the side, and kneaded his earlobe with one hand. And the look on his face was hilarious; he was so unimpressed.

So I laughed at the face he was making, and he looked up and recognized me and passed me this indecipherable smile. I had seen that smile before, and I got this glimmer in the corner of my mind: I didn't know where I remembered the director from, but I did know that the memory was fraught. So I leaned over to Julie and whispered:

"Can we go?" And this is exactly the context when it is such a nightmare to have Julie LaSalle along, because she takes such pride in her, like, bravado. I was like: "Can we go?" And she was like:

"No way. I need another virgin caiphirinia."

"No, Julie, I'll explain later. We have to go."

But Julie shushed me and wouldn't move. There was nothing I could do but sit there and surreptitiously try to figure out who this director was.

And, I work on Wall Street. I see a lot of guys and how they dress. The joke at Hoffman is, if they aren't fashion-phobic, they're fashion-fetishistic: it's either 100 percent beige khakis and blue shirts, with the wrong size inseam and the wrong size collar, or 100 percent Paul Smith and Thomas Pink and Hermès and Versace. But this director, who had smiled at me. He was very tall, and very skinny, and had on these gorgeous vintage clothes. This plaid linen jacket, orange and white with blue details, and these pale blue linen pants, with handsome white chalk stripes, which must have been bought at the same store as the jacket fifty years ago, because the tailoring and the colors all kind of matched. And a black tie. It was, like, frivolous clothes, but from an era when frivolity meant something different than it does now. And a boater, with a silk ribbon that matched the pants. The sort of outfit that instead of making the person in it stand out makes everyone else in the room look underdressed. He looked so much like someone who took life seriously, and in good humor at the same time. Which . . . of course, of course, since he was the one who made the movie about clothes.

And he was tall and cute, and I guess I was sort of gazing at him again, because he caught me staring a second time. He gave me the look guys give you when they have something to say to you and they want you to stay put so that they can come over and talk to you. But I still had the feeling that there was something very . . . fraught about him, so I told Julie again:

"Seriously, we need to go. I know that guy, and we need to go."

Julie just squinted her eyes, kind of defiantly, and threw her hand up in the air and started waving it around like she had some urgent question.

JULIE LASALLE *hits the nail on the head again (early August 2000)*:

I had given no thought whatsoever to what I would ask if called upon, but nonetheless I was waving my hand in the air like a sycophant in second grade, as a way to tease Jennica, who would have had to climb over my lap to escape. In an audience of sedate East Village cinephiles my overeagerness stood out, and the moderator called on me, obliging me to improvise. So I asked a question of doubtless staggering unintelligence, and I posed it to the director who Jennica said she knew. Specifically, I asked him how he managed to synchronize the music in his film with the action, because it was, after all, quite impressive, the way, for example, the woman who was crying would wipe her nose in time to this one leitmotif in the music. It was, in other words, not an insightful question.

The director was very gracious, however, and explained that no, in fact, the entire movie was shot on silent film with a hidden camera and he had composed and performed the music himself after gathering and editing the footage. It was, for me and I suspect for Jennica as well, a stunning revelation, because while I know nothing whatsoever about classical music, the music to his film had not sounded to me like something composed in the twentieth century (or, more to the point, it had not sounded like something that could have been composed by someone who lived in the twentieth century). The director said, however, that before making his film he had worked for many years as a composer for the piano, and that directing a movie seemed like one way to encourage people to sit through his music, which previously, he said, they had not seemed inclined to do. It goes without saying that Jennica, in the James Ivory world of her imagination, was swooning.

MAYNARD GOGARTY *recalls the first words he exchanged with Jennica, when he hurried up to her after the Q & A (early August 2000)*:

I said, "Pardon me. Do we know each other? From the subway with the—."

She said, "You do know me from the subway. And I know you from the subway."

That devastating feminine understatement! Her friend smirked and left, as if to say, No need for me to hang around and help; she'll be able to humiliate this sap on her own.

I said, "I do apologize for that—ill-managed scene."

"Scene? Was it staged and filmed?"

Feminine unflappability!

"No! No, it was not on film. Everything that happened was just me being—me. And I'm sorry for that. Though if it had been filmed, you would have been, ah—. You had on those picturesque pants and sandals. It made you very gorgeous and serene."

There occurred some sort of thaw then.

"You really wrote the music for your film yourself?"

"I really did. My name is Maynard, by the by."

"Jennica."

"J—."

"Jennica."

"Well—Jennica—shall we at last be friends?"

"Maybe."

But she was smiling.

JENNICA GREEN *recalls the first words she exchanged with Maynard when he hurried up to her after the Q & A (early August 2000)*:

He came up in his mannerly way:

"Pardon? Pardon, hello? Do you and I know one another from the subway?" And I was like:

"I knew I knew you! And it is from the subway, isn't it?" And Julie makes herself scarce, which, I'm like: Thanks, Julie. Thanks for the solidarity. Anyway, he said:

"I apologize for that." Which, why was he apologizing? I had been daydreaming about George Hanamoto at the time; what had happened on the subway again? But then it all came together: filmmaker, hidden cameras. So I said:

"Wait! That whole thing wasn't being filmed, was it? Because there is no way I would come out any better than any of the other people in your movie." Which, of course he thought I was asking for a compliment.

"No, it wasn't being filmed . . . and nonsense, you would have looked wonderful! Serene. As picturesque as a . . . peasant."

"A peasant?"

"Peasant . . . in the good way! The sort of peasant one sees in nineteenth-century French pastoral paintings. In a flouncy shirt, holding a basket of flowers, with a good complexion and exuberant hair under a bonnet, milk-fed, celebratory, frolicking in blossoming meadows. I seem to be . . . bungling my compliments."

"Nonsense yourself. I'm flattered you remember me. And I thought your movie was a masterpiece. So intelligent, and so emotional, and the music was . . . Until you said it wasn't, I thought it was something by Chopin."

"No, just something by me. Speaking of whom, may I introduce myself? Maynard Gogarty."

"Jennica Green. Maynard is a great name. Very proper!"

"Until twelve I went as Manny."

"I don't like that as much."

"Neither do I. It was my grandmother's idea. She was a fan of the mambo and thought Manny sounded . . . Latin and debonair."

"Maybe I can find another nickname for you."

"So maybe we shall be friends, then?"

"Maybe." But, you know, I was laughing. And he said:

"In the meantime, J—? Jennica! . . . Shall we get a drink?"

MITCHELL *and* SUSAN GREEN *explain their daughter's name (early August 2000)*:

S: We made a hybrid of Jennifer and Jessica. Both of which were names we liked, but both of which were too popular.

M: We wanted a name that would be unpopular.

S: Do you want to tell your favorite joke?

M: It's a good thing the names weren't Lucille and Jennifer!

S: His favorite joke. He has never had any taste for these things. I felt it was important for her to have a pretty name, but also something singular. And we have never heard of another Jennica. But still, doesn't it sound like something you might find in a baby book? When she was little, she wanted sisters, and she decided that she was one of a set of quadruplets separated at birth. The other three were Jennifer, Jessica, and Jessifer. Her imaginary friends.

M: I'll tell you something interesting. She says that people, when they see her name without having met her in person, think she is black. And that being perceived as black is sometimes an advantage. Who could have planned for that in 1972? We were actually concerned about whether Jennica sounded sufficiently Jewish, whether she would fit in at synagogue. Some concern that was.

S: Why you are so concerned with her meeting a Jew, I don't know. I'm just concerned that she should meet anyone she likes. At this point. To tell the truth.

The passage of time, as observed by CERTAIN CICADAS *(late summer 2000)*:

She-eee-eee. He-eee-eee.

GEORGE HANAMOTO *talks about rue (late September 2000)*:

She was obviously the sort of girl you don't let get away, and I let her get away. That's my luck for you. I mean, in my own defense, it's not like it was a beach balls and Bacardi summer in the Equities Division. I mean, have you seen these articles in the *Journal* about the election? The ones asking, "Would Anyone Rather Have a Beer with Gore"? Because I am the one Democrat in my group, everyone hectors me with this bullshit. As if it were a huge surprise that the *Wall Street Journal* supports George Bush and would rather have a beer with him, who doesn't even drink, than with Al Gore. They e-mail me these "Who would you rather have a beer with?" articles every time the *Journal* publishes them, and this summer my reaction, honestly, was, "I'd just like to have the time for a beer, period, you assholes."

I'm only saying that I didn't mean to neglect the Jennica front, but it was a busy summer, and August was a total loss. I did e-mail this buddy of mine from b-school who's at Hoffman Ballin and told him to send me Jennica's page off Hoffman's employee-only intranet, no questions asked. Which he did, no questions asked. And she really is pretty amazing. I mean, her résumé. Plus she's pretty cute, with interesting beauty spots.

But I say all this with rue, because when I finally did e-mail her seriously this week, suddenly she was busy. Friendly, but busy. She didn't say it, but you know the story. She met some guy. Maybe things won't work out with this guy in the long run, but they're working out well enough in the short run that she's not going to bother with me. That's my luck for you. Not that I'm giving up all hope; at the very least I'll see her at Nadi's wedding next year, and who knows, maybe we'll both be single then. But still, in the interim, that's my luck for you. The one month I am busy is the one month she meets some guy.

MAYNARD GOGARTY, *in a fine mood, chats about cats (September 12, 2000)*:

I bought her the cat. I dashed uptown from my last lesson of the afternoon, went to the cat emporium on Lexington in my old mint-green seersucker suit and my old Bourbon tie, paid in cash, and left with Representative Maine Coon Cat, Democrat of New York, sitting nattily in his handsome antique carrying case. The carrying case was another hundred dollars, but on the accouterments of pet ownership one must not scrimp.

It had taken some doing to arrange. Jennica first told me about the cat on one of our early evenings out, in the middle of August. Already Jennica was convinced that the cat, the waif, would have been sold to another customer. She refused so much as to visit the cat shop with me—the prospect of going, only to find that her favored kitten had already been sold, made her too anxious. "I should have been more decisive, and now it's too late!" Well, it is never too late if your beau is willing to play the private dick. And as it happens, as I learned, August is a slow month in the long-haired kitten trade, and the kindly proprietress at the cat shop not only remembered Jennica when I described her but remembered which cat she'd come—three times!—to pine over.

"Oh, *no,* that little guy's still here. But she is a *prize,* that girl of yours. You better show her you're *committed*, or you look out, she will find herself another *man.*"

So I put down a deposit. I bought a one-month option on the cat.

"Oh, she will be *so* happy. But I am telling you, against my better interest, don't you worry about giving her a cat—what you need to worry about giving her is a *ring.*"

In fact what I was worrying about was finding the money to pay for rent. But then the check from ITD Records arrived and I cashed it. It wouldn't have covered rent anyway—it didn't even cover the cat—but I went to the pet store, cash in hand, and bought the beast. The shopkeeper gave me a complimentary flea collar, a complimentary pamphlet on the proud Maine coon breed, and a 10 percent "preferred customer" discount on the rest. But still, with tax, six hundred ninety dollars. I commend myself into the hands of the gods, as far as paying rent in October. You gods! Help me make rent!

And yet what an elated state I was in on the way back downtown. And what a creature, this Maine coon. He has gray stripes, enormous and hyperactive ears, a decadent squint, and brave mewls. And green eyes. And uncontrolled riots of hair, a mane of hair, really—a feline triceratops. Whiskers, which are a fascinating flourish. And, as we headed downtown, Congressman Cat seemed just as elated as me. Terrified and wide-eyed there in his antique cat-tote, keen to meet his constituents. We were fast friends, he and I.

And—may I digress briefly? Because one feels, discoursing on love, like some hard-luck graduate student, wearing undersized blue jeans, skipping haircuts, and discovering hourly that every topic he wants to draft a dissertation on has already been dissertated. Everything to say has been said! There is nothing new under the reading lamp! Similarly so—similarly so—you meet a woman, you are so certain of your own unique pleasure in love, and yet, check the card catalogue. Check a teen magazine, check broadcast television. It turns out that everyone knows the pleasures of, say, buying your girlfriend a cat. To say nothing of—a first kiss.

So! A digression on a first kiss. A digression:

The—. The very hour that she met me, there at the screening of *Unseemly*, Jennica uncovered that I had never—sung karaoke. My abstention from karaoke was well considered: to sing a formerly popular song, written by some formerly popular singer, in a small room full of probably unpopular people, who, when you are done singing at them, will then sing back at you, all accompanied by prerecorded instrumentals? What could better illustrate your failure in life? But I had taken a vow to try to be nice, and Jennica was adamant that karaoke ennobles the spirit. I made her promise it—I made her promise "karaoke ennobles the spirit" before I would agree to anything. But phone numbers were traded, phone calls were traded. And the Thursday after the screening of *Unseemly*, Jennica and I met at—a karaoke bar.

It was on one of those dead-end streets down where Chinatown rubs up behind City Hall. And it was drizzly but hot that night—the weather for which the plaid short-sleeved gingham shirt was invented. And indeed, I was in a plaid short-sleeved gingham shirt, cork on white, and Jennica was in some of her office things. A tight white blouse unbuttoned to the point of décolletage and Burberry trousers and black Mary Janes. And we went down a narrow staircase into a boiler room, a gussied-up boiler room, with a karaoke screen and a karaoke microphone set up on a wooden stage the size of a shower stall.

Now, the night we were there, the boiler room was suffering from—a birthday party. Two girls, who looked like sophomores at NYU but who apparently both were turning twenty-six, had invited all their friends down to—sing Madonna. And there was also one gray-haired fellow there, a Chinese gentleman in an overpressed two-hundred-dollar suit, very drunk on whiskey but holding it well, who after every third song by the birthday girls would lay down his dollars and take his turn. Frank Sinatra, Bobby Darin. He must have had some training, because he sang in an unearthly basso profundo, and so he managed some dignity, waiting patiently in the corner for his turn, chatting in Chinese with a friend in a more expensive but less pressed suit.

Jennica and I sat on two stools and drank white wine—because why not drink white wine?—and during her second glass, she leaped up, infiltrated the birthday party, absconded with the binder listing the songs programmed into the karaoke machine, and announced she wanted to sing "Girl." Why "Girl"? "*Rubber Soul* was my favorite album when I was little, and 'Girl' was my favorite song. I thought that it was about me. Because in our family, I was the girl. I also thought that 'Run for Your Life' was about me, but I don't like the lyrics to that one as much." So there you are.

And after three more songs by Madonna and a memorable performance of "Not for Me," the miscellaneous drunks parted and there was Jennica on the tiny stage, looking me in the eyes and singing, "Is there anybody going to listen to my story?" Well—she was good! A clear, clean alto. A funny impersonation of the little sucking noise that John Lennon makes through his teeth during the chorus. "Thththth." An improvised dance of wiggles when the music faded at the end, making her Burberrys sway. So perhaps I have found an original, untouched dissertation topic for myself: the pleasure of watching the girl whom you are about to kiss for the first time, with a microphone in her hand and a frown under her beauty marks, as she bravely sways through the fadeout on a karaoke stage. And so what else was there to do when she sat back down on the stool but kiss her, quickly? And tell her that she was wonderful? And tell her that I would never, never in my life, have that kind of—karaoke courage?

"But don't you want to try?"

"Gah." A quick second kiss. "Perhaps next time."

I believe I was digressing, but if so, what was I digressing from?

Cat, Jennica, splendid!

It was an ideal evening in the paragon days of late summer, the day I bought her the cat. The sky was sky blue! And warm. With a courteous breeze off the Hudson, and with every tower on Manhattan Island expressing the same saffron opinion about the sunset. The pleasant odor of the brackish rivers, and of the after-work cigarettes of back-office boys smoking in garage doors, and of the cologne samples drying behind the ears of the office girls who had freshened up at the Bloomingdale's counter on their way to their six P.M. cocktail dates, and of cat urine!

Because poor, delighted Congressman Cat had peed in his antique carrying case and now was apologizing loudly, saying, "Ow? Ow? Ow?" And I had the elation of knowing I was about to make my girlfriend very, very happy.

JENNICA GREEN, *also in a fine mood, also chats about cats (September 12, 2000)*:

Everyone who I've told about Arnie and the kitten has wanted to warn me. My mom was like, "Isn't that presumptuous? A cat can live fifteen years," and my dad was like, "You don't want this man to think he can just impose a lifestyle on you." And then Julie LaSalle said, "It's analogous to an unplanned pregnancy, Jennica. He is now the father of your cat." And Gabe said, "Is having a cat and a boyfriend going to become your new excuse for never going on a vacation ever again?" I guess I appreciate the concern, but I think . . . I think that in the end everything is going to be wonderful.

Like, you move to New York City when you're twenty-two years old. It's June of 1994. And your most beloved pastime is walking through downtown, alone. You're subletting the same furnished room you did when you were just a twenty-one-year-old summer intern, a room with furniture but no windows in some blah and expensive neighborhood, and you own exactly one pair of blue jeans and one black cotton T-shirt that don't make you feel ugly, but you've never been more inspired. All the flower shops, all the drop-off laundries! So you forage for cuter apartments and noteworthier shoes, and you invest all of your attention in reading about the city. Like, reading restaurant write-ups in *New York* magazine. Which you can't really afford because you still haven't gotten your first paycheck from your no-longer-just-an-intern job at the investment bank. And you read . . . free museum newsletters, and bizarro nightclub fliers, and the personals in the *Village Voice*, and the wedding announcements in the *Times*, and the class notes in the *PAW*, and the weird movie reviews that they print in the schedule at the Anthology Film Archive, and the omnibus cultural overviews in the *New York Review of Books*. Which you also can't really afford, even when you do start getting your paycheck. And you're always how many months behind on your *New Yorker*s? But you go to Central Park on Sunday and read "The Talk of the Town" on the grass. And you're always how many weeks behind on telephoning your friends? But you sit in a café off of 2nd Avenue and write them messages on the backs of the weird free postcards that you got from the dirty rack by the café's bathroom.

Two days before Thanksgiving, you fly home to San Jose, and everyone is like, "You look so cosmopolitan." Which just makes you feel worse, because you see how far you are from being cosmopolitan, and it's embarrassing that your family can't see it too. And then three days after Thanksgiving you fly back to New York, and in your taxi, on the way in from the airport, you realize you moved here because you wanted to be somewhere that wasn't nowhere, and if you don't want to be nowhere, you're going to have to stay here forever. And you'll never make it, you'll never be able to leave, because this is not where you are from.

Until you meet the right boyfriend. And then New York is where you are from.

Like, let me tell you about this kitten, whose name I am not going to share with you yet. The plan for that night had been to eat healthy. Arnie was going to come over to my apartment and make me trout in a white wine sauce and a pear-and-walnut salad. We were supposed to go shopping after I got home from work, and then I was going to get to sit on the couch and drink wine while Arnie cooked for me and told me funny stories. That was the plan, which I was feeling pretty smug about. But when he arrived, when I opened the door for him, he was standing there in his southern gentleman's getup, with a wooden cage in his arms and the kitten sort of peering out, going, "Ow?" And Arnie said:

"I brought you a present, who needs a towel and perhaps a bath."

I was . . . wowed. We cleaned the kitten up in the kitchen sink and let him go on this, like, expedition around my apartment. Putting his nose onto spots on the parquet to smell them. He'd creep up on a spot and make little pecks at it, sniffing, but the instant his nose actually touched the parquet, he would, like, recoil, and then gallop behind the kitchen island or the CD towers or whatever. And then silence. And then a minute later he would stroll back out like nothing just happened, with a dust ball on his face, with his tail in the air. Stalking my unread *New Yorkers*. I have a stack of them, and they were flapping from the fan, which was on high. The kitten would make an ambush, race up, put his paw on the corner of the magazine to stop it from flapping, and then he would run away behind the philodendron. I kept thinking, This is such an easy, good thing, owning a kitten, but I couldn't do it for myself. Arnie knew me better than I knew myself.

Or, like.

Through some prestidigitation, and because he has a whole huge family history of connections, every other week Arnie gets us free tickets to Avery Fisher Hall. It will be some girl from Korea or some boy from Russia, playing Saint-Saëns or Schubert or Beethoven. And if it's beautiful, we sit there holding hands, almost alone in the auditorium, and if it isn't, we run away at intermission and go to one of those bars on Broadway for mussels and breadsticks and beer, and Arnie will flirt with me in his shy way.

But after the first time we went to Avery Fisher, we took the subway back to my place together. It was one of those nights of the-world-and-its-mistress bustle, like, where at eleven P.M. Broadway feels like the Great Gatsby's lawn. And when our subway reached Times Square, the conductor announced that we were being held for connecting passengers. So Arnie and I sat there, yawning from the mussels and watching to see who would make it into our subway car before the doors closed on the platform. And just as the train was getting ready to go, this old woman appeared, this . . . little Chinese granny, coming down the stairs to the track. We were both rapt. Like, could she possibly catch the train?

She was such the template of a granny . . . with her walking shorts and her heavy red shoes, and her hair in some kind of perm, and her pinched face, and her double handful of orange shopping bags. She was making her way down the stairs as quickly as she could, but probably not quickly enough, because she was taking the stairs so carefully, as if her knees and ankles were stiff. She was right in the middle of the staircase, too. So of course on both sides of her all these kids, all these athletes, were cutting her off, slowing her down, bounding down the steps two at a time, because they wanted to make it into our subway before the doors closed. But Arnie and I both had the same instinct: to root for the granny.

The doors did their warning chime, and the conductor said, "Stand clear the closing doors," and the little old lady had only reached the bottom stair. The doors had already started to close as she shuffled across the platform . . . she was so not going to make it. But just before the doors sealed, she reached her foot out and clomped one thick red shoe right in the middle of the slicing doors.

You wouldn't have thought she could do it, with her stiff legs. But she got her foot in place, and the doors stuck on her shoe, and the train couldn't depart. It was so simple. So small and flawless. The subway conductor had to reset the doors, which gave her the chance to hustle into the train. It was like watching a perfect dismount in Olympic gymnastics. You wanted to cheer.

Arnie immediately jumped up to offer her his seat. And . . . I loved that. Not just his courtesy, but the way, like, when the train was moving again, he caught my eye and gave me this silent nod . . . to acknowledge our admiration of the old lady. As if to say, "We are in the presence of a champion." That nod, that knowing nod. He knew that I knew how perfect a performance we'd just seen. I had to stand up and be next to him right then, it was so adorable, that nod. Like, Hello, hello, hello, you . . . man who makes me feel good.

Or the *Sunday New York Times.* You can't explain to someone how to love and hate the Vows section, where they print all the wedding announcements. Or why most Saturday nights it is less fun to go out than it is to stay in and buy the *Times* and figure out which couples in Vows are actually the happy ones. Or you can't explain to someone what it's like to come from San Jose, where there are no jaywalkers and no sexy boots. But Arnie, the first time we went out, to karaoke, when we were leaving the bar and going to dinner, he was like, "Has anyone ever told you that you are an exceptional jaywalker? So daring and so calm, and in such sexy boots!" Or, like, the first time Arnie saw my apartment and he said immediately, "Jennica, what a treasure! With original parquet!" I was like:

"But there are mice. And it's never the right temperature. And it's so loud. And it's susceptible to burglary. And it's too expensive." Because no matter how much you like your apartment, you always feel like a real New Yorker would have gotten a better deal. But Arnie said:

"If you say so. Shall we find you something more perfect, then?" Like, that confidence, that irresistible male confidence. That perfect sense of anything is possible, because New York City could be where I am from.

So, I don't need all these warnings people are giving me about

Arnie buying me a cat. I am not the sort of person to fall in love recklessly. I know there are issues with Arnie. Including that he wants me to call him Maynard, which is ridiculous, instead of Arnie, which is a perfect nickname for a shy and gentle and tall boy, a prep school boy. But also that he is eight years older than me, and that he has all that debt, and that it isn't clear how interested he is in, like, adulthood. Fine. But when he was standing at my door and holding the kitten out for me, he had this look on his face like, Is it all right for me to like you this much? And I was like, Yes, please, like me that much.

MAYNARD GOGARTY *explains about the naming of cats (September 12, 2000)*:

On the train downtown from Practical Cats, a long-legged black girl wanted to know the cat's name. She was sincerely charmed by Congressman Cat. And her boyfriend, dressed like a gangster, was smiling amiably and humbly and even apologetically at me. It was like being in church, the air of fellowship this cat brought out.

The black girl said, "What is your cat's name?"

"Actually, he doesn't have a name yet."

"You got to name your cat."

Congressman Cat said, "Me?"

And I said, "But I only just this minute bought him. I'm giving him as a gift to my—girlfriend. I think she gets to name him."

"He look like he a bobcat. He ain't no normal cat. He huge. You tell your girlfriend she need to call him Simba."

Simba? A terrible name for a cat. But the ease with which these kids talk about girlfriends and boyfriends, and the ease with which you can join the ranks of the happy. I say girlfriend, people take me at my word. Forget race, forget money. The real divide in New York City is between the content and the discontent. I am ready, I am ready! I want to be a member of—that upper class.

JENNICA GREEN *explains about the naming of cats (September 12, 2000)*:

And so while the cat was prowling around, Arnie and I had this great sparring match about names. Which I love, that feeling of having a boyfriend to, like, match wits with. Because I thought we should call the cat either Wolfgang or Amadeus. And Arnie was, like, vehemently opposed. I was like:

"But we like Mozart." And he was like:

"It's true, Jennica. You and I, and all people, like Mozart. Let me see the fellow's face. I need inspiration."

"He's hiding from you because he thinks you don't like him. How about Ludwig?"

"Absolutely not."

"You yourself said that not everyone likes Beethoven." And Arnie is like:

"We could call him Camille."

"But he's a boy, Arnie."

"So was Saint-Saëns. Whose music you like, and whose first name will not sound like a . . . deliberate allusion."

"But what's the point of naming the cat after something if no one will get it?"

"Because if you name a cat after something, and if people get it, then they will know that you named your cat after something. A fact that would be humiliating. How about Knudage? After Knudage Riisåger the Danish modernist."

"You're just trying to be pretentious."

"Pretentious! You, my half-naked little hypocrite, are the one who insists that we name the cat after an artist."

Which, whatever. I was not half naked. I had taken off my shirt so I could mop up the cat. Arnie was like:

"The name should be simple and whimsical. We should name him Mumpus. Or Grumpton. Or Tuskatonic. Or Abdul."

"Mumpus? You don't know anything about naming a cat. What about Wharton?"

"Jennica, if we name the cat Wharton, everyone who comes to your apartment will think . . ."

"What, Arnie? What will everyone think?"

"They will think that you have read Edith Wharton."

"So what? I liked *House of Mirth*. How about . . . Horatio?"

"Horatio?"

"Everyone likes Horatio."

"The danger is not that people won't like the character the cat is named for, the danger is that we will be perceived as lauding our cultural credentials. And that our cultural credentials will amount to having seen *Hamlet*."

"So what are your suggestions?" And Arnie was like:

"Call him Uku!ola," which was supposed to sound like a word from an African click language.

"That's how you talk to horses, not cats."

"Call him Uku!ola. And if anyone asks, you can tell them that it means something nice in some exotic tongue. You can say, 'In the Xhosa language of southern Africa, *uku!ola* means perfume.' You'll stun people with your erudition."

"I can't even make that noise, and anyway he doesn't smell like perfume. How about . . . Brahms. Brahms the Cat. Or . . . Schubert! Schubert the Cat. Schuby!"

"Jennica, do I get one veto?"

"Yes, but only one."

"I veto all musicians."

MAYNARD GOGARTY *explains about the naming of cats (September 12, 2000)*:

So she goes to her bookshelf.

I didn't care about the name of the cat, but still, sometimes, even with something so trivial as the naming of a cat, you get a glimpse of someone's inner nature. And you see that the person you love is so—. It is awful to say—. But with the naming of a cat, you see that she is so—.

She goes to her bookshelf and starts reading the names of the authors off the spines of her books, as proposals for what to call the cat.

"Emerson. Coleridge. Woolf. Proust. Marcel!"

"Jennica, no."

"Marcel!"

"No!"

"Yeats."

"Why must the name be literary?"

"Don't you think that cats are the most literary animals?"

"I—? I—? No!"

"You think dogs are more literary than cats?"

"What—? No!"

"What do you think the most literary animal is, then?"

"Do I have to choose between cats and dogs?"

"What else is there?"

"Pigeons? Prawns? Parazoans?"

"You think that the most literary animal is the prawn?"

"I think that the most literary animal is the human."

"That's ridiculous. You can't name a human baby Coleridge, but it's a great name for a cat. When you think of a bookstore, you don't think of people. You think of a cat. A big, lazy cat. Curling around the bookshelves. Cats are the most well read of animals. And the most authorial."

"Jennica. Cats—shit—in boxes."

"Well, you do it in a bowl."

"But I wipe, and I flush."

"Not always, you don't flush."

She thought she had me. She thought the fact that I once forgot to flush her toilet meant that I would have to let her name our cat Amadeus.

"What's wrong with Coleridge?"

"Let's call him—Jimmy Carter."

"I want to call him either Marcel or Coleridge."

"Coleridge detested cats."

"He did?"

"Yes. Call him Geoffrey. That's a good name. Lots of nice men are named Geoffrey. Or even Geoff-with-a-G. You could say to people, 'This is my cat, Geoff-with-a-G.'"

"You have no idea whether Coleridge hated cats."

"Call him Samuel if you want to name him after Coleridge."

"But then no one will get it."

"That's the point!"

"You are such a snob! No wonder people hate you! Finnegan."

"But Jennica, neither of us has ever read *Finnegans Wake*!"

"I have so! Excerpts."

"If the cat's name alludes to something, we—*we!*—*we!*—have to get the allusion!"

"Leopold. I have read *Ulysses*, which is more than most people can say. How about Leo?"

"No! No Leopold, no Leonardo, no Ponce de Leon."

"Chatterley."

"Good! Call him Lady Chatterley's Pussy."

"Don't be dirty. How about Salinger?"

"Call him the Alien and Sedition Cat. Call him the Stamp Cat. Call him the Sonny Bono Copyright Extension Cat of 1998."

"I am willing to call him Portnoy."

"Call him Herr Doktor. Or Mein Führer. Or Il Duce. Il Duce is an excellent name for a cat."

At this point she went back to her bookshelf and retrieved a flubby tome—a certain flubby tome. A certain flubby paperback tome. Second edition, Princeton University Bookstore sticker still on the cover. You know the book I mean.

And she said, "Zooks. Zooks the Cat." And now she was flipping through the pages. "Longfellow. Longfellow the Cat. Hiawatha the Cat. Ozymandias the Cat."

"Jennica. We can't get a name for the cat out of *The Norton Anthology of Poetry*."

"No, but Hiawatha was from *Maine*, right?"

"What does Maine have to do with anything?"

"He's a Maine coon."

"Jennica—consider Il Duce."

JENNICA GREEN *explains about the naming of cats (September 12, 2000):*

I was like:

"We cannot name him after a fascist. He's Jewish." And Arnie was like:

"A Jewish cat. I hadn't thought of that. Well, then . . . Pol Pot."

"How about Marcel?"

"See, he came right to me when I called him Pol Pot."

"What's wrong with Marcel?"

"Marcel is neither obscure nor sinister."

"That's your rule, Arnie? Obscure and sinister?" And he was like:

"First of all, why must you call me Arnie? And second of all, look at his sinister fangs."

"How about Kafka the Cat?"

"Jennica Green! If you want to display your learning, display your learning."

"Maynard Gogarty! I went to Princeton, I majored in English, I have earned the right to name my cat after anything I want."

"You went to Princeton so you could name your cat Horatio?"

"And what was your best idea? Mumpus? Pol Pot? If we call the cat Pol Pot, then everyone will hate me, just like everyone already hates you."

"When did it become a given that everyone hates me?"

"If we call him Mumpus instead of Marcel, can we call you Arnie instead of Maynard?"

"Gah! If we call me Arnie, can I take off your bra?"

Afterwards, it was too late to buy the trout anymore. And while we were trying to decide what to do . . . Get Chinese delivery? Pick up Lebanese takeout? Make apple pancakes? . . . we realized we didn't know where Mumpus was. Not behind the CD towers, not under the philodendron. And it actually took us a few minutes to find him, because he had climbed over my recycling bins, up the radiator, over the stovetop, and into the kitchen sink, where he was lying on his belly, staring down the drain forlornly. It was the sorriest, most hilarious thing, the way he looked at us from the sink, like, "I know what you two were up to in the bedroom all this time."

MAYNARD GOGARTY *describes the pungency of it all (September 12, 2000)*:

I—. I am no Don Juan. If anything, I'm a failed celibate. There have been whole years when I've been abstinent, continent—marooned. It's like plashing back into the waves after a long ebb tide, these past few weeks. So forgive me if I gush. And forgive me too if I resort to water metaphors. But that flood of ardor when you get to get wet again! I know Jennica is feeling giddy too. She's more discreet about such things than I am, but as I was saying, sex with Jennica—.

How to begin?

Perhaps with some—demonology? Because it sometimes has seemed to me that I, as a lover, am being persecuted by evil spirits. It has seemed to me sometimes that all my previous girlfriends, all my few previous girlfriends, were the victims of unholy possession. It has sometimes seemed to me that in bed, each of my previous girlfriends channeled one or another of two malevolent supernatural beings: the Sissy and the Anti-Sissy.

The Sissy. The Sissy is a demon who—renders you anemic. As a man, you can suffer terribly in bed: a lady accidentally knees your balls; you have to wear those nonoxynol tourniquets on your cock; you abrade your groin; you sprain your back. You must endure the awful half-hour that sometimes follows extreme exertion, when you must stand over the sink coaxing scalding, halting droplets of urine out of your penitent penis. Well? Pleasure is an arduous pursuit! If you want pleasure, you must resist the Sissy! You must carry on! And should you ever sleep with a woman who is possessed by the Sissy—oh, it is grim. When a woman is possessed by the Sissy, if her left breast is inconvenienced by a draft from the air conditioner, her libido is shot; if you come in her mouth, her night is ruined; if you tangle her hair, you are scolded, roundly, for weeks on end. In waking life, this may be a woman who wins triathlons, who ignores blisters and cramps and sprains, who relishes hardship. But in bed and possessed by the Sissy, she is reduced to telling you, "Not too hard, not too fast, not just yet." And so you must weather forty minutes of neck spasms because her special clitoris is more tentative than an inchworm and more subtle than a glowworm and glimmers more elusively than a will-o'-the-wisp.

But then there is the Anti-Sissy. The Anti-Sissy is a demon who makes women speak in tongues. Perfectly articulate women —radio journalists, adjunct lecturers—who, when in their bra and panties and when possessed by the Anti-Sissy, begin to recite—hot talk. Hot talk and smutty commands and teenage cussing learned from television. And if you laugh at what one of these women says, she will slap you. "Fuck me! Faster, faster, faster!" You think to yourself, Is it sex, or is it an exorcism? Sometimes the Anti-Sissy will try a trick—spitting on your cock before giving you a welterweight champion's hand job and grunting, "You like that, don't you?"; flapping her tits around your cock and telling you, "I like it this way!"; flipping her hair and looking at you over her shoulder before commanding, "Do me"—*pant, pant*—"in the ass!" *Mon dieu.* You stand there, cock a-bounce in your boxer shorts, thinking, I can only fail.

I don't know whether I am proud to be able to offer these observations. They are simply the field notes of a—mostly wholesome lad who has seen some evil nights. But those days are over!

Jennica—! She goes to bed with the simple attitude of, Do to me what you will. Absolute permissiveness, spiked with irreproachable hauteur. For example, her whimpering. Certainly, certainly, her whimpering is one of the great accomplishments of Western eroticism. A perfectly soft little moaning or gasping. You feel the terror of the impermissible. It's very, very provocative. She whimpers, and you think, I am getting something I shouldn't be getting. And yet if I stop, she will hold it against me forever. She whimpers, and you think, She does not condone what I am up to, but she wants me to keep going. This is what her whimpering conveys. And you can feel her whimpering—in—her—cunt!

And—! Is it something they teach in yoga, that sexual alacrity? I salute you, you anonymous yoga instructors—you, my nameless benefactors! Never again will I disparage those Manhattan women in their cotton-and-elastic body armor and with their foam yoga mats strapped over their shoulders like quivers of arrows, striding off to their yoga classes. The thought alone gives me a stiffy. Jennica—my yogini, my mistress of the hunt.

I adore her, and I think she adores me too. On her back, curled like a little starfish, with her legs spread in some sort of contortion unknown outside of ashrams and vaudeville, my enveloping, juicy succubus. And did I tell you about her breasts? And midway through, when she is wrapped around me like some snail out of her shell—. When she's so soft and so suddenly dispossessed of her affects, a little pleasure oyster—. When she is like a happily sedated squid, suddenly I will find myself in the midst of a sensational squall of bouncing surf to realize that in my open-mouthed pleasure, I am in fact weeping and drooling simultaneously into her shoulder.

What grand fun! I come like a standpipe, like a hydrant in Harlem. They have to call in the fire department to shut down my cock. I believe she—I believe Jennica feels the same. She's a shivering, sopping wreck, which is just gratifying.

The pungency of it all!

This is

THE THIRD PART.

It is short, consisting of some succinct statements from the winter of 2001 as well as the partial transcript of a pop song. It might be thought of as an intermission between the longer Second and Fourth Parts. Please enjoy a complimentary mai tai from our luau bar.

DAVID FOWLER *gives us a tour of the lobster (the early morning hours of February 9, 2001):*

You want a tour of the lobster, I'll give you a tour of the lobster. But I'm going to have to whisper, since court is in session. Here, the tour starts with Gogarty's paperwork. Look at this: "Criminal mischief in the second degree" and "Cemetery desecration in the first degree." And this is the room where they do the lobster. It's a typical 100 Centre Street room. Scummy linoleum floors, scummy lighting, scummy windows high up on the walls, bad heating. But nice wooden benches, you've got to admit. Tonight it's a bit slow because of the snowstorm yesterday. Sometimes it's a threepenny opera in here, or a two-and-a-half-penny opera, with the relatives sitting in the galley moaning and groaning while Mac the Knife gets arraigned. But tonight it's quiet, which is why Gogarty is getting out in less than eighteen hours.

On the right is the sap from the DA's, on the left are the Legal Aid folks. And back behind that door is where they keep the defendants while they're waiting to be arraigned, the holding cells and the peepshow booths where the attorneys can talk to their clients, which is where I went when I went to talk to Gogarty. He's waiting back there now, with maybe twenty other defendants, all of them eating peanut butter sandwiches.

Tonight presiding we've got Judge Leon D. Lushprod. Never been in front of him before. The way the lobster works is, every night it's a different judge from a different borough. Lushprod's from Brooklyn. When it's a judge from the Bronx, you know you've got a softy, and when it's a judge from Staten Island, you know you've got some reactionary clone of Giuliani. Brooklyn is a toss-up in terms of judges, but I've been listening to the proceedings for half an hour now, and this Lushprod sounds pretty reasonable. Look at him. He looks like the guy who used to be on Mutual of Omaha's *Wild Kingdom.* But you never know with the lobster.

"The lobster" is just what they call night court. "The lobster shift": one A.M. to nine A.M. The story I heard, the etymology, is that the court takes a coffee break at four A.M., which is the same time that the lobster boats come in at the Fulton Fish Market. But that doesn't make any sense, because what lobster boats? In New York City? And what, criminal court judges are wandering over to the Fulton Fish Market at four A.M. to eat fresh lobster on their coffee break?

Gogarty should be arraigned by two-thirty. If they didn't have the lobster shift he'd have to sit in the Tombs all night, and he wouldn't be arraigned until maybe noon tomorrow. That nickname, "the Tombs," really spooked what's-her-name, Jennica. She calls me in a tizzy: "David! You have to help us! They're taking Arnie to the Tombs!" The Tombs are where they process people after they bring them in from the station houses. It's across the street. Go inside, you'll know why they call it the Tombs.

So, Gogarty. I just went back there and spoke with him. He looks exhausted, but he says he's making friends with the dope dealers. It's a whole bunch of kids in do-rags back there, and Gogarty in a suit and a tie and a nineteenth-century hat. The cops had a search warrant, picked him up at home, and tore his place apart. They're saying that he intentionally poisoned a tree in the old German Lutheran Cemetery. It's great: the warrant application has a cop testifying that an anonymous tipster called the city to report the crime. Nothing more about the identity of the tipster. So someone has it in for Gogarty, and the question is, who?

But Gogarty tells me that he did it. That he killed the tree. And that this is the second time, too. Here's what he tells me:

A couple of weeks ago he waits up until three-thirty in the morning, goes into the alley behind his building through the rear service door. Tosses an extension cord over the wall between the alley and the cemetery, leans a ladder against the wall, hops over. Carries a power drill with him, in a suitcase. The kind of power drill they use for putting holes in cement; he borrowed it from his building's super. Why did he have it in a suitcase? Because he doesn't own a backpack—they come in the wrong colors. Fine. So he's in the cemetery and spends half an hour boring half a dozen holes into the trunk of this tree, just above the root line. "Do you want to know the names on the graves from which the mulberries grew, David? Pichlmayr and Bass. Do you suppose they both ate mulberries as their last meals?" So probably half the building hears him drilling into this frozen tree trunk, but he tells me no one will be able to ID him because of his ingenious disguise, i.e., that he wore a black scarf around his face. "No one can finger me, David, I'm sure! Tell them I want a lineup!" Christ. He gets served with a warrant, but he wants a lineup. He was bragging to me about how he scoped the whole thing out in advance, how he knew he could climb back out of the cemetery by scrambling on top of some crypt that abuts the cemetery wall. And how for the last three weeks he has been strolling over into the cemetery during park hours with one of those blue "We Are Happy To Serve You" coffee cups filled with herbicide. He says he pretends to be an artist wandering among the graves, sipping coffee and looking for inspiration. But then he pours the herbicide into the holes he drilled in the trunk. Every day he tops off the holes with herbicide and then heads uptown and teaches kids piano.

I ask him the obvious question: "Gogarty, what do you have against this tree?" Know what he says? He killed the tree for the view. The tree was blocking the light to the rear of the building, so the superintendent asked Gogarty to kill the tree in exchange for a break on his rent. And Gogarty did it. In other words, Gogarty wants to plead the Manhattan real estate defense. At least he had the sense not to say anything to the cops.

Oh, here's what's-her-name.

JENNICA GREEN *ignores pride (mid-February 2001)*:

The courthouse was just . . . straight from Marvel Comics. Twenty-five stories, sort of late art deco, sort of totalitarian, but basically a big black looming fortress out of Gotham City. Right there in the middle of downtown. And when I finally got there, David Fowler was sitting in the courtroom, waiting his turn, looking at the judge like a stray dog that's hoping to be fed. Except fatter.

I mean, Arnie could spend four years in jail. Four years! And they searched the apartment. They rifled through . . . everything. Everything. And it's like, Was Sal the Super the anonymous tipster? Is he looking for an excuse to kick Arnie out of the apartment? What if Arnie loses the apartment? And of course Arnie is maddeningly . . . not blasé, but maddeningly reticent about it.

Anyway, at one-thirty A.M. David Fowler finally called me up and told me to come downtown and meet him at the courthouse, that Arnie was going to be arraigned during night court. He said, "I'm sure that you two can make a nine A.M. flight to California, if that was your plan . . . *But only if you can make bail!*" I had withdrawn the limit in cash from my money market account that afternoon, after I called David from that hotel on Times Square. I took out four hundred dollars, which was all my bank would let me withdraw, even when I tried to trick it by going to ATMs from different banks. I asked him if that was enough, and he said, "I can't promise what the judge will do." I don't trust him, as a lawyer. I mean, "*If you can make bail!*" Get over yourself. So while I was waiting for the cab to take me downtown, I called the airline. I ignored my pride, and I explained that my boyfriend was unexpectedly arrested. The woman at the airline was like:

"Hon, my husband was arrested for DUI once, I know what it's like." She got us a flight straight to Hawaii on Saturday. Which meant we'd still get our vacation, if Arnie got out on bail. But which also meant we wouldn't get to stop over in California on Friday, so Arnie wouldn't get to meet my parents or my brother.

MITCHELL *and* SUSAN GREEN *explain when they expect to meet their daughter's boyfriend (mid-February 2001)*:

S: Well, she was obviously in distress that night. I told her, "Listen. Don't worry about seeing us on Friday." I told her, "Go on your vacation to Hawaii. Just follow your heart, and stand by your man, and go on your vacation. Don't worry about hurting our feelings."

M: She wanted to know what to do if his bail was set at some amount higher than what she had in cash. And I do not hesitate to tell you, I had no idea what to say. Bail? Bail? And what happened to this wealthy family he is from? Why aren't they paying for his bail? I mean, cemetery desecration!

S: Mitchell. We know this fellow isn't a hoodlum, and we don't know what sort of family situation he is involved in. I told her, "Jennica, just follow your heart. And if you think you should stand by him, then stand by him."

M: You know what Jennica said? "But if you do it to improve your view, then isn't cemetery desecration a white-collar crime?"

S: When have we ever heard her so happy as these last couple of months? He bought her the cat, and he helped get her into her new apartment on the Upper East Side and out of that awful firetrap in the Village. And when has she ever gone on a real vacation? To Hawaii, no less? She is obviously in love. I told her, stand by him.

M: You want to know what counts for something with me? That it was a German cemetery he desecrated.

S: We told her, if you can't bring Arnie out to see us in San Jose, we'll just fly out to meet him in New York. Of course, anything between now and June is out of the question, because Gabe and Rachel's baby is due in April. And I refuse to visit New York in July or August. So I made Mitchell get us tickets for the fall.

M: And the prices you can get this far in advance are superb. We fly into New York on September fifth and fly back out on September eleventh.

DAVID FOWLER *goes on the record (the daylight hours of February 9, 2001)*:

That assistant DA last night was so full of shit. What did he say? "The tree was more than one hundred years old, very serious quality-of-life crime, shows a manifest disregard for government property and community standards." He asked for twenty thousand dollars bail. Twenty thousand—such bullshit!

I told the judge, "Your Honor, this is a man I have known personally my entire life. Not even a traffic ticket to his name. Professional filmmaker and musician and teacher, his whole career is here in this borough. Same apartment, fifteen years. Runs a business out of his apartment. All sorts of community ties. His fiancée lives in Manhattan and is sitting right back there." Which I think the judge liked.

Actually, that was something interesting, calling Jennica his fiancée. Because before I said it, I asked Gogarty if I could. And Gogarty said, "Will the judge like that?"

I said, "The judge will love it. It shows you won't jump bail. My question was about Jennica. Will she be okay with it?"

And Gogarty said, "I suppose we'll find out what she thinks. Though you and I still need to talk about my divorce."

I wondered whether I could really get up there and tell the judge that Gogarty was engaged to Jennica, given that he is still married to that Ana woman. But a man can be engaged to one woman pending a divorce from another woman, right? So it's not misleading the court to tell the judge that Jennica is Gogarty's fiancée, right? Anyway, I thought it was interesting how cavalier Gogarty was about the entire thing. Fiancée, not fiancée—all the same to Gogarty.

In any event, I also told the judge, "Your Honor, I have serious doubts about the merits of these charges against my client. The charge is that my client killed a tree. It is the middle of winter, Your Honor. The tree in question is still standing. There is no way the State can say the tree is dead. So this is a baseless charge. And the warrant that was served on Mr. Gogarty is certain to be ruled invalid; it's based on testimony from a single anonymous source, no indicia of reliability." Which I think is a great argument. "Bail should be waived, Your Honor."

But the judge tells me, "I am not passing on the merits, counsel. I'm setting bail at five hundred dollars." But then he tells the assistant, practically *sua sponte*, "I do note, however, that I have serious doubts about this warrant."

I don't know. I told Gogarty that I couldn't afford to take his case pro bono, but I do feel like I owe him a favor. And this issue about the validity of the warrant is an interesting one. An anonymous tipster, and Gogarty has no clue who it might be.

JENNICA GREEN *doesn't complain (mid-February 2001)*:

On the way down to the courthouse, at two in the morning, I made the taxi stop at two more ATMs. It was after midnight, so I was able to get another four hundred dollars. There I was, withdrawing money for the first time from an account that I opened five years ago, to save up for a down payment on an apartment. I'm not complaining, I'm just . . . noting. Which, running around town in the middle of the night with eight hundred dollars in cash in my purse?

Anyway. I got to the courthouse, and they set bail at five hundred dollars. David went with me to the bail clerk, to help me pay. And I told him:

"Arnie and I aren't engaged, you know." And David was like:

"Well, he said it was okay for me to call you his fiancée."

"Oh, did he? He said it was okay to say that . . . to a judge?"

I let it drop with David. And of course I wasn't going to say anything about it to Arnie. Because. It's not like I haven't thought about . . . whatever, marriage. But we've only been together five months. Still, he is the father of my cat. And he did help me find my new apartment.

And we did do Thanksgiving together. Arnie's mother, Joan, always hosts this Gogarty family Thanksgiving up at their cabin in the Berkshires. For Gran Rose and Arnie and Arnie's cousins. And Joan, unlike my mother, is a traditionalist about the food. So in October I told my parents I wasn't coming to California, and then Arnie and I went to Massachusetts together for Thanksgiving weekend, and I met his family. And, you know about Thanksgiving. You and your boyfriend take his little second cousins for a walk in the snow on Thanksgiving afternoon while the turkey cooks; you and your boyfriend eat the leftover pumpkin pie in the kitchen on Friday night after everyone else is asleep; you and your boyfriend whatever. And you think to yourself, Is this what we'll do every year from now on? You don't say anything, but you look in your boyfriend's eyes while you're chewing the pie, sort of, and . . . you're both thinking about marriage or the equivalent.

And the other Gogartys were obviously thinking about it too. Because, which was adorable, Gran Rose pulled me aside into the bathroom and had a little talk with me. We were driving up to the cabin on Wednesday afternoon, on the Taconic Parkway. Arnie drove, and I sat in back so that Rose could have the front seat. It was the first time that she and I had met, and I think Rose liked the fact that I wouldn't let her sit in back. That, and the fact that I recognized that her coat was Chanel.

But Rose kept having to use the bathroom, so we kept stopping at little gas stations on the parkway. And at the second stop Rose said, "You're coming with me, young lady," so I escorted her to the bathroom while Arnie bought trail mix for us in the convenience store. And Rose is energetic, but she's an old lady. When we got to the bathroom, she told me:

"Sometimes it takes me a while to get warmed up in there. And I do not like it when people knock while I am getting warmed up. People are so impatient. You can stand guard." So I stood guard for her while she peed, and made the other people who came to the bathroom form a line and wait patiently. And then, when Rose was done, she couldn't figure out how to get the paper towel dispenser to work. It was one of those dispensers that operate like an upside-down box of baby wipes, except the nozzle that is supposed to feed out the towels was clogged, so I had to fish a paper towel out for her. And Rose was like:

"I don't think it's a very sanitary invention if it makes you do all that work just for one paper towel." I said:

"It certainly isn't. I think it's a case of someone trying to sell a better mousetrap but ignoring the public weal." And Rose said:

"Hrmph! I hope Manny realizes what a sensible girl you are. And I want you to know that the two of you are welcome to use the cabin whenever you like."

She's the kind of little old lady who, even in some wet, cold, overlit bathroom on the parkway, is on a mission. In her red Chanel coat. And she hooked her arm through mine and marched me back to the Mercedes, past the people who were waiting in line for the bathroom, like I was already her granddaughter-in-law.

And Arnie must be thinking about it too. I mean, he's going back to work as a teacher at Chatham, and when he accepted the job, he told me that the reason he's doing it is so that he can be a more respectable boyfriend. But is he planning something big when we're in Hawaii? Anyway. I'll spare you my speculations.

MAYNARD GOGARTY *tells about his pleasant day (mid-February 2001)*:

May I offer a preface to the tale of my arrest? Because I want it to be clear that I respect the police department and the mayor. Rudolph Giuliani may dislike democracy, but he has briskly done what no mayor before him has dared even slowly to do, namely, act as though nothing in New York City were sacred. A mayor *sans esprit de pays*! An admirable tyrant!

Here is my preface: The firemen are, we are made to understand, "New York City's Bravest." And the trash men are "New York City's Strongest." Now, I have seen Canal Street on trash night, and personally I would have reversed those two, but let that pass. Just yesterday I learned that the corrections officers are "New York City's Boldest." From what I saw, "New York City's Bulkiest" is more like it. But the police! The police are "New York City's Finest." As in, "Fincst Nab Creep in Sick Tree-Slay." This concludes my preface.

Through a softly falling snow—pianissimo, please—I had gone to the Chinese grocery looking for prunes and sunscreen. When I returned to my apartment, there was a squadron, a detachment, of New York City's Finest at my door. And Sal the Super was standing there among them with his—bold ring of keys, letting them into my apartment. Naturally Sal knew why the police were arresting me, and so naturally he avoided my eyes and faded off into the background without a word. Well, Sal, I won't rat you out. Even though the conspiracy to kill the tree was your invention. I am an honorable man—I will keep mum. Unless my attorney advises me otherwise.

So—! Four cops, myself, one tube of SPF 25, and one carton of prunes, in the hallway outside my apartment. They showed me their warrant. They wished to search for

> Drills, awls, bores, and/or affiliated materiel; and/or
>
> Herbicides, fungicides, pesticides, and/or other deleterious floratoxins and/or affiliated agents; and/or
>
> Funnels, pipes, and/or any other gardening and/or construction implements; and/or
>
> Other such tools and/or devices as may have been used to prepare a hole for, and/or to otherwise assist in, the intra-arboreal delivery of liquids; and/or
>
> Liquids for intra-arboreal delivery.

It's good of them to provide you with your own copy of the paperwork. After half a day in custody, I am grateful for small considerations. For example, that Jennica cleaned up the apartment for me. And rearranged our Hawaii flights. This girl is unprecedented!

As I was saying, four cops in oversized rain jackets, three ladies and a gentleman, all of whom had the demeanor of elementary school crossing guards who had gotten promotions—handed in their whistles for service revolvers, so to speak. Teasing each other but humorless with me. I was the kid who had crossed against the light and was being made to sit in detention. I looked at the warrant without removing my jacket or my hat and asked if I could please call a lawyer.

The male officer, he laughed at me. He looked less like a crossing guard than like some miscreant cafeteria assistant. With that violent, runt-of-the-litter look to him that scrawny young men sometimes have, the wiry fury of the picked-upon. Sadism and pride of uniform. He laughed at me and said, "You can make your calls at the station house."

Apparently, so long as they aren't asking any questions, you don't get a lawyer. I said, "Then allow me to invite you in."

"Oh, we're coming in," said Officer Runt.

"May I take your coats? Do they always issue them to you that large?"

They searched the apartment. Like mice, wiggling themselves into every little corner, looking for crumbs. They put the youngest officer in charge of me—a sweet girl, Puerto Rican, I believe, maybe twenty years old: Officer Isabel Muñeca. She looked like a sorority girl dressed up as a New York City cop for Halloween. Her pants needed tailoring, and her rain jacket was three sizes too large for her. When her fellow officers found the drill and the herbicide, she seemed genuinely sorry to learn that I was in fact—a tree-slaying creep.

She asked me, "Have you ever been arrested before?" and sounded so apologetic. But then she cuffed me, behind the back, and read me my rights, and then for two hours she sat next to me in the piano studio while her fellow officers searched through my effects.

"You got a nice place," Officer Muñeca kept telling me. "You listen to all those records you got on the wall?"

"I don't mean to be rude, Madame Officer, but if I haven't a lawyer, I mustn't converse."

"You play the piano, though? This is a nice piano. I used to know 'Chopsticks' and 'Hot Cross Buns' and 'Mary Had a Little Lamb.' But I could never play the piano for real. You mind if I put on the radio?"

"Not at all."

She put it on Hot 97.7. And—. Hot 97.7 played—a song. A song, or a ditty, or a jingle, or a travesty, or a hit. And it was as though—not as though my heart skipped a beat, it was more gruesome and euphoric and disorienting than that. It was as though, after thirty-seven years of pouring blood into my body, my heart, like a giant mineral water dispenser, had its first bubble. Are you familiar with how, when you draw water from a water cooler, every glass or two a huge bubble will jellyfish its way to the surface? Well, it took thirty-seven years, thirty-seven years of pouring my body full of the clean red stuff, but finally my heart did precisely that—had a bubble. I thought I would die. But then I became too distracted to think about death, because I was trying to make out the words.

PUPPY JONES *lays down two verses and a chorus (mixed for radio December 2000)*:

[Intro]
Y'all can't rhyme for [*scratch*]. Puppy's got a list,
And he's gonna learn y'all, yo. Uh-oh, here we go:

[Verse]
Airfare, blame game, brain drain, Care Bear,
Fake bake, hair bear, late date, hair care.

Waylay, mayday, name game, naysay,
Pale Male, pale ale, plain Jane, payday.
Fat cat, gal pal, backtrack, fag hag,
Handstand, grandstand, pass gas, ragtag.
Bed head, pegleg, birth dearth, deadhead,
Hell's bells, jet set, med head, bedspread.
Cheat sheet, deep sleep, dream team, Fleet Street,
Geek chic, green bean, Greek Week, heat treat.
Kiwi, real deal, sneak peek, near beer,
Speed read, sweetmeat, TV, steer clear.
Big Dig, big rig, bigwig, chick flick,
Chill pill, ill will, picnic, Pickwick.
Spit pit, [*scratch*] fit, Slim Jims, Ring Ding,
Swiss Miss, white knight, white flight, spring fling.
Talkin' time for a mai tai. Talkin' prime-time rhyme.

[Chorus]
Here's my manifesto to contest who's the best
And who's a novice.
This ain't no creed about the street, it's a screed
About rhyming's office.
It's a triptych of philippic against a bad aesthetic
From a most poetic medic
On a diatribe.
I'm Jeremiah, you're my tribe.
You got a soul to save? Listen up, slave!

[Verse]
Hari-kari, "Later, skater," Wabi-Sabi, Wavy Gravy,
Handy-dandy, hanky-panky, Laffy Taffy, lardy-dardy,
Namby-pamby, razzle-dazzle, fenderbender, gender bender,
Helter-skelter, herky-jerky, Jelly Belly, heebie-jeebies.
Jeepers creepers, legal eagle, teeny-weeny, wheelin' dealin',
Chilly Willy, silly-billy, willy-nilly, hippy-dippy,
Artsy-fartsy, "party hearty!," pocket rocket, walkie-talkie,
Hocus-pocus, hokeypokey, Holy moly!, local yokel.
Hootchy-kootchy, loosey goosey, pooper scooper, rootin'
tootin',

Super-duper, flower power, wowie-zowie, Chubby Hubby,
Chunky Monkey, culture vulture, double trouble, funny money,
Hurdy-gurdy, Fuzzy Wuzzy, Hubba Bubba, Humpty Dumpty.
Talkin' mother-[*scratch*] OshKosh B'Gosh, yo. Talkin' prime-
time rhyme.

[Et cetera.]

JAMES CLEVELAND, *age thirteen, assesses Puppy's hit "Prime Time" (mid-February 2001)*:

It is mad complicated. He uses mad samples, from some old piano record, and he is talking so fast you can't understand what he is saying until the twelfth time you hear it. But serious, it sounds like Beethoven. We played one Beethoven in orchestra, which I'm in this year. Puppy's samples sound like the same thing.

Maybe it isn't complicated but just addictive. Which is why so many stupid idiots like it. It goes so fast, you keep wanting to hear it again just to be sure you heard it all. But honestly, I'm more interested in jazz these days, because this year I'm also in jazz band. Miles Davis was a genius, son.

MAYNARD GOGARTY *tells about his pleasant day (mid-February 2001)*:

It was the first time I'd heard the song.

I mean, the label, ITD Records, had sent me that dreary check for a few hundred dollars, so I knew the song was circulating. Still, what does etiquette demand? Do I send Mr. Jones a note congratulating his—effort? Do I tell him that if he had told me what he was after, I might have custom-designed something for him and spared him the toil of scavenging the third movement like he did? Perhaps we could work together? Perhaps my recent arrest gives me legitimacy on the street as a killer?

Jennica, naturally, refuses to discuss any of this with me. She told me, which I didn't like to hear, "Arnie, it makes me very uneasy that you aren't more concerned about the possibility of jail."

I said, "I promise everything will be all right." I told her I was grateful to have her. I told her I was eager to be in Hawaii.

"You can't let David be your lawyer, Arnie. Why do you think he's going to do a better job with keeping you out of jail than he did with advising you on that contract? The song has been on the radio twice since we started listening. This Puppy person is a millionaire, and you got four hundred dollars, and the only reason the song is catchy is because of your music. And now you think David is the person to keep you out of jail. For four years? You're not thinking clearly."

In any event, shall I complete the story of my arrest and detention?

When the police were done searching my apartment, they took me to the precinct house, and then, at night, to—the Tombs. It would have been horrifying if it weren't so boring. The other arrestees thought I was a pastor. A loquacious lot, overall. Talking about getting to the methadone clinic on Riker's Island as if it would be paradise. Officers bustling in and out, taking very little interest in me. Sit there, stand here. They read me my rights—I kept count—seven times. I told them, "Yes, thank you for reading me those rights. I would like to call my attorney now." That amused them.

Finally a woman arrived, the Queen of the Crossing Guards, a redhead from Long Island. Her uniform actually fit her properly. And she let me make four phone calls. One to David's voice mail, one to Jennica's voice mail, a second one to Jennica herself, which was awfully stressful for the both of us, and which I believe she told you about, and a final one to David's voice mail again. An articulate plea, I thought.

DAVID FOWLER *plays us his voice mail (the daylight hours of February 9, 2001)*:

Listen to this. Listen to who I've chosen as a client.

> David, once again it is Maynard. Thursday evening, the eighth of February. And once again I am calling from the station house for the Thirteenth Precinct. How are you this afternoon?
>
> I wanted to add to my previous message a note about my disappointment in this precinct house, aesthetically. Comparable to a United States post office. Scraps of paint peeling off the wall, stains on the floor tiles—and stains on the ceiling tiles too, come to think of it. Can't your profession collectively do anything about this? Ideally these places would be outfitted with mahogany and marble. Beaux Arts mosaics, plaster friezes of the Roman gods. Magistrates sweeping along the hallways in powdered wigs and floor-length cloaks and buckled shoes. The constabulary armed with sabers. Perhaps you and I could organize a movement.
>
> But—fine! I understand something must be sacrificed by way of taste for the sake of the city budget and overall judicial economy.
>
> Nonetheless, I don't want to spend the next four years in this grim place, four years being what they tell me I could get for a Class E felony, which is what they tell me I am charged with, so perhaps you would be so kind as to help me be arraigned this evening around one A.M., which is when they tell me I can expect to be arraigned?
>
> Thanks muchly!

My client.

MAYNARD GOGARTY *poses a question (mid-February 2001)*:

So now that I am free and headed for paradise, one question remains. Who? Who was the anonymous tipster?

ROBERTA GLADYS *reads two poems (mid-February 2001)*:

I wrote two poems about what I saw. I think my style is developing. The second one is one of my favorites.

I, saw, you, in, the, night.
What, you, did, was, not, right.
You, drilled, into, the, tree.
You, drilled, into, me.
Because, the, tree, was, ours.

I, saw, you, in, the, night.
What, you, did, was, not, right.
You, put, your, poison, in, the, hole.
You, put, your, poison, in, us, all.
Because, the, tree, was, ours.

BY, ROBERTA, BRANDI, AND SABRINA

Brandi and Sabrina are my two cats. They're hiding right now. They don't like company.

I, saw, you, in, the, shadows.
I, saw, you, in, the, shade.
I, speak, for, the, shadows.
I, speak, for, the, shade.

BY, ROBERTA, BRANDI, AND SABRINA

I saw when the police came to arrest him. I never liked him very much. He looks down on other people. And so did his wife. They were meant to be together.

ANA KAGANOVA *heads for the hills (mid-February 2001)*:

This idea of marriage was spontaneous. It was in 1995. I told Gogi one morning that I would pay the rent if he married me, and he said yes, and this afternoon we went for a license to the city clerk. He needed the money and I needed the visa, and anyway we lived already together, and the rent was not so much. In this way I probably paid for his debt from the movie about dog shit. Gogi even bought me a ring, of copper. And we held a fake wedding that I will tell you about.

The reason for the fake wedding was so that we would have photographs, to prove it to the INS that it was a real marriage. Several of my Russian friends knew of a bungalow colony in the Catskills, and for free we were able to go there during the Fourth of July weekend. It was very shabby. There were rabbit burrows under the tennis courts and mice droppings in the bungalow cabins, and the gazebo was hunted by wasps. The owner's lemonade tasted like soap. And the swimming pool was not heated and did not have enough chlorine, so that in the morning the owner's nephew had to use a net to scoop out the toads.

But there were hundreds and hundreds of guests squeezed into the bungalows. All of the guests were poor, poor Russian Jews from Brighton Beach, the old grandmothers and grandfathers brought over to America as retirees, who live now in Soviet-size apartments in Brooklyn, all of them too ignorant to know that this tiny bungalow colony in the Catskills was not the Elysian Fields. We bought them soapy cocktails, and they pretended for our photographs to be our friends and relatives, and afterwards we went with them swimming in the pool, with the dead toads.

The moment I said "INS," they all volunteered to help fake the wedding, because these Russian Jews are all enemies with the INS. But still they all teased me: "Why are you marrying the gentile when there are good Jewish boys? Aren't you Russian, aren't you a Jew? But how is it you speak with a German accent? Where are you from? And this husband, he is British, no?" There is never any peace in this world—always you must explain to people what your passport says, and what your parents' passports say, and your grandparents'.

Maybe I will explain it to you later, when I am in a better mood. The story of Ana Kaganova, the Russian German Israeli American Jewish half-orphan. But in the end, in 1996, my Alien

Relative Petition went through without any trouble, and then I had permanent residence, and now I will be a citizen soon. *'Ne echte Ami, hey!*

> Oh beautiful, for spacious sky, for amber waves of grain,
> For purple mountain majesty above the fruited plain:
> America, America, God shed His grace on thee . . .

Shed, like a dog. Still, it will be nice to be a citizen, as then there is no deportation, even if I get caught for something naughty. For example, today with the cabdriver, which is why I am now a fugitive, and which is why I am now going to Gogi's grandmother's cabin for a few days.

You must believe that I did not enjoy this today, during the sleet storm, to get out of the cab and not pay the Russian driver. But I had not expected that the *schiki-miki* girl would leap out first. I had only been downtown to return the donkey head to Hano and to ask him about this Lower Manhattan Council, because I want to be able to arrange some studio space for myself in Tower One, so that I am not always dependent on other people for their space in this regard. Hano thinks that he and I perhaps should apply for space together. But after I met with Hano, as I walked uptown, the sleet started, and I thought that I would join the *schiki-miki* girl in her cab. Obviously she was *schiki-miki* enough to afford the fare. But when she got out of the cab at Times Square, I had to flee.

So I thought I might lie low at the cabin for two, three days.

Do you know about his cabin? Gogi has a grandmother who has a cabin in Massachusetts. They call it a cabin, but it is an *echt* farmhouse. No mouse droppings or wasps, *weiß' du?* Just a subscription to the *New Yorker*.

When Gogi and I were together, we visited the cabin perhaps five times a year, or ten times a year, and no one else ever was there. The soap in the bathroom was always the same bar that we had left the last time. So even now, when we are broken up, sometimes I go to this cabin. Not in the summer, when sometimes Gogi's mother and aunt stay there. But I kept a key, and so

I still go to the cabin. Gogi does not know. I am careful to leave no trace, and it is my weekend away.

So yes, I do like to disappear. I think of it every time I have a month such as this one, when I run around and around and make no money and must always answer more phone calls. It is nice when nobody knows where I am, and I do not have always to explain to people, "Oh, what an interesting accent you have, where are you from?"

MAYNARD GOGARTY, *in paradise, tells us something he isn't certain of (mid-February 2001)*:

There are geckos in Hawaii. And what a piece of chance the gecko is—what a splendor of cumulative chance! The marvel of evolution, the quintessence of protein! They have excellent skins, toes that defy gravity, the triangular tongues of angels, and the all-seeing eyes of a god. There is a family of them that lives next to the lamp, out here on the balcony of our cozy, bargain-rate condo, the Keauhou View. But every time I approach the geckos to inspect their perfections—they leap! They leap across the walls, three and four times their own body-length. It must be how they catch their meals.

The lamp on the balcony attracts goofy Hawaiian flies, and the goofy flies attract the geckos, and the cozy condo attracted frugal Jennica, and frugal Jennica attracted me! And I rather like the Keauhou View: wall-to-wall carpeting, a tropical fish motif in the kitchen and bath, and access to a beach of black lava rocks, where colossal sea turtles feed at high tide, and where at low tide compact black crabs pounce from pool to pool. The animals in this state jump more frequently than you would think. Also there are carob trees. Carob—on trees! A state where chocolate, or at least a chocolate substitute, grows on trees! The only thing that doesn't grow on trees here is cell-phone service. The balcony is the only place I can find reception for my cell phone, which I used today to call David.

His first question: "Gogarty, if you're in Hawaii, why are you calling from a 917 number?"

"It's my cell phone."

"*You? Gogarty?* You have a cell phone?"

"They're quite handy, David."

"I know they're quite handy, Gogarty. Everyone knows they're quite handy. But when I first got one you denounced me. You said you expected me to be a holdout, and that it was a disgrace to my utilitarian aesthetic, and that I had disappointed you. You said you disowned me. And now you've gone and got one yourself."

"Inconsistency—is that the worst you can accuse me of?"

"Gogarty, does this Jennica girl have any idea how insufferable you can be?"

A fair question. Naturally the cell phone was one of Jennica's innovations for me. She bought me the cell phone and told me she would pay the first month's bill, but only if I would promise to use it. And naturally after that first month I was, shall we say, hooked. Because it's so grand, promenading down the street, one elbow ratcheted up—chatting on the phone.

She also paid for my first yoga class, and came along with me even though it was Introductory Hatha and Jennica normally attends classes for the advanced. She came along with me and staked a claim to two secluded spots at the rear of the studio, so that we could unroll our mats side by side and so that no one would be able to hear me moaning in horror—. Should I feel the need to moan in horror—.

But I did not. Jennica had scouted out an instructress who wasn't given to spacey pontifications about—chakras, what have you. Jennica even bought me my very own cotton pants from Thailand and my very own foam yoga mat, in salt white and forest green! She said she'd use them herself if I didn't want to come back. But it turns out that yoga feels good. No one told me that it would feel good, or that it would offer the compelling opportunity to watch your girlfriend do poses in her yoga huntress gear. I am, naturally, an embarrassment to the sport, because I have no talent for bending—at least, not without breaking into a horsy sweat. There is no panting stallion pose in hatha yoga, but if there were, I would be good at it. In any event, at the end of the first class, I had a conversion experience while lying there in corpse pose, my horse musk mixing with the rubbers of my mat and the cottons of my pants. Our instructress was moving around the studio, anointing the foreheads of her students with sweetly scented oils, and I realized, This is actually quite dignified. And the Thai pants show off my calves to advantage.

Needless to say, now I am the one paying for our yoga classes.

Jennica is good for me, and I suppose David is good for me too. He had told me to call him from Hawaii to talk about my arrest, and so there I was, calling him from Hawaii, and he was saying that he would take my criminal case pro bono. Not only that, but he'd found a good and inexpensive attorney to handle my divorce case—which gave him an opportunity to upbraid me again for not yet having told Jennica about Ana.

David was saying, "Which island are you two on again?"

"The Big Island, as they call it."

"And you're having a good time."

"The wildlife is horrifying. Maybe you're right, though. I need to tell Jennica about Ana. Maybe Valentine's Day would be a good time."

"You are insufferable, Gogarty."

"Speaking of insufferable, you know what Jennica wants to do on Valentine's Day? Attend a genuine luau."

"She talked you into going into a luau? *You? Gogarty?* You must be in love."

It is so curious to hear someone tell you that you are in love. Still, I was feeling expansive, so I told David, "I suppose I am, I suppose I am. Jennica brings out my—. How to put this? She makes me feel calm. She is so comfortable with the idea that fun and happiness are—attainable. Forget luaus. She got me to try—caramel-flavored coffee. What else? She wants me to try fleecewear. And smoothies. And karaoke. And—therapy. Sooner or later she'll probably come out in favor of moving to Westchester. All these things that preposterous people enjoy, when Jennica recommends them, I find myself willing, and grateful. It used to be I would worry that I shouldn't have fun and be happy until I had proven that I wasn't a failure. Now I am eager to accept that I am a failure, so long as I get to have fun and be happy. And— and so long as I still get to disparage the preposterous people who actually enjoy life."

And then David asked me the question of questions: "Gogarty? What is it that you have against other people?"

"An indictment! From my own lawyer!"

What could I say, other than that I am now resolved to be a nice person? And that I intend to see that resolution through? But no, I am not certain Jennica realizes just how—. Insufferable? How misanthropic I can be.

JENNICA GREEN, *in paradise, tells us something she isn't sure of* (*mid-February 2001*):

Valentine's Day.

It's some kind of cliché, right? To want Valentine's Day to be perfect? Like, to want the day itself, February 14, Saint Valentine's Day, to be ideal and romantic? I'm not sure Arnie realizes how sentimental I really am. Like, conventional and sappy . . . ? Or maybe he does realize. The day before the day itself, he told me there was something "a bit perilous" that we needed to talk about, but that he needed to find the right words. Which could be Arnie-speak for talking about marriage. It was hard to believe, but was he going to propose to me on Valentine's Day?

That morning, Valentine's morning, we woke up, kicked off the sheets, and it was another sunny day in our humid condo, with papaya and cottage cheese for breakfast. There was a mongoose under our rental car when we came outside, looking like one of those corkscrew animals in *Through the Looking-Glass.* Arnie tried to, like, befriend it with our salami, but it bounded away once we got close.

We drove our silver rental car to Snorkel Bob's, which is the local snorkel monopolist, and then to Kona Kayaks, and we rented these bright orange snorkels and flippers and a bright blue sea kayak, which you can strap to the top of your car with nylon, and then we drove across the ridge to Cook's Cove. Down past papaya trees and banyan trees, and past a coffee plantation, out onto this concrete breakwater at the edge of a bay. The water in this bay is turquoise, and eighty degrees. It's a whole different ocean than the one in Santa Cruz. And it's so calm that you can paddle across it in your kayak, with your snorkel and your flippers and your salami and your sunscreen.

It only took Arnie fifteen minutes to paddle us across. And at the other side of the bay is this monument, this cenotaph, which supposedly marks the spot where the Hawaiians killed Captain Cook after they discovered that he wasn't a god. You beach your kayak on the lava and hide your salami from the mongooses, and then there is this reef right there, under two feet of water, with thousands and thousands of fish. Arnie bought himself a book and figured out all the names, but I can't remember them. There were parrotfish and groupers and tangs and wrasses and durgons and . . . butterflyfish, and angelfish. And the state fish of the State of Hawaii, which is *muhu . . . muhumunu* . . .

And in the afternoon this family of dolphins comes into the bay to feed, and you can watch them jumping around while you eat your avocado. Your one-dollar avocado that is the size of your boyfriend's grandmother's four-hundred-dollar handbag from Fendi. And, may I just say, you cannot be sarcastic about dolphins. Because they are so much more majestic and graceful than anything human, the way they swim. We saw them pass underneath us when we paddled back. And, I mean . . . halfway across a bay, with the warm waves slapping over the bow of your plastic kayak, and the dolphins under you, tricking your eyes? Arnie stopped paddling so we could watch them underneath us. And he said, which was such the perfect way to express it, "This must be why Debussy put the brass in *La Mer.*"

Humuhumunukunuku apua'a!

That was our Valentine's Day day. And on the way back to Kona Kayak and Snorkel Bob's, we stopped at the coffee plantation and got real kona coffee and real coconut ice cream. And I got to scream every time Arnie almost got us killed with his insane driving.

And then the luau. Or, the *luau.*

The point is, all day I was thinking, Is he actually going to . . . not propose, necessarily, but suggest we get married? In Hawaii? On Valentine's Day?

GABRIEL GREEN *tenders some obnoxious advice (February 15, 2001)*:

Yesterday, Valentine's Day, at four-fifteen, Jennica calls me from the beach in Hawaii. She says, "Gabe. I can only talk for as long as Arnie keeps snorkeling. But I think he's going to propose to me tonight when we go to the luau."

Like . . . what?

"There are indications. He said there's something we need to talk about."

"He said there's something you need to talk about, ergo, it's marriage. That is a solidly supported theory, Jennica."

"There are indications. I think he might have hidden the ring at the bottom of this carton of prunes he brought along. Because why else would he bring prunes from New York to Hawaii? Unless he knows I don't eat prunes and thought they would be a good place to hide a ring?"

"He brought a carton of prunes, ergo, he's going to propose marriage. I mean, it is a theory, Jennica. Another theory is that he gets constipated." I mean, to me? To me it seems impossible for a guy to be both sophisticated enough for Jennica to find him attractive and lame enough to actually propose marriage, in Hawaii, on Valentine's Day, at a luau. But that's just me. And also, I sometimes have to adjust what Jennica says to account for her romantic inflation. She can't just be in Hawaii because she and her boyfriend decided to splurge; she has to be there because she's getting married. I told her, "Do you want my marriage advice, Jennica? Be here now."

"Gabe! That's not advice, that's an obnoxious slogan." And she starts explaining her nuptial epistemology to me, her theory of how she will know who she should marry. "Do you know the feeling that you should only marry someone who isn't like everyone else? Someone who is going to be unique and intriguing their whole life? Every guy else I've ever been with, even if I sort of admired what he did with himself, I always felt on some level, whatever, any other guy could have done the same thing. Arnie's the first man who seems like a suitably impressive resolution to the Jennica Green marriage problem. I feel elevated when I'm with him. Like we inhabit an impregnable kingdom up high among the volcanoes, above everyone else's annoyances."

"Okay, Jennica? Illustrious is good, but can we be here now?"

"And the thing is, if we did get married, we could probably get free tuition for our kids at Arnie's school, which is huge. Plus his family is wealthy and might help us buy a house."

"Okay, rich is good, but be here now."

"So obnoxious! And don't be dismissive of money issues. And it's not even about that. He's bottomlessly devoted, and he wants me to be happy, and I am happy, and there is something irresistible about devotion. It's like, that's what love was supposed to be, and . . ."

"Wait, can you repeat that? 'He wants me to be happy and . . .'"

And there was this pause, which was, like, she's standing in her swimsuit on the lava in the sun at some snorkeling spot in Hawaii and realizing she's happy. She did repeat it too, except she did it in this grudging voice, as though I had forced her to admit something she didn't want to admit.

I tell her, "I'm sorry I haven't met him."

Which sends her into this long explanation. Jennica is coming out to California in May, to help us out after the baby is born, but Arnie can't come then, because he is working as a teacher and Easter is his only vacation between Ski Week and July. And he and Jennica will be in California in September for Nadine Hanamoto's wedding, but that's so far away. So maybe they can come out to California in July, but Jennica is running out of vacation days, especially if she wants to come out to California over Hanukkah. Like, Jennica is on the beach in Hawaii and she's worrying about when she'll get to go on vacation.

And then she had to hang up, because Arnie was getting out of the water. I made her promise to call me and let me know what happened at the luau. And forget about being here now. I am so eager to hear what happened that I haven't been able to get any work done all day. I have to assume he didn't propose marriage on Valentine's Day in Hawaii. But I've never been to a luau. Who knows what goes on?

JENNICA GREEN, *in paradise, tells us something she is sure of (mid-February 2001)*:

But okay, the *luau.*

The luau was at the King Kamehameha III Hotel. Which is this vast tourist hotel from the 1960s on the harbor in the town by our condo. With, like, triple-wide grand hallways with six-foot-tall oil portraits of the entire Hawaiian royal family, and the taxidermied body of a 680-pound swordfish that was caught in 1988 by the women's world angling champion. Arnie made me stop and read the plaque. And the luau itself was held in the hotel's garden on the beach. Five hundred guests, with kerosene torches burning and a stage for the Polynesian Dance Revue, which I'll tell you about. People from the hotel trying to sell you flower leis for three dollars. Other people from the hotel demonstrating traditional crafts. Palm carving, hula hooping. Other people from the hotel dressed up like native Hawaiian priests and reenacting the landing of a royal Hawaiian flotilla. What else? This chubby Hawaiian emcee, a total ham, wearing a hotel uniform and a flower lei, running around with a microphone shouting, "*Aloha* means hello!" and "*Mahalo* means welcome!" and "*Ohana* means family!" Totally unctuous.

A free mai tai bar, serving the weakest mai tais in the world.

A ceremonial unwrapping of the roast pig that was the centerpiece for the feast. These two topless actors leaped into the roasting pit and exhumed the pig, which was smoking hot and wrapped in banana leaves, or taro leaves, or whatever they use to wrap the pig. And meanwhile the emcee stands at a microphone and lectures all five hundred guests about Hawaiian history. Like:

"Until 1819, the ancient laws called *kapu* forbade men and women from eating together, but today everyone is *mahalo* at our *luau!*" And all five hundred guests are wearing three-dollar leis and slurping weak mai tais and saying, "*Mahalo!*" and "*Kapu!*"

You get the idea.

Arnie . . . speechless with horror. I mean, they just dished out one cliché after another. We were both dressed entirely in white, Arnie in his boater, me with a white scarf over my hair, and we couldn't stop laughing.

The sun set, and then the all-you-can-eat buffet opened on the patio. You carried your plate to an assigned seat at a long communal table, and you ate by torchlight. Arnie was like, "Torches, ahoy!" Roast pig and seaweed salad and kava and pork buns. For the adventurous. And for all the big midwestern couples who were there for their, like, fortieth wedding anniversaries, there was fried chicken and three-bean salad and Jell-O, and pineapples, and shrimp scampi. During dinner, a three-piece band playing Hawaiian standards adapted for electric guitar, with this skinny Hawaiian kid in a King Kamehameha III Hotel uniform playing the ukulele and singing traditional falsetto ballads. Arnie was laughing and laughing. He was like:

"*Mon dieu.* I'd karaoke to that!"

And then, while we were still eating, they started the Polynesian Dance Revue. By torchlight. It had about seven different acts, but it was always the same ten dancers, who were constantly ducking offstage to do costume changes. Into, like, the traditional garb of Fiji! The traditional garb of Borneo! The traditional garb of Tahiti! The traditional garb of New Zealand! And then they would do the traditional dances of Fiji or Borneo or Tahiti or New Zealand, all of which were indistinguishable. And the emcee would tell us how to say *hello* and *welcome* and *encore* in Fijian and Borneoese and Tahitian and . . . Maori. All five hundred guests clapping drunkenly along, shouting, "*Bulah! Bulah!*"

And here is the punch line of the luau.

All the older couples around us at our table thought we were newlyweds, and they wanted to see my ring. On one side of us was a family from Texas, and on the other side were three women who went to high school together in Indiana in the fifties, and their husbands. And they all thought that Arnie and I were newlyweds. Newlyweds from Britain, because of Arnie's supposed accent, and because we were wearing white. But I told them we eloped, and so the wives pretended to be shocked. Like:

"Didn't you want to have a big wedding?"

"No! Because we're blowing all our money on the honeymoon instead!"

"But what about your mother? Isn't she upset not to see her daughter in a dress?"

"No! Because she eloped too!"

They didn't know what to make of me. Arnie cleared his throat and said:

"You'll pardon my wife; she gets like this whenever she eats *scampi.*" Which he said with an Italian accent.

Meanwhile the men, the Indiana men, all wanted to shake Arnie's hand and congratulate him. And so Arnie shook their hands in his . . . preposterous fashion. He raised his eyebrows as high as they could go, and frowned seriously, and raised his boater off of his hair with his left hand, and shook their hands with his right hand, saying:

"Thank you! Thank you! *Bulah! Mahalo!*" Which, watching him and feeling like I was going to bleed from holding back the laughter too long . . . I mean, there are only so many moments when you are that conscious of how much you're in love with a man. Like, how just being with him makes better everything else that ever happened to you. But, the punch line.

At the end of the Polynesian Dance Revue, the emcee made all of the couples stand up, based on how long they'd been married. People married fifty years, forty years, thirty years. Half the crowd had been married that long or longer, including all of the Indiana couples and the people from Texas. And then the emcee asked if there were any newlyweds, and without hesitating, Arnie pulled me up from my chair and kissed me, while the emcee was like:

"Everybody say *hoomaikai* to our youngest *ohana!*"

A perfect day!

No mention of anything "perilous." But we're going to Nadine's wedding in a few months. And I'm sure it will be talked about by then. But, kind of, I'm happy to leave it untouched. I like things as they are, I don't want them to change.

This is

THE FOURTH PART.

It is longish, and yet not overly so. The statements here date from the weeks following September 11, 2001, the day on which religious fanatics assaulted the World Trade Center towers in Manhattan with hijacked commercial jetliners, killing innocent thousands. No one we heard from in the first three parts of this comedy was injured in the attacks. Again there are press clippings.

MAYNARD GOGARTY *says some totally unacceptable things (autumn 2001)*:

Patriotism is always in such—bad taste.

Don't get me wrong. The flag—this ugly flag of ours—is the least of it. Nonetheless—! It is my understanding that the ancients used horse urine to age their copper domes, to turn them that pleasant shade of green. Maybe a bit of the same here, for our flag? Take some of that ugly Crayola four-pack brightness off the red-white-and-blue? Because at present it is such an unsightly thing; it ought to ashame us. And you who have flown a flag since the tragic events of—your most sacrosanct day. You flag-fliers, you in the tricolor "Never Forget" T-shirts, you with the American flag pins in your lapels. Each of you is personally—gah!

And now both the New York tabloids are running full-page flag advertisements. Full-page, full-color American flag advertisements, with panting instructions to the reader: "Show America's Determination. Show America's Pride. Show America's True Colors." And you people—are obeying. You weepy tabloid readers, taping up full-page flags from the *New York Post* in your windows. Fine—in the doorway of an Afghani deli, there, I sympathize. I sympathize with those hapless fellows. Those poor, meek Afghani immigrants, here in the City Where Chauvinism Never Sleeps. But in the bay windows of West Side brownstones? In the twenty-eighth-story balcony door of a white brick apartment tower on the East Side? Behind the antiburglar bars of a garden apartment's front door in the Village? Oh, yes, how sobering it must be for the terrorists to see America's mortgage-holders and leaseholders united in taping newspaper flags to their windows.

Even the MTA, the workaday MTA, has pasted permanent flag decals, two feet wide, on every one of our subway cars. What is the message? "Fuck you—this uptown No. 6 train is an *American* uptown No. 6 train?" Flags on every fire engine. Because—those chaps who put out our fires? "Fuck you—they are American."

I should never have told any of this to Jennica.

Or can it be that there are certain things only a native of Manhattan can understand? Yet, a native of Manhattan? Really? Am I certain that Manhattan is where I am a native of? Because I woke up one morning and found out that I lived not in Manhattan but in—America! The *New York Times* was so pleased to announce the death of irony, which was almost accurate. It was the death of any discrimination at all. A holocaust upon the discriminating class, the death of Manhattan's—un-American ability to disbelieve.

Obviously—mentioning this to Jennica when she was so shaken—was a catastrophic lapse of judgment.

But it must have been a—*tragedy.* Ignore your ability to discriminate between a tragedy and a bloodbath. This must be a tragedy, because we feel so sad! And our tragic flaw? Our tragic flaw is our—*freedom.* They killed us for our—*freedom.* They must have been—*heroes,* those firemen. Do not attempt to discriminate between the heroic and the merely unlucky. They cannot simply have been rank-and-file union members who never heard the order to evacuate. They cannot have been dupes, because "when others ran out, they ran in."

The *Times* needed a new section, so what title does it mount against the onslaught of events? "A Nation Challenged." Not "The Nation Challenged"—that doesn't sound historical-tragical enough. Not "A Challenged Nation." That's too Third World for—America the Grand! This is our role as a nation. We have perfected the production and consumption of the cliché. And New York City, the national cultural holdout, the national scold and arbiter and educator, has surrendered. Everyone in America is infected with the *esprit de pays*, and "nothing will ever be the same again."

The *New York Times* has apparently decided to run an obituary for every single person who died on September eleventh, 2001. Every single infinitely unique and irreplaceable person. This has been going on for weeks! But they are not called obituaries, these things the *New York Times* is running. They are called "Portraits of Grief." What is a "Portrait of Grief"? One hundred and fifty words, two hundred words, proclaiming in the most dire platitudes available the hallowed uniqueness of every one of these stockbrokers, stock traders, stock characters. This one was unique because he was—a doting father! We must never forget this—doting father! This one was unique because she—always made people laugh! We must never forget this—funny, funny gal! They're all dead, and it's so sad! It's so sad that—this man whose most unique and noteworthy characteristic was that he loved to have a good time and hang out with his buddies is now lost to Western civilization. It's so sad that this unprecedented human can never be replaced in our grieving, weeping republic! Our united republic! Oh, revenge, revenge!

These dead people. What do I know—? I didn't know a single damned one of them. But just assuming that these dead people were a good sample of the citizenry of this credulous republic, then we can be certain that—their deaths merit no mention at all.

Who knows if they were wasting their lives? Certainly there is no evidence in the "Portraits of Grief" that they weren't. No, no, no. From all the evidence, these were the sorts of people who, when you saw them on the subway, you thought they'd be better off dead. But unlike the dead in any other event, ever, they must all, individually, one by one, be applauded and wept for.

You there, weep! This exercise in blubbering and treacle is all for the benefit of—you!

JENNICA GREEN *assesses the situation (achingly early on September 17, 2001)*:

He said some things . . . totally unacceptable. It's like he doesn't even begin to understand how awful it is. Like, who is this person that I am supposed to move in with in two weeks? Which is only one of the forty-six reasons I can't sleep. I'm serious. I made a list of forty-six reasons I can't sleep. Let me get it out.

MAYNARD GOGARTY *says some totally unacceptable things (autumn 2001)*:

But I read the "Portraits of Grief," and so I weep over the *New York Times* every morning. Everyone in the city does. And I will tell you why: because grief is the happiest emotion of them all. You all are so—eager to cry. You want to cry, you monsters. You tear-thirsty bullies!

Within a week, missing posters by the thousands across Manhattan. "Jack Jones. Loving Father. Last Seen WTC 2, 95th Floor." "Bill Black. Grandson, Son, Brother, Father, Grandfather. Last Seen WTC 1, 79th Floor." With photographs of Jack, of Bill, in fifty-nine-dollar rental tuxedos. More and more posters—even after it was clear that no one was missing, that everyone was dead. And everyone in the city wanted to read them all! No one had seen anyone who was missing, but still, everyone wanted to read them all! Because everyone was so delighted in their very souls—to grieve.

Everybody—especially you out there who have never lived in New York—everybody was so very pleased to be able to ask, "How can we have Christmas ever again?" "How can we sit down to a Thanksgiving feast—ever again?" Oh—the pleasure all of you take in your misery! You all are so happy to eat your stomach-turning "comfort food." You all are so pleased to be "glued to your TV." How many thousands of people took up smoking again, the instant the towers fell? And called up old, abusive lovers? And stopped exercising and put on sweatpants! Oh, what a thrill you all got—! You got the chance to grieve! You got the chance to be the children you always aspired to be!

And to grieve for a loss that isn't even yours. You—who are nowhere near New York—you who have nothing to fear—you who are the greedy and ideological monsters that the world hates—. You there, outside the city, with your ignorant theology and your jingoistic television and your lust for cars! You bellicose, illiberal, immodest Americans, you patriots, you "United We Stand" bigots, it is you whom the world wishes to destroy—! You, who lost nothing, are the ones who brought this on humble New York. They killed us because they hate you, and now you have the infernal chutzpah, the diabolical arrogance, to use the death you brought upon us as an excuse—to eat raw cookie dough in front of your television!

"We are all New Yorkers now." You rubes—you have always coveted citizenship in the capital, and it was denied to you because you were weak. The price of being a New Yorker? You couldn't afford it. You couldn't afford—the exuberant vermin; the feral addicts; the mindless thugs; the cosmic filth; the ceaseless noise, the heedless noise; the butchering rents; the roads, the public works, the libraries, rusted and stained and stricken with consumption; the parks, rank and unweeded; the friends who give up and move to San Francisco or San Diego; the usurious whims of fashion; the insults; the decades of bad coffee; the decades of bad plumbing; the appalling poor, wailing at you on the subway; the appalling wealthy, kneeing you in the shops; the blasphemous demolition, year by year, of everything you love; the recidivism of the public schools; the rapacity of the taxes; the spite of the blue laws; the indignity! Or—the dignity! Not a one of you can afford the emotional tax of not being as discriminating or worldly as your neighbors! You failures couldn't last here a week!

But you say, "After September eleventh, we are all New Yorkers—we're all in danger!" What do you think? That nasty Osama is going to poison your well water in Rotten Oaks, Michigan, or Stripped Pit, Minnesota, or Bleak Lanes, Missouri? For you it's playtime fear, it's dress-up fear. It gives your life meaning to think you might share in the horror. It gives your life so much meaning that—you wish it had happened to you.

You monsters, with your violent insistence that it is your tragedy as well—you actually wish it had happened to you, don't you? You would be so happy if it had happened in your danger-free home towns—out there where the sidewalks are not used—out there where the supermarket aisles allow shopping carts to pass two abreast—out there with your Internet access and your pickup trucks—out there with your lawns—out there in—San Jose, California. You are not all New Yorkers, you are all shit! I don't want your solidarity, I want my towers back—to block off my view of America.

ANA KAGANOVA, *safe in the Berkshires and inspired with a fraudulent scheme, attempts to conscript her husband into her plot (September 12, 2001)*:

And then I drove half an hour to a pay phone and bought one of these calling cards. I spoke with myself for a minute in order to get the accent correct, and then I called my husband to tell him that his wife is dead.

It was an answering machine. This was the first surprise, that Gogi has an answering machine. On the answering machine, he said that he can also be reached by cell phone. This is the second surprise. Has he finally made some money?

I decided, however, that if I were truly a Russian in Israel, and if I wanted to find Ana, I would call also the cell phone. I called therefore his cell phone, and he answered.

"Hello?"

"Hello, I speak with Ana Kaganova?"

"Hello? Pardon me?"

"I call from Israel for Ana Kaganova."

"Ana? Is this you? Where are you calling from?"

"No, I call for Ana. She is not at home, and I see on television the explosion at the buildings where she has work."

"Ana? I must have a bad connection. This cell phone is notoriously inept. Let me go into another room."

"No, you do not understand. I call in order to know is Ana okay, because of the explosion."

"Okay. I'm in another room now. Ana, start from the top."

"This is not Ana."

"It is so Ana, doing her impersonation of her Israeli relatives. An impersonation I used to laugh at, only to be accused of anti-Semitism and made to wash the dishes. Dishes that were always hard to wash because the whole reason Ana was doing her impersonation in the first place was because she had burned the strange Israeli lamb dish she was cooking us for dinner that night."

I did not know what to say to that.

"Hello? Ana? Hello? I know you're there because I can hear the traffic."

I told him, Listen, Gogi, you are my husband, and so you must report me missing. I will go underground into hiding. I have a space in Tower One, and no one knows whether or not I was in this building when it fell down. This is America, and the Americans will pay millions of dollars to the victims. You are my husband, so you collect the money. We will then split it half-half.

He said, "You're mad."

"We will talk about it later. Today you must only report that I am one of the missing. You must call the police department and tell them that you are my husband and that I never came home today and that I had an office in Tower One. And then you must meet me at your grandmother's cabin. I will need cash."

"Ana, you're mad."

"Today you must only report me missing. Later you can change your mind and report me not missing, if you do not later want to play along. Meet me at the cabin, and we work out the details."

"Why, you lunatic, do you want to go underground?"

"Will you report me missing? It would mean we would not need to get a divorce, because I am dead." And this for him seemed to be the winning argument, and so he agreed that until he could reach the cabin he would play along.

JENNICA GREEN *shares her list, compiled on the red-eye back to New York from Nadine's wedding at Goat Rock Beach, California, of forty-six reasons she cannot sleep (achingly early on September 17, 2001):*

Or forty-four, if you discount for items 17 and 28. And I only stopped at forty-six because the list wasn't being helpful. In terms of me sleeping on this red-eye, I mean. Anyway.

> REASONS I CANNOT SLEEP:
> (1) Dry airplane air; (2) Tiny airplane seat; (3) Fear of hijackers; (4) The heroes on Flight 93; (4a) Would I have that kind of courage?; (5) Need to buy nail scissors & nail file;

The reason for 5 being that the security people confiscated mine when I checked in at Logan Airport on Saturday morning, on the way out to Nadine's wedding. Which still did nothing to reassure me about item 3, I might add.

> (6) Schedule appointment with gynecologist; (7) Tell A. about wedding & about G.; (8) Decide about moving in with A.; (9) If I am going to move in with A., we need a lease; (10) Fear of A. going to jail for four years; (11) Fear of a military draft; (12) Need to schedule trip to see Gabe & Rachel & baby again; (13) Fear of nuclear terrorism; (14) Fear of biological terrorism; (15) Anger at stewardess re: refusing to let me change seats; (16) Anger at stewardess re: refusing to let me turn my BlackBerry on; (17) Need to list things to do for work;

Which I started to do.

> (18) Need to finalize e-mails re: terrorism & time off & compensation to all staff; (19) Need to check with Executive Comm. re: purchasing emergency kits;

It looks like Hoffman Ballin is going to buy everyone on staff . . . and I do mean everyone . . . these "emergency kits." Each kit is a fanny pack that has a flashlight and a smoke hood in it, and little emergency flares. Things an employee might need in case of an evacuation. But then there is the question of who gets which kind of kit. Because there is the normal emergency kit and the more expensive executive emergency kit. So can we give the secretaries the cheaper ones? Which don't have the iodine pills that you take to prevent thyroid cancer after a dirty bomb? Or would that be too inequitable?

> (20) In-flight movie is *Casablanca*, (21) which obviously is a concession to the fact that everyone is scared to be on a plane & *Casablanca* is supposedly comforting; (22) Headphones were $7; (22a) I was too stingy to buy them & it's too late now; (23) Need to spend less money in the fuel-based economy; (23a) hydrocarbon consumption is bad for the environment; (23b) & it promotes terrorism; (23c) Need to look into purchasing farmland & leading a more simple & self-sufficient & organic life; (23d) exposure to plastics & hormone-mimicking chemicals reduces fertility; (24) My feet are cold; (24) My nose is dry;

I guess I have two items numbered 24. I guess I'm pretty exhausted.

> (25) If I am not going to move in with A., I need to cancel with the movers; (26) What if WTC smoke contains asbestos?; (26a) How far north did the dust land in Manhattan? (26b) Will dust affect fertility? (27) Need to convince A. to refinance his debt; (28) Need to make a list of issues from fight with A. at the cabin; (29) Need to schedule time to discuss fight at cabin with A.; (29a) Out of vacation days from work; (30) A. is insensitive; (31) And rude; (32) And condescending; (33) A. needs to go into therapy; (34) A. needs to be in control of career & emotions; (35) Need to make decision about moving in with A.; (36) If I am going

to move in with A., we need apartment insurance; (36a) & we need to make sure the apartment insurance covers terrorism; (37) Fear of car bombs; (38) Stomach slightly upset from airplane food; (39) Have to watch less news coverage; (40) Thirtieth birthday in January; (41) Market is likely to crash on Monday; (41a) need to hire financial adviser; (42) If market crashes, need to move quickly to purchase co-op, interest rates cannot stay low forever; (43) Need to apologize to Mom & Dad re: fight at cabin; (44) Need to look into careers in philanthropy; (44a) Peace Corps; (44b) United Nations; (44c) organic farming; (45) Need to get specifics from gynecologist on age & birth defect statistics & infertility; (46) War.

It hasn't been my best week.

GABRIEL GREEN *promises this is relevant* (*mid-September 2001*):

The question is whether Jennica is freaking out. Because my parents were *definitely* freaking out; my dad called us at seven in the morning on September eleventh to say, "Don't get in a car with the baby until the government says it's safe." Like, what? But with Jennica, she has a particular way of acting in a crisis. I guess every disaster reminds you of every other, so of course on September eleventh I was thinking about Loma Prieta, and about Bob Bersen, and about the collapse of the Cypress Structure. And about how Jennica reacted.

Loma Prieta was an earthquake. It struck on Tuesday, October the somethingteenth, 1989, at 5:04 P.M., and was magnitude 7.1. You never forget the statistics of an earthquake. The epicenter was just north of Santa Cruz. The Giants and the A's were supposed to play game three in the World Series at Candlestick that night, and so later on you could buy commemorative "Earthquake Series" T-shirts, which was an excellent T-shirt for assholes to wear, because, Hey, why not have a T-shirt celebrating the day that fifty people died? The landfill under the Marina in San Francisco liquefied, and the buildings on top collapsed and burned, and a portion of the eastern span of the Bay Bridge collapsed, and big stretches of downtown Santa Cruz were pulverized. And a quarter-mile of a double-decker freeway in Oakland called the Cypress Structure collapsed and crushed the commuters on the lower deck to death in their cars. It was pretty ghastly. But you could buy commemorative T-shirts.

Five-oh-four P.M., Tuesday, October somethingteenth, 1989. The year I was fourteen.

Jennica and Nadine and I were home alone when it came. The floorboards of my bedroom did something I'd never felt them do in any other earthquake; they leaped up, like the keys of a cartoon piano when they get pounded by some cartoon piano player. I hid under the computer table in my bedroom, which was scary enough, but Nadine and Jennica were in the kitchen, which must have been terrifying, because we lost one whole cabinet of glassware on the Mexican tile. They screamed when it came down, and as soon as the earthquake was over, I went to make sure they were okay. There was glass everywhere, and all our Tupperware had fallen out of the cupboard, so there were pasta wheels everywhere too. Jennica had the broom out, but instead of sweeping up she was rummaging around trying to find batteries for the radio. Nadine was trying to get a dial tone on the phone. And Jennica told me, "Gabe, you go turn off the gas."

Our parents had always told us, If you are home alone and there is a big earthquake, then turn off the gas. There was this particular set of steel pliers that we kept on a nail against the side of the house, behind the birch trees, specifically for turning off the gas, which we both knew how to use. But classic Jennica, delegating responsibility, told me, "Gabe, you go turn off the gas."

Which I did. I got the pliers and went out onto our front lawn and turned off the gas. And because it was the biggest earthquake anyone in San Jose had ever felt, and because everyone had lost electricity, the entire Rose Garden District was out on the street, bragging about where they were standing when it happened, talking about how many dishes they had lost. And then there was a commotion, because around the corner from our house something strange was happening.

Water was streaming down the first-story windows of this particular two-story house. The owner wasn't home. At least, her car wasn't there. She was this single woman who nobody liked because she had done such an ugly renovation. And all the neighbors were trying to guess where the water could be coming from, that it would be pouring down her first-story windows. It was very strange to see, these rivulets of water flowing over the glass. Someone said that probably the water heater in her new second-story bathroom had toppled over. Schadenfreude. But everyone was arguing about whether to break into her house and try to stop the flood, and there were sirens, and the dogs were all howling, and you got the sense that nobody was willing to take action. So I said, "Well, I'm at least going to turn off her gas." But as soon as I said it, Bob Bersen decided that no, he was in charge.

Bob Bersen. Old Man Bersen. He was this widower who lived about two blocks away from us, in the one Eichler in the neighborhood. He'd been in World War II, and then he'd worked for FMC, and now he was retired. He was rangy, a big Reagan fan, the sort of guy who has a perfect lawn and who is proud of being a son of a bitch. The sort of guy who campaigns against . . . *school bonds* and *bicycle lanes* and who leaves his lights off on Halloween. He'd cursed Nadine out once about parking her Peugeot too close to a fire hydrant, and it was Nadine who came up with the name Old Man Bersen.

So we were all standing in front of the house with the busted water heater, and I had announced that I was going to turn off the gas, and Old Man Bersen started yelling at me. "That gas line is PG&E property, young man, and if you touch it, you're committing vandalism and endangering the public health. You could create air bubbles in the pipes that lead to an explosion. You don't know what you're doing, and you can only make the situation worse."

I was like, "Look. Her water heater fell over. If it's a gas heater, there is currently methane pouring into her house. My parents always said you should shut off the gas after an earthquake." The other neighbors didn't have much to say to that, so I walked over to her gas outlet, which was easy to see from the street, because she hadn't thought about hiding her utilities boxes behind a bush after her renovations were done. But as I was kneeling down to figure out how her gas worked and where the knob was, I put the pliers down next to me. And Bersen came over and snatched them away from me and started shouting, "I'm calling the police!"

It was so stupid. First of all, the phones were down; he couldn't call anyone. And second of all, I could turn off her gas without the pliers anyway, because her gas box was new and the handle was easy to turn. But instead of just turning off her gas and leaving, I decided to get the pliers back from Bersen. I left her gas on and ran after him and tried to snatch the pliers back. So there I was, in the middle of the street, with aftershocks from the earthquake still rumbling, grappling with Bersen over the pliers.

Bersen must have been in his mid-seventies, so he couldn't have been that strong, but he was willing to punch me, and I wasn't about to punch him. He slugged me about three times . . . in the chest, with his free hand . . . pretty fucking hard, too . . . until I let go of the pliers. And the neighbors were all like, "Gabe, Gabe, relax." Everyone sides with the old bastard who slugs the fourteen-year-old. And is there anything worse when you're fourteen than realizing you are about to cry in public?

I told Bersen to go fuck himself, it was his fault if the lady's house burned down. But I felt so belittled, like Bersen had insulted my parents, insinuated that they were the old fools, telling their kid to turn off the gas after an earthquake. Bersen was like, "Don't you cuss at me. And don't think I won't let your parents know what kind of language you're picking up at the swimming pool." Swimming pool? But that's what he said. What a shit. And he did, too. Later that night Bersen came over with the pliers and informed my father that I was a foul-mouthed delinquent; who knows what Dad told him to make him go away.

Anyway, I got back to our house after being defeated by Bersen, and Nadine and Jennica were sitting in Nadine's Peugeot with the doors open, listening to KGO on Nadine's car stereo, since the power was still out. And Jennica had been crying too. Jennica told me, "The Bay Bridge collapsed and the Marina is on fire. And Nadine's brother George lives in San Francisco. And we don't know if he's okay." So we listened to the radio for a while, until Jennica said, "We should be cleaning up the kitchen when Mom gets home."

Not "have the kitchen cleaned up when Mom gets home," but "be cleaning up the kitchen when Mom gets home." More classic Jennica: upset, but not so upset that she isn't making sure to get credit for being a good daughter. When we got inside, and when she got a good look at my face, Nadine asked me if I was all right. I told her I got in a fight and didn't want to talk about it. And I think that impressed Nadine, at least until Bersen came over that night and Jennica and Nadine figured out who exactly the fight had been with. Nothing like being fourteen.

So that was October somethingteenth, 1989. And when I got off the phone with my dad on September eleventh, 2001, my first thought was, Why does Dad think I shouldn't get in the car with the baby? Because terrorists might have planted car bombs in Santa Cruz? Thanks, Dad. Should I also turn off the gas?

But now I have a theory about what the whole turn-off-the-gas thing is about. What makes you tell your kids to turn the gas off after an earthquake is not the safety imperative, for your kids, of them turning the gas off after an earthquake; it's the psychological imperative, for you, of believing your kids will still be alive after the earthquake in the first place. It's the self-deception of parenthood. And what the fuck . . . just exactly what the fuck am I supposed to tell Simon to do, when he's older, if he's ever in a hijacked airplane? Crash it into a farmyard outside of Shanksville, Pennsylvania? I don't even want to think about it.

But there is *another* reason the Old Man Bersen story is relevant. Namely, that until the day after Nadine Hanamoto's wedding, which was the Sunday after September eleventh, Loma Prieta was the last time I saw Jennica cry. I mean. Well, Jennica had brunch with us in Santa Cruz on Sunday, the morning after the wedding, and . . . something was wrong.

MITCHELL *and* SUSAN GREEN *recall the decision to go to the cabin (mid-September 2001)*:

S: That we should have this tiny inconvenience of spending a couple of nights in Massachusetts.

M: Unthinkable, what people suffered.

S: Until Tuesday morning, our trip to New York had been absolutely lovely. Gorgeous weather. Jennica had lined up one restaurant after another for us to try. And Arnie. The point of the trip, of course, was to meet him. Such a gentleman, considerate and charming. But of course the morning we were supposed to fly back was Tuesday morning, the morning of the hijackings.

M: We were never in danger personally, thank God.

S: Even before we had left our room at the Ritz to get breakfast, they had evacuated the airports. And the airline was saying . . . What did that one woman say?

M: "America is at war, sir."

S: And what do you say to that?

M: Especially when she's right.

S: We had been staying at the Ritz using Mitchell's points, his hotel points. And this is not merely some Ritz-Carlton, this is *the* Ritz-Carlton. Central Park South. The shower in this room was heaven. But we didn't have any points left, and the Ritz wanted five hundred dollars a night for the room. So we moved into Jennica's new place on the Upper East Side, and she went to stay with Arnie.

M: It wasn't ideal.

S: She needed her clothes, she needed to check her answering machine, she needed to use her computer. I was allergic to the cat, as we discovered, and had trouble sleeping, because my sinuses were just plugged. Everything there was a mess.

M: In other words, her place was too small for the two of us. With her moving boxes everywhere, since she is moving in with Arnie. And what is there to do in the city, which is suddenly at ground zero of a new war?

S: Thursday morning, Jennica and Arnie said to us, Let's get out of the city, let's go to the cabin in Massachusetts, maybe the Boston airport will reopen first. They were both supposed to go out to Nadine Hanamoto's wedding, which was on that Saturday, and so they were worried about when the airports were reopening too. And with good reason, because in the end Arnie couldn't get rebooked, so Jennica had to go alone. In any event, we went to the cabin in Massachusetts. And that same night, Arnie's mother and grandmother came up.

M: And, some cabin. When someone talks about a cabin, I think of those tents you can rent on the floor of Yosemite Valley, in Curry Village.

S: It's a farmhouse, is what the cabin is. Spacious, but a little funky. Someone must have done some work on the bathrooms and the kitchen in the 1970s. Ugly tiles in the bathrooms. A little musty, a little dank. But five bedrooms, and does it ever sit on a gorgeous plot of land. Gorgeous trees, and owls at night. There is a pond, with ducks that the neighbors breed. Idyllic. And it belongs to Rose, who is . . . Arnie's father's mother.

M: She's the one with the money.

S: We arrived at this cabin on Thursday. And Thursday night, the instant Mitchell had a captive audience . . . He couldn't have waited until a better moment, when everyone was a little less shaken.

M: Life goes on.

MAYNARD GOGARTY *describes the arrival at the cabin (September 17, 2001)*:

The cabin, yes. I haven't heard from Jennica since then, you realize. She left on Saturday for Nadine's wedding, and so it's still, well—unresolved.

So yes, the cabin. We drove up to Massachusetts on the morning of the thirteenth, Thursday the thirteenth. It was myself, Jennica, Susan, and Mitchell in the one car, my mother's cigarette-ridden Honda, and then my mother and my grandmother came up later that same day in my grandmother's Mercedes. It was a warm day, with a breeze occasionally startling the chestnuts and the walnuts and the whatnots—. But we saw no cars once we left the pike, heard no birds chirping, experienced no weather. There obtained—an ominous stillness. As we came around the last bend on the road to the cabin, I saw, parked in the driveway—Ana's car, her unmistakable Plymouth.

I said, "Oh, it must be the lady who waters Rose's plants."

We took in the luggage. Jennica established herself on a kitchen stool and started phoning the airlines, searching for tickets on flights that could get us to Nadine's wedding. Her parents took an admiring tour of the cabin, cooing at everything, making inventories of the kitchen and the library. I told them that I was going to look for the watering lady. "Make sure she isn't stealing Gran Rose's china." That was the beginning of my new stint as a private dick.

I sniffed my way around the yard, peered into the windows of Ana's Plymouth to see what I could see, and was about to test the car's door, to nose around in her glove compartment, when: "Hsst! Hsst!"

Ana was crouching in the woods, behind the berry shrubs that line the driveway.

"Ana!" She didn't move. "There is poison ivy back there, you know."

"I am not allergic."

This is the extent of her evil—poison ivy does not affect her.

She said, "No one must see me alive except for you!"

"I've already told everyone that you are the woman who waters Gran Rose's plants, so you might as well come out."

Out she came. She was wearing jeans and a shirt that had been missing from my closet for five years—one of my favorite French cuffed numbers, with my initials monogrammed on the pocket, no less. She wanted to know if I had brought her cash, because she didn't want to use her bank card; she wanted to know if I had brought her clothing, because she didn't want to return to her apartment in New York; she wanted to know if I'd brought her a different car that she could use, because she was nervous about the plates on her Plymouth being spotted. Apparently she had been sleeping in Gran Rose's cabin, without permission, using a stolen key, and now she was demanding that I give her money so that she could stay at a motel, so that she could live underground. I told her she had gone mad.

She said, "This girl you have with you, is she the one who is the reason why you want to divorce me? Because if you are not giving me money for a motel, you are having to introduce me to her."

So? I gave her sixty dollars. She then handed me her bank card and said, "It is imaginable that my husband would have my ATM card and would know my four-digit password, no?" And then she told me exactly where to meet her the next day in order to bring her more cash. The conspiracy was rapidly maturing. She wanted to know if I had reported that she was missing in the collapse of Tower One, and I said I had.

"You lie poorly, Gogi." Gogi. Why can no one call me by my given name? "You are my husband. I am missing now two days. You must report me missing. If not, I will have to come here and say hello to your girlfriend."

I told her that I had no interest in her villainy and that I didn't want her dead, I wanted a divorce. But then she said something that I, in my role as private dick, instantly recognized as—a clue! She said, "If you divorce me, Gogi, I will get half of your apartment."

"It's *my* illegal sublease, Ana. You will get nothing."

She gave me a pitying look and said, "I see that I am better friends with Sal the Super than you are, Gogi. Don't you know that you own this apartment? Your grandmother has bought it for you. But if you want a divorce, I will get half of this, because it is the communal property of our holy marriage, you know. But if I am dead, then you will keep the apartment, and you will also keep half of the restitution that they will pay to you because your wife is dead in Tower One. The other half of the restitution you will give to me, as your partner in the underground. On the AM radio, Gogi, they say they will pay to each of the victims, in restitution, millions of dollars. Do not be a stubborn donkey. Go report me dead."

Stunning! Stunning! What—a villain!

ANA KAGANOVA, *safe in the Berkshires, waxes autobiographical (September 12, 2001)*:

My father had a theory of villainy, an *echt* Soviet theory of villainy, you know. But I will tell you now how I became a proud American girl and villain—my autobiography, so to speak.

I was born in Kazan, Tatar ASSR, in 1961. Look on a map. It is the capital city of Tatarstan: population 1.5 million; on the Volga River; one thousand years old. I was born there, but I have never seen this city, and my mother knew no one in this city except for my father. She followed him there after he seduced her.

My mother has her whole life been naive in this way. She is tall and a redhead, and always people steal from her, because she doesn't know better and gives them her money. She lives in Haifa now, and is very much New Age. She believes that extraterrestrials land in the Negev desert and that Kabbalah predicts the future.

In 1958 and 1959 she was a naive teenager. She lived in Voronezh, which is another city I have never seen. She was from a Jewish family, with two older sisters, and in 1958 or 1959 she applied to the most prestigious university in Moscow, to study poetry, and of course she did not get in. She now will say that this was because of anti-Semitism. And it is true, this Russian anti-Semitism is famous. In 1958 and 1959 the Russians had quotas for how many Jews could attend the prestigious universities. If the fifth line on your Soviet passport said "Jew," then you could study only in the provinces. But I do not think that my mother was a victim of anti-Semitism. I think that she was a victim only of herself. All of her sonnets used the same words and mentioned the poet's own red hair. She was simply not smart enough to go to Moscow. Instead she had to study at the Pedagogical College in Voronezh.

My father was then a professor at the university in Kazan. He came to lecture in Voronezh, and he met my mother. He was thirty-eight years older than she was, and he was a Russian, not a Jew. And he was not just a Russian, he was an establishment Russian. He was a widower, two times so, with two grown sons, my half-brothers. He had a friend high in the Communist Party who brought him special tobacco and cognac from Armenia. And he had another connection, a French Communist in Paris, who sent him ties and handkerchiefs. Once he was sent silver-framed eyeglasses with a tortoiseshell case from Spain. He was vain, but always with this pretend show of culture. My mother thought probably that it was romantic to be his mistress, but then she became pregnant with me and went with him back to Kazan. This is Russian honor for you, to marry the girl who is forty years younger than you so that she will come home with you to be your secretary and your maid. After I was born, my father got a permanent position to teach Russian literature at Humboldt University in Berlin, and my mother followed him there too.

A professor's position in Berlin was a job that the Soviets would give only to someone of the strictest Marxist-Leninist philosophy. Probably my father reported also for the KGB. We do not know. My mother took me to see him lecture once, in the dingy auditorium at Humboldt University, where the heating came from hot water through these painted pipes, from electrothermal plants. With his students, he spoke in booms and blasts. It was the same as how he spoke with my mother. Always *lya-lya-LYA, lya-lya-LYA! Weiß' du?* He insulted his students for their mistakes in Russian pronunciation. He told his students, "You sound like the water in the electrothermal pipes! Spit out that cigarette, speak with your throat!"

And he insulted my mother's German. She spoke no words of German, nearly. My earliest memory of her is that I was her translator. When I was five years old, we went for a vacation on the Baltic. My mother had an argument with the attendant at the shower house on the beach. She was one of these ignorant attendants who live in the world everywhere, who are stubborn and lazy. My mother wanted another towel, and the attendant said in German that if my mother wanted another one, then she had to get it from the desk at the hotel. I tugged on my mother and told her in Russian, "We have to get it from the desk at the hotel," but my mother would not leave, because she was too naive to understand that the attendant had insulted her. *Weiß' du?* Such fury I felt, and humiliation.

In Berlin, I went to a special bilingual school for the children of Russian bureaucrats and the highest East German Communists. It is sad to think how shy I was. I did not make friends well when I was twelve and thirteen. I did not feel like a German, but I did not feel like a Russian either. The fifth line on my passport did not say "Jew," because my father did not want me to be a Jew, but my mother, when I was seven, tried to teach me a hippy version of Judaism that she was learning from her sisters, who wanted to leave Russia and go to Israel.

DMITRI LARIONOV *(1902–1978) lectures seductively on his Marxist-Leninist theory of villainy (spring 1960, translated from his original Russian)*:

A villain can be a villain only relative to a class, and the efforts of playwrights to justify and of heroes to eradicate villains must be understood in the case of the former as an effort to *accom-*

modate within the strictures of bourgeois art anxieties concerning class struggle and in the case of the latter as an example of class struggle *represented within such strictures.* [. . .]

We may therefore define the *Capitalist Playwright,* of which as I have indicated our principal example will be William Shakespeare, as a playwright who owns the means of theatrical production. [. . .] Such a playwright will of necessity seek to obscure the class-relation and exploitation-relation exposed by the villain through *aesthetic accommodation/obfuscation,* as for example in the case of the *villain* Don John's inability to say anything more than that he is merely evil in *Much Ado About Nothing* ("There is no measure in the occasion that breeds," et cetera), or as for example in the case of the *inverse villain* or *hero* Antonio's inability to explain his sorrow in *The Merchant of Venice* ("In sooth, I know not why I am so sad," et cetera). [. . .]

We may therefore define *bourgeois aesthetic decadence* as the insistence by a playwright upon the prerogative to leave villainy unexplained. [. . .]

ANA KAGANOVA *waxes autobiographical (September 12, 2001):*

In 1978, I was seventeen and my father was seventy-six. He had a stroke and could not teach, and the doctors then found that he had cancer. He demanded to go to Moscow to be treated. The hospitals were better in Berlin, I believe, but he demanded to go to Moscow and insulted my mother until she agreed to take him. It was done without paperwork, and my father's connections in Russia were not so good as before. *Weiß' du?* He had been abroad too long to be of use to anyone. My father was only able to find a bed in a bad hospital in Moscow, and my mother and I lived in the worst apartment, across the street from the radiology clinic. We did not have the authorization in our passports—*propiska,* there is no translation. So we had to rent a room illegally. And from the moment we moved out of our beautiful apartment on Karl Marx Allee in Berlin and into this awful apartment in Moscow, for me the question was, How do I escape from Russia?

My mother never had the ability to operate there. She would come home and cry because she had been insulted on the subway or at the hospital when she asked a childish question. By this time my mother's sisters already were in Israel, so no one would hire my mother, because there was a great taboo against you in Russia if you were related to an émigré. I, at age seventeen, was the one who handled the gifts, the bribes.

I had to write a pathetic letter to the old friends and have them mail us more Armenian cognac so that I could bribe the doctors at the hospital to get my father a better bed. My half-brothers did nothing for us. They thought that they would destroy their career prospects if they helped us, because my mother's sisters had gone to Israel.

I do not know what we would have done if my father had not died. But he did die. Until the very last day, he insulted my mother. In front of my half-brothers, her own stepsons, my father told my mother that she was a conceited, brainless slut, and he said that she had slept with half of his colleagues in Berlin and that she had been a fool in front of the other half. He said she had ruined his career and had given him diseases and was a failure as a wife. And then he died. Only then did my half-brothers do anything for us. They paid the bribes to help my mother and me get visas to Israel. They wanted to get us out of their way. *Weiß' du?* That was the last I had to do with them. So at the age of eighteen, I turned from a Russian and a Berliner into a citizen of Israel.

And quickly then the question became, How do I escape Israel?

SILVI KAGANOVA *explains how she learned about ions (early September 2001, translated from her original Russian)*:

It gives me a shudder even now, remembering my first sight of Eretz Yisrael. But for Ana it was different. From the very first hour that we were there, she was filled with anger and resistance. I think that Russia had choked off her spirit, and that Ana was scared to listen to her own longings. So many women of Soviet Jewry are like that, and choke off their own spirits.

She was with me when I went to the Dead Sea for the first time. We had been in Israel for only a few weeks; still, it was one of the last days we spent together as mother and daughter, which as you know is a very special relationship, especially for Jews and for Russians. But the day of our trip to the Dead Sea was one of the last days we had together before Ana decided to go her own way, away from me. We took the bus from Tel Aviv, which also stops at Masada. We were so new to Israel that we had to borrow beach towels from my sisters and a backpack to carry water while we hiked up Masada.

Once we were on the beach at the Dead Sea, Ana was interested only in her American and French magazines. She stayed in her long pants the whole day and refused to put on a swimsuit, and told me that my swimsuit looked *Ossi*. I have never understood German, but I know that *Ossi* is a bad word.

Still, I didn't care how my swimsuit looked, because I was still feeling the shudder of being in the Holy Land and of being near Masada, the ancient site of so much courage and faith and spirituality. The oldest synagogue in the world is at Masada. And it is very healing to float in the Dead Sea. The Dead Sea's waters have twenty-one minerals, including several that occur nowhere else in the world. There are bromine ions, and magnesium chloride and potassium chloride, and the air at the Dead Sea has reduced UVB radiation and almost no pollen. I learned the science later, when I was living with Robby at the spa in Haifa, but even before I understood the science, my body and spirit felt the power of the Dead Sea water instinctively.

As I was floating in the Dead Sea for the first time, the urge overcame me to submerge myself entirely in its waters. So I curled myself into a ball and plunged myself under the water. What I did not know then was that unless you are wearing goggles, the waters of the Dead Sea will make your eyes burn terribly, because of the intensity of the salts and minerals. I had to come out of the water and stand under the shower rinsing my eyes, it burned so much. The day was in part ruined for me, and I was in great pain.

When I sat down next to Ana on the towel to recover, she said, "Mama, I told you not to dunk your head," but it wasn't true. She knew I couldn't understand English or Hebrew, but she hadn't read me any of the warning signs. In fact, she wouldn't even read all the signs at Masada for me. I found out that the oldest synagogue in the world is at Masada only because there was another tourist there who spoke Russian, and who read the Hebrew sign for me.

Ana said, "Mama, I said that the salt would sting your eyes, and that's why I didn't want to go in." But she was lying; she hadn't told me. She took pleasure in watching me suffer.

My sisters and their friends and the friends of their friends have always been kind to me, too kind to me. They understand the spirit of the Russian *aliyah* and of Eretz Yisrael better than Ana ever did or could.

ANA KAGANOVA *waxes autobiographical* (*September 12, 2001*):

I stayed only a few months in Israel. It is a loathsome nation. Yeah, how anyone, once they have seen Greece, can consider this land holy, I never understand. *Weiß' du?* There is nothing cosmopolitan about the Israelis, they are Mediterranean trash. And Jewish trash is the worst trash of all. I am a German Jew, I am allowed to say such things, believe me.

My aunts had moved to Tel Aviv, and we lived with one of them. She found work for my mother as a cleaning woman at a hotel. My aunts at least spoke a little Hebrew, but my mother was terrible. She would go to the supermarket only if someone went with her, to translate. But she found a Russian synagogue and was overnight a hippy born-again Jew, in hand-me-down summer dresses and her ugly black rubber East German sandals.

This was 1979. My aunts were confused about what to do with me. I had not graduated from high school anywhere, and there was no school in Tel Aviv quite for me. I now saw how shy I had been in Berlin, as a girl. So this was how I used my Israeli resettlement money: on clothes and shoes, and on haircuts, and on manicures and makeup, and on magazines. I wanted to look like Brigitte Bardot.

I met an Israeli boy who I liked a little bit, enough to sleep with him even though I had never slept with anyone before. He was about to go to Europe for two months, and he paid for me to go with him to Rome and Paris and West Berlin. And in West Berlin I realized how I would escape from Israel. I said goodbye to my boyfriend, who was anyway not so interesting after six weeks because he turned out to be jealous. And I practiced my *Ossi* accent, and I put on my oldest clothes, and I walked out of the youth hostel where we stayed in Wedding, and I crossed the street, and I walked into a police station and said, "*Guten morgen,* I have just escaped from East Berlin, I am a refugee."

What did they know that I had not been in Berlin for almost two years? And that I was a citizen of Israel, and that before I was an Israeli I was a Russian? I had the East German accent and the East German clothes, and this was all that mattered. They asked me how I made it across the wall, and I made up the story about the ape. The policeman said, "You should sell this story to *B. Blick.*" *Berlin Blick* is the tabloid.

The journalist from *B. Blick,* Stefan, knew that it was a lie, naturally. We came very clean with each other, and we split the fees from the sale of the story. So this journalist became my friend, and he found work for me as a photographer. I lived then for a few years in Berlin and traveled for my photography. But in 1991, I had no more interest in staying in Berlin, because suddenly everyone in Berlin was going to be an *Ossi.* So I came then to New York. If I wanted to be a fashion photographer, it was either New York or Italy, and the Italians are too much like the Israelis. This is my opinion. And also New York is the first place where most people did not care the first damn where I am from. For example, in a cab: "Where is that accent from, lady?"

"Russia." "Israel." "Germany." "South Africa." It doesn't matter what you say. "Oh yeah, I have always wanted to go there, I hear it's real nice there." Yeah, eat shit.

And now I am an American girl. An American! *Weiß' du?*

So you see then how it is? These accidents of where you are born, they determine everything about where you can go and who you can be. If the INS thinks that you are a Russian Jew, they might admit you as an asylum-seeker. But if they think that you are an Israeli Jew, then not. When I came to America, the INS thought I was German, and so I could be admitted only as Gogi's wife. And even then it took five years before I am a citizen.

And so also with where you die. If I die in Gogi's grandmother's pond because the kayak flipped over, because I had to row out into the pond to drown my floating Finnish cell phone, *weiß' du?*, then my life is worth nothing. If I die on the ninety-first floor of the World Trade Center, then my life is worth millions of dollars, probably. If I die on the ninety-first floor and I am an American. If I die on the ninety-first floor and I am a German or a Russian or an Israeli, I am probably not a millionaire. Such stupidity is what runs the world. *Tja.*

I happily will go underground for a few years, if then I never need to deal with the bullshit again, of all these artists and photographers and bureaucrats. And Gogi will help me, too.

JENNICA GREEN *tells about the trip to the cabin (early, albeit not so achingly anymore, on September 17, 2001)*:

Actually, I am going to postpone telling you about the cabin, because I have just walked into my apartment from my red-eye. Like, just. And I need a shower. And, there is a special kind of jet lag that you get on a red-eye. You open the front door to your apartment, you put down your carry-on bag . . . And even by the time you get out of your teensy shower and are hunting, in your towel, with your wet hair, for clean and unwrinkled work clothes . . . Even by the time you are looking in your neglected refrigerator to see if there are any scraps left for breakfast, even then . . . Even then, it is forty-five minutes earlier than it would be if you had gotten out of bed on a normal morning. You feel like you are trespassing in time. It's so disorienting. Like:

Whose apartment is this? In my bedroom, the morning sunlight never comes in from that angle at this time of year. In my living room, I don't remember leaving all my books packed into moving boxes. In my kitchen, I don't remember the linoleum being so, like, dull and empty and inhospitable.

Maybe it's another kind of homesickness, an exotic kind that you can only contract on a red-eye and that you can only feel when you are actually in your own house: the sorrow that the place where you live is still temporary, that you have yet to do whatever it is a person needs to do in order to stop playing with water.

Anyway. The one thing I want to tell you, before I get in the shower: Mumpus is wearing an American flag flea collar. I had Julie LaSalle come over and feed him while we were in Massachusetts, and she must have bought him the collar. He actually seems strangely happy in it. Which is touching. He is such a haughty cat. So disdainful and austere. It's good of him to show some patriotism.

After my shower I'll tell you about everything.

MITCHELL GREEN *tells* SUSAN GREEN *some things she didn't know (mid-September 2001)*:

S: We arrived at this cabin on Thursday. And Thursday night, the instant Mitchell had a captive audience . . . He couldn't have waited until a better moment, when everyone was a little less shaken.

M: Life goes on. And here is what I see in the paper. I see Palestinians dancing in the streets of the West Bank when they heard about the attacks in New York. I see Muslim clerics claiming that the Jews all had advance warning, and it was all a conspiracy by Mossad to start a war between the U.S.

and Iran. This kind of insanity, this kind of anti-Semitism, boiling up. And these things matter. If Jennica is moving in with him, he should know my feelings. From the outset, I want it clear that any grandchildren are Jewish, and if he has a problem with that, he should say so now.

S: Well, you certainly made that clear. And you couldn't have waited, could you?

M: Life goes on. And it wasn't as though this was the first word I said about it, ever. I had spoken to him when we walked to the co-op.

S: This I didn't know.

M: I had been planning on saying something earlier in the week too, but didn't have the chance.

S: This I didn't know. I wish you had asked me. I would have told you it was a bad idea, if you had asked me.

MAYNARD GOGARTY *describes the co-op (September 17, 2001)*:

The co-op is the only grocery store near the cabin. It is in part captive to some hick Massachusetts distribution concern—hence the brick ice cream and the 36-packs of single-ply toilet paper and the one ageless aisle of canned fruit from Mexico. But it is also in part captive to the fad-mongering of the local gentry—hence the four-dollar "Save the Rainforest" chocolate bars and the Tom's of Maine and the Dr. Bronner's and the Newman's Own and the Ben and Jerry's. And the decor: the shelves are covered in wicker-patterned contact paper, the walls are plank, and against the front window is a step-pyramid wrought from bold red boxes of the leading brand of color-safe laundry detergent, each box bleached pink on its southerly side, its window-facing side.

As for why it is called the co-op—I prefer to think it was a turn-of-the-century effort of the local yeomen to coordinate on their purchases of millet, barley, pulleys, yokes, whatever it was farmers bought. Certainly all the farmhouses I've ever visited in the neighborhood of the cabin have identical doorknobs—satisfyingly prismatic glass doorknobs—as if the entire township ordered its hardware collectively, at a wholesale discount. If a circumstantial string of sunlight tries to thread one of these doorknobs, the light frays itself into a rainbow. And the glass has a nice heft in your hand. Jennica's new apartment on the East Side has those hollow gilt aluminum doorknobs—concave, with depressible nipples in the center for locks. Disgraceful doorknobs. It is one of the things we both like about my apartment in Gramercy: the rickety iron doorknobs, thick with paint, each one with its own keyhole fitted for some long-lost key. Where was I?

The co-op. It's a few miles from the cabin, near enough for a walk, albeit an invigorating walk, if you decide to buy frozen organic cranberry juice and brick vanilla ice cream and canned extra-bitter chocolate syrup and fresh bananas and then decide to—schlep all of it home in plastic bags. As Jennica insisted we do the first time I took her to the cabin. Cranberry juice, because she insists on a precautionary glass of it after—amorous labor, and the other things because she had visions of fried bananas à la mode. Where was I? I fear I am somewhat distracted by events.

So—. Thursday afternoon at the cabin. Jennica was making phone calls to the airlines; Susan was taking a nap; Ana had driven off to some motel; and Mitchell and I walked to the co-op to buy dinner. And what they had at the co-op that day was eggs, milk, and stalks of Brussels sprouts.

MITCHELL GREEN *tells* SUSAN GREEN *some more things she didn't know (mid-September 2001)*:

S: This I didn't know. I wish you had asked me. I would have told you it was a bad idea, if you had asked me.

M: I knew what your opinion would be, which is why I didn't ask.

S: What am I supposed to say to that?

M: Let me tell you why I like Arnie. He is a very intelligent man. He is very interesting on the topic of music and culture. He has fascinating anecdotes about the opera. An erudite man.

We walked to this co-op together, from the cabin. A gorgeous walk, along the side of one country road after another. Lovely rolling hills. With such majestic trees, of a kind that cannot be found in California. We saw one walnut. Unbelievable. Twice the size of the famous one in Vacaville. And farmhouses, I suppose you'd call them, off the road. A very well-to-do parish. He and I compared notes on Mozart, Haydn. And so I said to him, "It's obvious to me that you're going to care deeply about educating your children, when you have them. And I do not want to make any presumptions, but you are moving in with my daughter." He says, "No presumption at all, Mitchell, it's a fair question."

S: I did not know this conversation occurred. You should tell me these things.

M: I said to him, "Should you two get married, it is very important to me that the children be raised as Jews, in a Jewish household. Is that something you're willing to consider? Is that something you and Jennica have discussed?" He said, "Well, it is something we've discussed, because we had to agree about how to raise Jennica's cat," which I thought was witty. I said, "I would ask you to consider converting." And he said, "Well, I have always felt Judaism to be an eminently dignified religion." Those were his words, "eminently dignified." He said, "What was it Disraeli said? About savages in Parliament and priests in the Temple of Solomon?" That impressed me, that he knew that quote. But he said, "But . . . we really should discuss it as a family."

S: I did not know this conversation occurred at all.

M: He said, "Because while I personally am happy to convert, I'd first need to ask permission from my mother," which I also thought was very witty.

MAYNARD GOGARTY *tells us what you can make for dinner with eggs, milk, and Brussels sprouts (September 17, 2001)*:

Quiche, spinach-bacon quiche. Canned spinach, frozen bacon. And vanilla custard. You simmer vanilla beans in the milk, whole vanilla beans being one of the oddities that they sell year-round at the co-op. And you roast the Brussels sprouts.

My menu exasperated Jennica, who was loitering around the kitchen, pacing, wrapping the telephone cord around her finger, on hold with the airlines. She was angry with them, and somehow angry with me by proxy. "I wish they could find you a ticket."

"So do I."

"You sure don't act like you wish they could find you a ticket, Arnie."

"Well—do you want to cook, and I can talk with them?"

"You can't deal with people, Arnie. You're only going to piss them off."

"Well, then, you deal with them."

"See? That's the attitude I'm talking about."

"Jennica, naturally I want to come with you to the wedding. I am not thrilled about getting on an airplane, but—."

"But what, Arnie? You think I am thrilled to get on an airplane? It's my best friend's wedding."

This kind of snappishness. I think I am being—fair, calling that snappishness? She was picking leaves off Gran Rose's kitchen plants and tearing the leaves into pieces and throwing the pieces at me.

She said, "Why did you have to make quiche? And why do you have to make the crust from scratch? It's such unpleasant work. It's like you picked the one thing I hate to cook, just so you wouldn't be the one who had to call the airlines."

"If you want me to make the calls, Jennica, tell me so."

"No, I don't want you to." She would hang up with one airline and call another, always loitering around the kitchen. She perked up whenever an operator picked up but complained about a headache whenever she was put on hold.

Now—a stalk of fresh Brussels sprouts. Have you ever seen one? It looks like a club or a mace. There is a central stalk, about as wide around as the handle of a tennis racket and about two feet long. Running up its sides are two tight spirals of sprouts, a double helix of sprouts. You pluck the sprouts off the stalk and you are left with a green vegetable billy club. Or if you leave the top few sprouts on the stalk, you have a mace, a blunt-force instrument from the dark ages of Belgium.

In any event, I was strolling around the kitchen waving my Brussels weapon. I said, "You know—I think I could subdue Osama with this thing! With two firm wallops from my—polyps."

Jennica frowned at me.

"Or I could hijack an airplane. Forget box-cutters—look at this beast!"

She said, "You're not funny."

And I said, "If I cannot make Brussels sprouts jokes, then the terrorists have won."

And she said—and she was quite serious, no humor at all—"Arnie, that's enough." And she walked out.

Sometime that day my mother and grandmother had arrived in Gran's Mercedes. For a while they were sitting out by the pond, talking with Mitchell and Susan Green, but then, after Jennica left me alone, my mother came in. She said she wanted to make herself a drink and "keep me company," a euphemism for having a cigarette, which she was shy about doing in front of the Greens. She sat next to the door at the back of the kitchen and blew smoke through the screen while I rolled out the quiche crust. I realized, as a private dick, that this was my chance. It was my chance to—interrogate the dame.

"Tell me, Mother. How was it that Gran Rose bought that place, that apartment, for you and Dad? The one on 72nd Street? How did that come about?"

Subtle, no?

But what does she say—what does my mother say, being herself? "Oh, I knew I wasn't the only one who'd been thinking about Scott this week!" And then what does she say, to top it off? "Have I ever told you? That we were having a hard patch in the marriage when he died? That took me a long time to deal with."

JOAN TATE *tells us what was on her mind (mid-September 2001)*:

Manny may not like it, but I do think about Scott when these sudden deaths occur. They always do remind me of him. No one used to lavish attention on death the way people do now. You should see how understated the *Times* was in 1974, when Scott died. But I suppose the newspapers know better than I do what will get them their ratings, or—well, I don't know what newspapers have. Circulations. They are the ones who have the sensitivity—or the sensibility for what's appropriate. That's one thing on my mind.

And though Manny wouldn't like to hear it, I also do wonder how he's doing. Manny went to therapy with Dr. Ibsen so patiently after Scott died, in 1974 and 1975 and 1976. Dr. Ibsen told me to keep Manny near his friends and in the same school, so that was the end of my idea of leaving New York, which had been one of the things Scott and I disagreed about.

Dr. Ibsen told me—no, you know, I think I *read* it, is how I heard it. Anyway, it doesn't matter. There is a phenomena—a phenomenon that child psychologists discuss. If one parent dies when the child is in certain stages of development, let's say the father, then the relationship pressure that exists between the mother and the son and that normally would find an outlet in the son's relationship with the father will be rechanneled into the child's own personality and into the child's habits, if the father has died. They've done studies. And I've wondered over the years whether Manny developed the habit of making all those resolutions as a way to talk about feelings he couldn't otherwise talk about with me. The proof, for me, is that fruition never—is that his resolutions never come to fruition. And of course that Manny has his music, which became so much more important to him after Scott was gone.

Manny won't let me ask those sorts of "How are you doing?" questions, though. Just like he won't let me tell him that he reminds me of Scott. And he does remind me of Scott. He fights like Scott did, for one thing. When I hear doors slam in the cabin, twice, at two in the morning, with Manny and Jennica arguing, that reminds me of Scott. Not that Scott and I fought so much, but that year before he died—.

In any event, that is—those are the things on my mind.

WHITING FREDRICK *reports in the Obituaries section of the* New York Times (*October 22, 1974*):

John Scott Gogarty, Child Prodigy, Dies at 38

John Scott Gogarty, who as a child during the Second World War entertained New York society with his piano virtuosity, died Monday afternoon in a barbershop on Seventh Avenue. He was 38.

Mr. Gogarty died when his throat was cut in an accidental fall, according to Sgt. J. Milligan McCollins of the New York City Police Department.

Mr. Gogarty's career as a childhood pianist was brief but spectacular. Beginning with small recitals in the living room of his family's brownstone on the Upper East Side and culminating in a series of appearances on the radio program *Saturday Regalia*, between the ages of six and ten Mr. Gogarty gave nearly two hundred public performances, according to his mother, Rose O. Gogarty, who survives him. In 1944, a *New York Times* critic who attended one of his private recitals called Mr. Gogarty's talent "remarkable" and described him as a "wonder" and "a little Little Mozart."

In his teens, Mr. Gogarty gave up performing in favor of composition. After graduating from Yale in 1958, he was the musical director of such Off-Off-Broadway productions as *The Harelip* (1960), *The Sexy Individual* (1962), *Songs from a Book by Audubon* (1965), *Gaius Phallus Nixon* (1968), and *Tet Fete* (1970), for which Mr. Gogarty trained a chorus of macaws to chant slogans opposing American involvement in Vietnam.

In recent years Mr. Gogarty took an increasing interest in city and national politics and was occasionally cited as an example of a new style of civic engagement emerging among New York City's leading families. "If anyone was having trouble funding downtown theater, Scott knew which uptown sponsors to reach out to. He always made the connection," said Marty Fowler, who directed several productions Mr. Gogarty was involved with, including *The Harelip*, as well as *The Clubfoot* (1960) and *The Rot-Nose* (1962).

Mr. Gogarty died while receiving a haircut at Ruby's Barbershop at 173½ Seventh Avenue South. According to Sgt. McCollins, after having been brushed off and offered Ruby's signature scalp tonic, Mr. Gogarty stood up from the stool, appeared to faint, and collapsed against a glass case containing the barbershop's baseball memorabilia. His fall shattered the glass, a shard of which sliced his throat. Mr. Gogarty suffered major blood loss from a severed left carotid artery, said Melvin Fitz, a spokesman at St. Vincent's Hospital, where Mr. Gogarty was pronounced dead Monday.

"He was in the stool talking about running for city council, and I was telling him he had my vote. And then the next thing you know," said Carmine Nardini, who owns Ruby's Barbershop and who cut Mr. Gogarty's hair on Monday. "Good guy, good tipper. It's a tragedy."

Mr. Gogarty is also survived by his wife, Joan Tate Gogarty, and son, Maynard; by his father, John M. Gogarty; and by his sister, Margaret.

MAYNARD GOGARTY *interrogates the dame (September 17, 2001)*:

My mother had avoided my question while I was making the quiche, but now I was on to the custards. More milk, more eggs.

"And, ah—so Gran Rose simply bought that place for you and Dad? On 72nd?"

"For Scott. This was before we were married."

"And you don't know the arrangements."

She thought about it for a moment and then said, "Arrangements? No, Rose and Jack just bought it for Scott, as an investment. It was a co-op, and we hated it, which is why we moved to West 10th with you. And then we sold it, because the co-op board was making it so difficult for us to rent it out. Who could have known what a mistake it would be to sell a three-bedroom co-op on 72nd Street in 1973."

I was going to need to try a more direct approach: "I'm trying to discover something obliquely, but I seem to be a poor dick, or gumshoe, or PI. Are you party to a conspiracy of silence—mither, mither?"

"I have no idea what you are trying to ask me."

"Then let me start over. I suspect that Gran Rose owns the apartment I live in and is secretly renting it back to me."

"It is a nice fantasy, Manny. It would be the first I heard of it."

"Ah."

"And in your fantasy, why would Rose do such a thing as secretly buying your apartment? So she can evict you? Ha-*ha!*"

"It's just a—hunch."

"It is a nice fantasy. If you want Rose to buy you a house, what you need to do is get married. That's when she bought those places for Margaret's kids—when they got married."

"Listen, Mother. How do you suppose I find out the truth?"

Now she was worried. "Manny, whatever you do, please don't ask Rose about money this weekend. Please? She's an old woman. She doesn't need to hear any sob stories about your credit card debt. You know her opinion of your movies and your career choices and, my God, your arrest. Every fight Scott and I ever had with Rose and Jack started the same way—money. She's an old lady, and she can do what she likes with her wealth."

There it was, the cardinal rule of being my mother's son: never demand anything from Gran Rose. But it occurred to me: "Mother—I take it Dad was never afraid to ask Gran Rose about money?"

"No, unfortunately he was not."

"Somehow we've always assumed, you and I, that I didn't inherit that prerogative from him. We've assumed that, like you, I don't get to ask Gran Rose about money. But why is that? I mean, if her son could ask her, why not her grandson?"

"Manny, please. Please? I do not want any fights with Rose this weekend."

Now—now I was thinking about my father. He must have had ideas about dignity and money, even if I don't know what they were. I'm almost as old now as he was when he died—. Why is it that no matter how wise one becomes, one's father will always seem to have died wiser? And how is one to carry oneself upright despite the ground forever giving way? So. I placed the custards in the refrigerator to set.

JOHN SCOTT GOGARTY *tells his half of what was not yet, in the spring of 1973, a famous story (spring 1973):*

Joanie said that he wanted a bowler and that I should buy him one.

I said, "A—bowler?" "Yes." "A bowler, the hat, a bowler?" "Yes." "Explain this." "He says it's the only hat he'll wear." "Joanie—why do you indulge this?" "I am not indulging." And she said it in her new, whining tone, which she never used to have, and which means that in her opinion the conversation is over.

I said, "You're not indulging, but when he said the only thing he would wear was—a bowler, you said that we'd buy him one." She said, "It's the only thing he says he'll wear, Scott. And I'm tired of fighting with him about this every morning. And I don't want to put him out on the bus stop with nothing on his head." "But a bowler isn't even going to keep his head half warm. A bowler is made of felt. It sits on top of the ears. And in two months his head will grow a hat size, and that's that." "Scott, I don't care. Just take him to buy a bowler."

Quod erat demonstrandum. The next Saturday, I took Maynard to buy a bowler.

I took him to the one remaining haberdashery on Lexington, at—83rd or 84th. We took the subway too, the filthy IRT, because Maynard loves the subways so much. He loves feeding the token into the slot, he loves the turnstile, he loves standing up and holding the pole, even if there are seats free.

The haberdashery we went to is owned by a German fellow—and he is not just German but *über*-German. Prussian, well fed, clean-shaven, in a prissy suit, with pearl cufflinks and a matching tie pin, with silk lining on the underside of his collar, smoking an ebony pipe, wearing horn-rimmed glasses. This fellow is the last surviving *Bürger* of Germantown, though no doubt he doesn't live there anymore. He must commute in from some prim little two-story castle on Long Island.

And the German has an assistant, a lanky black kid—polite, observant, maybe twenty years old, probably a Hunter College student. The assistant is also in a suit—a navy blue, chalk-striped suit straight off 125th Street. They've got some sort of understanding, the German owner and the black kid, because when you walk into the store, the first thing the black kid does is stand up and fetch the owner. "Hello, we're interested in looking at bowlers for my son." "Yes, sir. Let me get Mr. Berkenstrater for you, sir."

It was the middle of January, but the store was decked with Fourth of July bunting in addition to the Christmas lights and the Hanukkah menorah. And the place had the smell of tobacco, and the charred smell of a bad steam radiator, and the smell of incense, the kind they burn in cathedrals, as though the owner were taking cues from the pope or the hippies. I thought I was going to pass out just standing in there, the smells were so heavy. Until we walked in, the black kid was sitting on a stool by the door with a textbook open on his lap, pretending to read but probably hoping to gasp some fresh air from the street.

Herr Berkenstrater parades in from the back room. "Yes! A bowler for the young man, I hear! How old are you, young man, and what is your name, eh!" "Eight and eleven twelfths. Maynard." "Maynard! This is a good name, a stout name! A good name, eh! And why do you want a bowler!" "It's the most dignified hat." And the owner looked at me. It was like being boarded by pirates, the way this fellow looked at you. He looked at you as if to say, I am laughing, thus you too must laugh. He said, "Very good! And, young man, may I take your hat size?" "It's six and three fours, British, six and seven eights, American," Maynard says.

Which is the point of the story, from my perspective—that Maynard knew his hat size. Apparently after Joanie told him we'd buy him a bowler, he sat down with an almanac and a tape measure and figured out his hat size. He had asked me about converting fractions a few nights before, and I had thought it was his math homework.

The owner laughed and gave me another one of his grappling-hook looks and measured Maynard. But Maynard was right about his hat size. And of course it was smaller than the two bowlers this German had in the shop, and so of course Maynard was devastated.

You know the routine: the owner said he could make a special order but it wouldn't arrive in time for Maynard to have it for winter. "There is nothing I can do for you, young man! Your head is too small. Maybe next year, eh!" And the owner swaggered back out of the room.

Maynard looked like he was going to cry. And Joanie would probably cry too. I asked the black kid if I could borrow their yellow pages and their telephone to call a few other hat shops.

After a few of those calls, though, it was clear that no one in the city had any bowlers in Maynard's tiny size. But if you're willing to consider shops in Harlem, it takes ten minutes to call every haberdashery in Manhattan.

While I was making these telephone calls, the black kid was babysitting Maynard. He let Maynard try on an adult-sized bowler and see how ridiculous he looked in the mirror. Then he found a paper-boy cap that actually fit Maynard—a gray-brown herringbone paper-boy cap made from wool—and a gray-brown striped silk scarf.

Maynard seemed to trust this black assistant—I could see the admiration from the way Maynard was looking at him. The assistant knew what he was doing, knew how to handle children; he was squatting down on Maynard's level and speaking to him in a whisper and calling him "sir." "That cap looks very handsome, sir. Should we ask Mr. Berkenstrater what he thinks? Why don't you try tying the scarf for yourself while I get him."

In comes the owner again. "Very dignified cap, young man! Very dignified!"

At which point Maynard won't take the cap off, or the scarf. The black kid had to cut the tags off Maynard's neck in order to ring up the purchase. Meanwhile, I tried to extract some promises from Maynard. "If we buy you that scarf, will you promise not to complain about piano practice?" "Yes!" "For how long?" "Forever!"

Five minutes later we were heading back for the subway. Maynard was beaming. And I was thinking about how I was going to reveal my triumph to Joanie, that I had gotten Maynard into a cap—and a scarf.

On the subway Maynard was swinging around on the pole, making a nuisance of himself to the other people, and I was too tired to stop him. He asked me, "Dad, when do I get to stop practicing piano?" That shows you how much good it does to try to bribe better behavior out of him. "One year after your hands stop growing." "That's what you always say. How come you don't play piano anymore?" "Dignity." "That's my word." "That's why I'm using it." "You don't get to use it." "Well, dignity is a good word, and you don't have a trademark on it. Since I bought you the scarf and you're already reneging on your promise not to complain about practicing—may I give you fatherly advice?" "Walk quickly, run slowly, praise clearly, damn lowly." "Different advice?" "Wash your hands when you come indoors, wash your face when you go outdoors." "Very good. Different advice?" "No." "Maynard, sometimes your dignity commands your surrender." He chewed on that for a while. "When?" "One year after your hands stop growing." "That's stupid, and also it's your answer for when I get to stop practicing piano, and also dignity is my word." "Well, if you didn't want stupid answers, then you shouldn't have asked for fatherly advice." "I didn't."

So there you are with my half of the story. Joanie was flabbergasted.

JOAN TATE *explains her ideas about dignity and money (mid-September 2001)*:

Not that compared to some people now Rose is so wealthy, or that compared to what she and Jack had fifty years ago—. I think, compared to fifty years ago, Rose and Jack were better off, comparatively, for that time than Rose is now, comparatively now—you know what I mean.

The first time that Scott took me to the townhouse on 69th, which would have been in the summer of 1961—forty years ago, my God—it wasn't the first time I had been in a mansion, but still. There were marble tiles in the entryway, and silver Jugendstil candlesticks that I think Margaret has now, and black-and-white checkered onyx ashtrays distributed everywhere on the first floor, since we all still needed ashtrays then. But to see Scott move through it like a proprietor and just toss his shoes and socks into a pile by the piano and then rub ice cubes on the soles of his feet to cool them off, in the middle of the living room, that was something new for me. In the half-bath on the second floor there were caricatures of Margaret and Scott by Max Beerbohm. Someone who knew him had gotten them for Rose as a gift, and Rose had then gone and hung them where no one would see them, because she thought they weren't flattering. Well, it took me some time to feel comfortable in those kinds of surroundings. The Tates were "well off, nothing more," as my father always said, but we had never been barons.

Oh, I shouldn't go that far; I don't know if the Gogartys were barons—baronial. And Manny wasn't raised in the kind of circumstances that Scott was, not by a long shot.

But when I went to work at the foundation, I did start going by Joan Tate instead of Joan Tate Gogarty, because it was just too much to have to constantly explain my connection to a family that was so well known in those kinds of circles. People don't remember the name Gogarty now like they did fifteen years ago, but in 1985 it was easier to be a Tate than a Gogarty. Whatever money came from Rose after Scott died—Manny's tuition, his summer camp fees—I took with gratitude. But at the same time, I always reminded myself to assume I was receiving the last of it. And I want Manny to behave the same. That's dignity, if you ask me, never to put anyone into a position where they feel like you are making demands.

JENNICA GREEN *recounts how she put her parents in a position where they felt like she was making demands (September 17, 2001):*

Okay. I'm out of the shower now, but look at this. In my refrigerator, there's tangerine juice from Zabar's, and the large-curd one-percent cottage cheese, and a Tupperware container with diced cantaloupe and honeydew, and those little sections of mandarin orange that you get in a can . . . in a can, in syrup. Which, obviously this is all Arnie's doing. I mean, Julie LaSalle does not know about me and the canned mandarin oranges in syrup from Zabar's. So Arnie's trying to make up. He went shopping at Zabar's while I was out of town, and he stocked my kitchen for me. Which . . .

Anyway, the cabin.

We had dinner, all six of us, in the little formal dining room. By candlelight. One window of that dining room looks toward the shed where the owl lives, and one window looks toward the pond where the ducks and the lilies are. And no matter where you sit, you're banging up against the sideboards and the highboys, unless you're sitting with your back to the windows, where even on a warm night you get this funny draft.

And on Thursday night we had quiche, and custard for dessert, with raspberry compote. Which is what Arnie makes when he wants to spend all evening in the kitchen. He was obviously trying to avoid company. And my parents . . . they weren't drunk, exactly, but they were feisty. In California, except for the thimbleful of cranberry schnapps my mom, like, administers to herself when she's cooking on a cold day, they never drink, except to split one beer between the two of them with dinner. With my mom complaining about how sleepy half a beer makes her. But Thursday they'd spent all afternoon drinking a couple pitchers of Joan's bloody marys and sitting in the sun by the pond while Arnie and I cooked. And then, with dinner, they had beer. So by the time dinner was over, my parents were definitely . . . rollicking.

Anyway, Thursday night. We're done with the quiche, and Arnie has proposed coffee and custard, and everyone has sort of groaned that we aren't ready yet. And so there we are, in the formal dining room, hunched over our plates to avoid bumping the furniture. Joan is fidgeting for a cigarette. And my dad pours whatever is left in my mom's glass of beer into his own glass and then tells Joan:

"Your son and I had a talk about marriage." Which, I won't even go into the implications of that. And Joan's like:

"Oh!" And my mom, who maybe already sees where all this was headed, says:

"Mitchell. Maybe you should let them make their own announcements." So I say:

"We don't have any announcements." And I give Arnie this

look, like, We don't have any announcements, right? Like, You know this is not the way to spring a surprise on me, Maynard Gogarty, right? But my dad just plows on ahead:

"I'm not making an announcement, I'm posing a hypothetical question." As if the fact that he's just talking about hypotheticals absolves him of responsibility for what he's saying. And he says it with this smirk on his face, this I-am-the-smart-kid-in-class smirk; he has all the answers, and it would be irrational to dispute them. "I don't see why we can't talk about the possibility of their marriage, in the hypothetical." My mom says:

"Because it makes them uncomfortable, that's why." Which should have been the end of it. But then Rose pipes up . . . Gran Rose, my father's new ally. She says:

"They could use being made uncomfortable." And then she turns to Arnie, who is sitting next to her, and glaring right at the side of his face, she says, "You're thirty-seven years old. It's time for you to get married."

And there is this thing Arnie does . . . my dad does it too. I don't think it's exclusively a man thing; women are just better at it. The thing where to avoid an argument, you make a joke. Obviously, though, you can only make an argument go away with a joke if everyone wants the argument to go away. Otherwise, all the joke accomplishes is to make everyone angrier than they already were. And Arnie was . . . just one stupid joke after another that night. He just could not take anyone seriously. Anyway. So Rose says:

"You're thirty-seven years old. It's time for you to get married." And Arnie says:

"Gran, be fair. How old are you? And you're single?"

"Don't you sass me. This girl needs to know if you're serious." Which, then I have to be like:

"Oh, that's sweet of you, Rose. But don't worry about me. I've made Arnie talk about things." But Rose isn't satisfied:

"It's time to stop talking and do something about it."

"We are doing something about it. Arnie and I are moving in together as of the first of the month." And she says:

"That is something, but it is not what I'm talking about." And this is when my dad realizes he has an ally, and so he moves from his smart-alecky approach to a more confrontational one:

"You're talking about marriage and children, right, Rose?"

"Precisely." And then she turns to Arnie again and says, "Get to it, you!"

Right? Which puts my mom in an interesting position. I think she wants to change the subject, for my sake, but she can't resist the urge to, like, get in her point of view as well. So she says:

"As far as I am concerned, Arnie and Jennica can do whatever they want to." But then: "Though I'm not saying grandchildren wouldn't be nice." And then my dad has to say:

"Jewish grandchildren." And my mom is like:

"Well, any grandchildren." And Joan decides to get in on the act too. She says:

"It's true, Manny. Grandchildren would be nice." And my dad, plowing ahead:

"And I believe that Arnie and I are in agreement that the children should be raised Jewish." And then . . . it was so maddening . . . instead of just saying, "Why don't we talk about this later?" Arnie eggs them on. He says:

"Mitchell, to be fair, before I could convert to Judaism, I would need to ask the permission of my mother." And Joan is just drunk enough herself to actually believe that she might be two minutes away from getting her son engaged. You know, she actually thinks Arnie's religion is what is at stake. So she says:

"You've never asked my permission to do anything else, Manny." And then Rose says:

"It's a moot point anyway, Joan. Manny can't just become a Jew!" And so Arnie sees another joke. Like, the most inane joke in the gentile world:

"I've already been, ah . . ." So I tell him:

"Your jokes aren't funny." But not only is Rose not going to get a joke about circumcision, she's trying to make some bigger point. She says:

"They cannot just splash the water on you and say the prayer and make you a Jew. It's a whole outlook on life about which you know nothing, Manny. You don't have the bearing of a Jew. You aren't sensible enough to be a Jew. They even have a word for it." So Joan says the one word of Yiddish she can think of:

"Shiksa?" And my mom is like:

"Goy?" And my dad, who gets where Rose is going, says:

"Mensch." Rose says:

"That's the one. Mensch. You can't just become a mensch."

And now they've hit a nerve with Arnie. Because now he feels like his, whatever, his cosmopolitan identity is at issue. He says:

"I object! I am now and have always been a mensch!" And Rose is like:

"Oh, I'm sure they have a word for what you are."

And there is this pause while everyone decides whether or not to list off the Yiddish words that might apply to Arnie. Except for me, because I want to change the whole subject immediately, because I would rather not hear whatever point it is my dad wants to get to. So I say:

"This is a ludicrous conversation." And my dad says:

"It is not ludicrous." And Rose says:

"I concur." So I ask them:

"You both think that we need to decide tonight, at this dinner table, whether or not any hypothetical child that might result from a hypothetical Green-slash-Gogarty marriage should be raised as a Jew?" And my dad is like:

"That's right." So I tell him:

"And yet sixteen years ago it didn't matter to you whether or not I got a bat mitzvah."

"I admit I made a mistake about that. I didn't realize the importance . . ." And he has some point about heritage and tradition, or whatever. "I didn't realize the importance of giving a child a culture and a community to grow up in. I made that mistake, and I don't want you to repeat it. There is a culture that you cannot reject, even if you don't believe every word of the religion." And Rose says:

"I could not concur more." So I say:

"Actually, Dad, let me see if I have this right. There may be a whole list of things that you feel I am obligated to do for this hypothetical child, even though you didn't do them for me? Am I obligated to pay for this hypothetical child to attend college?"

"Yes!"

"Even though you didn't pay for me to go to college yourself?"

"What are you talking about?"

And, just to give you the background, my parents, when I was applying to colleges, decided that they would pay for me to go to U.C. Berkeley, but if I wanted to go anywhere more expensive, I would have to pay for the difference myself, with student loans. This was a point of pride with them, their frugality. So I tell my dad:

"What I am talking about is your 'We will only pay for a U.C. Berkeley diploma' policy. In case you have forgotten, I had to take out forty thousand dollars in loans in order to go to Princeton. Loans that I had to pay back myself." And he says:

"That was your choice." So I say:

"Oh, I see. Princeton was my choice, but how I raise my own child isn't my choice. Look, I won't hold it against you that I've already paid my Princeton loans off and that it took me three miserable years as an analyst at Hoffman Ballin to do it. I won't hold it against you how much it . . . perverted my sense of what I could do with myself while I was in college, that I had so much debt. I won't even charge you interest. No, actually, I will charge you interest! You want the child raised Jewish? Pay me fifty thousand dollars!"

"Now you're being absurd."

"Bullshit, Dad. You know what is absurd? Expecting me to raise a child in accordance with a religion that I reject." And, that got him.

"You do not reject it!" He was red in the face. Everyone else was horrified. Except Rose, who, like, relished every moment. But, telling my dad outright that I reject Judaism? Anyway, my mom says:

"She's not serious, Mitchell." And my dad says:

"She does not reject Judaism! It's intolerable how she talks. She can't even be honest with herself. She cannot tell me it doesn't sting her to hear that Palestinians are dancing in the streets because Jews were killed in the World Trade Center. Tell me it doesn't sting you personally, as a Jew." And my mom's like:

"Mitchell." So I tell him:

"It stings me personally as a New Yorker. Something I have become no thanks whatsoever to you." And my mom's like:

"Jennica."

"What? If you thought being Jewish was so important, why did you move to San Jose, where there are no Jews?" And now she has to say, which makes my father practically choke:

"I don't think being Jewish is so important." And here Rose has to chime in again:

"There you are wrong." And Joan, drunk Joan, whose one word of Yiddish is *shiksa,* is the only one with enough sense to say:

"Rose, maybe we don't understand." And then Arnie, so maddening, Arnie is like:

"Custard, anyone?" And it's Joan, drunk Joan, and only because she needs to go smoke, who finally has to put an end to the conversation:

"Manny, help me clear the table." And my mom sees what an inspiration this is. She tells my dad:

"Mitchell, since you have so much energy, why don't you wash the dishes?" But Joan says:

"Oh, Manny and I'll do the dishes, you just be guests. But maybe when the dishes are done we can all play . . . Scrabble?"

ROSE GOGARTY *explains the family's tactics (mid-September 2001):*

You can learn a lot from Scrabble, and don't you think I am not a shrewd player. Manny puts it past me, but I see things about people. This Jennica, she has a head on her shoulders, and all her ears are screwed tightly in. When Joan brought out the Scrabble board, the first thing Jennica wanted to know was whether we had any house rules.

I said, "In this house, we play by the only rules there are, which are the tournament rules."

What she wanted to know was whether, when she had her tiles in front of her, she was allowed to flip freely through the dictionary to see whether certain words existed. I said, "Who plays like that?"

Her parents, that's who. Mitchell said it made him nervous to play any game that penalizes him for consulting a reference book. And Susan said she would help Jennica, but in the end she just went to keep Mitchell company while he watched television. So much for those two.

Then Jennica asked, because she is cunning, "If I want to challenge a word that someone else uses because I think that the word doesn't exist, but if I'm wrong and the word does exist, then I lose my turn, right?"

I said, "Right." But you see what she was doing, this girl. She was very clever. She was making sure she would be able to get away with her system.

We drew our tiles. In the first round, I put down my word, Joan put down her word, Jennica put down her word, and Manny threw in his tiles. In the second round, I put down my word, Joan put down her word, Jennica put down her word, and Manny threw in his tiles. In the third round, I put down my word, Joan put down her word, Jennica put down her word, and Manny got a play-out. He played all seven of his tiles in one long row. In the fourth round, I put down my word, Joan put down her word, Jennica put down her word, and Manny threw in his tiles.

Let me tell you what was going on here.

When I play, I play to win. I look for where the triple letter scores are and where the triple word scores are, and I use them. I put my X's and Q's on squares that matter. XI is a word, not just

AX and OX. QADI is a word, and so is QAID. QOPH, a Hebrew letter. QIYAS, AJI, AJO. I know these words. And if I see a triple word score open up but I can't take it, I block it. I play to win.

Joan has no mind for the game. If she sees an AT on the board, the best she can do is make it into BOATS, wasting an S tile and opening up a triple word score for Jennica with the B. Joan takes BRA and makes it ZEBRA, using a blank tile for the E. I let her make these mistakes. And then I point them out to her after she has committed her tiles, and I show her where she could have done better. Instead of Z-blank-BRA, she could have put the Z on a double letter, playing ADZ one way and ZEA the other, collecting the double letter points for Z twice and saving the blank. I say, "Why are you wasting your blank tile like that?" But Joan never learns.

But Jennica is wily. She imagines words, is what she does. Maybe she really believes in her fabrications, or maybe she just bluffs well. Either way, she is convincing. To compound the knavery, that night at the cabin, she played her made-up words on all the double and triple word scores that Joan had opened up for her. WRENGI. She said it was a grazing animal on the Serengeti. I said I had never heard of it. She said she *thought* it was spelled right. I said I challenged. And she told me, the little fox, that if I wanted to challenge a Princeton English major on the spelling of WRENGI, I could go ahead and look it up in the dictionary, but I would lose my turn if I was wrong. I let it go, I let her have her imaginary word. KII, a Chinese philosophical principle. HOAB, a color, like dung or khaki, which she played on a triple word score, off Joan's BOATS. I looked all these words up later that night, and they were all complete fabrications. Well, let me tell you: she's used her trick on me once; the next time I play with her, I will know to challenge the big Princeton graduate on her so-called words. Because Princeton may have given her an imagination and confidence, but it didn't give her a vocabulary. Now I know, but that night she had all of us convinced. Except for Manny, who paid no attention to Jennica's words and who sat there, and who waited his turn, and who then threw in his tiles for the fourth time in five rounds.

I said, "Show me your tiles! If you need my help, you should say so, and I'll find a word for you. You must have a word!"

He said, "Nothing in the tournament rules prohibits me from throwing in my tiles even if I do have a word."

"What? You have a word but won't play it?"

"I play dignified words, or I don't play at all."

"What nonsense is that?"

He said, "It's not nonsense. A dignified word is one that requires all seven of your tiles. A play-out. Preferably without any blank tiles, and preferably neither a plural noun nor a verb in anything but the infinitive."

I said, "Let me give you some advice, mister. You don't win by getting a play-out once in a game. You win by putting down a word every single time. Show me your tiles."

He said, "I am not interested in demeaning myself with this scramble for points, as the rest of my family seems to be. I mean, Gran. QUA? What kind of word is that? XI? You should be ashamed of yourself."

"I am not ashamed, because I am ahead by ten points."

"Well, I do not play for points, I play for dignity."

"Where is the dignity in losing? You tell me that. You know what I think? I think *dignity* is just the word you use to explain your behavior when you decide you're too lazy to do what everyone else has to."

Even Jennica agreed with me. She told him, "Listen to your gran. Rose is right."

I said, "Of course I'm right. Show me your tiles."

He refused, and he threw in. And he went on to lose the game. I am not embarrassed to say that I came in second in the end, eight points behind Jennica, and that it was only because of her spectacular imagination. I told her the next morning, "That is some imagination you have for words."

And Mitchell, overhearing this, said, "You see why we play with an open dictionary."

JENNICA GREEN *reveals what Arnie was thinking about (September 17, 2001)*:

The cabin is picky about giving you any privacy. It doesn't feel like sound would travel that well . . . the whole place is so full of shadows, and even at the end of summer it is sort of pleasantly damp, with a heaviness and a coolness to the sheets and bedclothes, and this faint smell of loam, and the wallpaper always slightly chill to the touch, and the family pictures on the walls all slowly wrinkling up in their aluminum frames. So it's easy to forget how little privacy you have. Like, you'll be sitting in the living room downstairs, reading one of Rose's old *New Yorkers*, and suddenly you'll hear, perfectly clearly, that someone dropped the soap in the upstairs tub. You'll be lying in bed upstairs, and you'll hear that someone is unscrewing the cookie tin down in the kitchen.

Anyway, Thursday night, we're getting ready for bed. Arnie is washing his feet in the random little sink that's in the bedroom we were sleeping in. This white enamel sink, stained orange where the water leaks from the faucet. He can't sleep in the summer unless he washes his feet in cold water first. Which, whatever. It's one of his things that seemed so cute at first, and that finally was exposed as just . . . another deliberate neurosis. Anyway, he's like:

"I haven't heard from Ana."

And it didn't bother me when Arnie finally confessed to me, last spring, that he had married somebody for a visa. It was even sort of funny how embarrassed he was; I mean, whatever, it wasn't like a real marriage. He even showed me the wedding pictures that they faked, which were pretty hilarious. The old Russian women who they found to play Ana's family. And now we sort of look forward to seeing the *New York Times Magazine* each weekend, and to whether it will have another one of Ana's insane fashion shoots. Anyway:

"I haven't heard from Ana. Since Tuesday morning, I mean. She had . . . space on the ninety-first floor of one of the towers, donated studio space. And she did like working in the early morning . . . late at night and early in the morning. I called her, but I haven't heard back." It was like, Oh, that's why you've been acting so strange. He said:

"I'm sure she's fine. I'm sure she is fine and just isn't calling me back, which would be typical."

And so he'd been calling her. And, whatever. He's worried about her. Which is fine. But also isn't fine. Like, why are you worried about her, but ignoring me? The whole thing was weird. Anyway, that was Thursday night.

MAYNARD GOGARTY *blames the* New York Times (*September 17, 2001*):

It started with sexlessness, and with the Friday *New York Times.*

Sexlessness—. How is it one knows not to bother one's paramour? The uninviting tones of voice, the postures, the particular pajamas? It's communicated quite unambiguously. The day will take a certain key, in terms of who is touching whom, who is teasing whom, and then, once the key is set, sex either is or is not a note that can be played. I imagine that Tuesday the eleventh was the sexiest day of many people's lives, alternately listening to the feverish rumors on CNN and—fucking. But Jennica and I weren't sleeping together last week, for some reason. There you have it.

On Friday morning, Jennica's parents drove off to see Stockbridge, the Norman Rockwell Museum seeming suddenly relevant to them. My mother went along, to look at the shops. She said she would "get the jump on Christmas" and came back with a crystal wine decanter and a fondue set, obviously for herself. Gran Rose decided it would be a good day to give things to the Salvation Army and so was making piles of *National Geographics* in the library. *National Geographics*, moldy picnic gear, stiff raincoats and galoshes, and—the prize in her opinion—my grandfather's sixty-year-old beaver-skin hat. Jennica was once again in the kitchen, phone pinned under her chin, listening to the airlines' hold music, campaigning to get me a ticket for Nadine's wedding, using her thumbs to write e-mails to her colleagues on her BlackBerry.

So no one noticed when I took my walk to the co-op: "Stretch my legs! Buy some corn! Pick up the *Times!*" And get two hundred dollars out of the co-op's cash machine and hand it over to Ana, who was waiting, as arranged, in her car in a secluded gravel driveway—wearing sunglasses, drugstore sunglasses, and a handkerchief over her head.

"Have you reported me missing, Gogi?"

"Yes, yes, I have."

"I will have to make this surprise trip to the cabin and meet your girlfriend if you are lying. And I do think you are lying, still."

But I wasn't lying; I had reported Ana missing to Jennica. My trial effort, and my big mistake. I had only been assaying my own capacity for conspiracy—because having Ana dead was beginning to have some appeal. I seemed, however, only to be getting myself into trouble; so I handed her the money and—skedaddled.

Back at home, more pacing around, more beer, more Scrabble. Everyone was getting bored and jumpy. That night, Jennica wasn't able to sleep. We would have to leave at three in the morning in order to get her on her flight to California, and it made her anxious. She was sitting on our bed, filing her calluses with her pumice stone, and I was sitting across from her, looking at the pictures in the *Times*. The Friday *New York Times*.

There were photos of the missing posters that people were hanging all over New York. The bereaved were—papering the city with photocopied missing posters. "Beloved Father, Son, Brother. Scorpio Tattoo on Left Shoulder. Last seen in WTC 1, 86th Floor." This kind of thing. And Union Square was filling with flowers and candles. So, ah. Well. So I said, ah—.

JENNICA GREEN *recounts the argument (September 17, 2001)*:

"E-Shrines could be making a fortune this week."

That's what he says. Totally unacceptable, right? I told him:

"Would you please try not to make any more of your jokes? They're offensive."

"Well, look at the photographs people are using for their missing posters. Look at the photograph they used for this guy. That is at best, what? A fifty-nine-dollar rental tuxedo?"

Right? So I'm like:

"It's so sad. The fact that they call him 'missing.'"

"How about the fact that he had a tattoo of a scorpion on his shoulder, and that they broadcast that humiliating detail for the world to read on their missing poster? Is that sad?" And he just keeps going. "Why is it that the only photographs people seem to have available of their missing relatives are photographs from horrible parties? Parties that demanded . . . rental tuxedos. What a tragedy that these people died, because clearly while they were alive these people were having 'fun.'" Fun, of course, being a bad word for Arnie. And he was just going on and on, mocking the missing posters. "Look at that dress. It's the official I-am-an-American-bridesmaid dress. Look at that grin. It's the official I-am-a-girl-with-a-cocktail-and-you-are-a-girl-with-a-camera grin. Look at this one. This guy's family used his photo from the wedding page of the *Times* on his missing poster." And I'm like:

"That's . . . so . . . sad!" And he says:

"They could consolidate the two, actually, the wedding announcement and the missing poster. 'Missing: Lucy Lewis, daughter of Luke and Louise Lewis of Lunchstop, Louisiana. Ms. Lewis, 32, was an associate at the law firm of Kilmore & Keyes, where she worked on trusts and estates. She graduated cum laude from the University of Louisiana and received her law degree from Fordham University. She has a tattoo of a kitten on her left calf and was last seen in WTC 2. She will keep her maiden name." So finally I'm like:

"What . . . is . . . your problem?"

"My problem is the disingenuousness of it all. No one, least of all the *Times*, has anything to say that isn't . . . in style. They're photocopying each other's grief. Look at these pictures. Pedestrians in Manhattan are now wearing masks to protect themselves from the dust. Notice how they apparently all bought their masks at the same hardware store? They're . . . in style." Which, unbelievable!

"You are such a hypocrite, Arnie. A genuinely solemn occasion comes around, an occasion that actually calls for some dignity, and all you can do is make fun of it."

"Solemn?" And then, "Jennica, these are exactly the people who every Sunday you look at and tease when their wedding announcement photos are published in the *Times.* Exactly this class of person." He says, "You read their wedding announcements and you mock them for their tastelessness. Don't tell me you are offended on their behalf. These are people who you wished were dead in the first place." What am I supposed to say to that? So I tell him:

"That is personally offensive, Arnie. In case you haven't noticed, I have never laughed at your attempted jokes about dead people. In case you haven't noticed, this is not some . . . traffic accident, except times ten thousand. It's a global tragedy."

MAYNARD GOGARTY *recounts the argument (September 17, 2001)*:

Global tragedy—!

Is anything more infuriating than to have your girlfriend sexlessly inform you of prevailing wisdom? Was she hoping to incite me to riot? Well—she succeeded. I don't know quite what I said, because what can you say to such hokum? I said some things. What sorts of things? Oh, for example, "This is not a global tragedy, this is exactly what America was asking for—! This chaos, this horror? The events of September eleventh are to American excess as—Chernobyl is to Russian miserliness. Saudi terrorists are to the failure to conserve as bubonic plague is to—the failure to bathe."

And Jennica, naturally—well, what she said was, "That is so offensive. To me."

"No, it's not. You're just being mawkish."

"How can you—?"

"Because you don't actually feel offended. You have just deduced that you are supposed to feel offended. 'Everything is different now! Nothing will ever be the same again!' You just wish you felt offended because you delight in the idea that everyone should have to be sappy!" I should have known better than to tease her, but it was quite funny. "Jennica Green's dream come true—National Treacle Week!"

"That is so offensive. Why are you making this personal?"

"Because personally, we don't know anyone who died!"

And she was in a rapture of outrage. "Oh—!"

"What?"

"Oh—!"

"What?"

"That is so—, for so many—."

"What?"

"I mean, if nothing else—what about your Ana woman?"

And she had me. I had slipped. I had forgotten that Ana was supposed to be dead, according to me, possibly. And I must have blushed, or stuttered—I know I lost my composure. I said, "I know that Ana is fine."

And when Jennica asked, perfectly sensibly, "Have you heard from her?" I panicked. I felt caught, as if I'd been seen handing off the money that morning. I panicked, and I said, "No, I haven't heard from her!" I said it in exactly the wrong tone. I said it with vehemence, when I should have said it with—frightened submission. Jennica gave me a look. She didn't know what to make of me. So I took a breath and said, "I suppose I still am Ana's husband, on paper. I suppose I should report her missing."

And I think the argument might have ended there if I had kept quiet. Jennica was—maybe ready to be forgiving, maybe ready to make an allowance for me on behalf of this missing friend. But I didn't keep quiet—I kept talking, because I am who I am. I said, "I suppose if I wait too long to report her gone, and if she is dead, it will look awkward for me to seek compensation."

Jennica made a sound—of revulsion—and left the room. She said nothing, but—. She didn't exactly slam the door, but she gave it a push at the end, a jolt. A rebuke that traveled throughout the cabin. *Whum!*

JENNICA GREEN *recounts the argument (September 17, 2001)*:

And then it's like . . . where do you go? Once you leave the room? Anyway, I sat on my stool by the telephone in the kitchen. I put on the light that's under the brass oven hood and just sat there. It was practically midnight before he came downstairs. And he said:

"Do you want some tea?" And he put on the water. And then he said, "So . . . what exactly is this about?" Which, as if he didn't know. But I gave him the benefit of the doubt. I told him:

"This is about how you would react if my airplane got hijacked tomorrow and I died. Would you react the same as with Ana? Like, worried about how to get compensated?" And he said:

"Your airplane is not going to get hijacked, Jennica."

"That's so easy for you to say, who aren't even getting on a plane. Who aren't even interested in going to California in the first place." And he said:

"That's not fair." But I'm like:

"It's totally fair. You are so happy to let me go alone, so you can sit back here and make it look like you're in mourning for your wife or whatever, so you can collect your money." And he said:

"She's not my wife, she's not dead, I don't care about the money. What I do care about is, why are you being like this?"

"Because I'm scared!"

MAYNARD GOGARTY *recounts the argument (September 17, 2001)*:

Unbearable! For her to sit there on the stool and—play-act! Play-act that she feels fear that she does not feel.

"Because I'm scared!"

"Of what, Jennica?"

JENNICA GREEN *recounts the argument (September 17, 2001)*:

And I'm like:

"You even have to ask?" And he's like:

"I'm trying to have an honest conversation . . ." Which, unbelievable. I told him:

"No, Arnie, you are not trying to have an honest conversation. It is so obvious that underneath all this contempt, you're scared too. What you are trying to do *now* is not be honest but make everything okay, which is different. You want me to tell you that you haven't . . . totally alienated me, and totally pissed me off. Well, you have. Just because you have spent your whole life . . . dissimulating about what you really feel doesn't mean I will."

And meanwhile the water boils. And in his flippant tone, his British tone, he asks me if I want some tea. As if to say, Oh, I am just arguing with Jennica for fun, no one's feelings are at stake here. He was totally pulling a Mitchell Green. As if to say, Oh, I can turn off the argument at any moment, just like I can turn off this water once it boils.

"Do you want some tea?"

MAYNARD GOGARTY *recounts the argument (September 17, 2001)*:

I ask her, "Would you care for some tea?" And what does she do? She stamps her foot. She stamps her foot. She's sitting down on a stool, so she leans forward, just so she can stamp her foot. I had never before seen a full-grown woman stamp her foot. Forget petulant children—stamping your foot is play-acting a petulant child.

But—there is a form of vertigo, of argumentative vertigo—a feeling that the world is behaving perversely beneath you, the same feeling I imagine that they must have had when the floors buckled and the buildings began to fall—the vertigo of realizing that whatever it was you and your girlfriend were arguing about ten minutes ago, something fundamental has been broken, something has begun to cave in, and now the whole affair is in irreversible collapse.

JENNICA GREEN *recounts the argument* (*September 17, 2001*):

So I'm like:

"Arnie, I have to get on an airplane tomorrow. And it scares me." And he says:

"I don't believe you, Jennica. I believe you are play-acting. Somehow it makes your story more interesting for you to be scared, so you're saying that you're scared. But you, Jennica Green, frightened of getting on an airplane? Tomorrow? Tomorrow, the one day in all of human history when no one could be foolish enough to try to hijack anything?"

And what do you say to that? What do you say to your boyfriend looking you in the eye and saying, I don't believe you? I told him:

"You can't tell when to stop trying to make me laugh, Arnie. You can't tell when to stop teasing me. You don't even realize that you crossed the line half an hour ago." And he still seems to think we're in debate club.

"What line is there to cross?"

"What do we *even* have in common, Arnie? What do we *even* see in each other? What am I doing moving into your apartment?" Right?

He spends a minute putting tea bags into two mugs and pouring the water in, and then he gives one to me. As if this were the beginning of the conversation and not the end. I'm like:

"I'm just telling the truth, Arnie. I don't want any fucking tea." And he says, "Maybe . . ."

But I don't even wait to hear what he has to say. I just go outside and slam that screen door behind me.

MAYNARD GOGARTY *recounts how the argument ended (September 17, 2001)*:

I lay down on the couch. She went—elsewhere. And at three in the morning I drove her to the airport in Boston. I haven't heard from her since. And now it's Monday morning.

But—ah—two more arguments to recount, I fear, before we are up to date. The argument with Gran Rose on Saturday night, and the argument, if you will, when Ana arrived on Sunday morning to claim her place in my family.

NADINE HANAMOTO *describes the days leading up to her wedding (mid-September 2001)*:

First it's the caterer, calling me that Wednesday night at eleven o'clock, confirming that we're going to still have the wedding. This is the same caterer who on her answering machine says, "You have reached Russian Valley Inn Catering. Please leave a message after the beep and tell us how we can exceed your expectations." You could exceed my expectations by not calling me up at eleven o'clock at night, just when my baby is going to sleep, and giving me a guilt trip for coincidentally having scheduled a wedding four days after whatever they are calling it now. The Attacks on America.

She says, "A number of my clients have been contacting me to ask about postponing events. And obviously I understand when a hostess needs to be conscious of her guests' sensitivities."

I was like, "Actually, Ms. Caterer, I intentionally planned to have my wedding four days after the Attacks on America. That's why I am having the two cakes, in the shape of the towers, with plastic replicas of airplanes crashing into them. I had advance notice of the attacks from Mossad, just like all the rest of the Jews. Didn't you know that Hanamoto-Dicochea is a traditional Jewish hyphenated name?"

Then the photographer calls. Then the florist calls. The florist wants to know if we want wreaths, or perhaps a floral memorial to the World Trade Center victims. He has a four-foot-tall plaster cartouche which he can decorate with a color photograph of the towers, and on top there will be two doves carrying a banner in their beaks that reads "We Will Never Forget." Like, actually, do you have an eight-foot-tall version that we could use as a background for our portraits?

This is the thing about having a wedding on the cheap: you suddenly realize that everyone you've hired has only ever done trashy weddings. The only people who didn't call me to ask whether the wedding was canceled were the band and my seamstress. Our mariachi band, Los Cerditos. Who rocked. And the Vietnamese seamstress who altered my wedding dress. Who also rocked, and who, unlike my mother, loved the fact that I was getting married in the same dress twice. Which I admit is trashy, but it was either buy a new dress or have an open wine bar, so . . .

My seamstress was so cool. When I explained why I needed the dress altered, she was like, "Oh, second time! This time, happy!" We so should have gotten her to cater the whole thing. You know she's got the crazy good *bahn chung.*

JENNICA GREEN *recounts how the argument ended and tells us about Nadine's wedding (September 17, 2001):*

You know where this story is going, right? With me and George Hanamoto?

The point is, the airline people could only find a seat for one of us, so Arnie stayed behind in New York and I went to the wedding alone, which obviously was . . . fateful.

It was a flight out of Logan Airport in Boston, at seven A.M. on Saturday, which would only get me to the ceremony on time if there were no delays. And we had to arrive at the airport by five A.M. to go through the new, heightened security screening. So Arnie and I left the cabin at three A.M. on Saturday, and he drove me in the dark down the Mass Pike, like, how many hours after we'd had that argument? I pretended to sleep while he drove, but I was awake the whole way, keeping my eyes just open enough that I could watch the clock. When we were twenty minutes from the airport, he said:

"Jennica, we're almost there." He wanted to talk. "I am sorry I can't go with you. I do think it's brave to get on an airplane. I am sorry I won't be able to, ah . . ." It was like, Don't try to make nice at four-thirty in the morning in your mother's Honda when I'm about to leave for California. I said:

"Whatever, don't worry about it." Like, shuffling my things around, the way you do when you're getting ready to get out of a taxi. Digging out my ID, stuffing my old issue of the *New Yorker* into a spare pocket in my carry-on. But Arnie was still trying:

"Send my congratulations to Nadine and . . . Oscar." And I'm like, Please just get me out of here. He said:

"Will you . . . call me when you get there?"

Anyway.

The airport in Boston was . . . sobering. All the people in line at check-in were silent, or at most whispering, and snapping their eyes back and forth, watching each other. Normally the kids are hypnotized by their Walkmen and the parents are addressing their children through bullhorns, practically. But there were whole families, like, at military attention. And National Guardsmen standing in every other corner. In camouflage and boots, with their yes-this-is-a-machine-gun faces. Their scowls. I was chewing on my nails, which I thought I had given up. It was five-thirty, it was five forty-five, it was six, it was six-fifteen, and the lines were hardly moving. I must have been asked for my ID twenty times. And every single person who checked it was like, "You're from New York City?" And gave me this look, like, Tell me what it was like. It took an hour and a half just to get to the metal detector. And then they opened my carry-on and unzipped every single pocket. I told them:

"My flight is at seven. Is there any way to . . . ?" And they're like:

"Lady, this is the way things are now. You should have gotten here two hours before your flight." Totally maddening. But you can't say anything. They asked if I had nail clippers, and they confiscated those. Like, great, my fingers look like I'm eleven years old. They confiscated the wire hanger that my dress was on. Just to ensure that the dress got wrinkled.

Anyway, I got on board with about two minutes to spare, and then the flight was delayed. There was some problem with the passenger manifest. And delayed, and delayed. It was like, I can't believe that I'm going to miss the wedding; that after all that, I'm going to get to California too late for the wedding. So I opened my old issue of the *New Yorker* and instantly fell asleep.

PHILLIP T. FIELD *reports in the "Talk of the Town" section of the* New Yorker (*June 25, 2001*):

Hoity-Toity Department: Two Syllables, Rhymes with Yuppie

The New York Public Library was hosting a panel on "The Life Lexicographic," and while tickets were twenty dollars, the Finnish vodka was free. Geoffrey Nunberg was there (think *American Heritage*). Simon Winchester was there (think *OED*). And also there, leaning impatiently against a column next to the stage, drinking something clear and odorless, was Puppy Jones.

He was modestly insisting on the limits of his own expertise. He has written neither a dictionary nor a book about a dictionary. Rather, he is the man behind "Prime Time," the pathologically catchy, pop-chart-popping song featuring as lyrics a litany of words that rhyme with themselves.

"People want to tell me I forgot one. They want to tell me they got some other word that rhymes with itself. 'Puppy, you forgot *hip-hop!*' I have to tell them, '*Hip-hop* does not rhyme with itself, fool.' 'You forgot *teeter-totter*, you forgot *dilly-dally*.' These are vowel substitutions, these are not rhymes. If I wanted to do vowel substitutions, I'd do vowel substitutions. I'd be the Galileo Galilei of vowel substitutions, son. I would not be *comme ci, comme ça*. I'd be the *pu-ppy*, yo."

Uh, yo. A child of the middle-class suburbs of Long Beach, California, and a dropout from the undergraduate Department of Linguistics at UCLA, Mr. Jones is arguably as unlikely a figure on the hip-hop charts as he was at the library. But then, he is not one to be deterred.

"'Puppy, you forgot *fen-phen!* You forgot *muumuus* and *couscous*.' This is repetition, this is not rhyme. If I was interested in repetition, I'd be the Sirhan Sirhan of repetition. The Boutros Boutros of repetition. Then there are the people who can't count syllables. 'Puppy! Puppy! *Etch-A-Sketch! Eminem! Stitch 'n Bitch! Hugs Not Drugs!*' It's like, you want to rap? Write your own damn rap. You all are *hillbillies*. You all are *hoi polloi*. People think they're bringing me the news, but it's the other way around."

And what news is Mr. Jones bringing the people, exactly?

"*Poo-poo* is a noun, and *pooh-pooh* is a verb. So *pooh-pooh* is what you do, but *poo-poo* is doo-doo. Word."

Uh, word.

The panel began. Mr. Nunberg spoke about *bamboozle*. Mr. Winchester spoke about *impresario*. Mr. Jones spoke about *mutatis mutandis*.

Questions from the audience? A young woman in an earnest knit cap asked Mr. Jones where he learned Latin, and he responded with an etymology of *bo-bo*. Applause was given, hands were shaken, polite noises were made, everyone was flattered, and Puppy found his way back to the bar for one last drink. How did he want his free Finnish vodka?

"Straight up. Please."

JENNICA GREEN *explains in some detail about her arrival in California but prepares to gloss over other things (September 17, 2001)*:

I woke up as the plane was taxiing in from the runway in San Francisco.

That white California tarmac.

It was local time, ten forty-five.

And I was rested, but also, like.

Emptied of worry. Or.

Like, as a kid, when you wake up after a tantrum. As though my mind had been flushed and flushed with clean water, until it shone. Whatever my eyes saw, it arrived in my mind clean, and then it instantly dissolved to make way for the next clean thing.

I got off the plane and onto the concourse, and I yawned, and my ears popped, and everything sounded so soft and considerate. Even the security announcements, in that spacious SFO concourse, were, like, echoing and caring. Unreal. Outside, it was a breezy blue child of a day, playing with its red windsocks. I had just woken up from my first good sleep in forever. It was the first time since Tuesday that I felt like I was somewhere safe. But it was more than that. I was somewhere where I knew the meaning of everything that might happen to me.

I bought a cup of Peet's Coffee in the concourse, picked up my little green rental car, and drove off to Sonoma, drinking my coffee. Off to Goat Rock Beach.

Which is on Highway 1, right where the Russian River shivers out into the Pacific. Fresh black cliffs, and that chilly green-and-gold fog-grass on the hilltops, and redwoods, and raw boulders . . . beetling over into the clammy, spraying waves. The Pacific is always cold up there. And always quiet and always gray-green.

It's the same cliffs all the way from the Golden Gate Bridge to Goat Rock Beach, and the same salty, rugged . . . tranquillity. But then the cliffs relax a bit, sort of slouch, and the Russian River wiggles secretly out of its redwoods and its estuary from behind this low, rocky ridge. That's what you see if you are taking Highway 1.

But you don't take Highway 1 when you come from San Francisco. You take 101. The coast is purely theoretical when you're on 101 in your rental car. Your rental car that is the same color green as the uninsured Peugeot you took with your best friend the day you cut class to go to San Francisco. Your best friend who is getting married at the mouth of the Russian River. You drive up from the airport, past the spot in Hunter's Point where your best friend's Peugeot broke down in 1989. Your best friend who you haven't seen in ten years. Over Potrero Hill, where you get the instant, utopian view of downtown San Francisco. You cross the bay with the Golden Gate Bridge and go under that first mountain in Marin, through a long white-tile tunnel, the entrance to which is painted like a rainbow. The tunnel where, when your parents would take you and your kid brother inner-tubing on the Russian River, your kid brother would make your parents honk the horn for pleasure. You skirt past that dopey fjord at Sausalito, with the unmovable houseboats and the sleepy wood-frame houses, and then you are inland. In California, where you understand the meaning of things.

Santa Rosa is where you turn left for the coast.

Onto Highway 116, which is the sort of road where you will see a quietly expensive car, a Lexus or whatever, pulled over on the side next to a vineyard, or a pasture, or a field of lavender. And then, six miles later, you pass some topless marathoner in elastic black shorts on a training run through the heat. But then the road sinks and curves and follows the Russian River through the shade of the redwoods. Which is where the hotel for the reception was. The Russian Valley Inn. Where I changed into my dress and sandals.

PERLA HANAMOTO *prays (mid-September 2001)*:

I wish they could have done it in a church, even a Catholic church, if that's what Oscar wanted. To me, a wedding on a beach is not a wedding at all, it is a princess fantasy. God is not satisfied with just any vows. This is what Nadi doesn't understand; that she and Oscar should have said God's vows, in a church. I pray that this time she makes her marriage work, especially since she has the baby. I pray for his children too, because Nadi must be a mother to them. She is joining a big family, and she does not know what it is to have a big family. She always wanted her own room and her own car and her own rules, and I don't think she is used to having a big family, with no peace. But I pray that she is happy. I pray for the baby. I pray for all these things.

George never understood a family either. He should be married, but all he cares about is himself and money. He was always very selfish, and he still is. The day before Nadi's wedding he went to San Francisco and bought himself three new suits, one of them for the wedding. We were supposed to spend the day together in San Jose as a family, but instead George went to San Francisco to shop.

One thing that made me grateful was to see Jenny Green. I had not seen her since the girls were in high school, but I was the only one who was able to recognize her. We were all standing by the van where Nadi was waiting so no one would see her in her dress until her silly ceremony began. Jenny drove up in her rental car and parked, and got out in a very elegant dress. George said, "Who is that?" And Nadi looked through the window of the van, but she couldn't recognize Jenny either. I was the one who said, "It's Jenny Green." Her parents raised her okay. Jewish children are like that.

I don't understand why Nadi couldn't try to be more elegant, like Jenny is, instead of being silly, putting that ugly dress on the baby and hiring a mariachi band and sticking those figurines on her cake. So I just pray to God, you know.

JENNICA GREEN *explains in some detail about the rectangle in the sand but prepares to gloss over other things (September 17, 2001):*

The ceremony was performed by the accordion player, who, well . . .

Goat Rock Beach is this length of shoreline at the foot of this bluff. And halfway down the strand, out in the waves, connected to the shore by a spit of boulders, there is this remnant of cliff, this tall, natural castle. It's an outpost left over from when the cliffs stood a hundred yards farther west, I guess, before the ocean eroded them eastward. So that's the Goat Rock in Goat Rock Beach.

When I pulled up in my rental car, some people who I didn't recognize but who were obviously dressed for a wedding were getting out of their cars, looking, like, eager and deferential. So I followed them. They were wandering down from the parking lot onto the beach, toward this vast rectangle that had been constructed in the sand, marking off where the wedding would be.

There were a few people on the beach who weren't there for the wedding, just normal beachgoers, but they were all sitting as far away from the rectangle as they could get. As I walked down from the parking lot, there was an accordion player, playing Parisian café music. And that Nina Simone song, "Marriage Is for Old Folks." Dressed in a tunic, and grinning in that way that priests and rabbis do. That sort of wide, wise, welcome-and-rejoice! grin.

The rectangle in the sand: someone had had the idea of giving all of the children pails and having them mark off part of the beach for the wedding by making little sand towers. Like, where you fill the pail with wet sand and turn it over and you get a mold of the pail. Between the two families there were probably twenty kids under the age of ten, and they had staked out a quarter-acre of beach. The bigger kids were convinced that if the rectangle didn't reach all the way out into the waves, then somehow uninvited guests were going to disrupt the wedding. So I walked past the accordion player, with his big smile, and then someone's daughter, in a peapod-green dress, ran up to me and said:

"If you're not with the Hanamoto-Dicochea wedding, we ask that you please use the remaining beach!" I was like:

"And what if I am with the wedding?" And she said:

"Then! You have to go through the feather gate so that you don't break the wall!"

So I walked between two pail molds that had feathers sticking out of the top. The girl said:

"If you have to leave the wedding for any reason, you have to use the feather gate to leave. And if you have to cross to the other side of the wedding, you have to use the seaweed path. And you can't step off the seaweed path once you step onto it." I was like:

"Oh!"

And then, in front of me, holding an infant, was Theresa Hanamoto. Who I hadn't seen in literally ten years. Her face was a little longer, and her hair got wavier somehow, and she had the start of those two deep wrinkles next to the mouth that their mother always had. And obviously, once you saw how they looked at each other, the bossy little girl in the peapod dress was Theresa's daughter. Theresa told her:

"I don't think Jenny needs to know all your rules, Gabi." She called me Jenny. And then she said: "Welcome to *Lord of the Flies.*" And then she put the infant she was holding into my arms, saying, "Have you met Piggy?" It was Nadine's baby, Delilah. Who was wearing this ridiculous baby-sized prom gown: bright blue, taffeta and tulle, with lace.

And, here's what I meant when I said that in California I understood the meaning of things. It was like I understood the meaning of that dress. It was something Nadine found at some secondhand store somewhere and put on the baby as a joke. I understood the meaning of Theresa not exclaiming over my appearance after ten years and not even saying hello. She had inherited that from their mom, that undemonstrative manner. And I understood that when she called Delilah Piggy, like the kid in *Lord of the Flies*, it was a weirdly tender way of showing that even after ten years of having practically abandoned the Hanamotos, I was still . . . Jenny, and I was still loved.

And, Delilah and I? We understood each other. We gave each other this look, like, We're cool. And really, Delilah was the most placid baby you've ever met. This perpetual chubby frown. It was adorable how pouty she looked. Tiny black eyes, her hair just long enough that someone got two bows into it, to make it look like pigtails. She would sit there on your hip while you bounced her, looking at you, letting her arms flop. Unless you were Nadine or Oscar, she was unimpressed with you. Theresa said:

"Nadi said you had to pull some strings with the airline to get here. But George said that you work for a company with a lot of strings." I was like:

"George? Is he here?" And little Gabi meanwhile was sort of whining:

"Mom? How come I don't get to hold Delilah?" And Theresa said to me:

"I think George is with Nadi, who's hiding in a minivan in the parking lot. It's his job to keep our mom from bitching at her. Mom's mad that there isn't a real priest for the wedding. George is good at keeping her distracted." And out of the other corner of her mouth: "Gabi, you can't hold the baby because you're a flower girl. Look, go tell those Dicochea people where to walk before they step on your walls." And then to me: "Here, I'll introduce you to the groom. Notice, by the way, how much Delilah loves her prom dress. You should see her when she's grouchy."

And, Oscar. He was a tall man, a widely built man, barefoot, in a gray suit and a pink cotton shirt, no tie. His jacket was tailored very tight for his torso and arms. Big, proud, patient. And I understood the attraction to this guy who exuded so much power and gentleness. Dressed by Nadine to look like the owner of, like, some hip Oaxacan bistro. And with a smile that's actually not that different from the priestly smile on the accordion player. By way of hello, because he'd figured out who I must be, Oscar said, as he smiled at me and reached for the baby:

"Who's got my girl?"

The baby, who is suddenly smiling, and who is now holding her plump arms up because she sees her dad.

What do you do, witnessing all this love? Like, you arrive in a rental car after ten years, and everyone loves each other, and no one needs any explanation about where you've been, they just smile at you, genuinely? What do you do? And then the accordion player started playing the processional. He followed Nadine and her father across the beach, down from the parking lot, toward the feather gate, while eight little barefoot cousins in mismatched dresses threw poppy petals at their feet. And Nadine's father had one arm looped through Nadine's arm, while with the other hand he was drying his eyes. It was the first time I'd seen my best friend in ten years.

GEORGE HANAMOTO *makes two assumptions (mid-September 2001)*:

It was definitely a nice ceremony, and it was pretty funny that the officiant was the accordion player. In all the however many weddings I have been to of b-school friends, that was something I had never seen before: the ceremony performed by the band. I talked to the accordionist afterwards, and he was just some friend of a friend of Nadi's and Oscar's who got ordained online for twenty-five bucks. No wonder our mother was so mad. Nadi told me, "George, can you please convince Mom that the accordion guy is a man of God?"

It was hard to hear their vows, though, because there was no microphone, and everyone was whispering, and the breeze was coming in pretty good off the ocean. Unless you were right up there with your ear in their faces, you weren't going to hear a thing. But they traded rings, and Nadi was crying, and my dad was crying too, so it was definitely a nice ceremony. I mean, I assume my dad had already been drinking by that point, but he was definitely a bit weepy.

In any case, just as the ceremony was starting, I saw Jennica at the back of the crowd, sort of politely standing behind all the Dicochea people. She was definitely beautiful. She had on one of those sweaters that only covers your arms and shoulders, knitted from something puffy, and a gray velvet dress. Velvet is the tufty one, right? So I went over to her, just as they were getting started, to keep her company. She didn't know who I was; she was just standing there, straining to hear. I put my hand on her back and said in her ear, "Jennica," and then she recognized my voice and smiled and put her hand behind my back, and we watched the ceremony like that, with our hands on each other's backs. So already by that point I had the sense of, you know, she might be available.

JENNICA GREEN *explains in some detail about the Nut Tree but prepares to gloss over other things (September 17, 2001):*

The Russian Valley Inn.

Probably originally it was a vineyard, and then they added the tasting room, and then they added the restaurant, and then they added the hotel, sprawling down the same dry ridge. All the buildings were done in different versions of the same Town & Country Village architecture: the low wooden roofs, the sheltered walkways, the wood paneling, the earth tones, and the lacquered river-rock walls. With all of the parking lots on different terraces, and shaped liked kidneys and croissants and curlicues, so that the redwoods and the live oaks and the random olive trees wouldn't have to be cut down.

But in the back there was the original vineyard. Which, you got the sense that at this point the vineyard was only there so the hotel would have a nice view. I mean, at the reception they were serving wine from some "sister vineyard" in Chile, so . . .

But Nadine had rented part of their patio for her reception, and the hotel had screened it off for her by making a fence out of potted fuchsias, and so we all waited there for Nadine and Oscar to finally show up, looking at the view of the vineyard and drinking the Chilean chardonnay and taking off our jackets and sweaters, since it was so much warmer on that ridge than on the beach.

Anyway, after I'd gone to my room and gotten out of my velvet, George and I went around meeting all the Dicochea cousins. Who were from, like, Modesto and Stockton and Union City and Los Baños and Gilroy, with all these professions. An airline mechanic. An administrator at a women's maximum security prison and her husband, who works for the Water Board. A speech therapist. This one woman who ran a nursery school and bred fox terriers and was an accountant, and who wanted to hear all about Mumpus and couldn't believe the business model of Practical Cats. A guy who was in purchasing for some huge agricultural conglomerate and his wife, who taught massage.

They all thought we were a couple, George and I, which, we just laughed. But they were all so enamored of us when they heard we were both from Manhattan. Like, We all support you; we want to come help; our church is having a vigil; your mayor is amazing; I was in New York once twenty years ago and it is the greatest city in the world; you have to rebuild the towers, you have to stay there, you cannot ever leave. Totally sweet, and no pretense at all.

And then Nadine arrived, in her dress, and started coming around with her baby. When she finally made it past all the Dicocheas and came to where I was, back by the fuchsias, I hardly knew what to say. I was like:

"Did you see me smile at you during the ceremony?"

"It looked like you had sand in your eye. Delilah's got sand up her butt."

"I can't believe you have a daughter. She's so . . . adorable."

"And now she's legitimate. By the way, I made sure that the band knows 'Hava Nagila.' But you have to sing it, because they don't do Hebrew and you're the only Jew. And you have to make everyone do the dance."

"The hora? I can't believe how long it's been since I've seen you, Nadine. You look beautiful."

"Do you like this place, the Russian Valley Inn? Isn't it all Nut Treed out?"

Which, I will try to explain that joke to you. To give you a sense of what that whole day was like, Nadine's wedding day. She said, "Isn't it all Nut Treed out?" And, the Nut Tree was this institution in northern California. A family-owned theme park, a rest stop off of the freeway on the way to Tahoe. In this horrible nothing town called Vacaville. It started probably in the thirties, as a fruit stand next to a . . . very large walnut tree. And then the family built a coffee stand next to the fruit stand. And then they built a restaurant next to the coffee stand. And then a bakery next to the restaurant. And then they started erecting colossal roadside totem poles with their Nut Tree logo on it. Which was a black tree with the words *Nut Tree* visible through the branches. And then, by the time my parents were taking me and Gabe to Tahoe, in the eighties, this place had a gift shop where my parents wouldn't buy us the walnut brittle, and four restaurants, and a campground with RV hookups, and a private airstrip, and water slides, and a small-gauge railroad that my parents wouldn't pay for us to ride on. Like, some sad businessman dreamed of owning his own Disneyland and built the Nut Tree instead. A walnut-based theme park. It was this joke between Nadine and me: the Nut Tree was the place where the other one was doomed to end up. She said, "Isn't this place all Nut Treed out?" which, like . . . completely captured how charming but ridiculous the Russian Valley Inn was. And how ridiculous we would have seemed to ourselves, if we could have seen at age seventeen what we would be doing at age twenty-nine. Because here we were, all Nut Treed out, but happy. And Nadine's like:

"Make sure to check out the figurines on the top of the cake." And then she was immediately distracted and talking to other guests.

NADINE HANAMOTO *recounts the funniest thing from her wedding (mid-September 2001):*

Let me tell you what a wedding is: it's the day when the two people in your life who have the least in common sit at the same table and try to have a conversation. So Jennica and George, the two New York sophisticates, sit at the same table as Una, Oscar's trashy cousin from Santa Rosa.

It was after dinner before I finally was able to sit down and talk to Jenny. And I asked her if she saw the figurines on the top of the cake, the bride and groom figurines. Jenny said, "I didn't get close enough." So I told her they were black.

She was like, "What, the figurines were black?"

"Yup. Black folks."

And Jennica says, "Really," like she's trying to decide whether or not it is hilarious, which it is. But trashy Cousin Una, who is sitting there listening, takes this ostentatious swallow of wine, to show that she thinks it is unacceptable for me and Oscar to have black figurines on our cake. And Una's daughter, Heather, who is just being a kid, says, "Aunt Nadi! I didn't see. Aunt Nadi! I didn't see."

I found the black figurines in the cake place, and I told the cake people I wanted them. The cake people were like, "Well, well, normally we reserve those for our African-American brides and grooms." Like, oh? And what do you reserve for your half-Japanese, half-Mexican brides and half-Guatemalan, half-Mexican grooms? So I asked them, "Are you saying I can't have them?" And they were like, "Well, well, consider the value of the figurines as keepsakes for your children." And I had Delilah with me, so I said, "You mean this child? She can have the figurines from my first marriage." They were scandalized.

Anyhoo, Una makes this face. Una the racist, Una who thinks it's dirty to have black people on a white cake. But little Heather still doesn't understand what's going on, because Una hasn't taught Heather to be a racist yet. So Heather says, "Aunt Nadi, I didn't see, Aunt Nadi, I didn't see."

And Una sort of tugs her on the shoulder and hisses, "Heather, shh!"

It gets better.

So Jenny asks Oscar, "Did you know about the figurines?"

And he says, "I tell you one thing I've learned: whatever makes Nadine happy. All I care about is that the cake be good. But Jennica, I hear that you're not coming to brunch tomorrow."

And Jenny gives her lame excuse: "My brother and his wife have a baby I haven't seen in a while." Classic Jenny Green: she doesn't visit us for ten years, and then when she does visit us, it's for one afternoon and she can't make it to our wedding brunch because she has to get on a plane back to illustrious New York City. That's Jenny Green.

But Oscar is trying to tempt her, saying, "There will be mimosas and ice cream waffles."

So now trashy Cousin Una has something new to be scandalized about. She says, "You're feeding the children ice cream for breakfast?"

And Heather asks, "What's a mimosa?"

And *whap!*

Right there, in front of everyone, Una just wallops Heather across the face. *Whap!* And does her hiss again: "Heather, I said to shh!"

Heather bursts into tears. Jenny looks like she is about to pass out, she's so shocked. So that's what I want a sepia picture of in my wedding album: Jenny Green fainting while trashy Cousin Una clocks her own little daughter, innocent little Cousin Heather, upside the head. Hilarious. George told Una to go get herself a glass of water, and Oscar took Heather and told her that she hadn't done anything wrong.

Okay, it gets better.

After Una leaves and while Oscar is soothing Heather, George says, "Nadi, now that I bought the apartment, you all can visit us for a change, in New York."

And Oscar immediately accepts. "I think we should visit

them, Nadi. We could take the kids to see the Statue of Liberty. And Yankee Stadium."

Then I say, because Jenny is meanwhile taking a huge swig of wine, "And I can meet Jenny's mysterious boyfriend."

But Jenny shoots me this look. Like, Don't mention my boyfriend if he isn't here. Hilarious.

Anyhoo. Later on, Oscar and I are putting the kids to bed. It was only nine o'clock, but I needed to go to sleep immediately. I sat down on the bed, and even though the duvet cover that the Russian Valley Inn had given us had the same thread count as a hair shirt, it seemed to me like the most comfortable, angel-soft, downy bower ever.

I asked Oscar, "Is anyone going to care if I go to sleep this early?" Except for Jenny, everyone was either gone already or would be at brunch the next morning. "Jenny won't hate me, right?"

Oscar was like, "I think George can keep her company okay."

So Oscar picked up on it too. Jenny Green, seducing my brother, on my wedding night!

JENNICA GREEN *glosses over other things (September 17, 2001)*:

So, after the reception.

I mean.

The dinner ended, and there was dancing, and everyone with children vanished, and then it was just George and me, at the bar there at the Russian Valley Inn, drinking lemon tonics. The Town & Country–style bar. And, we hooked up.

What more do you want to hear?

I mean, I don't remember what we were talking about. About how he ran away. Their mother caught him with pot, and he had friends in San Francisco who had a room he could stay in, so he moved out of San Jose. And he was able to find a job that paid for his rent and his car. And their dad sent him money secretly, too.

He worked his way through community college and SFSU, and then the business school at Berkeley.

About how his company was going to have to abandon one of its offices that had been next to the World Trade Center. No one at his bank died, but their building was hit by falling rubble. He was in Chicago the day it happened. So we talked about that. How he had to go shopping in San Francisco because he had no clothes to wear, because he wasn't able to make it back to New York between Chicago and the wedding. I guess we were sort of half holding hands under the bar. And then we were talking about earthquakes, and San Francisco, and the teachers we'd both had in high school. Just pointless small things.

And at some point, we started kissing. And until it happened, I didn't know it was going to happen. Really.

But, it just seemed like . . . so much the natural thing to do. And, exhilarating. To just . . . go where things led and not worry. And, too, it was like, you know this feeling? At night, after a carefree day, and a day with so much family love, and you've been drinking? And suddenly you see, like, Oh, this is where everything was headed? Oh, this is so much the thing that is supposed to happen?

And so I was like:

"Should we go up to my room?" And he was like:

"I guess we should." So we did.

So it's two in the morning. He asks me if I want him to stay or go, which is sweet. And I said I just wanted to be alone and think, which, I'm not sure what I wanted to think about. Everything seemed so without consequence, what happened one moment to the next. I was still so . . . free from anxiety. And getting a little tired. He left and went to his room, and then a minute later called me on my in-room phone and was like, "Hey, since I won't see you at brunch, how about if I call you at work on Wednesday at three." Which I sort of liked. I mean, knowing exactly when he'll call.

And then I turned on my cell phone for the first time that day. Arnie had called twice, and my parents had called twice, and my brother. And I turned on my BlackBerry and it was like . . . eight screens' worth of new messages. Everyone at work in a panic over like, vacation time and sick leave and new security policies. I mean, you saw my list of forty-six things. So by two-thirty in the morning I was stressed out again. It began to sink in that there would be consequences. There would be . . . consequences.

GABRIEL GREEN *tallies his grains (mid-September 2001)*:

Well, Jennica had brunch with us in Santa Cruz on Sunday, the morning after the wedding, and . . . something was wrong.

She had stayed up in Sonoma on Saturday night and was taking a red-eye from San Francisco on Sunday night, but in between she drove down here to Santa Cruz, to see Simon. It's great. Because of Simon, people always volunteer to come visit us. Jennica came out for ten days in May, a couple weeks after Simon was born, and she came out for some random weekend in July, and now she was back. And these days, when she calls me at work, what she says is, "Gabe, I need a baby update." I tell her, "His new habit is banging his head on the floor." And then Jennica goes on the Internet and finds a complete pediatric assessment of infant head-banging for us. Like I said, it's great.

But since she was driving all the way down from Sonoma just to see us for a few hours, I told her I would make her my special french toast for brunch, because it's so delicious and wholesome and extreme. I make the bread myself, with multiple whole grains. Rachel and I got a grain mill from our wedding registry, and lately I've been grinding up a blend of mainly wheat berries, plus corn, barley, millet, and quinoa, and buckwheat. I use that blend to make the starter, and then I knead in some oats and flax seeds, so that's eight grains right there. It's tricky to bake it in our oven, but if I use two bread stones, one on the rack above and one on the rack below, then I can keep the heat steady even if I open the oven door to spray the loaf. When the bread is done and cooling on the rack, the whole house smells mouth-watering.

Then, Sunday morning, before Jennica came over, I cut the bread up into slices and let them soak in a blend of eggs and rice milk and soy milk. The rice in the rice milk is the ninth grain, if you want to keep count, and soy is a bean, but let's call it the tenth grain. I let the bread soak up all that fat and sugar, and then, when Jennica actually got here, I fried the slices on our cast-iron skillet, in organic butter. That's french toast for you. Ten-grain french toast, served with whipped butter and fresh fruit. I bought some *amazing* peaches at the farmers' market on Saturday, which I stewed, and I bought some blackberries too. I have no idea where the blackberries came from this late in the year, but who cares; if they came from *New Zealand* I would still buy them, they were so ripe and so fresh. I just washed them, put them into a jar, added a little bit of sugar to draw out the juice, and then I shook the jar like crazy. It made this sweet, thick, pure blackberry puree.

Jennica didn't eat any of it.

The bread, after you fry it, has this texture, with the crumb of the bread holding little pockets of the fried butter, and little crispy blackened corners where the oats and the flax seeds sat right on the hot skillet . . . and the whipped butter melts to foamy white . . . and then, when you pour the blackberry juice over it . . . oh, *man.* But Jennica wouldn't eat any of it.

Fresh coffee, fresh-squeezed orange juice, poached organic eggs with a little pepper, organic honeydew on the side. Some goat's-milk yogurt to mix with the leftover blackberries. Jennica wouldn't eat any of it. She drank the orange juice, but otherwise, she said she wasn't hungry. Jennica is normally the poached egg champion and the french toast champion. Something was wrong.

I mean, when the three of us are together, Rachel and Jennica team up against me. But, for example, during brunch Jennica was asking about Simon's head-banging, which is disconcerting but supposedly normal. When he's on his back, he likes to lift his head up and then let it drop back down, over and over, so that it knocks against the floor. We'd read about it in one of our books, it's within the bounds of normal infant behavior at five months, but still, it definitely had us concerned the first time he did it. And as we were sitting there, out on the deck with the french toast, Jennica asked about it. And Rachel said, "*I* think it's because Simon is teething, but *Gabe* thinks it's because it's enjoyable." Basically inviting Jennica to team up against me and tell me I am wrong. But all Jennica said was, "Hmm."

I said, "Hey, I admit that teething is a *possible explanation.* But I tried it myself, I lay on the mattress and tried banging my head up and down, and it *is* enjoyable. So that's another *possible explanation.*" And Jennica said, "Hmm." I mean, I was practically begging her to make fun of me, and all she said was, "Hmm."

I said, "And a *third* possible explanation is that head-banging is genetic, because according to Mom, I used to do it too." Rachel said, "Do you remember Gabe doing that, Jennica?" And Jennica said, "No." No? Jennica declining an opportunity to talk about being my big sister? Declining an opportunity to invent things I did as a baby in order to tease me? So *maybe* she was just tired, *maybe* she was just hung over . . .

And then there was this moment. After brunch, Jennica and I took Simon for a walk in his sling thing, up to Natural Bridges and back, along the water, past the lighthouse, so Rachel could get some work done. We were out past the lighthouse, talking about nothing in particular. Global warming, buying houses, hippies. And I said . . . all I said was, "So Mom called us last night to say they made it back from Massachusetts. She said they adore Arnie. She said, 'It looks like Jennica finally found the right man. But I guess her kids will be taller than yours.'"

A ridiculous Mom comment, right? That was all I said.

Except Jennica doesn't respond, and then I realize she's crying. So I stop, and I ask her if she's okay, and she says, "I don't want to talk about it."

And she keeps walking. I say, "Jennica, what's going on?"

And she says, "Gabe, I do not want to talk about it."

And so we keep walking. For a while she's quiet, and then she starts talking about looking for a job at a nonprofit, maybe in the arts or in environmentalism, finding work that's closer to her passions. Meaning, she changes the subject. But she's still crying. And of course the people we are passing on the sidewalk see the baby, so they think Jennica and I are married and that I am a horrible husband, making my wife cry. And I guess it was true. I had made my big sister cry.

After Jennica left for the airport that night, the first thing Rachel said was, "Do you think she's doing okay?" And that was just based on how Jennica looked at brunch. I said, "I don't know." Because Jennica does not deal by crying. If she's angry at you, she argues with you; if she's angry at someone else, she will explain to you why she's the one who's right and the other person is the one who's wrong; if she's worried or stressed, she makes lists, or she reinvests her 401(k) and then writes you an e-mail bragging about how well diversified she is. But she doesn't deal by crying. Crying isn't *productive,* and Jennica is all about productivity. I told Rachel about what happened when we were out by the lighthouse, and Rachel's theory was, "Maybe she's really scared about terrorism." It's a *theory,* but I think Jennica would have been willing to talk about that. And she did talk about it; we talked all about what's happening in New York.

It makes me feel . . .

I mean, if Jennica is crying, in front of me? Whatever it is that's happening to her, it must be awful.

JENNICA GREEN *considers whether to have an epiphany (September 17, 2001)*:

You do feel like you need to have an epiphany when you go on a weekend trip. Because otherwise, it's like, you scurry past the scrappy baggage claim at JFK; you've been in New York for less than two minutes, but already the city feels scrappy and already you're doing the scurry; you spill yourself into a taxi; you sit in whatever traffic debacle is happening on the Van Wyck Expressway; you are . . . affronted for the umpteenth time by that dreary roadside lake in Queens, and the hopeless brick yeshivas and apartment towers, and the cemeteries where your grandparents are buried . . .

And it's like you just spent however many hundreds of dollars to be at yet another wedding; your stomach is gassy and your nails are dirty and your ears haven't popped . . . And it's like you have less insight into how to lead your life than do the people in the old *New Yorker* that you just read on the plane. Not to mention that you have to enter Manhattan over a bridge that's being surveilled by armed National Guardsmen.

MAYNARD GOGARTY *recounts a different argument (September 17, 2001):*

So—.

I was back from Logan Airport by eight or so on Saturday morning, Saturday the fifteenth. There was time for one fried egg on a buttered English muffin before I had to drive Susan and Mitchell down to peaceful Hartford, Connecticut. They had strung a paper chain of flights home, via Hartford and Chicago and San Francisco—perhaps Denver too; I don't recall. So—I spent another few hours in the car, driving back and forth to Hartford, slowing down wherever the Connecticut National Guard had thrown up security checkpoints in order to stare at the resulting traffic jams. Susan asking, pointedly, whether everything was all right with Jennica the night before, Mitchell remarking, equally pointedly, on the vulnerability of the turnpike to terrorist attack.

With the consequence that by noon on Saturday I had spent hours in the car alone, driving back first from Boston and then from Hartford, and had heard hours of—talk radio. One woman—this was on a station in Connecticut—called up to share her vision of heaven. It was a religious program, religious talk, and the host was enthusiastic to hear from an "amateur angelologist." He said, "The Lord's visions come to the devout of all stations." It took me a moment to figure out what he meant by "stations." In this woman's vision of heaven, when the dead firemen from the Twin Towers crossed the rainbow bridge into the afterlife, they were met by little Dalmatian puppies that Lord Jesus saves in a kennel in the clouds. The spirits of the most loving little Dalmatian puppies that ever lived—angelic puppies, with little Dalmatian spots on their little angel wings. It is the job of these little angel Dalmatian puppies to run halfway across the rainbow bridge and greet the newly arrived souls of fallen firefighter heroes and lick the soot from their faces with their puppy kisses.

It choked me up—! This woman's pure, maudlin despair. No restraint! Over the radio! For every one of her neighbors to hear! When the Connecticut National Guard waved me through on my way back to the cabin, they saw a miserable man. Jennica had confessed her sorrow to me in the middle of the night, and I had lashed out at her, whom I love. But when Wendy from Windsor—or Cathy from Canton or whoever she was—called in to this AM talk-radio program with her angels and her puppies, I choked up. So by noon on Saturday, my remorse about what I'd said to Jennica was—.

Jennica had gotten out of the car at Logan Airport in Boston in such a fury. And now she still hasn't called me.

This business about sinking yourself in love up to the hilt? It is grim.

May I please start over?

On Saturday night it was just we three Gogartys—Gran Rose and my mother and I—at the cabin. We ate dinner at the formal dining table that night, by candlelight, having gotten into the habit when the Greens were still with us. Outside, down at the pond, the crickets and frogs were engaged in a clash of civilizations.

What the FROGS *and the* CRICKETS *were each insisting upon (mid-September 2001):*

FROGS: Knee-deep.
CRICKETS: Thigh-high, thigh-high, thigh-high, thigh-high.

MAYNARD GOGARTY *recounts a different argument (September 17, 2001):*

One never knows what is for dinner when one shops at the co-op. That night I concocted a curry—a lamb and sweet corn curry, with lemon spinach and rice. And to start, a poor man's arugula-pear-walnut-goat-cheese salad, where I was obliged to substitute iceberg lettuce, Granny Smith apples, almonds, and blue cheese dressing for the arugula, pears, walnuts, and goat cheese. Still, it all came out zesty and went well with the local beer. Cooking is one thing I can do about which Gran Rose has no vocal complaints; she makes faces, but she gobbles my dishes up. And while she is eating my meals, she says things like, "You know what I don't understand, Manny? Why it is, if your movie played in such a whoopee-do festival, that nothing came of it, not a thing."

"Sundance?"

"The one that involved Robert Redford. And not a thing came of it."

It is not easy to talk about dashed hopes with your own grandmother, especially when she chews with her mouth open and talks with her mouth full, as I am abashed to admit my grandmother does. Still, I tried to give an honest answer, because I was feeling so—chastened after the fight with Jennica.

"I wouldn't say nothing came of Sundance, Gran. My film played in other festivals as well—and I suspect that its success in festivals is in part because of the attention it got when it opened at Sundance. It played in Seattle and Chicago. New Delhi. Hong Kong. South by Southwest! And all the little ones. It's playing this week somewhere in Antwerp, I believe. And next month in Fairbanks, and—one other. Lansing!"

"And not one of these wonderful engagements that you were so clever to arrange for your movie, not one of them paid you half a Canadian dime."

"Short films are not the same as feature films. If you win an audience prize, sometimes you get a few hundred dollars."

"So you made no money from this movie of yours, just as you made no money on the previous one, and you made no connections. And now you have nothing but a job teaching music at Chatham, the same job that you left five years ago."

Did I mention that she dressed for dinner? With pearls and lipstick? She brought two suitcases with her from New York, with half a dozen outfits, all of them—all of them—either Chanel or Oscar de la Renta. Thursday night she wore her queen-bee outfit: a matching yellow top and bottom with black fur cuffs and seams. Friday, a white pantsuit inspired by Nehru. Sunday, when we were heading back into the city, a black dress, complete with decorative cape and cowl, and a gold dragonfly brooch, with wings of smoked glass. For dinner on Saturday—while she relished my curry—she wore a red turtleneck sweater, tight beige stretch pants, and a thick black belt. She probably would have worn the queen-bee outfit if she had known how well it would have matched the curry on her tongue. Nonetheless.

I asked her, "Were you hoping that by now I would be directing blockbusters, Gran?"

"I was hoping for something I could boil in a pot and eat. Someone gives you an opportunity, and you splash it on your rear like it's free perfume."

"Gran, whatever you may think, I'm hardly profligate. Having one short art film play at Sundance and not becoming famous is not the equivalent of inheriting a transcendent fortune and squandering it on snuff. Having a short film play at Sundance is more like—winning the blue ribbon at the state fair for your russet potato. Or for your—pet hinny. Sure, it's a wondrous spud! Sure, it is an outstanding—sterile ungulate! Still, your blue ribbon isn't going to get you into college. At least, not Stanford or Yale."

Gran Rose wanted to know "Just how much money did you spend making your movie?" but then my mother said, "Oh, Rose, it wasn't about the money for him." Me, though, I was ready to brawl; if nothing else, Jennica and her parents had shown me how it's done. I said, "Gran, to answer your question, I spent *plenty* making the movie." But my mother had learned something from the Greens too, and so she persisted: "It wasn't about the money, Rose, and that's why Manny's gone back to teaching at Chatham! Right, Manny?"

"Ever the optimist, Mother."

"What's wrong with optimism?"

"Mother, your brand of optimism is so—hopeless! Tell me, do you remember our lunch at Phoebe's?"

"This was the lunch, Rose, when Manny told me about Jennica for the first time, though he wouldn't tell me her name."

"And may I add, Gran, that but for my film, which you are so quick to disparage, Jennica and I would never have met."

Gran Rose said, "If that film is what impressed Jennica about you, then I advise you to hurry up and marry her before she has the sense to find another fellow."

So—enough was enough. I decided to explain, absolutely, for the two women who raised me, how I think about myself. I put my fork down, I drank one swig of beer, and I said, "Gran, the lunch at Phoebe's—this was the lunch when I tried to explain the following: That the proper aesthetic relationship between an individual of insufficient talent and his art is not a creative one—my mistake, at the forgivable age of ten or twelve—but an appreciative one. And that while I labored in error—the silly, unexamined error of a child of ten or twelve—for, say, twenty years, and while those years are lost, I don't regret them, and am now happy to be able to listen to, say, the first movement of Debussy's *La Mer* with only awe, and not with envy or regret. And that this generosity of aesthetic sprit extends for me into the realm of the moral, the day-to-day, the pedestrian, the unaesthetic, as well. And that as I resign myself to simply listening to Debussy, so too I want to stop demanding behavior—more tasteful, more stoic, loftier, and more dignified behavior—from my companions in life, and start simply enjoying whatever company their—company provides. And thus it is not with sorrow but with satisfaction that I want to lay aside my struggles and—be nice."

My mother said, "I have no idea what you're trying to say."

And Rose said, "He's saying he's a lazy fool, is what he's saying."

"Gran, is it possible that I am not a lazy fool?"

My mother, naturally, hoping to intercede, said, "Manny—."

But Rose, who was now swishing a mouthful of beer together with a mouthful of spinach, said, "Well, you seldom do anything contrary to being a lazy fool."

"And you thought my father was a lazy fool too?"

"No, Scotty was not a fool. Just lazy."

"Is it possible that neither of us is a fool, neither me nor my father, and that we simply feel subject to imperatives, the existence of which you refuse to acknowledge?"

"Listen to yourself. You talk like a lazy fool. And if you mean to imply that I don't have taste in music, unlike Scotty and supposedly unlike you, you are sorely mistaken, young man. If you aren't a lazy fool, how about making some money? Tell me that."

"Yes, Gran, money! Let's talk about money!"

My mother said, "Manny—" but Rose was not deterred, and neither was I. Rose wanted to know, "How old are you, and you had to go begging back to Chatham last winter, after you met this Jennica, for them to give you your last job back?"

I clapped my hand on the table, I made the silverware jump, and—"Rose, who owns my apartment?"

A pause. Outside—crickets, frogs. Rose said, "Oh, for pity's sake."

My mother was staring at me, I was staring at Rose, and Rose was staring at her plate. Rose chewed some lamb, mouth closed.

Crickets, frogs. She took another forkful of lamb and chewed that, mouth closed. She drank some beer. Crickets, frogs—owl. Rose looked up and saw that both my mother and I were waiting for her answer.

She said, "What is amazing to me is that it's taken you this long to find out." In other words, she was at peace with her own duplicity and was irked only by my tardiness in unearthing it. But then I had one of my—inspirations.

I said, "In fact, I've known for nearly ten years that you bought me the apartment." A brave lie, but a clever one. "I simply kept quiet out of curiosity as to how long, and for what reason, you wanted to deceive me. So, Gran—for what reason did you want to deceive me?"

She said, "Some gratitude. Jack and I bought you an apartment, and in thanks you accuse me of deceit."

"Gran, if you believe I have been ungrateful, I will instantly sign a deed conveying title back to you. In exchange, however, I would ask for one honest and unreserved compliment for either one of my films. And—an accounting of my rent payments."

I had spoken like a man who knows his business, and she was looking at me with—teary affection. She said, "Now you sound like Scotty." It was a sudden and loving concession. I had won my grandmother's small respect—until I lost it again mere hours later, when Ana arrived at the cabin to—force her perceived advantage.

DAVID FOWLER *hands it to Maynard Gogarty (late September 2001)*:

Calls me on my cell that Saturday night, the Saturday after September eleventh. It was after Becky and I had put the kids to bed. Becky was doing her puzzle, I was doing my fantasy league. Late, is the point. It was the first day when we had managed to avoid looking at the news on TV. Becky had been having trouble sleeping all that week. She would wake up in the middle of the night and not be able to fall back asleep. I'd hear her in the kitchen at three A.M., scrubbing the inside of the cabinets, cleaning behind the knobs on the stove, chipping the wax off all the candlesticks. Not an easy week.

Saturday night, my cell phone rings, it's Gogarty. Whose cemetery desecration case was not going so well, and who I had spoken with just a few days before. I assumed he was worried about his next court appearance and needed to talk, but no, what he says is, "Ana has gone missing."

It takes a minute for me to remember who Ana is. But then it comes to me: Ana, the maniac; Ana, who was the reason Gogarty needed a divorce lawyer.

"What do you mean, missing?" And Becky looks at me across the room like I am the grim reaper. The word *missing* was not a word to say within earshot of your wife that week.

"Ana had space on the ninety-first floor of one of the towers. And I haven't been able to reach her."

I say, "Oh, shit." It comes out inadvertently, but Becky hears the shock in my voice, and then she really is frightened. Gogarty, however, is chillingly indifferent. It can be unnerving, his sangfroid.

He says, "Well—perhaps she will—turn up. You know how Ana is. It's not as though I'd heard from her for a while anyway, except about the divorce."

"Have you called the police? Or anyone?"

"I haven't. Somehow I feel it isn't my role."

So we talk about that for a bit. And I'm trying to be comforting, but he doesn't seem to need it. Because apparently this still isn't why Gogarty has called me.

He says, "Listen, David, a twist has come up," and he launches into a story about his apartment. His grandmother bought it in the eighties sometime, it's being held in a trust, along with the money Gogarty's been paying in rent for the last fifteen years, and on and on. Until finally I say, "Gogarty, Gogarty, this is all fascinating about your apartment. But maybe you need to be calling the police department, about Ana?"

And he says, "But David, assuming she's not missing, and—

assuming I own the apartment because my grandmother bought it for me in the eighties, then—Ana would get half the apartment when we got the divorce, right?"

Does sangfroid even go that far? It was beyond sangfroid! It was beyond the pale! So I let Gogarty have it. I tell him that he's without a human heart. I tell him, who is he to call me in the middle of the night, worrying about money he didn't even know he had, when his wife—his wife, for fuck's sake—is missing in the World Trade Center collapse? Then he tells me to stay calm. Me! I was about to hang up on him for that. I was furious. I was furious because now Becky had left the room and I could hear that she was in the kitchen, watching CNN.

But then Gogarty unpins his grenade. "Listen for one more minute, David, please? You know how my grandmother is with money, how very exacting she is. She and I were talking, and it turns out that the amount I've been paying in rent for the last ten years is not the same as the amount Gran Rose has been receiving, in trust, for me."

"I didn't follow that, Gogarty."

"Listen. There is only one thing that could have happened to the difference between what I have paid and what Gran Rose has received. Our friend Sal the Super has been pocketing it."

I have got to hand it to Gogarty. Not one half as dense as he seems. He should have been a lawyer.

I say, "I see where you're going with this, and I like it."

MAYNARD GOGARTY *brings us up to date (September 17, 2001)*:

And then, Sunday morning, Ana came to the cabin, thus—ah—bringing things to a head, shall we say?

And now it is seven on Monday evening. Jennica left a message for me on my cell phone at around ten this morning, which is a time of day when she knows I can't answer any calls, because I'm in class, with students. Shall I play her message for you? Note the bald lie. Note also that there is no mention of the collar for Mumpus the Grumpus. How do I feel? I feel like vomiting.

JENNICA GREEN *returns Arnie's calls (September 17, 2001)*:

Hey. I'm back.

We need to talk.

But not tonight, because I'll be too tired. I'll come over tomorrow, after work.

Sorry I didn't call. My phone wasn't working.

All right, bye.

PUPPY JONES *explains the circumstances preceding his arrest (early November 2001)*:

Now, I am not an egotistical man. I am not an egomaniacal man. I am not all about *me*, is what I'm saying. But nigga open a fortune cookie and it say, *You die tonight, nigga!*, nigga's keepin' that fortune in nigga's wallet. I am a humble man, despite the clippings I keep, is what I'm saying. So here we go. Three clippings from your op-ed pages.

> Puppy Jones [. . .] is emblematic of the smug elites who came to dominate American popular culture before September 11: self-promoting, self-referential, self-satisfied, and utterly disconnected both from the real emotional life of America and from the real challenges of an increasingly violent world.

Ouch! Jones!

> After the tragedy of September 11, America has no patience for the stylish irony, the sarcastic posturing, and the relativistic post-post-postmodernism of such performers as [. . .] Puppy Jones.

Wow! Jones!

> It is strange to think back now on what we were concerned about just two months ago. Remember when deciphering

> the lyrics of that Puppy Jones single seemed like an important task for teenagers nationwide? If only we had put them to work learning Arabic instead.

Scapegoat Jones! High-tech lynching of a black man, is what I'm saying.

Because, as the ad said, "Puppy's debut album will appear in stores nationwide, Tuesday, September 11."

It tanked, is what I'm saying. The supertanker tanked. Puppy Jones's debut full-length, *Puppy Valdez, Supertanker,* tanked. I entertain the possibility that it was shite. I entertain the possibility that my debut album was shite. But in addition to the shite factor, there was another, distinct factor, an independent variable, is what I'm saying. And that independent variable was that somehow, on September twelfth, every newspaper in America agreed that buying the new Puppy Jones full-length was equivalent to treason. Scapegoat Jones.

By mid-October my calendar was clear. By mid-October I was not entertaining. By mid-October it was hard to find entertainment in New York City at all. But our hero, the Puppy Person, knew where to look, and our hero brought along his own supply of rocket fuel.

And so it was that upon a certain Saturday night in October of 2001, our hero found himself at a certain club on Coney Island. This is not according to your po-lice, this is according to me. Dudes lining up at the toilet stalls to go smoke a pipe of rocket fuel. Women at the bar pulling little tubes of rocket fuel out of the linings of their purses. And certain things were said at this club. Certain things were said about the prospects of our hero. Certain words were directed at our hero over the course of the night and the morning. Certain looks were directed.

And so it was that at approximately eleven in the morning on a certain Sunday in October of 2001, our hero, Puppy Jones, found himself parked in Coney Island, feeling like his rocket was in the air but his countdown was still descending, if you see what I'm saying. Our hero's countdown was getting down below zero. At around eleven in the morning on this certain Sunday, our hero's countdown had reached about negative seven.

I should mention that our hero was driving his Roadster that morning, his 1957 Jaguar XK140 Roadster. This is a beautiful vehicle, with the three-month-old tan leather interior, with the twin angled tailpipes, with the split front fender, is what I'm saying. And I should mention that our hero had a weapon in his Roadster. A .357 Magnum, Colt Python, six-inch barrel, nickel-plated, factory-engraved, ivory grips. This is a beautiful weapon, is what I'm saying.

Our hero was sitting in his Roadster across from the aquarium in Coney Island, listening to the radio. Listening to public radio. Listening to WNYC, because it is one station where there is no risk of hearing any hip-hop. Also, our hero was listening to WNYC because he is a member. Fifty dollars a year, because our hero believes in giving back. Our hero was sitting in his Roadster, feeling like negative seven might be the perfect state of mind to defeat Puzzle Master Will Shortz.

But instead of the puzzle master being on WNYC, what was on was the local program, that New York City program, the one for rich folks who like to listen to stories about poor folks, *The Next Big Thing.* This week they had a September eleventh special. They had set up a table in Union Square on September thirteenth, with a sign saying WHAT'S ON YOUR MIND? and they had recorded the stories that people told them. The stories the poor niggas had about September eleventh, you understand? And they were broadcasting these stories now, on a certain Sunday morning in October, for the rich niggas who are members of WNYC.

But there was one story they broadcast that was not true. WNYC had asked an old woman "What's on your mind?" and the old woman had told them an obvious lie. "I walked in while others ran out," she said. Anyone could have told you, this woman was not walking into anywhere. Even Puppy Jones, out there in Coney Island in his Roadster, at negative seven in his countdown, could tell you that this old woman was lying. Except somehow the editors at WNYC could not hear it.

The editors at WNYC were unaware, is what I am saying. And so our hero was thinking, How come WNYC broadcasts the lies of an old woman but not the truth about Puppy Jones? Puppy Jones, who only ever told the truth, with no self-satisfaction, with no self-promotion, with no self-reference, with no disconnect, with no stylish irony, with no sarcastic posturing, with no relativistic post-post-postmodernism? Puppy Jones, who is a fully paid member of WNYC? I believe what I said to WNYC was, "Who is this bullshit master?"

I reached negative ten, is what I'm saying. And then I looked out the window of my Roadster, and I saw that I had some company. About ten of them, strutting along the park across from the aquarium. Coming toward me, on foot. So I took my weapon out of its case and I exited my vehicle. But this now is according to your po-lice.

DAVID FOWLER *speaks from somewhere other than the courthouse steps (early November 2001)*:

Go ahead and guess. Go ahead and guess who calls me to be their lawyer, and guess how they got my name. Go ahead and guess. And since when did I start doing these criminal cases anyway?

Speaking of which, Gogarty's cemetery desecration case. After he and I talked that Saturday night, I looked into it. I called his grandmother's lawyer and got the trust statements. I got Gogarty to give me his bank statements. And I laid it all out on the table and started comparing the figures. And sure enough, there it was: Sal the Super had siphoned money right off the top. A few hundred dollars every month, for upwards of ten years. Gogarty would pay a rent check to Sal the Super, and then Sal would pay most of it to the trust that owns the apartment and pocket the difference.

This was good stuff, and so I called the shithead assistant DA who's in charge of Gogarty's case to tell him about it. This assistant had heard our story before, because we had filed a whole round of briefs to suppress the evidence from his illegal search warrant. For half a year I'd been calling this assistant and saying, "Look, you've got the wrong guy. Sal the Super is the ringleader here, half the building was in on the plan to kill those trees, my client is a fall guy. Let's work a deal so you can get the big fish." The shithead assistant just stonewalled me.

But now I finally had some good stuff on Sal the Super, and so I called the assistant to make a proffer of the evidence. Suddenly the assistant was interested. Maybe he was now under pressure to clear his cases, focus on terrorism, who knows? Long and short, within two days the assistant was calling me back to cut a deal. If Gogarty testifies against Sal the Super, we can plead Gogarty out on an infraction, which is great, because anything more than an infraction and Gogarty will lose his job at the school. But an infraction is nothing.

So while all this is going on with Gogarty's case, I get a telephone call. From the German psychopathic ex-girlfriend-cum-ex-wife, Ana Kaganova. She says, "I got your telephone number from our mutual friend Maynard Gogarty. I think we met once." Yes, Ana, we met once.

I tell her on the phone, "We were worried about you, Ana. Gogarty said you were missing."

She says, "No, I was not."

Why is she calling? Oh, she's been arrested and is about to get arraigned, in Brooklyn. Gogarty got arrested for killing a tree to get a better view, right? Fine, that's one crime I can understand committing. You want to guess what Ana did? It was probably Gogarty's idea too, come to think of it.

She's being arraigned in Brooklyn. She was arrested in Manhattan, but they drove her over to Brooklyn to be arraigned, because Centre Street is in the midst of all that World Trade Center mess. I get to the courthouse, over by Borough Hall, and in front of the courthouse are cameramen, TV crews, the whole bit. My first thought is, Bomb scare. And my second thought is, Anthrax. And my third thought is, Ana is a celebrity, she's more famous as a photographer than I knew, and I am going to have to speak on TV from the courthouse steps after she's arraigned.

I get into the arraignments room. There is more press inside, the print journalists. I ask one of them, What's the big story? He says, "We don't have any details yet, but Puppy Jones just got arrested on a firearms charge."

Puppy Jones, Gogarty's nemesis. Half the reason I've been doing all this free work for Gogarty is guilt over that stupid Puppy Jones contract that I told Gogarty to sign. Couple thousand dollars of free representation is the least I can do to make up for it. So this is a nice moment to be witnessing. This kid, Puppy Jones, is the official national symbol of pre–September eleventh decadence, and now he's been arrested on firearms charges. Although, tell you the truth, I liked that song of his. It was very catchy.

And while I am waiting for Ana to come into the dock, Puppy Jones is arraigned. They read the counts, a whole string of firearms charges, pretty serious stuff. Possession too. Apparently this idiot, Puppy Jones, was carrying felony amounts of cocaine in his Jaguar when he was arrested.

Me and the entire press corps are leaning forward in our seats to hear exactly what the DA will say. And then it comes out. Apparently Puppy Jones, after a night of some heavy partying, pulled an unregistered .357 Magnum out of the glove compartment of his classic Jaguar and attacked a flock of Coney Island seagulls. Fired all six rounds, reloaded, and still he didn't hit a single bird.

ANA KAGANOVA *explains some of the circumstances preceding her arrest (early November 2001):*

Tja, thank God that I am an American citizen, otherwise they now are deporting me as an enemy of the republic, to Israel.

I will tell you, the easiest thing was to get a new cell phone to replace the one I threw in the pond. I told the telephone company that I have lost my phone in the World Trade Center, and so I got a phone for free, and it was a camera phone. And I tell you the hardest thing. This was when I used for the first time my new camera phone to check my messages, after this week in the underground in Massachusetts. My mother left seven messages for me. Who are these people who need so much comfort? It exhausts me. "Where were you, Ana? Why didn't you call me sooner? I was so worried. I thought you were dead." Oh, grow up and be a tough cookie. I told my mother, "This is bullshit, that you thought that I was dead. If you thought that I was dead, why did you put seven messages on my voice mail?"

Hano is the only one who thinks straight. He and I have applied for a small business grant. We lost, after all, our space. We think that maybe we shall go into business as interior designers, and why not, if the Congress has for us, as small business men and women, the money?

So, I tell you the last conversation I had with Gogi.

When I still was underground and had the plan to play dead, I decided I would make Gogi choose, yes or no, whether or not to play along and pretend with me that I was a victim in the collapse of Tower One. I drove to the cabin, and I found him there. I told him to call the police while I stood there in front of him and report that Ana Kaganova was missing. If he did not, I would then tell his family and his girlfriend that I was his wife, and I would then demand half the apartment. This, however, did not impress him very much. He said that he would not anymore play along. He gave me back my ATM card, and he told me that he spoke to his lawyer and I will not get half of this apartment because of this trust that his grandmother created.

He said, "You may want to consult your own lawyer, Ana, but I believe that you will find that my lawyer is correct, and that the apartment is mine alone. Naturally, if you contact your lawyer to confirm this, you will no longer be able to pretend that you were killed in the World Trade Center. But that is your choice."

And that was somewhat true. But then at this moment the

woman who must be his mother appears in the background, and so it is my last opportunity to make Gogi do what I want him to do.

JOAN TATE *recounts a conversation (mid-September 2001)*:

Well, on Sunday morning, as we were packing things together to go back to the city, a woman drove up and parked in the driveway. She looked like she was in a hurry, the way she rolled her car to a stop up against the hedges. I was folding sheets out by the washer and drier and watched her through the little window in the pantry. She walked up to the screen door at the back of the kitchen, which is not the door that you would go to in the normal course of—not the door you would go to if you had just pulled up in the driveway for the first time and had never been inside the cabin before. She was wearing sunglasses and a scarf, though she was not exactly a Jackie Kennedy.

Manny was washing dishes in the kitchen, so I let him answer the door. But when I was done with the sheets, he was still talking to the woman, so I went to see who it was. And Manny was standing there, holding the screen open but not inviting the woman in.

I said, "Who is it, Manny?"

And he said, "Ah—no one, Mother!" But the woman he was talking to seemed very eager to say something to me.

She said, "You are the mother, and I am the woman who waters the plants."

I said, "Oh! Do you always come on Sundays? I think we've gotten everything pretty well watered." I am probably not paraphrasing exactly—not quoting exactly. In any event, Rose walked into the kitchen at that point too, and she also wanted to know who was there.

I said, "It's the woman who waters your plants, Rose."

Rose took one look at the woman and said, "Who, her? She doesn't water my plants."

And then Manny said, as if he were making a joke, though I

guess I didn't get it, "But if she isn't the woman who waters the plants, then who is she?"

To which the woman replied, "You really want me to tell them then I am who I am, Gogi? So, in this case"—and she took off her scarf for dramatic effect, but not her sunglasses—"I am Maynard's wife."

Rose cannot be flapped. She is unflappable. When the woman had stopped shaking out her hair and had straightened her sunglasses again, Rose told her, "You married Manny? *That* doesn't improve my opinion of you." And Rose left the kitchen to go about her business.

Well, the woman at the door was not so unflappable—she didn't seem to know quite what she wanted to say to me. Something along the lines of, "You are my mother-in-law. My name is Ana."

And only then did Manny say, "Ana and I were married for the sake of a visa, Mother, once upon a time."

I said, "Oh! Are you an Italian?"

And Ana said, "Never!"

Manny said, "I'll explain everything later, Mother."

And I said, "Yes, I'm sure you will, Manny." But Ana clearly was—clearly had taken umbrage at the idea of being Italian, so I tried to explain what I was thinking. I said, "It's just that Manny had all those visa problems when he lived in Genoa, so I thought you must be Italian. And some northern Italians are just as fair-skinned as you are. It surprised me so much to see all those Italian blondes, I never would have guessed. Where are you from?"

She said, with her funny accent, "The Upper East Side."

Manny said, "I will explain everything later, Mother." Well, he was trying to get rid of me.

I said, "Ana, would you like some custard? We're just cleaning out the fridge, and Manny made some wonderful custards the other day from real vanilla."

"No, Ana was just leaving, Mother."

"Don't be rude, Manny. I'm happy to give her some custard that's otherwise going to go to the ducks."

"No, Ana was just leaving, Mother."

Obviously he didn't want me there, so I left, but I told him, "Don't think Jennica and I won't be holding an inquisition"—no—"holding an inquest about this wife of yours." And Manny did explain it to me later, and I suppose it goes to show that at least as far as girlfriends go, he's come quite some way.

ANA KAGANOVA *explains the rest of the circumstances preceding her arrest (early November 2001):*

His mother was not interested in a meeting with her daughter-in-law. And the cat was coming out of the bag, so to speak, that I was alive, and so this was the end of the possibility of a life underground for me. Gogi said, when his mother was gone, "Apparently my own family's expectations of me are so low that not even a secret marriage surprises them. Thank you, however, for telling me that I own the apartment, Ana. David Fowler has found a way to make that fact very useful in my criminal case."

And so this is how I remembered David Fowler when I was arrested, which I will explain.

I was in 1990 and 1991 in Berlin, and I saw what people did with the *Mauerstücke,* the pieces of the Berlin Wall. The street vendors forged certificates of authenticity and sold the *Mauerstücke* to the American tourists as souvenirs. Why should it here and now be so different, with the American tourists in New York in 2001? So while Hano and I waited for the small business money, I decided that I could make the quick buck, *weiß' du,* with baggies of dust for sale to the tourists, with certificates of authenticity to prove that the dust is coming from the World Trade Center. This is what I am up to at the time of my arrest.

At first the policeman wanted only to give me a ticket for vending without a license. I told him that it was bullshit, that he should look at the old woman who was right next to me, who was vending her poems about the World Trade Center and who did not have a license. He said that she had First Amendment rights. I told him that I did too, because vending the dust was my performance art. He asked me really if it was dust from the World Trade Center in my baggies that I was vending, because if it was not, then he would arrest me for fraud. I told him that it was, and then he said he would arrest me for stealing government property.

Echt Scheiße, weiß' du? So I told him, "This is *echt Scheiße,*" and I left behind my baggies on the sidewalk and began to walk toward the subway. He followed me, but I believed that unless they read you first the rights, you did not need to stop when a policeman told you to stop.

JAMES CLEVELAND, *age fourteen, witnesses an arrest (early November 2001)*:

Because me and Chief went to see how close we could get to Ground Zero. We weren't supposed to, according to Chief's mom, but we did, first of all because that shit is fucked up, but second of all because two of Chief's cousins are in the navy. I don't mean to say "f—ed up," but there is no other word for it.

Except Chief was out of money on his Metrocard when we were trying to get back home, so we had to wait in the subway station for the eighteen minutes. I have the month pass, and if you have the month pass, you can swipe it twice at the same station to get two people in on the same card, but you have to wait eighteen minutes between the first swipe and the second swipe or else the turnstile stops you. The point being is, it's illegal to swipe a card twice, but who's going to wait around for eighteen minutes to prove you did it?

We were waiting there for the eighteen minutes, with me on one side of the turnstile and Chief on the other. What Chief was doing while we were waiting was looking for Metrocards that other people had thrown away, to see if there was money on any of them. He had this big old stack of thrown-away Metrocards, and he was testing them at the turnstile one at a time and not letting anyone else use the turnstile while he did it.

And it was one of the tall, bread-slicer, revolving-door turnstiles, the kind with all the tongs, the kind they made so that people would stop jumping the stile. And it was the only turnstile in that little corner of the station, because all of the other ones were the one-way kind, that let people out but not in. Chief kept saying, "Oh, excuse me, pardon me, I will only be two minutes, excuse me," whenever someone came up to use the turnstile, and he made them go to another turnstile around the corner. It was funny, and because it would have shown people that Chief was messing with them, I couldn't laugh, which made it funnier.

So we were standing there when this woman comes sprinting down the stairs and through the station at us. She was shouting, "I have the right to run!" Some old white chick wearing a wild old white rubber coat with fur on the collar, screaming with some crazy accent, "I am an American, I have the right to run!" She was coming straight for the turnstile where we were at, with her card out, screaming, "Move, move!" And this time Chief decided to get out of the way, because this woman looked like she would kill somebody, with her coat flapping around behind her. He said, "Damn, Gump," but he got out of her way. And as soon as she was at the stile, we saw why she was so crazy, which was that she was being chased by this cop, this Dominican cop.

But Chief had swiped so many cards at the stile that the computer was confused. The screen was saying, "Swipe Card Again At This Turnstile." The point being is, it was one of those times where the computer is so confused that you have to pull the turnstile toward you before you can swipe again, to reset the computer. The crazy woman saw what was wrong with the computer, and she went to pull the stile toward her. But Chief puts his boot between the tongs. He was wearing Timberlands, and he put his foot between the tongs of the bread-slicer. And he gave me a mad funny look when he did it too, like, "Oops," so I was laughing out loud.

But the woman didn't see what he was doing. She was pulling the turnstile as hard as she could toward her, to make the computer reset so she could swipe. But the turnstile wouldn't move, because the tongs were stuck on Chief's boot, and so she pulled harder. And Chief was like, "Ow, the toes, bitch, the toes!"

And then the woman didn't know what to do, because she didn't know that Chief had put his foot there on purpose to stop her, and she didn't know that since he was wearing Timberlands there was no way that he was really hurt, and so she forgot to keep running. And that's when the cop caught up to her. And he arrested her hard. Her face in the subway floor, her hands behind her head, his knee on her back. She was saying, "Do not you dare to rip my coat, it is a one-of-a-kind," in her wild accent.

The problem was, then we had to wait for other cops to come and for the whole arrest to be over and for the cops to leave again with the old crazy white chick before I wanted to hand my Metrocard through the bars to Chief. So even though more than eighteen minutes had gone by, we watched the whole arrest. And it was some funny shit. The woman was crying now, and saying, "I am an American, I speak no English, I want my free attorney," and then she was cursing in some other language, and you could just tell that she was calling all of us niggers, including the Dominican cop. Chief was like, "Damn, bitch, use your right to be silent." I couldn't stop laughing.

ROBERTA GLADYS *addresses WNYC's listening audience (September 13, 2001)*:

Today I am selling my poems. I have them in a chapbook called *Two Trees.* The trees are a symbol of the towers.

[Audible cut.]

I have lived in the same apartment for thirty-six years. And there were always two mulberry trees outside my window. But then they cut them down. Those trees were twin sisters, and I wrote poems about them. Because for years I had seen them, and then they cut them down. And so I had a chapbook of poems about the twin sister trees that I never shared with anyone except my cats, Sabrina and Brandi, who are also sisters, but not twins.

[Audible cut.]

I saw the planes hit on television. So I went outside, and I started walking downtown. And the towers fell, but I got closer and closer. People were saying that there was money on the street, that had fallen out of the towers. I thought, Maybe if I go closer I can find money on the street. And so I got closer and closer. Everyone was running out, but I walked in.

And as I was walking into the dust, I saw a ring on the ground, in the dust. It must have been from a man's finger. It was a wedding ring. And I picked it up. I thought I could sell it. But then I remembered that the ring had to have belonged to someone who was dead. And then I felt sad. Maybe the ring would be the only thing that the family had left to remember him by. I wish I could find the person to return it to.

[Audible cut.]

I wanted to do something to help, because I found that ring.

So I went to Kinko's and I made copies of my poems. And now I am selling them as a chapbook, for five dollars. Would you like to hear a poem?

[Audible cut.]

JENNICA GREEN *says goodbye (late September 2001)*:

Just before noon on Monday the whatever, the seventeeth, the guys in Security buzzed me. The security guys at the Hoffman Ballin reception desk, who suddenly are so full of themselves. Since September eleventh, when I come in in the morning, they shout at me, "ID!" They've been ogling me for how many years? But now they pretend not to know me and are only, like, "ID!" Anyway, just before noon on Monday, when I was at my desk, they buzzed me.

"Green? This is Security. You got a delivery down here."

"Oh, thank you. Could you please send it up?"

"You got to come down and sign for it."

"Come down and sign for it? Why?"

"Why? Because go turn on a TV, that's why."

So I go down to the lobby, and . . . it's flowers. Two dozen irises in a glass teardrop vase, with ivy tendrils for color and one of those teensy triple-cream envelopes attached. Obviously it was Arnie, trying to make up with me. And, it got to me in a way that the food from Zabar's and the American flag collar on Mumpus hadn't, because . . . Arnie would rather anything than feel average, and for him to send me flowers? Flowers being the most conventional gesture imaginable? Somehow, that was how it finally sank in: I was the one who had done something wrong. I was the one who should be sending flowers. All Arnie had done was say some stupid things in the middle of the night up at the cabin; I was the one who had, whatever. Committed the betrayal. Seeing the irises and knowing they had to be from Arnie . . . it made me feel just so, so sad. But I asked the security guys:

"You couldn't send up *irises* without my signature?" They were like:

"You want the flowers or not? You want them, you got to sign for them. And we need to see ID."

Totally absurd, right? As if flowers were a security threat. And, there is this feeling you get . . . I don't think it has a name, but there is this feeling you get when an event occurs and you want to remember to tell your boyfriend about it. This twinkle of, My boyfriend will love this. You feel your memory putting one of its Post-it stickies onto that page of your day, to flag it for future reference. And there were stickies all over my interaction with the security guys: the fact that they apparently think terrorists are going to bomb Hoffman with bouquets; the grammar of "because go turn on a TV, that's why"; the fact that those ogling creeps are suddenly so proud of themselves. Like, it doesn't matter that he and I are in the middle of a maybe breakup-magnitude fight, I'm still noticing things to tell Arnie about.

But so anyway, in the elevator, I pull the teensy card out of the envelope that's attached to the irises. It was handwritten, obviously by the girl at the flower shop who had taken the order. This looped-out teenage handwriting, in purple ink. To match the irises, I guess. And it said, "Fond Thoughts, George." George had sent me the irises. Which was . . . as infuriating as if George had barged into a room where I'd gone to be alone with Arnie. So I destroyed the card before I even got to my desk.

But my secretary, the one secretary that everyone in Personnel shares, and who spent all day Monday on the phone with the other secretaries talking about how "weird" it was to be back at work . . . as I walked past her desk, she saw the flowers. And she was like:

"Ooo, Jennica, irises! After the big wedding in California! What do irises mean?"

"You know, I don't know that, Roxanne. Do you want to find out for me?" Three minutes later, she's in my office:

"Jennica. I looked it up on the Internet. Irises mean hope and ivy means wedded love. Did Arnie ask you to marry him?"

So then I had to spend half an hour online, looking at flower Web sites. And, whatever. Irises also mean my compliments, and ivy also means friends. As if George thought about any of this. I'm sure he just asked the teenager with the loopy handwriting to pick something pretty for him. But Roxanne's excitement about an engagement, and her Long Island accent, and her immediate interest in what flowers "mean" . . . that whole exchange would have had Arnie stickies all over it too. Except, of course, not.

At five, after Roxanne left, I stuffed the irises into the trash in the photocopy room and put the vase into the recycling bin. And then I left the office myself, at 5:05, for once in my life.

The whole reason I'd called Arnie's voice mail that morning and told him I couldn't see him until Tuesday was that I had assumed that after work I would be falling asleep. I hadn't slept on Friday because of our fight at the cabin, and I hadn't slept Saturday because of Nadine's wedding, and I hadn't slept Sunday because of the red-eye. But in fact, when I left the office on Monday and was out in the sunlight, I felt . . . alert.

I mean, I'm sure it would have been different if my office was downtown, on Water Street, where our traders are, with all the National Guard tanks and all the smoke. But my office is in midtown, where there wasn't much sign that anything was wrong at all, except for all the cops and all the flags. The last thing I wanted was to go to my apartment, where I would just be alone with Mumpus with my books and my dishes and my clothes all half packed for the supposed move to Arnie's apartment. I wanted to see the ruins, the World Trade Center ruins. I just wanted . . . to see them. Mumpus could wait for his dinner. So I walked over to the subway at 51st, past the cops who were standing around making sure you didn't take any irises on the subway or whatever, and I asked the MTA ticket agent lady:

"What lines are running downtown?" She was like:

"Ma'am, where you going?" As if I were a tourist.

"I just want to . . ." I didn't know how to finish, but this MTA lady had obviously heard it before.

"Ma'am, National Guard won't let you through. If all you want to do is look, go to Brooklyn and look."

Brooklyn never seemed to me like a place I could just go to, without, like, advance planning. But I got on a train and went to Brooklyn. Which, it is so beautiful over there, right next to the Brooklyn Bridge. So elegant and safe. Whole streets of London plane trees and ginkgos and pin oaks and lindens. When I got there, the sunlight was striking their branches from this particular angle: the tops of the leaves still had that huge green authority that they get in late summer, but the undersides, which are normally shadowy and sheltered, were lit up . . . pink.

Anyway, you make your way past these grand townhouses and lovely streetlamps and narrow churches, all of them weathered and peaceful, and you arrive at this stone promenade that looks out over the harbor. There are benches and railings and these trees that I didn't recognize but that had little placards nailed to them saying that they were honey locusts. And from this promenade you can get a view of the sunset and the Statue of Liberty. And the skyline, with its smoke and its gap. So people had built shrines there. Like, they had taped photos to the steel railing, including photos of what the skyline used to look like, which was another observation for Arnie: that he was right, e-Shrines could be making a fortune. All around me, people were grieving for September eleventh, and I was thinking about my maybe ex-boyfriend.

If Arnie was willing to trade apologies, I was willing to forgive him. But it wouldn't be as simple as just trading apologies, because if Arnie's whole dignity thing means anything, it means he'd rather be lonely than be . . . betrayed. So if we were still going to be a couple, it would be because I had decided never to tell Arnie that I'd slept with some other guy. I'd have to learn to have secrets, keep my peace, whatever. Anyway. It is always a conundrum, trying to figure out why you are unhappy, but at least it was clear to me that it didn't matter who apologized to whom, as between Arnie and me. The problem wasn't that he'd said a few mean things to me at the cabin in the middle of the night; it was something very different. And then my phone rang.

It was George, calling from Chicago. And, you know that click you sometimes hear when someone calls you from work? Especially a banker? Like, the click that means that when he dialed your number, he had his speakerphone on, but that when he heard that you had answered, he grabbed his handset from the cradle to talk to you privately? It makes it sound like you're one of his clients . . . maybe his favorite client, but still his client. I was like:

"Oh . . . hey! I thought we were going to talk on Wednesday at three." And he was like:

"I wanted to make sure you got the flowers."

And, fine. I am sure that most women would be, whatever, thrilled by his enthusiasm. But you know how I am. I like to have things be orderly. If you promise me that I get to have until Wednesday to sort out how I feel about you, don't call me two days early. And don't call me just to make me say something grateful to you about your flowers. Anyway, I told him:

"I did get the flowers. Thank you so much. I love irises."

Which, when some guy calls and asks you if you got the flowers he sent, there is no way to answer that doesn't make you sound like such a girl. That lilting voice, saying, "Thank you so much. I love irises." He said:

"The woman at the flower shop said that in the age of chivalry, irises meant 'May I request another assignation, my lady?'"

How am I supposed to respond to that? After I've sort of told him that he's calling me two days early? I was already feeling mad at myself for having been all, "I love irises." So when he said, "In the age of chivalry, irises meant 'May I request another assignation, my lady?'" I said:

"I thought they meant, 'I have no left ear.'"

"What?"

"Van Gogh." And, either he didn't hear what I said or he did hear but didn't get it and was trying to cover for himself, because he was like:

"There's this really loud breeze in the background. Are you outside?" It's like, you did call my cell phone, where did you expect me to be? So I said:

"Yeah. I wanted to get out of the office."

"Are things crazy there?" And he said it in that flat banker way, where what *crazy* means is *busy.* I'm sure George was trying to ask me about how I was doing. But he had phrased it with that tone bankers use when they are frantically overworked and they are calling someone who is a little less frantically overworked. Everything he was saying was irritating me. Which was this reminder of, like, what it means to start over. That's the constant dilemma of love. However much the man you're in love with disappoints you, the only alternative is to begin afresh with some other guy. Who maybe will make you more perfectly happy, but who also maybe will just turn out to be . . . some other guy. If you want to stay in love, you have to learn to expect so little from it. And that was it: I wanted to stay in love. I was tired of feeling like nothing in my life was . . . permanent. Obviously, I needed to get out of the conversation with George immediately. I was like:

"When your flowers came, the guys at our security desk made

me go down and sign for them, physically and in person, as if the flowers were going to be booby-trapped with explosives. When I asked them why they couldn't just send them up to me, they were like, 'Because go turn on a TV, that's why.'" And George's response? He's like:

"Crazy." Apparently he does not have a sense of humor. I told him I had to go.

His phone call had burst my thoughts and scattered them, and I wanted them recaptured. So I was sitting there, trying to remember what I'd been thinking about. The sun was getting lower, making these tranquil shadows on the harbor, but it was still too early to call Gabe. So I was wondering how old the honey locusts were, and who had had the bad idea to plant them there, because they are pretty ugly trees, and then it was like, Oh. Oh. That's the thing I really want, isn't it?

I had no idea what Arnie would say, and not knowing sort of thrilled me. Like, if he said yes, of course I'd give him another chance; and if he said no . . .

But it was still Monday night. When I got home from Brooklyn, Mumpus was sitting in the sink, staring down the drain. Hunched over, with his big shoulder blades pointing up at the ceiling and his red-white-and-blue flea collar down practically at his ears. My sad, hungry, patriotic cat. Who for once decided to curl up with me in bed that night, probably because he could sense something momentous. I slept like the world had ended. And then Tuesday night, the eighteenth of September, I went over to Arnie's apartment. By which point I was practically shimmering with eagerness to hear what he would say.

MAYNARD GOGARTY *says goodbye (late September 2001)*:

May I offer a preface?

Imagine, if you will, a fortuneteller's deck that was made specifically for Manhattan. A deck of cards, of tarot cards, each card painted with a symbol of the city.

Not a bad way to make money, perhaps—selling those cards.

Certainly there would be a demand for the things, because there is no block in Manhattan that doesn't have a fortuneteller's shop. With the symbol of the trade, the neon hand, glowing down from a second-story window, along with a neon sign:

$5 Readings
One Flight Up

The neon hand, understood worldwide as the symbol for—high school graduates who can foretell the future. There must be thousands of these women who know the fates of men, and certainly many of them are tired of that medieval tarot deck. I mean—the Hanged Man? The Wheel? The Six of Pentacles? What is a pentacle? Imagine the possibilities: "You have drawn the Nine of Taxi Medallions and the Three of Subway Tokens. I foresee great change. Now you have drawn the Chinese Food Delivery Boy, inverted—your home life is at risk. And here, the Three of Dogs crossed by the Co-op Board. Beware, beware! And here, the Twin Towers—! I am forbidden to say anything more—!"

There's money in this idea. Instead of Death, the deck would have—the Staten Island Ferry. So,there's a shtick for you, if you need a shtick—the Manhattan tarot shtick. Where was I?

My point was that two of the cards in this deck would need to be the Pigeon and the Rotary Ventilator.

The Pigeon. The pigeon you are familiar with. The pigeon represents the drudgery and the docility of the weary Everyman. The pigeon represents the schlepper—harassed, impoverished, miserable.

The Rotary Ventilator. The rotary ventilator maybe you are not familiar with. They are also called whirlybirds. They are the spherical turbines that cap the tops of some chimneys; the turbines spin in the breeze and thus—create suction and thus ventilate whatever is at the bottom of the chimney pipe. These rotary ventilators are ubiquitous in Manhattan; like mushrooms, they sprout along the rooftops. Look out the window of any fifth-floor apartment and you'll see—dozens, dozens of them.

Rusted, blackened, spinning in the breeze. The rotary ventilator represents the dazzle and the spin and the movement of the city. The dizzying way everything in the city has of whirling around, without ever going anywhere. The rotary ventilator represents—mortality, futility, vanity. This concludes my preface.

That afternoon, at seven o'clock, I was standing in my apartment, waiting for Jennica. Outside the sun was still up, but inside the light was failing. I had not, however, turned on my lamps. I was walking from window to window, in the piano studio, in the bedroom, in the kitchen, rehearsing things to say to Jennica—auditioning, really. I still felt like vomiting, though, so I put on some Verdi to calm myself.

It was that time of dusk when there is a—deepening of the interior shadows. It is a melancholy time: all you need do is switch on one lamp and the inside and the outside will separate, held apart by the reflections in the glass, and evening will begin.

I could say, "Jennica! You won't believe it—I own this apartment! Gran Rose bought it for me. And—all the rent I've been paying? It's been put into a trust, and it's enough to pay off my debts, more than enough. Think of it. We could live here rent-free. We could sell this place and use the proceeds to buy another! Or—we could rent this place and use your savings—and my savings—as a down payment on a second place! We could launch a real estate empire! We could—!"

But it wouldn't work.

Because—it's maddening, it's endearing, but—Jennica earnestly believes that things happen to her for a reason. She likes nothing so much as—an explanation. She loves to feel—gah!—a plot! In Jennica's mind, the reason that there was a mouse in her recycling that night was so that she would go uptown the next morning to buy a cat so that—she would meet me. The reason I spent years going into debt to make a movie on the subways with a hidden camera was so that—she would meet me a second time. The reason we went to a luau on Valentine's Day was so that we could leave Hawaii without my proposing marriage. The reasons don't always have to make sense—they just have to be there.

And—I could already hear what she would say. She would say that September eleventh, her going to Nadine's wedding alone, our fight, everything—everything happened as it did in order to—prove that Maynard Gogarty was Mr. Wrong. It's so—sweet, so aggravating, the romance of her outlook! That thousands of innocents should die and that the world should go to war for another hundred years, all in order to serve the destiny of Jennica Green. But—there you have it.

To know this about the girl you love! To know that all you have to do to win her back after a fight is make the fight part of the plot of how you are falling in love. If I tried to make up with her by telling her that I owned the apartment, that would make our fight at the cabin seem like part of a plot involving money, not love, and that would be too crass for Jennica Green. But—what to say to convince her that everything that had happened had happened for love?

"Jennica—. The reason I was so upset and said all those things—. Seeing all those people dying—and seeing all that grief—I realized—. Seeing all that grief—. For the first time in my life, I saw that I am—I saw that I am just like everyone else. That I finally have someone whom I love more than I could bear to lose. It's you. Please forgive me! It's you. It's you! Please don't leave me, please don't leave me!"

It is all so very factitious; but if one wants to be nice, one has to be—nice! And what horribly undignified things nice people have to say. But there it was for me. Was I or was I not willing to be nice for Jennica forever?

So! I was—walking around my darkening apartment, listening to Beverly Sills sing *La Traviata,* standing in different dark windows, waiting for Jennica, trying to decide what to say. As I was trying out the sounds of different apologies, looking out the window of the piano studio and over the German Lutheran Cemetery—the somewhat treeless German Lutheran Cemetery—I saw something I had never seen before, something I had never even heard mentioned before. Something—perfectly simple, yet utterly novel, and therefore an omen.

Atop a roof, across the cemetery, there was—a rotary ventilator.

On it had landed—a pigeon.

And the ventilator—was spinning.

The pigeon—was riding the ventilator!

Never before seen! Like a child on a sit-and-spin—a pigeon on a whirlybird! I saw it and thought, Oh, surely the pigeon will fly away this instant. I saw it and thought, This cannot last. But no—the pigeon stayed put. Was it enjoying the ride? Or miserable but transfixed? A few seconds passed. A few more. I started counting the rotations. Five, six, seven times around. Eight times around. Nine times around. I needed to document this moment, because who would believe it? You, for example. You don't believe me, do you? You don't believe that I actually witnessed a pigeon taking a ride on a whirlybird, do you? Where was my camera? Did it have film? But I was too anxious to move. I knew that I couldn't leave the window until the pigeon left the whirlybird. To leave the window would break the alignment of portents. I was weeping with excitement and honor. And I was so enraptured that when Jennica let herself in—I had forgotten what I was going to say.

And, to finish things off, here is

THE FIFTH PART.

It consists of a single statement given by Nadine Hanamoto and Oscar Dicochea early in the winter of 2002. Yes, they do know that they are getting the final word.

NADINE HANAMOTO *and* OSCAR DICOCHEA *get the final word (early winter 2002):*

N: Jenny just spun out of control. Started partying, lost her job, burned through half her savings. We had to put her in a clinic in Marin. It's been really rough for her, and for all of us. *Sob!* But she's turned the corner now—we pray to God that she's turned the corner! She got a job as a waitress at the Nut Tree, and . . . they're like a family to her now, the Nut Tree. They take such good care of her . . . they're . . . *sob!*. . . they are giving her the love we never could!

And she's fixed up her room at the halfway house with some nice macramé. She's totally into macramé now, and cats.

O: And you and me are getting a divorce because I met someone younger and prettier.

N: Right. Okay, that's a good place to stop.

O: You forgot to tell them about your brother.

N: Right. George wasn't into Jenny's whole methamphetamines and macramé thing, so now he's dating this friend of Jenny's.

O: Julie.

N: Right. And no one has heard from that Arnie guy. No, wait. That Arnie guy is living in Central Park, in a giant peach pit, the one that James Henry Trotter lives in at the end of *James and the Giant Peach.* Okay, that's a good place to stop.

O: You should tell them about the day we went over to meet Jenny's parents.

N: *Mi amor*, you are such a pain in my ass. All right, here's the truth.

In early December, Gabe Green calls us up. And he says, "My parents want to host a play-date for your baby and our baby. Are you going to be in San Jose over the holidays?" He's kind of being conspiratorial about it. He has something up his sleeve. But we always do our family stuff on Christmas Eve, and the Greens obviously don't do anything at all, so Gabe and I agreed that we would make Susan cook us dinner on Christmas Day.

I told him, "Tell Susan I want the potato pancakes. Tell her I want latkes."

"Okay."

"Gabe, listen to me, no *Schmüchlblärchl.*"

"What are you talking about?"

"You know what I'm talking about, Gabe. I want latkes."

Gabe asks me, "So, have you heard Jennica's big news?"

"No! I haven't! Is she marrying that Arnie guy?"

"No, no. Not that."

"Is she pregnant?"

"No, no. Not that either."

But what could possibly happen in Jenny Green's life that would be big news other than that she's getting married or that she got knocked up? "Did she and that Arnie guy break up?"

"I should let her tell you herself, Nadine. Forget I said anything."

The first thing I do when I get off the phone with Gabe is call Jenny in New York. She doesn't answer, she doesn't call me back. I call her again, a week later. She doesn't answer, she doesn't call me back.

So on Christmas Day, in the middle of the afternoon, we go over to the Greens' house in San Jose. They're still in that same place in the Rose Garden District. And it was perfect Christmas Day weather too, chilly and clear skies and everything looking a little soggy, and with long shadows. In San Jose, Christmas Day should be the one day in the year when you need to leave the heat on in your car, even in the middle of the afternoon.

There is nobody out. The streets are pale and vacant, except for one or two kids on the new bicycles they got that morning as presents. You know, lonely kids, sitting on the seats of their new bicycles, not pedaling, not going anywhere, just sitting on the seats of their new bicycles on a corner of the deserted sidewalk, gazing off into the distance and talking to themselves. You can see their lips moving even though they are alone. Telling themselves make-believe adventures. I looked at this one girl as we drove past, under a sycamore on Park Avenue. She was maybe nine years old, and when she saw that I saw her, she started and then stared at me. She was embarrassed. Because just by looking at her, I had broken her daydream.

Do you like how I am setting the scene?

O: Yeah, good job.

N: Oscar and I had seen Jenny at the wedding, but I hadn't seen any of the other Greens since . . . 1990? Since high school. And now it's Christmas Day 2001. We park at the Greens' home, get grumpy Delilah out of the back seat, go and knock on the Greens' door, and who should answer but Jenny Green herself. Ho ho ho, big surprise, Gabe didn't tell me you would be in San Jose for Hanukkah, ho ho ho.

O: Nadine's acting like she wasn't surprised, but she was surprised.

N: That was why Jenny hadn't been returning my calls. She wanted it to be a big surprise that she was in San Jose for Hanukkah. Ho ho ho. But Jenny is looking as impeccable as ever. Some space-age pair of ridiculously expensive jeans and a cashmere sweater. And pointy shoes. Every bit the New Yorker.

So I ask her, "I hear you have some big news."

And she says, "I do?"

"Your brother said so."

"I wonder what he meant?" Ho ho ho, keeping Nadine in the dark, ho ho ho.

Anyhoo, we go inside, and it smells like something weird. Susan Green is in the kitchen, and she says, "Nadine, I'm making a goose! Two gooses, actually. I mean, two geese!" She's got a bottle of red wine open for herself.

I told her, "Oh, Susan, wow. I hope Gabe told you that we would be happy with just latkes."

"Nonsense, Nadine. One goose is in a spicy Thai plum sauce, and the other I'm making Santa Fe style, with sweet jalapeños and cornmeal."

"Oh, uh, great, Susan!" And I'm thinking, Why? Why? Why are we eating weird goose dishes?

O: Man, those geese were good.

N: Those geese were weird. Mitchell, meanwhile, is standing there with a tumbler of gin. He's drinking it without even any ice. And here's the thing: he looked good, but he also looked older. When we were in high school, he was always sort of plump, with dark hair, bald like a monk, and full of energy. Now he looked skinnier, and his hair was more white. And he looked resigned.

O: A tonsure is the thing monks have.

N: You think you're smart, *amor*, but you're a pain in my ass. My point is, Mitchell Green looked . . . ten years older. You could see him developing the elderly man's hair and the elderly man's face.

O: I thought he looked good. And he wasn't skinny at all. He said he swims forty-five minutes every morning.

N: I'm saying, compared to how he looked in 1990. Plus he's drinking. He says, "Nadine, Jennica reintroduced us to the cocktail when we were in New York."

Jenny's like, "My dad thinks it's sophisticated to drink straight gin."

And Mitchell's like, "If I have to host a *Christmas* party, can I at least drink in peace?"

So there is this crazy round of introductions. Because

the Greens have never met Oscar or Delilah, and none of us have met Gabe's wife or baby, Rachel and Simon. And then Jenny's like, "Oh, Gabe's out in the backyard, let's go get him." So Jenny and I go out back. And there's Gabe, playing croquet under the cherry trees with this man in a hat.

Little Gabe Green. He has a tummy now, and a beard, and he's wearing this shabby sweater, and he looks like such a little daddy. And he got new glasses that make him look like Mitchell used to look. That's what I mean about Mitchell; Mitchell looks older because Gabe looks so much like Mitchell used to.

And the man in the hat is Arnie. He's a handsome guy. Very tall, big brown eyes. Wearing this . . . boating hat, and shiny new custard-yellow pants, and a shiny new pink polo shirt, and a shiny new silky white scarf. One hundred percent preppy. And extremely polite, and just sort of . . . cheerful. They were both pretty cheerful, actually. Jenny and Arnie both.

Anyhoo, the first thing he says is, "Nadine, it is such a pleasure to meet you. And mazel tov! Mazel tov on the wedding! I am so sorry I couldn't come." And immediately I realize he has no idea about George. Jenny is giving me this look, like, Keep quiet. Hilarious.

Blah blah blah, we're standing there in the backyard, and I say to Gabe, "I've been going crazy for a month. What was Jenny's big news? She won't tell me."

And Arnie practically explodes. "Jenny! She lets you call her . . . Jenny!" Like he's learned a valuable secret.

Jenny tries to change the subject, saying, "Aren't you cold in that pink shirt, honey? My mother got him new clothes for Hanukkah, Nadine, which he insists on wearing, even though it's cold out."

And Arnie is meanwhile saying, "Jenny. Jenny. Think of the syllables I've frittered away!" He's funny in that way Jenny would like.

O: He's a good guy.

N: Definitely. But Gabe says to Jenny, "I told Nadine that you two have big news."

And Jenny shrugs. Ho ho ho, keeping Nadine in the dark.

But Arnie says to her, "You can play the wily mongoose with them, Jenny, but not with me. Nadine, next summer Jenny and I are moving to California."

So that's everything. And it's the truth too, totally the truth. And the geese were weird. Totally the truth.

Here is

A LIST OF THE SPEAKERS IN THIS COMEDY.

To be fair, it includes a few people who do not speak but who are spoken about. Daggers indicate the deceased. This list is provided only for your ease in reading, so please refer to it as much or as little as you like.

THE GOGARTYS

MAYNARD GOGARTY, born in New York, New York, in 1964

JOAN TATE GOGARTY, Maynard's mother

JOHN SCOTT GOGARTY,[†] Maynard's father

ROSE GOGARTY, Maynard's grandmother

JOHN MAYNARD GOGARTY,[†] Maynard's grandfather

MILTON GOGARTY,[†] Maynard's great-great-uncle

JOHN GOGARTY,[†] Maynard's great great-great-great-great-uncle

THE GREENS

JENNICA GREEN, born in San Jose, California, in 1972

SUSAN GREEN, Jennica's mother

MITCHELL GREEN, Jennica's father

GABRIEL GREEN, Jennica's brother

RACHEL GREEN, Gabriel's wife

SIMON GREEN, Gabriel and Rachel's son

THE HANAMOTOS

GEORGE HANAMOTO, born in San Jose, California, in 1964

PERLA HANAMOTO, George's mother

NORMAN HANAMOTO, George's father

THERESA HANAMOTO, the older of George's two younger sisters

NADINE HANAMOTO, the younger of George's two younger sisters

OSCAR DICOCHEA, Nadine's fiancé and then husband

DELILAH HANAMOTO-DICOCHEA, Nadine and Oscar's daughter

THE KAGANOVAS

ANA KAGANOVA, born in Kazan, Tatar ASSR, in 1961

SILVI KAGANOVA, Ana's mother

DMITRI LARIONOV,† Ana's father

THE OTHERS (ALPHABETICALLY)

YVETTE BENITEZ-BIRCH, an MTA conductor

FRANNY CLEMENT, an attorney

JAMES CLEVELAND, a public school student

PHILLIP T. FIELD, a journalist

DAVID FOWLER, an attorney

WHITING FREDRICK, a journalist

ROBERTA GLADYS, a poet

PUPPY JONES, an M.C.

JULIE LASALLE, a graduate student

STEFAN MAYR, a journalist

HANO MOLTKE, an artist

SAL RUGGERI, JR., a superintendent

As well as an aged MACAW, certain CICADAS, certain FROGS, certain CRICKETS, and one EMERGENCY BRAKE on a certain No. 6 train.

The following pages contain

THE ACKNOWLEDGMENTS,

SOME INFORMATION ABOUT THE AUTHOR,

AND THE DEDICATION.

They are what they are.

Jay Mandel, thank you.

Anjali Singh, thank you.

Everyone else at William Morris and Houghton Mifflin, thank you.

Rebecca Leece, thank you. Everyone who read drafts of this book, thank you.

Also, a few years ago I asked a friend whether I could make use of the sentence "I am sorry that I called you a fucking cunt" in this book, and she said yes, but only if I promised to cite her should the book ever actually be published. So thank you, Zoe Schonfeld.

And speaking of promises: the dust jacket says that a few more details about me appear on this page. I was born in San Jose, California, in 1975, and I attended its public schools, where I got mostly good grades. I had bright red hair as a child and liked apple juice, nature programs, and hiding. My mother was a sculptor, my father was an engineer, and my sister shared her caramels with me when my allowance ran out and I couldn't buy myself candy, which was good of her. At my bar mitzvah, I impressed everyone with my singing of the haftorah.

I went to Stanford and later NYU Law. I have made a living, miscellaneously, as a paralegal at the Antitrust Division of the United States Department of Justice, as a law clerk for the Honorable James R. Browning of the Ninth Circuit Court of Appeals, and as a litigation associate at the law firm of Simpson Thacher & Bartlett LLP. There was also one year in there when I lived in Berlin and earned money by selling subscriptions to my personal letters. This was profitable not because I had a lot of subscribers but because I charged each of them two hundred dollars a year and then mailed all of them identical letters. Still, the letters were occasionally salacious, so the subscribers probably got a better deal than they deserved.

I now live in a rented apartment in Brooklyn. It is a fine apartment, but the living room needs to be repainted, and I know it. My father is now retired, my mother is now in real estate, and my sister no longer eats caramels, because they give her headaches.

I dedicate this book to James Copeland.